MONDAY'S CHILD IS DEAD

MONDAY'S CHILD IS DEAD

James Elward

Carroll & Graf Publishers, Inc.
New York

First Carroll & Graf edition 1995

Carroll & Graf Publishers, Inc.
260 Fifth Avenue
New York, NY 10001

Library of Congress Cataloging-in-Publication Data

Elward, James.
    Monday's child is dead / James Elward.
        p.   cm.
    ISBN 0-7867-0130-7
    1. College teachers—New York (N.Y.)—Retirement—Fiction.
2. Clothing trade—New York (N.Y.)—Fiction. I. Title.
PS3555.L84M66   1995
813'.54—dc20   94-22382
                                                           CIP

Text design by Terry McCabe

Manufactured in the United States of America

For
J. H. A. L.

MONDAY'S CHILD IS DEAD

MONDAY

CHAPTER ONE

The killer looked down at the body in the bed. Not so beautiful now, are you, Rena? Her face was twisted; distorted in surprise and anger. The ugly smells of sudden death had already spread through the basement apartment.

It was beginning to get light out, not much, but it was time to leave. Soon people would be waking in the rest of the brownstone building, alarms would be going off, there would be the footsteps overhead as sleepy neighbors started their day, even this early. Even in the West Village. Somebody might just look out to check on the weather and see the killer leave the building. Not that any identification could be made. Not positive identification. The broad hat brim down, the full cape, the boots and jeans could belong to anybody. Three blocks to the car and then . . .

The killer looked around once more. The room was a jumble of overturned drawers, clothes closets stripped of searched and discarded contents, every cabinet in the small kitchenette emptied, each box and container ripped open and flung to the floor.

Only where the hell was it?

Suddenly the room was darker. Streetlights going out, the killer thought, pulling taut the gloves that had been carefully worn all night. Time to go. Let somebody else clean up the mess. Maybe they'd find it. Maybe not. Maybe having her dead was enough.

The killer opened the door to the hall, snapping the lock back so that anyone could enter if they tried. Let the police figure that one out.

Seventy blocks uptown in an apartment on West End Avenue, Horace Livsey was furiously wondering why life always seemed miserable on Mondays. He tried to remain motionless in bed. It was too late to try

3

to go to sleep again, not that he'd had much sleep during the night, even with the array of nonprescription tranquilizers in the little dish by his bed. He didn't like pills, and since he was perfectly honest with himself (if not with everybody else), he knew he was afraid of becoming addicted to them. It was bad enough that everybody was always telling him to give up smoking, something he knew he was never going to be able to do. He didn't need another addiction.

No, it was Monday that he hated . . . at least this Monday. No point in getting up yet, the papers wouldn't even have arrived. He forced himself to stretch out in bed. At least lying here, nothing ached. To be accurate, nothing much ached when he got up unless he tried to walk the mile a day his doctor had suggested with a smug smile. A mile a day indeed! That's what you got for advice when your doctor is what? Forty? What Horace needed was a doctor over sixty who smoked. Only he'd had them and they'd both died. Not, thank heaven, from smoking. So this time he'd gotten one young enough to be around when Horace would be ready for the end. Not that he wasn't ready now . . . or at least on Mondays.

He considered the day ahead of him. Ginny would be coming . . . presumably to drop off her suitcases while she went apartment hunting. Good luck with that! Rosemary, Horace's sister, had called the previous Friday to remind him. It's not that Horace didn't like his niece, he rather did. But at twenty-two, Ginny would be bright and bubbly at whatever hour of the morning she arrived, critically looking to see if he'd shaved and had breakfast, chattering away, full of energy. A morning person. How the hell did she expect to be an actress? Although Horace had to admit as he lay there that he supposed even actresses had to get up sometime.

Then there had been that message last night on his machine (about the only concession Horace had made to progress in the last twenty years) that Zoe had called. In for the winter in New York, she had announced cheerfully, staying at her usual residential hotel on the East Side. Please call or she'd call back.

Zoe. Horace sighed heavily. Surely one of the few pleasures of divorce was that you didn't have to see your ex-wife? Not that he didn't like Zoe, but after all, it had been twenty years—no, damn it, nearer thirty—since she'd wanted out and yet she still felt she had some sort of proprietary rights over him. He had no illusions that she was in any way in love with him, although in the odd times when she'd been unmarried, they had occasionally gone to bed together with considerable satisfaction on both sides. Surely she must be beyond that by now?

No. Not Zoe. She had a healthy appetite for everything. No high blood pressure (and the accompanying pills) that Horace had. Or gout (another batch of pills). Probably had injections of the essence of unborn goats, or whatever it was they used in Europe. He was reasonably sure she'd had a face-lift . . . at least one before she married husband number three, the Italian count who had to have been fifteen years younger than she was. Not that that had lasted.

No, it wasn't love that led Zoe to announce her winter arrival. She'd want him as an escort and there were not that many available men in her age group that had a tuxedo, could hold their liquor, and didn't feel emasculated if she picked up the check in restaurants.

Tuxedo. There was another glum thought. His winter clothes were out of their dry cleaning bags, and although he knew perfectly well clothes shrunk in dry cleaning, no matter what anybody said, there was considerable tightness around the waist in most of the trousers he'd tried on.

Walk that mile a day, his doctor would say. Swim. Exercise. God! Monday-morning thoughts. Not to mention that he was without a cleaning woman again. And the paint was beginning to peel in his bathroom. Both Ginny and Zoe would be united in deciding he needed to have his apartment repainted.

Then, of course, there were the other less urgent things that made getting out of bed a miserable choice. The notice of an income tax audit on his desk. Which meant more money out of his savings. A notice for jury duty, he'd have to do something about that too, an extension of course, but that would mean a letter or something. And last night the television had predicted rain.

And this was his undesired retirement?

All this was making him sleepy. Now, I'm sleepy, he mumbled to himself. Why couldn't this happen at two in the morning, when he had to get up to go to the bathroom, one of those things men over sixty seem to have to do that he had never thought would happen to him? Not that he was that much over sixty. Not old enough for Social Security but too old to get another job as a teacher. Professor, he reminded himself. Not that the title did anything for his ego or his pension. Damn the modern world and progress.

He turned over and decided to doze. Ginny could see him in his bathrobe and the hell with everything else!

It was well after ten when he finally got up. Not that he was in any better mood, but at least the newspapers would be there at his front door. He put on the trousers he had discarded the night before and yesterday's shirt. A look in the mirror as he brushed his teeth (at least he still had all of them) told him he definitely needed a shave. But

Ginny could take him as he was. Besides, Zoe had said something about dinner that evening and he'd certainly have to shave for that. If he couldn't think of an excuse to get out of it.

He was deep in the papers and his second cup of warmed-over coffee when the buzzer rang from downstairs. Damn it, they must have a new man on! All the regulars knew enough not to buzz him before noon and Ginny had her own keys. He slouched angrily over to the intercom. Odd. It was Ryan on the other end. He knew better. . . .

"Sorry to bother you, Professor, but there's a Mr. Franklin here. Says he needs to see you."

Franklin? Horace couldn't remember anybody by that name. "What does he want?"

"He says he knows you." Ryan appeared to be lowering his voice, which made it about as soft as a rasping foghorn. "He's got another guy with him, looks like a cop to me."

Ryan had been a marine for twenty-five years and after his retirement and a couple of years of boredom had decided to work as doorman in Horace's building. His opinion of the police was not high.

"I guess you'd better let them up," Horace said with a heavy sigh. "Oh, Ryan, my niece is due, you can send her up anytime." He was about to hang up, when he added, "I don't suppose the mail is in yet?"

"In New York? You kidding, Professor? Two this afternoon, earliest."

Horace hung up and went back to his cold coffee. He debated if he had time to clear the table before the elevator brought the visitors up, and decided not to bother. Of course this would happen on a Monday, he thought, putting his copy of the *Times* pretentiously on top of the tabloids. Mentally he was wondering what he could have done to attract the attention of the police. He didn't own a car, didn't even drive one. His bills were paid. They couldn't be from the IRS already and he still had a month before he was supposed to report for the jury duty he had no intention of fulfilling. I lead a dull life, he thought, not for the first time.

When the doorbell chimed he answered it. Out in the dark hall— when was the landlord ever going to paint it?—stood two young men. One looked somewhat familiar: maybe five ten, certainly less than Horace's over six feet. Somewhere in his twenties. Suit. Tie. That was a change. Probably jogged five miles a day, Horace thought sourly. Flat stomach undoubtedly. And muscles. Still, the hair was retreating a little at the temples, a problem Horace didn't have. The man behind him was bigger, heavier, with a full mustache. Ryan had been right. Clearly a policeman. Horace remembered when policemen were clean shaven.

Well, they hadn't always been, not in the nineteenth century, Horace's area of expertise, so he should grant them the right to grow hair where they wanted now.

"Gentlemen, what can I do for you?"

"Could we come in, Professor Livsey?" This was from the one who didn't look like a cop. He had a small smile tugging at his mouth as if he knew this was not the best time in Horace's day.

Horace stepped aside, ushering them past the open archway to the dining room and into the living room. This at least was reasonably neat. He had a fear that with retirement he would turn into one of those crotchety old men who collected newspapers and lived in dust. Grouchy he had always been, but clean.

"Why don't you explain what all this is about?"

He took his usual place in his wing chair by the fireplace. At least he had a working fireplace, even if he often forgot to light it. The two men perched somewhat uneasily on the sofa on the other side of the room. All three men were aware that Horace was at the advantage; his chair had its back to the windows and what light was coming into this room (no rain yet, thank God!) was on their faces.

"I won't offer you coffee. Mine's terrible."

"That's perfectly all right, Professor." The young man smiled openly now, as if he had once experienced Horace's version of coffee.

"Do I know you, Mr. ... is it Franklin?"

"I was in your class: European Civilization, 1814 to 1914, about seven years ago."

Would have to be nearing thirty, then; that class was only for seniors.

"I'm sorry, I don't exactly remember you. What mark did I give you?"

"B plus." The young man smiled openly again. "We disagreed about the cause of Louis-Philippe's downfall."

"Undoubtedly you were wrong." He looked at them carefully. "Surely you haven't come here to ask me to change your grade?"

The other man let out a short, sharp laugh. Horace gave him a look that told him he would have received an F.

The man changed the laugh to a semi-cough.

"Actually, we're here on sort of unofficial business." Franklin shifted in his seat, glancing at the other man, who clearly thought this was *very* official business. "A girl's been murdered."

"A former student of mine?" It was the only response Horace could think of. Damn it, where were his cigarettes? Breakfast table, of course. He decided he could hold off until he found out more.

"Possibly. But we don't think so."

A thought came into Horace's mind, a little late, he realized. That's what happened when he let people talk to him before he had finished breakfast. "Shouldn't I be asking you for some kind of identification?"

"Yes, sir." Both men efficiently pulled out their wallets; Franklin, Horace noted, kept his in his inner upper jacket pocket like any sensible New Yorker. The cop, obviously feeling no one would dare to pick his pocket, fished his out of the back of his trousers.

"I'm Mark Franklin and this is Detective Margolus from Homicide." Like twins, they opened their wallets to show ID. It looked official enough from where Horace was sitting, although Mark's had no badge.

"All right. He's with the police and you're . . . ?"

"I'm with the district attorney's office." Franklin flushed a little. "I mean, I'm going to be, I think, after a couple of weeks of training."

"At murder?"

"Not exactly, Professor. You see, it's a new program, set up to give us possible assistant D.A.s some idea of what the police go through each day."

"Everybody accuses us of brutality. And being dumb." It was the first words out of Margolus's mouth and they came out louder than he had apparently expected. "Not meaning you, Professor." But he said it in a way that implied just the opposite.

"How does this have anything to do with murder? Or me?"

"Part of my job is to follow various investigating divisions around, see how they work—" Franklin broke off. "Today something happened that I thought I could help Detective Margolus with . . . since I know . . . well . . . who you are."

Horace was sure he had intended to say "since I know you" and then changed his mind. Whatever the young man had learned in European Civilization, he obviously still stood in some awe of Horace.

"All right. Although I don't know very much about murder. Ask me about the Praslin murder of 1847 and I could possibly help you." Now he needed a cigarette. He stood up and noticed Margolus had automatically started to rise as well. "I'm just going into the dining room to get my cigarettes, Detective," Horace said with an affected affability that held more than an edge of ice. "I assure you, I am not about to make a break for it and flee to Brazil." That ought to hold him, he thought as he headed for the dining room. Behind him he could hear the detective mutter, "Better not."

Maybe this was serious? He came back, cigarette, holder, and lighter in hand. Mark's face was expressionless as he lit the cigarette, but he could see the grimace Margolus was making.

"Sorry, Detective Margolus, if you don't like smoking. But it's my apartment. You can open a window if you like."

Margolus got up heavily and, as Horace hoped, went directly to the window that had been stuck for months. Let him use his heft on that, Horace thought with some amusement, only to be surprised to see the window open easily under the detective's pressure. When he was seated again, Horace noticed the younger man had taken something out of a manila envelope that he must have had concealed under his open raincoat.

He might at least be polite; after all, Margolus had gotten the window open, which was more than Horace or the super had been able to do.

"Would you like to take off your coats or anything?"

"Not now that the window's opened." Horace had the feeling Margolus wasn't any more of a morning person than he was.

"Would you take a look at this, Professor?" Mark Franklin handed Horace a glossy photo he had removed from the envelope.

Horace got up and took the picture. He took it to the window and studied it carefully. It was no snapshot, but obviously the work of a professional photographer specializing in models or actresses.

The woman in the picture was striking. Long dark hair carefully brushed around her face, high cheekbones, wide-set eyes. Her full mouth pouted somewhat insolently and there was a look about her whole face as if she had decided to defy the world and was sure she was going to win.

Horace had never seen her before in his life. Still, there was something . . .

"Recognize her?" Margolus was almost at his shoulder, as if searching for some reaction.

"Truthfully? No. But there is something . . ."

"Perhaps you saw her picture someplace?" Franklin asked tactfully.

"Don't prompt him, Franklin." Margolus's voice was not pleasant; this was his territory and the young would-be assistant D.A. had better not forget it.

"Well, I certainly never knew her. Or taught her." That Horace was positive about.

"How can you be so sure? You didn't remember Mr. Franklin." Margolus was obviously not going to be impressed by a retired professor.

"Mr. Franklin was in my class seven years ago," Horace replied crisply. "Seven years ago this girl would have been in . . . what? Grammar school?" Despite the provocative look on the girl's face, she couldn't have been much more than twenty. "Any girl this young would have had to have been a recent student. I assure you, my memory of young women has not disintegrated that much.'' He walked over to Franklin and handed him the photograph. "What's the girl's name? And was she the one who was killed?''

"Smothered. After being hit on the head.''

Margolus turned to study the professor again. Horace could see the detective's technique was skillful. He hated to think what he would be feeling if he had been guilty of anything.

"The girl's name is . . . was . . . Rena Varmont,'' added Franklin.

"European?'' Horace sat down again, flicking his cigarette on the ashtray beside him.

"No. She was a model, a high-fashion model.'' He went on, perfectly aware that Margolus would have liked to stop him. "You might have seen her face in a magazine ad, a newspaper story covering fashions. Modeling at shows, the new seasons for designers, that sort of thing. Just becoming successful.''

"She was found dead this morning by the head of her modeling agency.''

"Philip McKay.'' Margolus actually had a notebook out and was reading from it. Just like television, Horace thought. "The Classic Agency.''

"It seems she missed what they call a 'shoot' last night. A magazine spread for a designer.'' Franklin didn't need a notebook; he had clearly remembered all the important points. "There were some other problems that delayed the session, so nobody got too worried, although they tried to call her.

"Then this morning, when they still hadn't reached her, Mr. McKay went to her apartment. Apparently she was a reliable girl and this wasn't like her. The door to her apartment was unlocked. He went in and discovered the body. He called 911, but of course she was already dead.''

So young, Horace thought. He couldn't say he found the face in the photograph attractive; striking perhaps and to some people probably beautiful but a bit too hard and calculating for Horace's tastes. But a girl like that . . . who knows what her future could have been? And here he was, a useless poop, still walking around.

"Tragic.'' He hadn't meant to say that out loud but it was what he felt. Then he shifted in his chair so he could see both men. "Only . . . where do I come into all of this?''

"We could start by asking where you were last night.'' Margolus was not about to dismiss Horace from his idea of a possible suspect.

"I was here until about seven,'' Horace said thoughtfully. "I'm working on a new book.'' He added with a wry smile, "Slowly." There wasn't any reason to explain he'd done only about half a page yesterday even though the career of the British prime minister Disraeli was one of his favorite subjects. "I got cleaned up and went downstairs to the restaurant next door for dinner. I go there two or three times a week. You can check with them. I have my own table and my own light to read by. I came back up here about eleven."

"Long dinner." Margolus was beginning to get on Horace's nerves. Deliberately he lit another cigarette, although he was trying to cut down to one an hour.

"The owner of the restaurant is a very charming lady who offered me a brandy when I was through. We talked for a while, then I came back up here and was in for the night."

"With the lady?"

"Margolus!" Franklin may have been in the less powerful position of the two of them but he was not about to see Horace insulted.

"Absolutely not. She has a perfectly good husband who runs the restaurant with her. We're all old friends."

"So nobody knows that you stayed in?"

"Margolus!"

The policeman looked at Franklin with barely concealed contempt. "You'd better start learning, Mr. Franklin, the way the police get things done is to ask questions."

"It's all right, Mark . . . I may call you that, mayn't I?"

Franklin nodded. He was prepared for Livsey to explode with one of his famous outbursts of temper which could be brought on by the stupidity of the generals in the Crimean War or a broken shoelace. However, Horace's face was strangely serene and his voice, when he spoke, dangerously pleasant.

"I don't know if you live in a building with a night doorman, Detective Margolus," he said, phrasing his words carefully, "but in this building we have a Mr. Hexford on the door from eleven at night until seven in the morning. Mr. Hexford and I do not like each other. In fact Mr. Hexford generally doesn't like many people. He is also as deeply suspicious of the activities of human beings as I imagine the police are."

Margolus made a move as if to speak but Horace froze him with the glance that had terrorized students for nearly forty years.

"Mr. Hexford makes it his business to know who lives in the building, when they come in, and who accompanies them, at any hour during his watch. And *watch* is the word for it. Nothing and no one escapes his notice. I assure you, if this unfortunate young woman"—Horace waved his cigarette and holder at the picture still in Mark's hand and went on—"had lived in this building, you would by this time know who had visited her, when he arrived, and when he departed. Which would make your life a great deal easier, I'm sure."

Horace dropped the thin affability he had assumed and sat forward. "Now, just where do I come into all this?" His voice was firm and authoritative. Margolus took his seat quietly. Horace noticed Mark was unable to keep a smile from pulling at his mouth; a good district attorney was going to have to hide his feelings better than that.

"Professor—" Mark was determined to be efficient about this. He could sense Horace's temper was fraying. "Something curious was found in going through Ms. Varmont's apartment. The place was a mess. Obviously somebody had been searching for something."

"Any idea what?"

"No, sir. Could have been something small. All the food packages in the kitchen had been emptied on the floor."

"Could have been to put us off." Margolus was not going to let Franklin take over.

"Possibly." Mark acknowledged the other man's experience. "Emergency had to wait for the Sixth Precinct to be called, and they notified Homicide. I came with Detective Margolus."

"They left the body there all the time?" Horace found himself growing curious. He'd never known anybody who had been murdered.

"She was dead. Had to wait for the photographers to take pictures."

Horace found himself regretting Margolus's choice of words. What a sad ending for a beautiful young model, the last pictures of her murdered.

"We . . . Detective Margolus and I had time to examine the apartment after it had been dusted for fingerprints."

"She must have been discovered early." Horace had no idea how fast the police worked but it was still before noon.

"Mr. McKay was there around seven. In looking around, we noticed the girl's appointment book. The page for today was ripped out. But she had obviously written down an appointment with a sharp pencil or pen. We could see the imprint on the next page."

Horace had the image of the two of them tracing the paper underneath with a soft pencil. He used to do that as a kid.

Mark cleared his throat. "There was only one entry for today. It had your name, address, and phone number."

"How curious. Still, I am in the phone book." He put out his second cigarette. "Why would she have put that down? I didn't know her."

"Suspicious, uh?" Margolus was still eyeing him steadily.

"Strange perhaps, but hardly suspicious. It seems she wanted to contact me today. Only she was killed yesterday." He paused to look at Mark. "Was it yesterday? You said only last night."

"We won't know the exact time of death until we get the coroner's report." Mark stood. He obviously felt they had covered everything they could from the professor. Reluctantly, Margolus joined him.

"We'll have to check your story, Professor," he said. "In the meantime—"

"Don't leave the city?" Horace had seen his share of detective stories on television. "Don't worry, I'm not going anywhere." As he said it he felt the sad truth of his words.

After getting the name of the manager of the building (presumably to check Horace's story with the night doorman), the two men left, leaving cards with phone numbers if Horace remembered anything more. A selfish, irreverent thought came to Horace's mind. Was being a possible suspect in a murder case sufficient cause to get off jury duty?

It was almost a quarter to one before Ginny arrived. Hernandez, the houseman, carried up her three suitcases, and seemed more pleased with the dazzling smile Ginny gave him than the tip Horace had ready. Ginny did have that effect on people.

By now he was sufficiently awake and interested in the day to greet his niece warmly.

"Horsey, you haven't shaved!" she said, frowning a little when he released her from his embrace.

"Didn't have time. I've had a busy morning."

Ginny glanced through the archway at the dining room table, still spread with the plates and cups from Horace's breakfast and the scattered newspapers.

"Obviously," she said with a lifted eyebrow, trying to give the one word the sort of reading a Noël Coward play might require.

"Don't get snippy. It's been a good bit more exciting than usual. Now come into the living room and tell me what you're planning. You're not moving in here, you know."

"Now, Horsey . . ." She'd said it again. It was a nickname she had first used when she was a small child and he would carry her on his shoulders around his sister's house, both of them roaring with laughter. He disliked the nickname, although he suspected several of his students over the years had also used it. Still, he'd learned to tolerate it from her.

"Actually, you could do a lot worse than having me here. Remember when you had your back operation?"

"Don't remind me." It had been over a year since then and he dated most of his troubles from that time. Having to miss a semester of teaching, a growing sense of pains in his legs if he walked any distance, the consequent enlargement of his waistline, the narrowing of his department until he was quietly and unwillingly retired. Still, Ginny had volunteered to stay with him the first weeks, doing a much better job of housecleaning than any daily help he'd managed to have and even cooking meals that Horace liked, once he firmly refused to eat anything healthful or organic.

"Now, don't worry! I'm not moving in, I'm just dumping my stuff here until I get straight about my apartment. I didn't want to pop in too early—"

"You've already got a place? Your mother didn't tell me."

"It just came up over the weekend. Saturday I got a call from this girl I knew in college. Well, the first year of college; she dropped out after that." Ginny looked around the living room. It *did* need painting; hopefully the new apartment would be cleaner.

"Anyway, to my surprise she said she needed a roommate ... at least for a while. She's a nonsmoker." Ginny sniffed delicately in Horace's direction, knowing he would ignore the criticism, which he did. "It's a floor-through, with a garden and what I guess is a room about the size of a closet for me and it's only one fifty a month."

"I didn't know there were any bargains like that anymore."

"Neither did I. Naturally I leaped at it." She stared at him, a deliberately malicious smile on her face. "Especially since my only relative in the city wasn't offering to take me in."

"No, he wasn't. And isn't."

Ginny decided to ignore this. "So I'm to call her this afternoon, get the keys, and move in." She ran a finger over the coffee table. Probably hadn't been dusted in a week. "What's strange is we were never all that close. I didn't even think she liked me very much. Nor anybody else either. You know, one of those quiet girls."

Which Ginny could never have been accused of, Horace thought with some amusement. "Maybe she needs help with the rent?"

"A hundred and fifty dollars a month? That probably wouldn't pay her phone bill. Anyway, she's a successful model. You've probably seen her picture."

Horace felt his stomach sink about ten feet. "What's the girl's name?" he asked quietly, although he had a definite feeling he knew the answer. She must have heard something strange in his voice, for Ginny looked at him with a puzzled expression on her face.

"Rena Varmont. Why?"

CHAPTER TWO

For the next hour Horace had no chance to avoid a discussion of the murder with Ginny as she energetically proceeded to sweep through his apartment doing basic cleaning, including emptying and washing out his array of coffeepots. He had seven, which with careful reheating got him from one visit of the cleaning woman (where was he going to find another one?) to the next. It was the one household chore Horace hated, always managing to spill the grounds on the floor, digging into the damp containers to get the last of the dead coffee out. Since Ginny knew this, he was more or less at her mercy as he stacked the odd parts into the dishwasher. Breakfast had long since been cleared away, and for once Ginny was too preoccupied to think about lunch.

Ginny had a constant flow of questions about the murder for which Horace had no answers, some of her theories clearly derived from detective stories she had read, various crimes from classic plays, and a smattering of what Horace could only guess were current movies. Only after giving the hall table a final swipe with a paper towel was he able to get her to sit down in the living room and answer a few questions.

"We should call the police," she said for about the fifth time.

"First I think I'd like to know a little more about this girl. How did you come to know her? That's what the police will ask you about."

"Actually, I don't know much more than I've told you." Ginny nibbled her lower lip thoughtfully. "Except it was so strange about her becoming a model. She never even seemed pretty. You know, not the campus prom queen."

"Too tall for the guys?"

"Mmm. Even slouching. Sort of hiding her face under a lot of hair. Thick glasses . . ."

"Contacts could have changed that." Horace thought of the picture he had seen that morning.

"No makeup. She was even a little awkward. Pants and turtlenecks, no curves to speak of."

"Good for high fashion, maybe?" Horace tried to remember things Zoe had told him about models. "Did she date anybody?"

"I don't think so. Not steady or anything. She was the kind of girl who faded around people."

"You said you only knew her that first year?" Horace saw Ginny thinking, not exactly refusing to answer his questions but obviously worrying about something else. "Ginny? These are the questions the police are going to ask. Let's get your head straight."

"We both hated biology, so sometimes we'd study together. Since we were both day students, there wasn't a question of our being room-mates or anything."

"Yet that's exactly what you were going to be." Horace found himself getting a little impatient. Usually Ginny was more forthcoming than this.

"I know. That's what's so ... odd. See, she never really wanted to go to college but her parents were dead and she was being raised by this really strict aunt who insisted she get an education. The grim type, I met her once. A retired nurse. You know, the sort that wakes you up in the hospital to give you a sleeping pill."

Horace thought back to his operation. "Not exactly Florence Nightingale?"

"I don't think Rena's aunt ever smiled in her life. Well, the aunt died that first summer and Rena called me to say she wasn't coming back to college, she was going to New York."

"To be a model?"

"No. At least, she didn't say anything about that. I think she just wanted to make a new start or something."

"You stayed in touch?"

"Not exactly. Christmas cards and things. Maybe lunch once or twice when I came into the city for a play."

"By this time she wasn't Cinderella sitting in the ashes, but glamorous and beautiful?"

"Kind of. Horsey, it's not easy to explain. She still didn't wear any makeup although she must have for pictures. But somebody had taught her to slick back her hair and she was ... striking. When she smiled, I mean. Or turned it on." Ginny was obviously trying to remember the changes that had taken place. "Still the same skinny pants and sweaters, only now, of course, they were all Italian or Japanese or cashmere. I could still see the same girl, but when a guy came by, a waiter or a salesclerk or something, it was like inside she turned on a switch and she was a real knockout.''

''Get to the part about your sharing her apartment. That's what the police are going to want to know. Even I remember seeing her pictures in magazines and newspapers. Obviously she was a success; why did she need you to help pay the rent?''

''That's the funny part. I hadn't seen her for maybe a year; then last February, when I came down for the Juilliard audition, I called her. We didn't have much time to talk and I got the feeling she was sort of bored with me. But when I knew I was coming to New York this September, I did what every actress does—''

''Would-be actress.''

''Actress,'' Ginny said firmly. ''Anyway, I looked up everybody I'd ever known who was in Manhattan and told them I was looking for a share in an apartment. Brooklyn and Queens I figured I could handle on my own.''

''Did this list of people include young men?''

''Don't get snoopy, Horsey.'' Her tone was clearly ''Mind you own business.'' ''Anyway, nobody had anything to offer, not specifically. Rena didn't even answer me. Then over this last weekend, when I was contemplating someplace really dreary like a women's hotel ...''

''I don't think they have them anymore.'' Horsey realized that had probably ended with the sexual revolution. Or antidiscrimination. Or one of the things he wasn't sure he approved of.

''She called me at home. She had this real neat deal, a small room in her Village apartment, for like peanuts. I couldn't believe it!''

''Maybe that should have warned you.''

''About what? Murder?''

''A successful model ... needing a roommate.'' He reached for his cigarettes but stopped, thinking further. ''That means no live-in boyfriend.''

''Maybe she had just dumped him? And was afraid of being alone in case he broke a door down?''

''You have a melodramatic mind.''

''Oh, God!''

Horsey stared at her. ''Now what?''

''*Mother!* If she hears about this on television or the radio, she'll have a fit.'' Ginny hurried for the telephone. Horace could only watch his niece silently. He loved his sister but her mothering instincts would make a pregnant tigress blush with shame. He couldn't help hearing

Ginny's end of the conversation, dreading the words he knew were about to be spoken.

"No, Mother, of course not! Anyway, the police probably have it all roped off." Here it comes, he thought, grimacing slightly. The thin wedge in the door . . . or was that a foot? "I'll stay here with Uncle Horace until I can figure out what to do. I've got that scholarship audition the day after tomorrow, so I really can't go apartment hunting until after that."

Pushing the door farther open, Horace thought wryly. That and Zoe back in town and the police, it was becoming the perfect Monday.

"Yes, of course it's all right with Horsey if I stay here." She looked over her shoulder at her uncle with what she thought was a winsome smile. Although it was, he still sighed heavily. "He understands. Do you want to talk to him?" Ginny nodded to her uncle.

Horace could hear the anxiety in his sister's voice as soon as he picked up the phone. Her worst fears for her daughter . . . a single woman being murdered in New York had now been confirmed and Ginny had only been in the city a couple of hours.

"Yes, Rosemary, she can stay," he finally managed to say. "For a while. A *short* while," he added hastily. "I'm not running a theatrical boardinghouse." Better to get that in now. "Now, untie the apron strings and let Ginny get on with her life. My best to Eliot . . ." It was still several more minutes before he could get his sister calm enough to hang up the phone.

"Gee! Welcome to Bleak House." Ginny was grinning wickedly at him.

"Don't get the idea I'm going to be some pushover for struggling actresses. You get past that audition, you find your own place."

"If you were really a loving uncle, not to mention being my very own godfather, you'd let me stay here. All this space, just going to waste."

"It's my apartment and it is *not* going to waste!"

But Ginny did have a point. It was a large apartment, rent controlled still, picked when Horace had first obtained his position at the New York college that was to become his life. Those were the days when he thought he wanted a family. Not that children were particularly attractive to Horace, who liked peace and quiet, but he had assumed it was one of the reasons Zoe had suggested marriage. He had been wrong about that, of course, as he had been wrong about a lot of things concerning her.

However, the place *was* large. Three full bedrooms, one that was now his alone, one that was his office (he could only hope the IRS would still believe that considering he hadn't published a book in five years), and one that he had thought would be a nursery one day that had become a general storeroom through the years. There was also the dining room, a "butler's pantry" (not that even Zoe had ever imagined that they would have a butler), and, tucked in back of the large kitchen a small maid's room (they never had a maid either) and bath. Two other baths. A long hall. And almost every space held piles and shelves of books. Horace considered that he needed every inch.

But to be fair, Ginny had been only a mild problem as a houseguest after his operation once they had reached a suitable compromise as to what music should be played, at what hours, and at what level of volume.

"I'll give you to the end of the week," Horace said, exaggerating his reluctance. He was not going to be persuaded by Ginny even if in his own way he loved her.

"Yes, Uncle Horace." He wasn't fooling her for a minute. But before he could repeat his ultimatum in stronger language, the intercom buzzed.

"Good Lord, can the police have tracked you down already?" He moved toward the hall, uttering loudly. "I'll never get back to Disraeli."

"He died ages ago, he can wait," Ginny called after him as he went to the in-house phone.

"What is it, Ryan? Oh. Well, I guess you'd better send him up." He put down the phone and looked at Ginny, who had followed him from the living room. "A messenger. With a package for you."

"Me?" Ginny looked puzzled and suddenly very young. "Nobody knows I'm here. I haven't even had time to shop for anything to be delivered."

"Did Rena know?" Horace was thinking of his name being scrawled on the appointment pad in the dead model's apartment.

"I guess I did say something about stopping by."

Before she could add anything more, the door chimed. The elevator must have been standing empty on the ground floor. Usually in an old building like this it took several minutes for a visitor to arrive. Horace reached in his pockets. Did he have any money on him for a tip? Something crinkled; he could only hope it wasn't a five.

When he opened the door he found a short, slight young man in front of him, holding a large, square, almost flat package.

"Sir? You have a Miss Karr here? A Miss Virginia Karr?" He spoke quietly with a slight hesitation. It was obvious English was not his first language. Horace stepped aside to let Ginny meet the man.

"I'm Virginia Karr." She was almost as hesitant as the slender delivery man in front of her. It was seldom she was called by her full name, Horace realized.

"Here. This is for you." The young man presented her with the large package. His black hair was slick with the rain that must have started outside, spotting his dark cape.

"I was supposed to deliver this last night, but there was . . . were"— he searched for the right word—"difficulties." He made a small polite bow. "I hope the delay did not . . . does not make a difference?"

"No, I just got here." Ginny held the package awkwardly. "Who is this from?"

"Please. I know nothing."

"But . . ."

"Nothing. Excuse me." He darted away down the corridor toward the elevator. He must have propped the door open, Horace thought, because before either he or Ginny could move, he could hear it start to descend.

"A secret admirer?"

"It couldn't be." She looked at the package that had been so rapidly pushed into her hands. It wasn't heavy but was large enough to be awkward to hold. Without looking at Horace she went into the dining room and put the package on the now-bare dining room table. Horace flipped the light switch. One of the problems of his apartment was that few of the rooms looked out on anything but the walls of neighboring buildings, making electricity vital nearly all day long, except in the living room, Horace's office, and the maid's room in the back, where you could sometimes get a view of the Hudson River on a clear day.

Ginny looked at the package. "It's for me, all right." Scrawled on the brown paper wrapping was her name, care of Professor Horace Livsey, with the West End Avenue address clearly printed. "To be delivered by hand," she added.

"Where's it from?"

"No return address." She looked at Horace. "Don't delivery guys usually ask you to sign for something like this?"

"I'd think so." He tried to remember the last time he had used a messenger service. "They'd at least wait for a tip." But Ginny was already struggling with the twine that held the wrapping together. The paper was definitely dry. The young man must have kept it under his cape. The rain that had been predicted was splashing against the windows.

Ginny managed to get the wrapping off and spread the package on the table. It was a large folder, about two thirds of the size of a card table, Horace thought, black plastic, zipped closed around three sides.

An envelope had been Scotch-taped to what was apparently the top of the large folder, again addressed to Ginny, care of himself.

She ripped the envelope open. There was only one sheet of paper inside. "Listen to this," she said to Horace after swiftly reading the one page. "It's from Rena." She read the words out loud. " 'Sorry to bug you, but I think this might be better with you or at least your uncle until I talk to you. I'll call tomorrow afternoon, Rena.' "

"Nothing else?"

But Ginny was already unzipping the sides of the package. She unfolded it onto the bare dining room table.

"It's her portfolio," she said. "Her model's portfolio."

"Why would she send you that? I thought they were practically sewn to a working model's hands."

"I don't know." Ginny was turning the pages rapidly. The pictures of Rena were excellent, each one obviously of some different aspect— some sullenly seductive, some innocent as a virgin (these were less successful), some buoyantly vital, some regal as any princess could wish to be. It was obvious to Horace that whatever the girl had looked like in person, the camera clearly improved her. Her high cheekbones, clear jawline, wide-spaced eyes, all conveyed whatever impression that was needed, and in addition made her stunningly beautiful. A few of the pictures had a young man in the background, holding a fur coat or fastening a necklace.

Not perhaps the girl you would take home to mother, Horace thought as they turned the pages, but a girl that could clearly turn the head of any man or jealous woman when she walked into a room. When she turned the "look" on.

"See what I mean?" Ginny asked in almost an awed whisper. "That's what I'd like to be as an actress. Magnetic."

"I wouldn't worry. There's never been a great actress who was a conventional beauty. Too limiting."

"Horsey, you always say the right thing." She turned over the last picture, disclosing the back of the folder. "That's it?"

Horace could sense her disappointment. "You mean, just the photographs? What were you expecting? Compromising letters? A diary? A secret code?"

"I don't know." Ginny wasn't responding to his attempt at humor. "*Something*. I mean, if this is so valuable, she has to send it here so it would be safe before I moved in—"

"She said *better*." Horace was rereading the note that had come with the portfolio.

"She meant *safe*." Ginny's curiosity was now aroused. She was feeling the edges of the binding. Nothing hidden there. Slowly she started going through the plastic-covered pages of the portfolio again, as if the arrangement or the order of the photographs had some hidden meaning.

"Maybe she had an appointment in this part of town today. Didn't want to lug it around last night?"

"She wasn't anywhere last night. She was in her own bed. Dead." It seemed to hit Ginny suddenly and she sat down quickly on one of the dining room chairs.

"Horsey, this is *weird*."

"We'll call the police, let them work it out." But he didn't move away from the table. What was there about the photographs that bothered him? "We probably shouldn't have touched it anyway. There might have been fingerprints."

"Hers. And ours. She wrapped it herself obviously. And the delivery boy had gloves on. Didn't you notice?"

"No." But Horace wasn't paying attention. He went through the collection of pictures one more time. Suddenly he began to see what had caught his attention earlier. "Ginny, take another look at these pictures."

Ginny stood and moved closer to him. Together they watched as he turned each page slowly.

"Notice anything?"

"She looks different in each one?"

"No. At the bottom. The name of the photographer. Axel Gruen."

"Is he famous or something?"

"He used to be. Maybe he still is. He was just beginning when I knew him."

"You know him?"

"I did once. Zoe and I met him that year I was in Paris doing that book on the Second Empire." His one big success, Horace remembered, since there were enough sexual scandals in that era to catapult the book onto the best seller list. A long time ago. Horace sighed, pushing away memories of his favorite city: gray-wet streets, blossoming trees, little cafés, nights of talking about everything in the world. Zoe was still in love with him then. Or so he thought . . .

"Horsey?"

He was back in the present, more than twenty-five years later. "Zoe and I met him somehow, some party. He was very helpful in getting pictures from archives for the book . . . period things and then some of the places he would photograph as they are today. Well, twenty-five years ago. Not that Paris changes that much." He resolutely put aside images of the modern skyscrapers that had begun to loom on the edges of central Paris, like dinosaurs waiting stealthily to move in and devour the beautiful past. "I haven't seen Axel in years."

"Would you mind coming back from Memory Lane, Uncle Horace?" There was a practical tone in Ginny's voice that reminded Horace she was his sister's daughter. "Doesn't it strike you as a little strange that all of these pictures are by the same photographer?"

"I'm not following you."

"You're not paying attention! Look, even I know models go to lots of different photographers. They'd have to. I mean, certain magazines only hire certain photographers. They're under contract. They can't photograph for anyone else." She bit her lower lip again, thinking. "At least, I think they can't. I read it someplace. But actresses and models go to different photographers to get a different point of view, a different look." Ginny frowned. "Only all these are by just one photographer." She turned to face Horace. "Do you think maybe this Axel Whatever was her secret lover or something?"

"Axel? Not likely."

"Why? Didn't he like girls?"

"Ginny, you don't have to be so frank about everything. Of course he liked girls. Women. I think." Horace hesitated. Just exactly what did he know about Axel after all these years? "But he was middle-aged then and practically a gnome, with a heavy accent. Plus he never seemed to change his clothes." He rubbed his chin reflectively. He *did* need a shave. "No, I can't see him involved with somebody like Rena."

"Maybe she was using him to advance her career?"

"Surely she'd be beyond that point?" He started toward the hall table, where he had left the cards the detective and the young lawyer had given him. "Time we got in touch with the authorities. That'll give me a good excuse to get out of dinner with Zoe."

"She's back?" Ginny had followed him into the hall. He knew without looking that there was an excited gleam in Ginny's eyes. She had always been fascinated by her aunt, or, rather, ex-aunt, he reminded himself.

"For the winter, damn it. Now, where are my glasses?" He fumbled in his shirt pocket as he reached for the phone.

Zoe Masters Livsey Banning, the Countess Sirelli, looked around her suite at the Hotel Stanforth with satisfaction. In a world that seemed daily more muddled or modernized and sometimes both at the same time, the Stanforth never changed. Located on a quiet street in the East Sixties, it had been her winter home ever since her second husband had died. Avery's lawyers had recommended it after the funeral, reminding her that the Fifth Avenue apartment was not only much too big for a woman alone but without an expensive staff, impossible to maintain. And since she had to stay out of New York at least six months and one day every year to exempt her large income from New York State and City taxes, it made more sense to move into a hotel.

She glanced at the telephone. She had no illusions that dear Horace was going to return her call. That she knew when she had left the message about dinner. She didn't really need him as an escort tonight; in fact, with all the excitement of settling in she was looking forward to a quiet evening with a light meal sent up from the hotel's excellent kitchen. Besides, she needed to get her hair and her nails done, a pedicure, a facial, a thousand things before she was ready to face her first husband and, more important, her New York friends.

She went over to the antique chest that discreetly hid the television set. It was time for the late afternoon news. Not that she enjoyed world news much these days but it was important to keep up, to be able to respond sensibly to the latest gossip and rumors and topics that everybody else would be discussing. She'd call Horace at six, just late enough for him to be worried that he had misunderstood her message. By then he would have thought up a good excuse as to why he couldn't join her. Also, probably one for the next night, Tuesday.

That was perfectly all right with Zoe; she didn't really need him until Celeste's dinner party on Thursday. She knew her first husband well enough to know even he couldn't think up that many excuses.

Dear Celeste! Such a charming girl!

Zoe made a fast mental note to herself: Nobody female was a girl anymore, even if they were under twelve. And Celeste had to be at the most only about fifteen or sixteen years younger than she was. Unmarried, but Zoe supposed that was what happened when you worked toward a career. Not for the first time, Zoe was happy she had never had any such ambitions. Although she knew if she told Horace that, he would say her career had been husbands.

The television set blazed into color.

Some model had been killed in the West Village. The police fortunately had already caught the murderer. She saw the police leading a small Latino-looking youth in a black cape into a station house, his hands cuffed behind him, his hair shining, probably still wet from the heavy rain that had fallen earlier that afternoon.

She turned up the sound. If a model had been murdered, it was sure to come up at Celeste's dinner party, especially now that she was the executive director of the fashion magazine *Elegant*. Must remember to get the latest issue, Zoe thought, Celeste would be so hurt if she hadn't read it.

"Quick, Horsey! He's on the news!"

Horace had retreated to his study for most of the afternoon, not that he had accomplished much. Ginny had dumped her luggage in the spare room but had tactfully elected to sleep in the maid's room at the back of the apartment. However, it meant he was constantly hearing her footsteps in the hall as she went back and forth, obviously unpacking enough for a longer stay than a few days.

Not that she was the real distraction. Disraeli's influence on parliamentary law seemed incredibly dull that afternoon, and he found his thoughts wandering back to Paris. Paris and Zoe and, he had to admit, Axel. He hadn't been quite accurate in telling Ginny he hadn't seen him in years. Occasionally, at one of the fashionable parties Zoe was always asked to, he would catch a glimpse of him and they might nod, but somehow there was never time for a conversation. Also he had been wondering why the police hadn't returned his call.

Calls, to be accurate. For he'd tried both Franklin's number and Margolus's as well as the precinct down in the Village and the district attorney's office. And here it was late afternoon . . .

"Horsey! Come on!" Ginny's voice had real urgency. He went into the living room. She was hunched in front of the television set, switching channels almost desperately.

"What's wrong?"

"I just turned on the news to see if there was anything about Rena's murder." The news, he remembered, started at five. Was it that late? He should call Zoe . . . or was she to call him?

"Horsey! Pay attention! They say they've arrested the murderer!" She found a channel that was recapping the story. Together they watched two plainclothes policemen escorting, if that was the right word, a young Latino-looking man wearing a black cape up the stairs of the police station, his hands behind his back. He was keeping his head down, perhaps because there was still a fine drizzle of rain. Then, as he was about to enter the building, he twisted around to face the camera.

"Did you see him? That's our delivery man!" She flipped the channels again, picking up another shot of the young man's face. It was the boy who had brought the package that afternoon, all right. Horace reached forward to turn up the sound.

". . . and apparently neighbors heard the young man quarreling with the beautiful model last night. One of them, who asked not to be identified, was looking out the window when he left, carrying a large package. The neighbor identified the alleged killer, Paco Navarez, at the Sixth Precinct this afternoon. Navarez was employed by Franchard, the dress designer for whom Ms. Varmont had recently started modeling." The camera was now on the woman reporter standing in front of the station house. "Navarez has refused to speak except to deny he had anything to do with the model's death. Now back to you, Jim." The camera cut to the television studio and a report on a windstorm in Texas.

"That was fast work." But Horace didn't say it with any conviction.

"He couldn't have been the killer, Uncle Horace. You don't believe that any more than I do."

"They have a witness."

"That he was at the apartment, yes. That he picked up her portfolio. Not that he killed her." She stood up, her whole body indignant. "Horsey, this doesn't make sense! You don't kill a girl, then the next day deliver a package she gave you, with Ryan downstairs and you and me here to identify him. No killer's that crazy. Or that conscientious."

"We shouldn't have opened that package." But before his niece could answer, the phone rang in the hall. Let it be Zoe, he thought for the first time all day.

But he knew it was the police.

CHAPTER THREE

"Professor Livsey? Mark Franklin."

Horace felt a small relief. This would be easier to explain to the younger man than the detective from Homicide. Mark went on without waiting for Horace.

"I'm sorry it took so long to get back to you, but we ... I mean, the police have been rather busy all day...."

"Yes, I know. We saw it on the television."

"Look, I'm really sorry for having disturbed you this morning, but apparently Homicide has to follow up every lead."

Was it Horace's imagination, or was Franklin just a little brusque? Of course a day with Margolus could do that to Mother Teresa. "I understand, Mark." Horace kept his voice deliberately neutral. He wasn't going to get involved with this any further than he had to. Fortunately Ginny wasn't standing at his shoulder. A flicker of suspicion crossed his mind that she was probably on the extension in the office, although he hadn't heard the receiver being picked up. "Only there *are* a couple of leads I think you haven't looked into ... and that maybe somebody should."

Ginny's voice broke in; she was on the extension. "Like maybe you guys have arrested the wrong man!" She had clearly worked herself up to a state of indignation. Or was it acting? Once again, with Ginny, Horace couldn't be sure.

"I'm sorry?" Franklin's voice on the phone sounded startled and the brusqueness was gone.

"That's my niece on the other phone," Horace explained. "Mark, I don't like to bother you but there are a few strange things that have happened since we talked."

"*Strange* isn't the word! The cops have made a mistake. You're harassing an innocent guy!"

"Harassing? Who?" Franklin sounded completely confused.

"Ginny, get off the phone!" But Horace heard no click. "A package was delivered here today for my niece by the man we think you arrested."

"We know it's the same man!" Ginny sounded as stubborn as her doctor father now when he was advising a reluctant patient to change his habits. It was a tone Horace was very familiar with.

"We don't know it positively but we're fairly sure. Mark, could you possibly come up here, there's something I . . . we think you should take a look at."

"Actually, I'm kind of busy. Navarez isn't talking and I've got to find a Legal Aid lawyer or somebody doing pro bono work for his defense."

"Maybe you should come up here like a good little district attorney and see what we have first?" This was Ginny again, her voice dripping with what Horace could only think of as sweet acid.

"Ginny, there's no reason to be rude, Mark is just doing his job. Still, Mark, it might explain why my name was on the dead girl's appointment pad. And I really do think we ought to turn this package over to someone in authority."

"I don't understand this about a package. . . . How does this connect with Ms. Varmont's murder?"

"Because she sent it to me," Ginny broke in, her voice crisp. "And I was going to be her new roommate." There was a definite click as Ginny hung up the phone in Horace's office. She clearly knew what she considered a good exit line.

"Her roommate?" Horace couldn't help grinning at Franklin's change in voice. It was the sort of tone he had heard for years from students when he announced a surprise quiz.

"We'll be expecting you, Mark," Horace said amiably. "It might be better not to bring Margolus along."

Without waiting for an answer, he too put down the phone. He rather imagined he'd have time before Mark arrived to write his usual letter to the City and County of New York explaining that as a free-lance writer dependent on his own time and efforts to earn a living he was able to claim an exemption from jury duty (but not from federal, he reminded himself; must put that in).

As he headed for his office, he found himself humming. What a remarkable satisfaction it was to do your duty as a good citizen twice in one day!

*   *   *

"Just who is this Mark Franklin anyway?"

"He's a young would-be assistant district attorney, a former student, as I explained, and you behaved very badly to him."

Ginny had been banging things in the kitchen ever since the phone call. Being a good citizen, even if the law didn't seem ready to believe her yet, had not improved her temper. Fortunately she had stayed out of Horace's way while he wrote a letter to the New York county clerk, a letter as subservient as Oliver Twist asking for more porridge, and then called his tax man about the audit. Luckily, George had only sighed and asked Horace to send the notice on to his office. All in all, it wasn't turning out to be such a bad Monday.

"I was perfectly justified. I'm a 'concerned citizen.' I'm not going to let some poor young man be railroaded into prison just because he's a minority."

Horace watched his niece with a mixture of amazement and awe. The slight matter that the police were considerably more efficient at solving crimes than civilians and that there had (apparently) been witnesses seemed merely to have hardened her vague suspicions.

"You sound like Joan of Arc attacking the English." Horace said it as docilely as possible. "Is that what you're doing for your Juilliard audition?" Ginny on the theater might be a calming influence before the lawyer arrived.

"I'm not going to Juilliard. I know I told you that." Ginny still had her back to him, her dark red hair swinging indignantly as she took ice trays out of the refrigerator. She seemed to be preparing to offer poor Franklin a drink when he arrived.

"You were all excited about it. Wasn't that the last time you saw Rena? When you came down for the audition last February?"

"Juilliard is a four-year course, Uncle Horace." The official use of his full name signaled instantly that Ginny was not going to be any calmer talking about the theater. "A fact I thought I could get around when I took the audition. It also costs as much as another full college education and I certainly wouldn't put Daddy through that again."

"No scholarships?" Horace asked mildly. Might as well get out clean glasses as long as he was in the kitchen. And he seemed to remember somewhere there was a mostly full jar of mixed nuts.

"Scholarship? With Daddy a successful doctor in Connecticut? They'd laugh in my face." She turned to face him, genuinely angry for the first time. "Of course, if some people"—she left no doubt whom she meant—"who happened to see me in my high school plays had been encouraging about my talent instead of persuading my parents that

I should have a full college education first, I could have gone straight to Juilliard then.''

"I thought you were wonderful in your high school plays." Horace remembered her Rosalind in *As You Like It*. Not as breathtaking as Katharine Hepburn's perhaps, but filled with a youth and humor any star might envy. "I just thought you needed a college education to prepare you for life. Your parents thought so too."

"I was prepared for life," she snapped. "What I wanted was an opportunity to act. Which now lets out going to the Neighborhood Playhouse, they only have a two-year course, like the American Academy, but they won't let you act in anything outside the school until you finish." Her anger disappeared almost as fast as it had arrived. "By the time I'd be allowed to go for a real acting audition, the only thing they'd cast me as would be mothers." She glanced at the side of the shiny ice bucket she had polished earlier that day, then looked at her reflection earnestly, as if she suddenly expected to find gray hair and wrinkles.

"Two years, you'd only be twenty-four."

"Twenty-one," she answered crisply. "I intend to stay twenty-one for quite a long time."

"Then where are you going to get this scholarship? You're not staying on here indefinitely, you know."

"You've made that point very clear!" The thought obviously still rankled. "Anyway the Natasha Kinn School has as good a reputation as any of them, plus several endowments as well as some housing accommodations. I have to see about that if I pass the scholarship auditions. They don't believe in having parents support you. They believe in your going out and looking for work right away. So when I passed the entrance audition last June, with Madame Kinn's staff, they gave me an appointment to meet her personally, and if she likes me—"

"Natasha Kinn. I haven't thought of her in years." Horace remembered the evenings he had spent in the theater, years ago, when she had been one of the brightest new stars on Broadway along with Julie Harris and Geraldine Page. "I thought she retired?"

"She couldn't find scripts that she liked. Now she teaches. She has several wealthy backers." Ginny looked up at him, her anger for the moment gone. "Did you know, Horsey, that her grandmother was supposed to have been Stanislavsky's next-to-last mistress? Stanislavsky of the Moscow Art Theater!"

"I know who Stanislavsky was, Ginny. I *did* teach European Civilization." He couldn't resist adding, "And I don't think you learn to be a great actress in bed. Not that would pass on two generations."

"Don't be coarse, Horsey, it doesn't suit you." Ginny frowned a little. "Of course it won't be the same as a Juilliard training . . ."

Horace realized what he was about to say was the same thing as dangling a dangerous toy in front of a child to stop her tantrum, but he went ahead anyway. "But think, if you hadn't gone to college you would never have met Rena Varmont and be up to your neck in a juicy murder."

Ginny put down the ice bucket, her eyes widening. "You're right. And when they catch the real killer, I'll probably have to testify at his trial. It'll be wonderful publicity!" She hesitated, clearly thinking. "What should I wear? Something demure, of course. A Peter Pan collar . . . they must still have blouses with them someplace."

"Meanwhile you might think about something to wear tonight. Or are you going to meet an assistant district attorney in jeans and that sweatshirt?"

"Why should I care how I look for some pedantic kid? He probably still has acne and a wife and three children in Brooklyn."

"I don't think those things go together." Horace decided it was time for a tactful retreat. "I'm going to shave and take a shower. Afterward, we'll go out for dinner. Or were you planning on something vegetarian here?"

Not waiting for an answer, he ambled out to the hall.

Zoe was contentedly having her dinner in her suite at the Stanforth. A plate of thinly sliced cucumber sandwiches, a pot of hot tea. And one . . . only one . . . glass of dry white wine (why waste calories when you're eating alone?). The waiter had also brought up a copy of *Elegant*. Now, with the waiter gone, her face in a herbal mask, her appointments with all the other people who she needed to work on her appearance settled, she could relax and leaf through the magazine with one eye on the television set to see if there was any more news on the murder of the model. They had shown the girl's face almost constantly on the various channels and she was searching the magazine to see if there were any pictures of her in it. Apparently this Varmont girl hadn't reached that point of success yet, or at least not in this issue.

What was more important were the pictures the magazine showed of the latest fashions. Celeste had concentrated a lot of this issue on the American scene, and Zoe had the depressing feeling that everything she had brought with her, now carefully hanging in her bedroom closets, was hopelessly out of date. God knows she couldn't find anything she liked this last trip to Paris. The designers there had passed through their ripped-clothes stage and their frightened-waif period and had, by almost unanimous consent, if such a thing could ever be said of European designers, decided that women should all wear dark brown, making the runways look like a parade of tall cigars.

Brown! Zoe shuddered. It was the one color she loathed and she looked bad in. Even when wearing mink was automatic for every woman she knew, she had always had it either in pale gray or totally black. Tomorrow, she thought, I've got to get a new dress. At least something to wear to Celeste's party. Once there, she could make her own mind up on what was current and attractive. Thank God, the teeny-tiny-skirt phase had gone. Zoe knew she had good legs but nobody her age should expose the backs of her thighs. She started circling the names of various designers whose dresses were photographed in the issue, when she caught sight of a name listed for the next month's issue: Jean-Claude Franchard.

Good heavens, she hadn't thought of Franchard in years! Perhaps it was only a year or two, she amended. But in fashion that was the equivalent of decades. Hadn't there been rumors of bankruptcy and a drug habit? Apparently he was back. She remembered a dinner dress he had made for her once. Yes, definitely she'd have to see his latest collection, and before Celeste's dinner. And wasn't he the designer the dead model had worked for?

The most important question of the evening, however, was should she call Horace again? She'd tried about five-thirty but the line was busy. At least that meant he was in the city, although Zoe couldn't remember a September when he hadn't been. No, she decided. She'd let him fret about her, tomorrow would be soon enough. By then he'd be properly guilty. And anyway, she had tied up the phone quite a bit herself all afternoon.

"Miss Karr, you've got to admit the police have a right to at least consider Paco Navarez guilty."

Mark Franklin sat in the same place on the living room sofa as he had at noon, looking steadily at Ginny. In fact, Horace noticed with a certain amusement, Franklin had been looking steadily at Ginny ever since he arrived at the apartment twenty minutes before. This, despite the fact that Ginny had made no concession to his visit besides putting on a little lipstick. Horace, clean and shaved for the first time that day, leaned back in his wing chair and watched the young pair as he sipped his plain tonic water. Martinis were only for dinner and he had a feeling from the way Ginny was presenting her case, that might not be for some time yet, whether they went out to eat or not.

"Mr. Franklin, no murderer would deliberately tie himself with Rena the same day he killed her. It just doesn't make sense." She gestured toward the model's portfolio lying on the coffee table between them. "Especially delivering this here."

They had already discussed her relationship with the dead model. And where Ginny had been Sunday night. However, either Mark was confused by her evidence or was under the impact of Ginny's charm, for he had the dazed look of a man who opens his bathroom door to find an elephant asleep in the tub.

Horace had to admit to himself that Ginny was making a persuasive case, not that he intended to interfere. Since Mark's arrival, Ginny's attitude had abruptly changed and she was making every effort to appear calm, reasonable, and at the same time charming. The charm was clearly working. He wasn't so sure about the reasonableness.

"But witnesses saw him leave her apartment. This after hearing a terrific argument."

"About what? Do you know?" But she pushed the dish of slightly stale salted nuts closer to Mark. Really, she was going to have to make a shopping list for Uncle Horace tomorrow, these things were inedible.

"No, nobody could hear the exact conversation, just the voices." Mark was being edged down from his opinion of Paco's guilt and Horace could see he wasn't happy about it.

"So you don't even know if it was Paco?" Ginny had clearly decided to take the delivery man's case personally.

"He was seen leaving her apartment." Mark sighed. Horace could see his jaw tense. Ginny was going to have a tougher fight on her hands than she thought. "We have witnesses."

"That was on the news. What witnesses? And when did they see him?"

"I'm not allowed to give out names. And it was around midnight."

"And when did Rena die?"

"They're still doing the autopsy. Look, Miss Karr—"

"Call me Ginny. Everybody does." The charm was back on but Horace had seen a very clear change in Mark's attitude. Maybe he'd make a good, tough attorney after all.

"All right, Ginny. Now first you've got to understand something. This isn't one of your mystery plays. . . ." Horace couldn't remember exactly when it had come up in the conversation that Ginny was an actress but obviously it had registered with Franklin. "You know, where they pinpoint the time of death between nine-fifteen and nine-thirty. It doesn't work that way. It's give or take a couple of hours."

Horace had a feeling this was recent knowledge that the lawyer had acquired. Probably from Margolus that day. The young man was a quick study.

"He slammed out of her apartment building just before midnight. Four people saw him."

"Was he carrying anything?" Ginny had clearly caught the change in atmosphere and was switching back to direct questions, minus the charm.

"He was wearing a big floppy cape. The same one, I guess, you saw him in this morning. He could have been carrying a television set under it. In fact, that's what one of the witnesses thought he had. There's a lot of break-ins in that neighborhood."

Horace could only be grateful Ginny's mother wasn't there to hear that.

"But they didn't call the police?" Ginny's voice was getting harder.

"People quarrel. And New Yorkers tend to mind their own business." Mark's remark was clearly aimed at the newly arrived New Yorker sitting opposite him.

"If that was intended for me, Mark, you might as well forget it." She went on with only Horace realizing they were now both on a first-name basis. However, that wasn't making their conversation any easier. "Now, let's just go over this. Rena sent this portfolio to me. He delivers it at noon."

"If the delivery boy is the same man we arrested. That's a big 'if.' "

"No, it isn't! I saw him on television, just as clearly as I saw him today. Now, why would he bring me this package? It ties him to her. And it's not as if it were something important to me that I would have made inquiries about. I didn't even know it existed."

"Just maybe he's smarter than you think? Bringing it here, letting people see him . . . if it was the same man . . ." She started to interrupt, but he put his hand up like a traffic cop and went on. "That could convince a lot of people, as it obviously has convinced you, that he had nothing to do with her murder."

Without missing a beat Ginny swerved away from a possibility she couldn't answer, and started a line of attack Horace thought she had already exhausted. "Why would Rena send me this portfolio in the first place? Saying it would be *safer* here?"

"Better," Horace interrupted.

"You know what I mean, Horsey. And so do you, Mark. I was to see her today. Move into her apartment. Why would she send it all the way up here care of my uncle—you have to admit that, you told me about the appointment pad."

"I don't know." Mark's jaw was definitely set now. "Maybe that's
what they were quarreling about, asking Paco to take it."

"You don't kill somebody because they ask you to deliver a package!
And where was he between last midnight and noon, when he got here?
I mean, if he was so wild to set up that he was innocent, wouldn't he
have hightailed up here as fast as he could? Just to have an alibi for
when the autopsy report came in? To stop all these so-called
witnesses?"

"Look, I don't have all the answers. I didn't say I did. I'm a lawyer,
I'm not the police."

"You're certainly acting like a cop!" Then, realizing she may have
gone too far, she turned on a gentle smile. "Concerned citizen" again,
Horace thought. "Look, Mark, why would she send me a pile of pictures, all by one photographer, if that didn't mean something? How
about considering that, leaving out whoever delivered it."

"I don't know that either." Mark was beginning to look thoroughly
miserable. He flipped through the pages of the portfolio. "Maybe she
was suggesting that this photographer, this Axel Gruen, might be the
one to do some pictures of you. Actresses have to have pictures,
don't they?"

Ginny was not about to be deflected by this. "She would have written
that. I don't care how much of a hurry she might have been in. Or the
messenger might have been in. Can't you face the fact that somebody
else could have come to her apartment and killed her? When was her
body discovered?"

"Sometime after seven this morning." Mark's voice was turning as
sulky as a student who had been called in to explain why his assignment
hadn't been completed and was finding his excuses weren't being
accepted.

"That's a long time from midnight, isn't it? It's a quiet street, isn't
it? Any witnesses would have gone to bed."

"So the real murderer managed to kill her without any fights,
screams, shouting? You don't really believe that!"

"Ginny does have a point, Mark." It wasn't that Horace wanted to
get involved in this crossfire of questions without answers, but he was
constitutionally unable to sit for almost half an hour letting other people
talk. Too many years as a teacher, he supposed. "I saw the young man
this morning too. Cape or no cape, he seemed a slight, not very tall
and certainly not very menacing figure. From what Ginny had told me,
the late Ms. Varmont was tall, spare, and I imagine in excellent condition. How would Paco have managed to crack her skull from behind

and then smother her?'' He turned to Ginny. "Would Rena have been about a foot taller?''

"Almost.'' Ginny was clearly glad to have Horace come in on her side. "And she worked out at a gym. She told me that.''

"I don't know how he did it!'' He ran his hand through his hair. No, Horace noticed, it wasn't a receding hairline, he had what used to be called a widow's peak. "Maybe she asked him to change a light bulb and he was up on a ladder?''

"While they were fighting? And he was carrying something heavy enough to knock her out?'' Ginny's tone was clearly contemptuous.

"Okay, so it doesn't make sense.'' He stood, his expression more baffled than angry.

"Not to mention the place was a shambles, you told Horsey that yourself. Why would a delivery boy be searching her apartment?''

"I don't know.'' Not having answers was raising Mark's voice in volume. "Maybe he was angry. Destructive.''

"Why was he there in the first place? Did she call him?''

"I don't know.'' He was clearly searching for something more intelligent to say. "Look, she missed a session to be photographed. Maybe her agency or whoever was taking the pictures or somebody sent him over to find out what was wrong?''

"At midnight? Wouldn't that be a little late for a photographic session?'' Damn it, Horace thought to himself, I wasn't going to get involved with this!

"And the photographer? Was it this Axel Gruen?''

"Nobody knows yet. Maybe Rena was having an affair with Paco.''

"Not likely.'' Ginny sat back almost smugly. "From what I know of Rena, if she was having an affair, it would be with somebody rich. Or powerful. Or both.''

"Would you like another drink?'' Horace felt a little quiet conversation was in order.

"No, thanks, Professor. Anyway, I don't think there's anything more I can tell you or any answers I can give you. The best thing I can do is get the man a lawyer. Maybe this Paco will speak to him.'' But he didn't move, just stood staring down at the portfolio. "If it'll make you feel any better, I'll take this down to Homicide. Tell them what you've told me.'' He picked up the portfolio carefully. "Do you still have the wrapping paper? They might want to see that too.''

"It's in the dining room.'' Horace got out of his chair and as he left the room he heard Ginny, charm back in her voice again.

"Just promise me you won't let them close this case? I mean, the evidence is so flimsy.''

"I don't have the power to open a case or close it. Even if I do make assistant district attorney, I'll probably spend the next two years handing papers to whoever is prosecuting traffic tickets."

"I don't think it'll be that long before you start trying cases." Ginny was standing now, reasonable, affable, and just a bit condescending. "But if you were prosecuting this case just on what you have against Paco now, any good defense attorney would chop you to bits."

That emphasis in her tone on the word *good* brought Horace back into the room faster than he had planned.

"Ginny, you leave Mark alone. He's come up here on his own time and we both should be very grateful to him." He handed the wrapping paper to Mark, who zipped it into the portfolio of pictures. "I'm sorry for the inconvenience, Mark, but I did think you and the authorities should know about all of this. Now I'm sure you don't want to hear any more arguments from anybody today."

With that, Horace took the young attorney firmly by the arm and led him to the door.

"He isn't going to do a damn thing." Ginny hadn't moved since the door closed behind Mark.

"Watch your language, Ginny. Anyway, I think you've said more than enough tonight. Now, put on a skirt or something presentable and I'll take you to dinner." He noticed the thoughtful expression on her face as if she weren't listening. "On the sole condition that we do not say another word about this murder. Otherwise, you can sit here and eat tofu."

"I wonder who will bury her. The aunt was the only relative." She looked at him thoughtfully. "You've got to see Gruen."

"Ginny, be sensible! I don't know the man. Not really. Haven't for years."

"I suppose I could go." Ginny was clearly not listening. "Just say I was an actress who needed pictures. Mark said something about that."

"You are doing no such thing! And you make any attempt, and I'll send you right back to Connecticut and your parents. I mean that!"

"Yes, Horsey."

He had clearly made his point. "Now I want a very dry vodka martini on the rocks, maybe several, and my dinner. And no talk about murder."

"Can we talk about Mark?"

Horace was getting used to her swift changes of conversation. "He seems a nice young man, much too nice to be bullied by you."

"He isn't married."

"How did you draw that conclusion?"

"No wedding ring for one thing, not that that matters these days. But he didn't ask to call his wife saying he'd be late." Horace was prepared to interrupt but she went on remorselessly. "No smell of aftershave lotion which means no girlfriend buying him presents. And he had one black sock and one navy blue." She headed for the hall, her back as straight as Horace imagined Sherlock Holmes might have looked if he were a twenty-one-year-old girl. "I'll put on a skirt. To-night I want a steak."

As she disappeared, Horace felt his eyebrows rise.

TUESDAY

CHAPTER FOUR

As he got dressed Tuesday morning, Mark Franklin realized the previous day had been a total disaster. Margolus was no joy to begin with and the two interviews with Professor Livsey had been uncomfortable and, what was worse, unrewarding. Not to mention the niece who kept asking questions that had no answers, at least not for him. Another actress! God, hadn't he gone through enough with Cheryl, his last semiserious romance that had ended this summer when she decided her future lay as a lounge singer in Miami? All right, so she wasn't exactly an actress, but it was the same thing. He decided he was going to keep several long arms' length from the professor's niece.

Only why was he ending up with one clean black sock and one clean blue one, the last in his dresser drawer? Laundromat tonight, he thought. And he'd have to get the stack of clean shirts back from the Chinese man at the corner; he was down to his last two.

He was also starving. Dinner last night had been a quick hamburger after he had visited the Sixth Precinct. He knew there'd be nothing in the refrigerator this morning, glumly remembering it had been his week to buy groceries. That was the problem sharing an East Side apartment with two other guys—nobody planned ahead for emergencies. A party had been going on when he had finally returned, and while he generally got along with his roommates, it seemed a dumb thing to do on a Monday night even if Jerry had finally gotten the cute blonde from six to come up. Mark slipped on his mismatched socks (What had he worn yesterday? Had Ginny noticed?).

He sighed heavily. At nearly thirty, he was getting too old for this fraternity-house style of life. He swiped his black shoes in an attempt to give them back the shine they'd had before yesterday's rain and

41

thought about the morning ahead. He'd have to face Margolus again and it wasn't an interview he looked forward to. Not that he hadn't done everything by the book.

He'd carefully lugged the portfolio down to the Sixth Precinct, only to find Margolus and the prisoner both gone. Margolus off-duty—there was a thought to depress anyone. Home to a *Mrs.* Margolus? Probably some hatchet-faced harridan with a flat chest. No. Margolus would have a faded blonde ex–prom-queen or manicurist, beaten down by life with the stocky detective.

And Paco was in jail downtown. He had debated whether to try to see him that night and knew it would be useless and he'd get ripped up and down if he spoke to the suspect without the detective's permission. Still, he had gone down to Margolus's office and checked the portfolio in—that's what you're supposed to do with evidence, if that's what it was—leaving a note for the detective.

He debated wearing the red tie or the brown one. The red was too cheerful. Cheerful wasn't what Mark was feeling. As he knotted the brown tie, he heard outside the door of his bedroom (the smallest in the apartment) the desultory sounds of Jerry and Bill cleaning up the living room. That he didn't have to bother with; you gave a party, you cleaned it up.

Okay. Breakfast someplace. Then down to his office and report yesterday (package, the professor and Ginny and everything) to his supervisor. He could only hope he had handled everything correctly although he knew Margolus for one was not going to take kindly to any questions about the delivery man's guilt. But the supervisor first, since he still had to be cleared by the Bar Association before he officially became an Assistant District Attorney. Fortunately he couldn't think of anything in his past that might cause doubt. He'd cleared all his cases at the small law firm he went to after passing the bar. While they regretted seeing him leave, they knew he wanted more than suing deadbeat landlords.

He thought of his older brother, who was already a successful dentist. Maybe he should have gone in for medicine after all. Bet dentists got out in time to pick up their clean shirts.

"I'm supposed to get excited about some dumb collection of pictures?"

However Margolus had spent the night (and Mark was beginning to doubt there could possibly be a Mrs. Margolus) his mood this morning was worse than yesterday's.

"It's just that the professor and his niece felt it strange, it being delivered to them.'' Mark tried a tactful smile. ''I was sure you'd want to see it.''

''Okay. I've seen it. Now it's time to try and get something going on with this Navarez guy.'' He glanced out the window and reached for his raincoat. Today didn't look any clearer than yesterday.

''He still hasn't said anything? I mean, since he was at the station?''

''Name, address, and serial number.'' Margolus pushed the portfolio to one side of his desk. ''But he's sure causing a lot of flak! First I get calls from downtown: His boss wants him released, this French guy . . .''

''Franchard. The designer,'' Mark added helpfully. Margolus just glared at him.

''Then Franchard's lawyer. One of those yo-yos from a big law firm, the kind of upper-class dope with three first names and a couple of numbers after it, willing to post any amount of bail as soon as we can get a magistrate to set it. All this about a delivery guy? Something funny going on.''

''You haven't exactly arrested Navarez for murder . . . ?''

''We read him his Miranda rights. So now it's down to suspicion of murder, accomplice, I don't know. You're the lawyer. Phone's been ringing off the hook since I got here with witnesses spotting suspicious-looking people around the dead girl's apartment till eleven yesterday morning. Jeez, it was probably the police by then. Doesn't anybody ever sleep in the Village?''

Margolus headed off with the clear indication that Mark was not welcome to join him. Although he knew the detective would disapprove, Mark made his way over to the Tombs, where Paco was being held. Apparently the fact that he was (almost) an assistant district attorney carried some weight, for after waiting for less than an hour he was shown into an interview room and allowed to sit behind the glass partition until Navarez was brought in.

And I thought I had a bad night, Mark thought to himself. The young man was shivering although the room was warm, even for late September. Paco was clearly frightened, too frightened to remember seeing Mark the day before. Calm him down, Mark thought, after he showed him his identification.

''I didn't kill her!'' Paco said at once, his voice stronger than he looked.

''I understand that. And I believe your employer is getting a lawyer for you.''

''Then let me out! They believe me!''

"We can't until the police finish investigating you." Mark hesitated. "You weren't exactly helpful yesterday."

"I told you my name. I showed you my green card. I tell you where I lived . . ." His voice quivered. "What more can they investigate?"

"You live alone?"

"Alone." Paco's face settled into a sullen mask.

"What did you and Ms. Varmont quarrel about?"

"I didn't quarrel! She was acting very nervous. She shouts. I'm not responsible she shouts."

"This package she asked you to deliver—"

"I took it up. A favor! I'm no delivery man!" He was both angry and dignified now, but there was a wary look in his eyes. "She was fine when I left her. I never touched her!" His anger faded away as suddenly as it had come. "Please. I don't do anything wrong. Please get me out of here."

"I'm sure Mr. Franchard is doing the best he can."

Paco leaned back a little, still wary. "How long can they keep me here?"

"Twenty-four, forty-eight hours. Maybe seventy-two. Unless they actually file a charge of murder against you."

"But that would be wrong! In this country you do not allow wrong things."

"What country do you come from, Paco?"

"Colombia." The prisoner stopped, shutting his mouth swiftly, as if he had let out some terrible secret. His eyes were frightened again. What's he hiding? Mark thought. Unfairly, perhaps, but Colombia was the one country known best to the law for drugs. Better not get into that, Mark thought. Not now.

"Have you been here in New York long?" Mark tried to sound casual.

The sullen look had come back on Paco's face. "I don't say anything more. Not until I have a lawyer. You call Franchard. Tell him he'd better get me a lawyer fast." He sat back in his chair, folding his arms deliberately.

At least I won't have to get Legal Aid, Mark thought as he signaled to the policeman standing by the door that the interview was over. But as Paco reached the open doorway, he looked back at Mark.

"I said *fast*. Franchard, he knows what I mean." The policeman took him out. "And he knows why."

Maybe Franchard knows, but I sure as hell don't, thought Mark.

Horace faced Tuesday morning with cautious suspicion. Ginny had kept her word last night, directing the conversation to the theater and some of the performances Horace had seen (especially those of Natasha Kinn), then moving tactfully into a discussion of Horace's new book, a subject he didn't enjoy, and then on to world affairs. All the time devouring a huge steak.

Now, when he came out of his bedroom, he found the dining room table neatly set, his papers (apparently unread) by his place. Fresh squeezed orange juice was waiting as well as hot coffee (Ginny knew he liked it to cool first). There was even an ashtray for his first cigarette of the day that he had after breakfast.

I know what you're up to, Horace thought, but he couldn't help smiling. However, I am not calling Axel Gruen and you are *not* going to move in here. He could hear his niece singing in the kitchen and the thought that had been nagging at him since yesterday nudged its way back into his brain. It *was* a help having someone do all the things he hated doing. Breakfast, for one. Usually it was diet yogurt out of a container and reheated coffee, not that he wasn't hungry when he finally got up, anything more seemed like too much work. And Ginny had been helpful cleaning up yesterday. As she had been when she stayed with him after his back operation.

Don't give in, Horace, he told himself. Once she's here permanently, she's not going to have the time or interest to make his life easier. And there would go his privacy, probably forever. Not that he had any special need for privacy, he had to admit. His personal life was empty to the point of nonexistence. Of course, there was Zoe, but that didn't count. He wondered if it was too early to call her. Nearly eleven. She'd probably bought out three stores by now.

As he lifted the newspapers, fumbling for his reading glasses, he noticed a piece of paper lying coyly underneath them. Axel Gruen; address and phone number. Damn! He was *not* going to give in to Ginny. On anything.

She must have been watching from the swinging door to the pantry, for she breezed in with poached eggs, bacon, and a plate of cinnamon toast. She'd remembered all his favorites. Saying no to her was going to be harder than he thought.

"How kind," he said instead, determined not to give an inch.

"I thought you might enjoy a little change. Especially as you're out of yogurt. I'll shop for you this morning." She smiled demurely, settling herself down opposite him with her own cup of coffee.

"I won't ask you if you slept well, since if you didn't, you'll soon have a place of your own."

"Grumpy, aren't we?"

"I don't like to talk at breakfast and you know it." He picked up the newspapers deliberately. Predictably the tabloids had Rena's picture on the cover (story inside). The *Times,* he noted, had exercised its customary caution and merely had a reference to the murder to be found in Section B.

"If you're going to shop, you'll need money." The silence, brief though it was, had made him uncomfortable. He could at least be gracious. Besides, the world news was as bleak and incomprehensible as ever.

"I've got money, Uncle Horace." He lowered the paper enough to see her smile. "When I graduated, Daddy offered me a trip to Europe as a present, or the equal amount in cash. Naturally I took the money."

"Naturally." The poached eggs were delicious.

"Because even with a scholarship," Ginny went on, "New York is bound to be expensive."

"Very. So if you're shopping for me, I'll take care of it." He couldn't resist adding, knowing it was time to plant his flag, "You'll need every penny when you're looking for an apartment." She made no answer, just continued smiling as if she knew something better kept to herself at the moment. Horace had seen that smile often on women; men didn't smile that way. Sexist or not, Horace knew he was on the verge of walking into a trap. He picked up the slip of paper. "And what is this?" The direct attack. That ought to wipe off her smile. Only it didn't.

"Axel Gruen. He's in the telephone book. Eighty-ninth between Central Park West and Columbus. It'd be a nice walk for you today. Especially now that the rain's over."

"I'm not contacting him. I'm not walking anywhere. And while the poached eggs are delicious, I have not changed my mind about anything since last night."

"Of course not, Uncle Horace." She stood, coffee cup in hand, and started for the kitchen. "I never thought you would." How on earth could women manage to agree with you when you knew perfectly well they didn't and hadn't finished pressing to get their own way?

"You'll find the details on Rena's death on page three. They're quite interesting if somewhat contradictory."

With that the pantry door closed behind her, swinging barely at all.

Ginny was right. Horace gave up on world news and started on the stories of the murder. One report had her "savagely beaten." Another portrayed her as a helpless young blonde (totally inaccurate, Horace sniffed) simply trying to make her way in the city. One gossip columnist described it as a "crime of passion," while a hastily written editorial managed to condemn the growing violence of the city with an attack on the mistakes of the current administration for not protecting its citizens.

Fortunately it was too soon for letters to the editor. They would be a mixture of people blaming the dead girl herself for her murder by being too beautiful, and scathing criticism of the police behavior toward Paco simply because he was Latino. This, although there was no report of what the police had done the previous day.

However, all of the papers linked the dead model and Paco with Jean-Claude Franchard, the designer who was photographed with his hand shielding his face. There was even a small notice on the fashion page, obviously written before the murder, that Franchard was making a big comeback in the world of design, his previous financial problems delicately dismissed as "being behind him."

Financial problems. That was an element nobody seemed to have thought about. Horace was sure he didn't recognize the name, except from the stories about the model's death. But Zoe would know who he was. Must call her, he thought, not that she would know anything about the girl's death.

And he was definitely not interested in finding out even if she did, he told himself as he settled back with coffee and his first cigarette.

As if Zoe could still read his mind, an irritating habit that had not ended with their divorce, he heard Ginny pick up the kitchen phone on the first ring saying clearly enough for Horace to hear, "Why, hello, Aunt Zoe."

Horace took a last sip of his coffee. There was no escaping Zoe now. Before Ginny could call him, he went firmly into the kitchen and took the phone from her hand. Ginny smiled enigmatically again. And to think there were people who actually thought the model for the Mona Lisa had been a man!

"Good morning, Zoe," he said, determined to be affable.

"Horace, dearest, how lovely to hear your voice again!" This was Zoe being beguiling. Years of practice on three husbands and anyone else she wanted to do something for her and suspected they wouldn't had polished her style to near perfection. "I'm so delighted you're up and about, I always hesitate to call before noon. And how wonderful dear Ginny is staying with you!" Her voice suddenly became practical. "I hope this doesn't mean your back is acting up again?"

"My back is fine. I may not be ready for the polka but I'm mobile."

"That's tremendous news, darling. Because winter in New York just wouldn't be the same without seeing you."

Here it comes, Horace thought. She wants something. He tried to think up several excuses to get out of whatever it was. Some charity ball, probably. Or an "I'm back in New York" cocktail party to let her friends know she was in town and had a tame escort.

"You're frowning, Horace. I can feel it all the way across the park."

He *was* frowning. And Ginny was about to giggle, having heard Zoe's voice clearly.

"I hope you're well, Zoe," he replied as calmly as possible. "And I hope you're planning a nice quiet winter in New York." He couldn't resist adding, although he knew he was descending to weak sarcasm, "When you get to be our age, too much activity isn't good for one."

"I am not anywhere near your age, Horace, as you very well know!" That was more like the Zoe of the old days of their arguments. "I just thought you might be interested in going to a small dinner party given by a dear friend of mine." It was no time to remind Zoe that she considered most of the world, at least the wealthier part of it, her dear friends. "Celeste Lanier . . . she's the new editor-in-chief at *Elegant* magazine. . . ."

Elegant. Where had he heard that name? Oh, yes, weren't they supposed to be photographing the late Rena Varmont in Franchard's dresses last Sunday night? Horace dismissed the thought that New York, at a certain level, was a small world, and found himself curiously interested. A dinner party like that would have all the latest gossip about the designer, the dead model, the so-called "financial problems" . . . surely enough to repeat to Ginny and turn her attentions back to her career and apartment hunting.

"Just when is this party planned, Zoe?" he said cautiously. No point in encouraging her too much. From the corner of his eye he could see Ginny wasn't making any pretense of not listening in. At least she wasn't on an extension.

"Thursday night, darling. Which gives you time to get your dinner clothes pressed."

"They are pressed," Horace said. Zoe had graduated from "tuxedo" to "dinner clothes" during her marriage to Avery, the banker-diplomat. Horace hadn't.

"Good. Celeste always does things so perfectly. You'll get a very good dinner. You can pick me up around six-thirty, so we can get caught up. We're not due until seven-thirty." Horace could hear the satisfaction in her voice. She was probably checking him off her list of "things to do today" as they spoke. "Now I've got to pull myself together and get a new dress. I couldn't find a thing this morning." She mentioned several of the most expensive stores in Manhattan. "Nothing there but the current Paris abominations which I wouldn't be buried in, let alone let my favorite man in the world see me wearing."

Horace wondered just when he had become her favorite man in the world. Admittedly her two other husbands were dead, but she did have two sons by her second marriage, both grown and married, a fact she usually left out when mentioning them, implying they were still in a prep school somewhere. "So after Elizabeth Arden's, I've got an appointment at Jean-Claude Franchard's . . ."

Horace realized the conversation was tapering off. Impulsively he decided to continue it. "Franchard? I've just been reading about him. Wasn't that one of his models that was murdered Sunday night?"

"You've read the papers already? It'll be the *scandale* of the dinner party! Especially as Celeste is giving the party for him."

"Franchard?" Ginny was whispering in his ear. "Ask if you can go with her." She wasn't smiling now. "Please, Uncle Horace? For me?"

"Is that Ginny? What was she saying?"

Nothing wrong with Zoe's hearing, Horace thought. "Just something about my meeting you there. Absolutely nonsense, of course." Ginny was struggling to get the phone out of his hand. He gave her a stern look and she took a reluctant step back.

"What a perfect idea! Horace, you know I always feel so much better if a man's around when I pick a dress." She was clearly ignoring the fact that she'd bought hundreds of clothes without a thought of anything but her own taste.

"Zoe, I really have a lot of things to do today. . . ." He knew as he spoke it was too weak an excuse to stop the determination of his former wife.

"No, you don't, dear." Zoe was using her motherly tone. It had always tended to drive Horace right up the nearest wall. "You'll spend the afternoon smoking your head off and plowing through boring books on Victorian England. You haven't finished that book yet, have you?"

"No, and I never will if I keep taking time off." Before he knew it, he found himself telling her about all the events of the previous day.

"Horace, how fascinating! You'll be the hit of the party! And I'm sure Franchard would have heaps to tell you. Now let me talk to Ginny, dear."

What have I gotten myself into? Horace thought as he passed the phone to his niece. At least this would get him out of bothering Axel Gruen, not that that wouldn't have been preferable to sitting in some designer's showroom. Ginny was taking down the address and the time he was to appear. With several affectionate farewells, Ginny hung up the phone. The enigmatic smile was gone and she looked surprisingly thoughtful.

"I wonder if Mark has been to Franchard's," she said.

"I'm sure the police have asked the necessary questions of everybody that might know anything. And I would appreciate it if you would stop maneuvering me into something that is none of my business. Nor yours," he added.

"I was going to be her roommate. Your name was on her appointment pad. I'd say it was already our business." Ginny being logical, there was nothing Horace could come up with as an answer. He walked out through the pantry wishing there were something more substantial than a swinging door to slam.

He picked up the newspapers on the dining room table before heading for his office. Maybe the *Times* would have something more accurate than the tabloids.

Mark got back to his office by noon. He liked to think of it as an office, although it was merely part of a maze of cubicles that he could only hope was his temporary place until he had passed whatever training period he was undergoing. At least he had a desk, a chair, and a telephone. No secretary, of course, but somebody had placed a pile of phone messages on his desk. None of them, he noticed thankfully, were from Margolus. Two were from Jean-Claude Franchard. How did the designer know he had anything to do with the case? The papers or maybe television, Mark thought. But he hadn't spoken to any news people.

The answer was probably in the next set of messages. Jonathan Phelps Harrison III. That must have been the lawyer Margolus had dismissed so cavalierly earlier as having three first names. Not uncommon in Phelps's circle, Mark thought, smiling slightly, where all the young men either seemed to have three first names or three last ones. "Phelpsie," as he had been called at Harvard Law School, had joined his father's firm, one of the oldest, most distinguished, and certainly richest of New York's legal world directly after passing the bar exam. Since they had never been particularly friendly, the calls could only be about business. And since the only business Mark now had was Rena Varmont's murder, Phelps wouldn't be calling about anything else. The first message asked Mark to call back "urgently." The second was marked "Urgent! Important."

Without picking up the phone, Mark already knew two things. First, whoever was interested in this case must have money if they had access to this law firm, and second, if they were leaving it all in the hands of Phelps, they were prepared to wash their hands of it if it got messy. Obviously Paco didn't hire them, which left Franchard. He put the messages aside.

Underneath there were three more, all marked "please call" and "important." All of them were from Axel Gruen.

Curiouser and curiouser, thought Mark. He debated briefly whether he should contact Margolus before answering any of them, but he suspected Margolus had probably already received at least as many phone messages and from all of the same people.

Start easy, he decided, and dialed Phelps's number. Surprisingly, he was put through almost at once. Mark wondered if his fellow lawyer was in the same cramped space he had and then realized in that firm, even the phone booths were probably wood paneled.

"Phelpsie, I got your call," he said pleasantly.

Phelps's voice had a tendency to rise when he was disturbed and he was certainly that today. They'd probably never let him in a courtroom, Mark thought, he'd spend his life doing trusts for little old ladies. The conversation was brief and for Phelps remarkably to the point.

"When are you going to release Paco Navarez?"

"I don't have anything to do with that, Phelpsie old boy." He knew the other lawyer hated any playing around with his name. "I gather you've been hired by somebody? Or are you doing pro bono work these days?"

"Don't be absurd, Mark. Jean-Claude Franchard is one of our clients—"

"Since when?" Mark cut in.

"Fairly recently, but that's not the point. He wants this young man released ASAP." Trust Phelps to try and use that acronym. "So does Mother, who is one of Franchard's clients."

Mark had a quick image of Phelps's mother, whom he had met only once at the law school graduation. The kind of woman who had obviously been born to be empress of several large countries and found her current position in twentieth-century American life a distinct comedown.

"I'm afraid you'll have to tell your mother that it's out of my hands. Until the police have come to some sort of conclusion . . ."

"I know all that bull, Mark." Clearly this had not been a good morning for Phelps. "According to this detective you've been hanging out with, the police don't have any sound evidence. Not really. Not for murder one. Which is the only reason to deny bail, and you know it."

Obviously Phelps had been looking up Criminal Law, he hadn't been that bright about it in class. And Mark found himself smiling at the description of his relationship with Margolus. It sounded like they had met in a bar to share a few beers.

"You know there's a time period when the police can hold suspects for questioning, Phelps. And until we know the results of the autopsy—"

"Judge Gathers is an old friend of the family, Mark. I can have this poor young man released on bail half an hour after you police types get off your duff." Any hint of camaraderie had disappeared. "I shall expect to hear from you before the day is out. I'm having dinner with Mother at the Union Club tonight and I want to be able to report that this Navarez is free."

And Jonathan Phelps Harrison III slammed down the phone.

You're not going to have a very pleasant dinner, fellow, Mark thought. He crumbled up the messages from Franchard. No point in talking to him, he was sure Margolus had already done that. All Mark would get would be more throwing of weight around, and he didn't need that.

All this over a delivery boy? All right. Not a delivery boy, Paco had been firm about that. Only designers don't hook up with expensive law firms just because they have their employees' best interests at heart. And Paco had almost sounded like he was making a threat when he had finished talking to Mark. A threat about *what*? The length of hem-lines for next season? Mark knew perfectly well if he talked to anybody about this, Ginny for instance—and why had she popped into his head suddenly?—she would have a dozen theories, all highly unlikely and melodramatic.

He looked at the remaining messages. Axel Gruen. Margolus and all the rest of the police presumably had dismissed him and his portfolio. Mark couldn't be accused of intruding on procedure by returning a phone call, could he?

Anyway, he could always tell Margolus he couldn't reach him to ask if it was allowed.

As he picked up the phone, he realized he was doing exactly what the professor's niece had asked him to do the night before. Whatever he found out, it would give him a reason to call her, not that he cared what she thought. Still, he punched in the numbers written on the pink memo slip.

CHAPTER FIVE

"Mr. Gruen?"

"Yes?" The voice had a more-than-slight accent that Mark couldn't immediately identify.

"I'm Mark Franklin. You called me earlier?"

"Yes. The district attorney."

"Not exactly, but—"

Gruen cut in quickly. "You are involved in the death of my poor sweet Rena Varmont, are you not?"

"Sort of . . ." How do you explain a training program? "I happen to have been with the homicide detective who's working on the case. . . ."

"Never mind. Rena's portfolio . . . her portfolio of my pictures, where is it?"

So that's what this is about, Mark thought. "It's been turned over to the police."

"Ach, no!"

German, Mark thought. Or maybe Scandinavian. "What do they want with her photographs? To pin to their locker rooms and think dirty things? A disgrace! A disgrace to the memory of that lovely child. I must have that portfolio back."

"Look, Mr. Gruen—"

"Axel. Call me Axel, everybody does. Now, tell me, how soon can you bring me my portfolio? I will pay your cab fare."

"That isn't necessary, Mr.—Axel. It's just that it's in police custody. It's listed as evidence. Probably it won't be released until the murderer is convicted and the trial is over." Maybe he'd better brush up on his criminal law; he was beginning to sound as vague as Phelpsie.

"How can it be evidence? Just photographs, some of my best work.

I need those photographs!'' His voice was getting hoarse now, as if he were trying to restrain his anger.

"It's possible the police may decide the portfolio has nothing to do with the case and release it sooner. . . .''

"Good!''

"I'm just guessing now, Axel. Anyway, it wouldn't be my decision.'' He took a deep breath, expecting the photographer to break in. Only the man on the other end of the line was suddenly silent. "Surely you have copies of her photographs? Negatives?''

"I take many pictures, many pictures! I can't waste my time going through files. I need that folio *now!*'' This last came out more like an order than a request.

Mark found himself beginning to get angry. Was today going to be worse than yesterday? "Even if it's released, it's not your property, is it? It belonged to her.'' He knew he was fumbling but the man irritated him. "It's part of her estate.''

"They are not part of her estate! I keep the copyright on all my photographs. They are valuable. Works of art! They do not belong in some bin in a police station.'' Then abruptly, as if he suddenly realized anger wasn't helping him, his voice changed to a gentle pleading. "Please. I have a new assignment, I need to show how I photograph young people.''

"What assignment is this?'' There wasn't any reason for Mark to ask this, but the sudden change in the photographer's voice interested him. He must really want that portfolio badly!

"*Elegant* magazine.'' The answer came reluctantly, as if Gruen were starting to be cautious about what he revealed.

"You were to photograph her last Sunday night?''

"That shoot was canceled.'' The stubbornness had slipped back. Like Paco, Mark thought. There's more going on with this guy than a bundle of pictures.

"Why was it canceled?'' Might as well get as much information as he could before Gruen discovered how low in importance Mark was in the case. Not that Margolus hadn't probably asked the same question already. Still, if he hadn't, it might be something to throw in his cage to keep him from snarling.

"There were . . . reasons.''

Damn it, thought Mark. He's on guard now. Okay, let me try the sympathetic approach.

"You mean the girl was sick or something?''

"Rena? She was never sick. Never! And this was important to her.''

"You saw her Sunday night?''

"Of course not! I was at Franchard's, she never arrived. Somebody must have called and told her that it was going to be postponed." He added with a note of bitterness, "More courtesy than they showed me. Me, they think they can treat like dirt. No more. I'm through taking that. Me, I have a great reputation, a great talent . . ."

"But if you didn't see Rena Sunday night, how do you know she wasn't sick?"

"Because I saw her Sunday afternoon." He stopped, although Mark waited for him to go on. Obviously this was not something the photographer had planned to reveal. "All I want is that portfolio back. It is police brutality to deprive me of my work!"

"You say you saw Rena Varmont Sunday afternoon?"

There was a hesitation on the other end of the line. Finally when Axel spoke again his voice was carefully controlled. He wasn't going to let anything else slip out, Mark thought.

"Of course. You obviously know nothing about fashion photography. I naturally had to be given samples of the materials of the dresses she would wear, sketches of the dresses. We were all on a very tight deadline, I don't believe the actual dresses were quite finished. So they sent me the materials. I had to know what lights to use, some cloth soaks up light, some does not photograph with exact color, I needed to be prepared. . . ."

"So Rena brought up the sketches and the sample materials?"

"Of course not. She was no simple delivery person." The pleading had disappeared and the control, and Mark had a swift idea of the kind of hauteur Gruen would display to anybody he considered beneath his eminence. "The delivery boy, that South American one, he brought them up around noon."

So Paco was tied into this further. "Was Rena there when he came?"

"No. No, much later. Five or six." He continued impatiently, his accent getting thicker. "She should have been there at four. Careless of time, like all these lazy young American girls these days."

Wait a minute, Mark thought. What happened to "poor sweet Rena"?

"Just a minute, Mr. Gruen, I don't seem to be understanding this. Paco arrives at noon, Rena doesn't show up until about five-thirty . . . shouldn't they have been there together? I mean, if you were going to consult about things."

"You know nothing about models! Nothing about high fashion!" Gruen obviously considered this as a sign of total stupidity. "First I must look at what the model is to wear. Then, and only after I have tested my film, my cameras, my lights, then I always see the model. Suggest the hair, suggest the makeup—"

"I thought they had professionals to do all that," Mark broke in.

"Imbeciles! All of them! I knew Rena's face, her best side, how to photograph her so that whatever pitiful rags they put on her would seem beautiful, desirable, what every woman would want to buy because of the way Rena looked."

"And she wasn't sick?"

"I told you that!"

"Perhaps upset about something?" Mark felt like he was moving slowly through a dark and cluttered room.

"Rena was not a girl to get upset." Then Gruen in another hasty change of attitude became a doting, loving friend. "Such a sweet young angel! Such beauty, such a future ahead of her."

"When did she leave your studio?"

"About seven." The suspicion came back into his voice. "Later I left to go to Franchard's. I was there until one, two in the morning. You think I am a murderer? You think I need an alibi? Nonsense! Why would I kill a girl who I loved like a daughter? Besides, I came home straight from Franchard's. I had phone calls to make. . . ."

"At that hour?"

"Los Angeles. Europe. You don't understand. I must tell others that I am back in the fashion business. *Elegant,* it is known all over the world. So am I."

"I'm sure you are, sir." The photographer's vehemence made Mark cautious. "Tell me, do you have any idea who might have killed Rena?"

"Some drug addict. Some worthless person of the streets. Newspapers, they say her apartment was searched. Someone must have been looking for money. There was a garden back of her apartment, anyone could have gotten in."

Mark felt himself growing impatient. If the model had been a victim of a break-in, surely whoever did it would have taken her television set, her expensive clothes, her radio. He searched through the papers on his desk for the report on the death. Hell, there was even seventy-five dollars in her purse.

"I don't think the police feel it was a murder for robbery," he said cautiously. "There was money there. Other things that could be pawned."

"Some pervert, then. Why don't the police search for one of them? And return the property of a genuine artist?"

Back to the portfolio again, Mark thought. He sensed Gruen was about to hang up in frustration. "Mr. Gruen—Axel . . . the police have arrested the man you call the delivery boy. Paco Navarez. Do you think he could have done it?''

The reply was instant. ''Never! That frightened kid? Besides, he had met Rena only a few days before, when she went down to Franchard's for the 'look-see,' the interview models go through. Why would he kill her?''

Why, indeed? thought Mark.

''You get my portfolio back. Or I sue the city!''

And now Gruen did slam down the phone.

What the hell is going on here? Mark muttered to himself as he looked at the silent phone. Ginny thinks Rena was a shy, plain kid, Axel kept claiming she was a sweet, lovely girl, but then there had been all that about her being careless with time. That had angered him, Mark thought. And why would Axel be so quick to say Paco couldn't have done it?

And what was he, Mark, doing getting mixed up in this? He was a trainee, a lawyer, he wasn't the police. I'd better track down Margolus, he told himself.

But instead, he found himself punching in the numbers of Professor Livsey.

Horace had actually gotten some work done that day. Not perhaps very creative but at least he had the whole section dealing with Disraeli's maneuvers to have Queen Victoria made empress of India in order, which was a chore he had been putting off far too long. So when the phone rang, he was ready for a break. It was at least an hour and a half before he was supposed to meet Zoe, not that he had any real intention of going to a dress designer's. Ginny, wherever she was in the apartment, had been strangely quiet, although he knew she'd be in soon to start him on the excursion to meet his ex-wife.

He picked up the phone gladly. Even the sound of Mark's voice didn't change his mood.

''Professor Livsey? I hope I'm not getting you at a bad time?''

''Any interruption in my thought process is a bad time, Mark. I *am* trying to write a book, you know.'' Still, he tried not to be rude about it.

''Yes, sir.'' Mark sounded appropriately abashed. ''It's just that I've had a rather strange conversation with your friend Axel Gruen.''

''Axel Gruen is not my friend. Or at least he hasn't been for a good many years.'' Behind him, Horace could hear the door to his office open as he mentioned the photographer's name. Damn it, was Ginny listening at the door now? But he noticed her arms were full of grocery bags. No wonder the apartment had been quiet, she must have been shopping.

"Who is it?" she whispered.

"It's Mark. And take the groceries into the kitchen."

"Yes, sir." She disappeared. Of course she'd be on the kitchen extension, in two seconds.

"What did Axel want, Mark? And why are you calling me?"

"Frankly, Professor, I haven't the faintest idea. It all seems to be tied up with this portfolio that Paco delivered to you."

"To me." Ginny was on the extension.

"Hi, Ginny. Anyway, Gruen is all upset. He wants it back. I mean, he really wants it."

"What does he expect you to do about it? And what do you expect me to do? I presume you turned it over to the police?"

"To Margolus. But I don't think he's taking it very seriously." Mark's voice became less respectful. "I just thought, Ginny, you might like to be filled in."

"What else has happened?" There was no disguising the curiosity in her voice.

"You may be happy to know that Paco's got himself a very expensive lawyer. Courtesy of the designer he's been working for."

"Good. Now maybe they'll do something about getting him out of jail."

"I think that's probably going to happen anyway. Apparently there're witnesses all around Rena's apartment who swear they've seen suspicious-looking strangers coming out of Rena's building all through that night."

"I thought you were calling me, Mark," Horace broke in crisply. "If you want to talk to my niece, I'll hang up."

"No, sir. It's just I know this law firm that's going to represent Paco." He mentioned the name of the firm. Even Horace had heard of it, one of the last bastions of WASP power in the city and certainly not likely to be involved in worrying about a South American immigrant.

"Who's paying for it?" Damn, Horace thought. I wasn't going to get involved in this.

"Jean-Claude Franchard. The designer."

"How interesting." Ginny's voice had become cool with an edge of unconvincing sophistication. God knows what she'd be like if she saw a lot of Zoe this winter! "Uncle Horace is just about to go down there."

"I am not."

"Hold on. Did I miss a step here?" If Mark had been confused at the beginning of the conversation, he sounded totally lost now.

"Uncle Horace is meeting his ex-wife there. She's buying a dress." Ginny abandoned her attempt at casual poise and sounded her usual energetic self. "And I'll bet he'll find lots of things the police have missed."

"I am *not* going." But Horace knew his interruption sounded feeble.

"Yes, you are. Surely you're curious to see how Zoe looks before you go off to your grand dinner Thursday. She might be a redhead or a blonde by now."

Horace broke in. Enough was enough. "Mark, I'm quite sure the police and Margolus and his men have already questioned the designer. There is nothing I could possibly find out that would involve Axel or Rena or anybody else. And I don't appreciate being disturbed during my working hours." He put the receiver down on the phone. Not slamming it, that would be impolite. Just quietly and with finality.

Only he knew that Ginny and Mark were probably continuing to talk.

An hour later, Horace was in a taxi heading downtown. Oddly, he was finding it rather pleasant to have an excursion in the middle of the day ... well, the middle of his day, at least. Not that he looked forward to seeing either Zoe or the designer's workshop. Whatever they called it now. *Atelier?* That would be what it would be in Paris.

In one part of his mind, he thought as he leaned back, trying to find room for his long legs, he had been determined not to go. It meant interfering in a strange new situation to which he couldn't possibly contribute anything of value. The other part of his mind—and he was honest enough to admit it—was that he *was* curious. Not about Zoe. Whatever she might have done to her hair, she would be the same. It was the murder. Everything seemed to point to something to do with the Sunday photograph session that had been called off. By whom? Why? And if there was anything Horace disliked, it was having questions without answers. He didn't expect to understand computers or fax machines or atomic theories, he wouldn't even know the right questions to ask. But human beings, that he had reasoned had always been his speciality, for what was history except how human beings thought and consequently, or perhaps not, behaved?

So now he was on his way down.

Still almost summer, he thought as they went down Eleventh Avenue. Leaves not quite turning, even if it was late September. Knock it off, Horace, a voice said in his head. You're not thinking about leaves or the end of summer or the fact your gray suit still fits. You're just plain curious about a murder. No, that wasn't quite it. He was beginning to feel himself interested in today's world rather than a world where everything had been done and settled years before. Without being told, the driver swerved over onto one of the few fairly empty streets toward Seventh Avenue. Fashion Ave, it had been renamed, not that anybody ever called it that. Basic rule in New York, Horace thought, and probably every other major city: You could go from a long name to a short but not the other way around. Only a tourist would call Sixth Avenue by the more elegant name of Avenue of the Americas.

The cab swiveled its way through the Seventh Avenue traffic. For the first time, Horace became aware of the obstacles in the way. Huge delivery trucks (double-parked of course). Racks of dresses, all apparently identical and all covered with plastic, being shoved through cars and buses and dangerously near the feet of oblivious pedestrians. Fur coats on one rack. Did people still wear fur coats? Horace wondered, having no particular feelings on the subject one way or another. Trolleys being pushed by sweating men carrying bolts of cloth in a wide variety of colors. Oddly, the streets weren't particularly noisy. An occasional horn blast, a few of the standard four-letter words being exchanged with no particular emotion between those hurtling merchandise through the traffic and the drivers of temporarily stalled cars. But everybody somehow seemed to know what was happening was part of one of the major arteries of the economy of the city, and there was no point in getting upset about it.

"You're here," the driver said.

Once on the street, he took a long look at the building he was about to enter, standing impervious, like a true New Yorker, to anyone trying to get around or through him. It was, like most of the buildings that seemed to hold the heart of the fashion industry in this area, thoroughly practical, ugly, and grimy. He put his cigarette out carefully in a trash bin, pointedly ignoring the glare from a man who was fishing for an afternoon paper.

The lobby was as drab as the outside, not only narrow but crowded with cartons waiting to be picked up or delivered. Horace wondered how the trolleys and racks of clothes managed. Franchard's was listed on a panel covered with dusty glass to be on the third floor. Not very glamorous, Horace thought. Higher up might at least have some kind of a view. And sunlight. He stepped into the elevator (or, rather, pushed in next to the crowd already waiting) and pressed the right button. When did they start putting all these buttons so low? Probably some new law about access for the handicapped. Which I suppose I'll be if I don't exercise. He decided not to think about that.

For such a busy building, the elevator moved with incredible slowness. The people around him shifted impatiently and sighed, obviously used to this. Just to get to the third floor seemed to take five minutes, although Horace knew it couldn't have been that long. My God, I'm actually eager to get there, he told himself, and found that he was smiling. This was getting to be a lot more interesting than Queen Victoria. And besides, wasn't this simply another civic duty? Helping the police?

He stepped out on the third floor almost jauntily.

If Horace had expected the third floor to be bright with color and glamor, he was to be disappointed. The hallway was as narrow and grimy as the lobby downstairs. There were three doors, all closed. One, however, was painted a bright butter yellow. Horace marched toward it; this would be Franchard's. And on the door there was the tracing of a distinct signature with the designer's name. No buzzer or bell. Horace opened the door and walked in.

The reception room was also a bright yellow, faking sunlight that could not possibly have worked its way into the room from the one skinny window. A nervous-looking girl sat behind a receptionist's desk, twisting strands of her short hair as she waited for someone on the other end of the line. Her hair was a nondescript color done in the fashion Horace devoutly had hoped would have died out years ago: that of a wet floor mop. Whoever had devised that style, which had been popular for far too long, obviously hated women.

The rest of the room was empty, or, rather, full of scattered fashion magazines, yards of cloth spilling out from large bolts onto the two-seater sofa and one chair, a pile of costume jewelry in a huge dish on the small coffee table making the reception area look more like the entrance to a Gypsy fortune teller's than the reception room to a fashionable designer's workshop.

"Yes?" The receptionist had put down the phone and looked at Horace with the weary expression of someone who knew she was going to be asked to do still one more thing that had already made this day and probably the rest of her life totally miserable.

"I'm here to meet ..." Horace found himself hesitating. He was reasonably sure that Zoe had used her title to gain entry here but he still felt uncomfortable saying it. "The Countess Sirelli?"

"She's in the showroom with Jean-Claude. You Professor Livsey?" Horace nodded.

"Thank God. Not another cop." She waved a languid hand to the door behind her. "Go right on in."

Obviously any information she might have she was not about to repeat to Horace.

Through the door he found himself in a large open space. Here at least there was activity. Four ladies, their lips pursed from holding pins, were working on a mannequin draped in some sort of wispy material. Horace could only presume that the woman who would eventually buy it would be wearing something underneath it, although these days you couldn't be sure. From behind the dummy rose a man, almost as tall as Horace.

"If you are from the police or the newspapers, you are to get out at once." Despite his strong words, they didn't come out with the authority that he had clearly hoped for. "Or could you possibly be Professor Livsey?"

"Yes. And you would be ... ?"

"Jean-Claude Franchard. My God, what a pleasure it is to see an absolute civilian." Tall, Horace thought again. Taller than Rena had been.

From behind the closed drapes of an archway Horace heard Zoe's voice. "Horace darling, is that you? You found your way all right?"

Horace sighed. He had a feeling this was going to be a longer afternoon than he had planned. "Yes, Zoe. Ginny didn't have to pin the address onto my jacket. I *do* know how to get around New York, you know."

From behind the drapes Zoe's voice was lightly conciliatory. "Now, Horace, don't get cranky. Introduce yourself to Jean-Claude and be gentle with him. He's had a very bad day. I'll be out in a minute. Prepare to be dazzled."

Horace looked at the man now standing directly in front of him. Some gesture seemed to be required, so he put out his hand. The hand of the designer was surprisingly strong.

"Pleasure to meet you," the designer said. Although his name was definitely French, the man's accent was clearly New York, or at least that of someone born in one of the less-affluent boroughs, a fact that became increasingly obvious when he lost his temper, which he was already doing. "No! You imbeciles!" The four women working at pinning the dress looked at Franchard with the same expression on all of their faces: that of bored and overworked slaves.

"The side pleat must be higher. You're not designing it for that horse Rena now."

Another one not too fond of the dead model, Horace thought. There were small gilt chairs around the walls of the room and he settled himself uncomfortably in one of them. There was no need to make conversation, the designer and the four women assistants were muttering among themselves, completely oblivious of his presence.

Horace looked around the large room. Pinned to the padded silk walls (gray or perhaps just dusty?) were dozens of sketches, each with pieces of material attached to them. Future designs? Past designs? Horace couldn't be sure. Each of them had a slash cut off at the bottom, the same angle that booksellers make when the customer is buying the book as a present and doesn't want to advertise the price of the volume. On the other side of the bottom of the sketches was scrawled a large *F*, similar to the one that preceded the spelling of the designer's name on the front door.

Obviously he was going to learn nothing of interest here. He began to feel awkward and uncomfortable. What had he expected to see anyway? He remembered his years in Paris with Zoe. Not that they had had the money to visit couturier salons often, not even the less well known ones, but he remembered the men who waited for their ladies to appear in some new outfit from the dressing rooms. Men with unhappy expressions on their faces and sometimes with a poodle in their laps, knowing full well that their only reason for being there was at the end of the session (and it could take hours) they would be expected to pull out a checkbook and a pen. Luckily, Horace didn't have to worry about that with Zoe.

One of the ladies involved in redraping the dummy detached herself from the group and came over to him. She was, he saw now, older than the others and was wearing a severe black dress instead of the cotton smocks the other fitters had on.

"Professor? Could I get you some coffee?" She was a plain woman with a tendency toward stoutness and a face naked of makeup. All of the women were plain, Horace noticed, at least to his eyes. Was it a deliberate decision on the designer's part to make customers feel more attractive, or had it just been a long day with no chance to refresh their faces?

"Thank you. But if you just show me where it is, perhaps I could manage on my own? I can see you're all busy."

"Not that busy. We still haven't picked a new model yet, which means sewing the hems is delayed." She smoothed her already neat hair as if some stray strand might have escaped her tight chignon. "Although I suppose we could go back to June now that Rena's dead."

"Go back? Wasn't Rena the first choice for the picture layout?"

The woman's face, already blank of expression, seemed to close up tighter. "Cream and sugar?"

Across the room the designer's face was reddening with anger. For the first time Horace noticed his blond hair was dyed, a mistake for a man who had to be at least forty.

"Berta!" Franchard shouted. "Come back here! There's no *frisson* in the chiffon where the waist drapes over the behind!"

"Excuse me," the woman he had called Berta said.

"That's all right. I'll pass on the coffee. But is there a washroom?" That would at least get him out of this workplace, Horace thought, not in the least embarrassed at mentioning bodily functions, which he might have been twenty years before. One of the convenient excuses of getting older, he thought. Berta gestured toward another draped archway and hurried back to the designer.

Exaggerating his stiffness, Horace walked to the other end of the room and pushed aside the drape. He found himself in a long, dingy hall. Whatever money had been spent to create a luxurious environment had obviously not been extended beyond the showroom. There was a water fountain, a rickety table with a hot plate, and the smell of strong coffee coming from the pot on it. The hall ended at a last door, halfway open. Horace could see the edge of a desk. Franchard's office, he presumed, and headed straight for it. As he passed the door to the one washroom he noticed that door was open as well. He closed it quietly. If anyone came in while he looked into the office of the designer, he could always say he had made a mistake about where to go.

The office had a window that managed to let some of the September afternoon sunlight in. The desk was neater than Horace imagined, certainly neater than his own. A large stack of what were clearly bills was on the left of the desk, efficiently held together by a thick bronze clip. On a shelf behind the desk, which Horace noticed on a closer look was an inexpensive copy of a French antique, was a shelf that held a statue on a base. An award obviously, and Horace moved closer to see the inscription. "For the Best Designer of the Year" it said ... but the year was five years ago. Only one award, Horace thought. For all he could see in the office, it was the one object that was free of dust, and carefully polished.

"Merde!" The designer's voice carried all the way back here. Another crisis, thought Horace. He looked quickly around the room. What am I looking for? he wondered. He noticed the dying plants on the windowsill, a swirl of fashion newspapers thrown onto the floor. A stack of pictures was on the other side of the desk from the bills. Obviously models Franchard was considering as replacements for the dead girl. There was a closed appointment book next to the pictures. He wondered if he should take the chance of opening it.

He took the chance.

Franchard's handwriting was not easy to read: Most of today's page had nothing but phone numbers. One of them had been heavily underlined, clearly in anger. The number was one Horace recognized, thanks to Ginny and the paper she had left on the breakfast table—Axel Gruen's.

He turned abruptly. He could hear a woman's heels coming down the corridor. As he moved swiftly toward the door, he only had time to notice a picture in the wastebasket by the desk. Even torn to pieces he recognized the photograph to be one of Rena, one that Axel Gruen had taken.

The hall was empty. Whoever had been coming down the hall must have been headed for the washroom. Think of a good excuse, he thought, then, noticing a fire door, he managed to reach it as Berta came out of the washroom.

"We were wondering where you were," she said, her voice flat, not expressing any suspicion. Horace was a good ten feet from the office by now.

"I thought I might perhaps sneak a cigarette out on the fire escape," Horace said, smiling with what he hoped was a sheepish expression.

"That door should be locked."

All right, so she doesn't believe me. Berta stood there, obviously waiting for him to pass her on the way back to the showroom. As Horace went by her, he remarked with what he hoped was casualness, "I suppose with a magazine shoot like this you're all rather busy?"

"Today? Today is nothing, even with the police. December, when we do our first runway show, that will be a madhouse. Today is ordinary hysteria."

Horace wanted to smile at her remark, but the blank expression on her face stopped him at once.

"Come. Your wife is ready."

Meekly Horace preceded her back to the showroom. What was it she had said? "Their first runway show?" But they had been in business for years.

He pushed aside the drape.

CHAPTER SIX

Zoe was standing in the middle of the long room. Her hair was still the same curly black cap she had always had, although Horace had long ago suspected that nature had been helped a bit regarding the color. She turned to look at him as he walked in, smiling as brightly as she had when she had been one of his students.

Horace couldn't possibly have described the dress she was wearing. He knew it was blue, a particularly vibrant shade, and was made of either satin or some kind of thick silk. It had delicate sleeves starting just below her shoulders and the skirt came almost down to her ankles. It wasn't a sexy dress, although Horace sensed rather than saw that there were edges of lace at various places that suggested the lady might be wearing black lace lingerie underneath. It was not a dress that called attention to itself, but to the woman wearing it. Franchard as a designer was both superb and subtle. Zoe had never looked better in her life.

Her smile turned into a grin of triumph. "That's it, Franchard. I'm taking it with me right now. I haven't seen my husband look at me like that since our honeymoon." She moved lightly across the room and kissed Horace on the cheek. Turning back to the designer, she used her most entrancing voice. "Now, you're not going to make any objections, are you, darling Jean-Claude? You don't need it for the *Elegant* shoot, do you? Promise me you'll let me have it. I want to wear it for Celeste's dinner party. After all, it's for you."

"You too are going to the editor of *Elegant*'s dinner party? How then could I refuse you, Contessa?" He bowed low and kissed her hand.

"I suspect I'll be buying other things from your collection, Jean-Claude, but not today. Dear Horace is going to get me a taxi and see

66

me back uptown.'' She didn't wait for Horace to make an answer, but twirled once more and disappeared back into the dressing room.

"You like the dress?'' Berta was standing beside him. Horace realized he must still have that silly look on his face. Dazzled indeed!

"It's a . . . beautiful. I—I don't really know very much about clothes but . . .''

"But a great deal about women?'' Berta went on before Horace could think of an appropriately modest (and truthful) answer. "When a designer is a genius . . . it is worth all the tantrums and trouble. I hope the contessa enjoys the privilege of owning the dress now. By next season I suspect cheap copies of it will be in every department store in America.''

"Does your firm . . . I mean, Jean-Claude . . . make a percentage on that?''

"We're not quite big enough for that yet.'' Even for such an expressionless woman Horace could detect a thin edge of bitterness. "But after the *Elegant* spread and the runway show in December, perhaps then we can get the backing for our own prêt-à-porter.'' She added the explanation, "Ready to wear.''

"But surely Franchard's gets something if somebody copies his designs?''

"A flat sum. Unless we can manage a contract to give us some percentage. Not so easy these days. Not like it was before.'' She looked away from Horace, her attention caught by Jean-Claude, who was studying a handful of sketches. These had not been clipped at the edge, Horace noticed. Probably works in progress. "Excuse me, I must go.''

Horace took a step that effectively blocked her path. "But surely you can't do just one dress and make a living out of it? Even at the highest prices.'' He smiled in what he hoped was an ingratiating way to take any possible offense out of his question.

"Jean-Claude will make twenty, maybe twenty-five copies, to be sold in one exclusive shop in different major cities. His name will become known again. That is what is most important. That's what brings in the money.''

"Berta!'' Jean-Claude's voice was firm in his command. He had no need to be polite to the ex-husband of a good customer. "These sketches!''

Berta barely raised her voice. "You have not finished those sketches, Jean-Claude. As one look should have told you.'' Whatever her position in the company, this was one woman the designer couldn't boss around.

"Would Rena have worn that dress last Sunday night?'' If anybody had information about the dead model and her death, Horace suspected it was the stolid woman beside him.

"Her? In that? She would have looked like a tricked-up circus pony. It takes a delicate woman to wear that dress. Like your ex-wife." She sighed as she watched Jean-Claude get down on his knees with the other ladies and fussed with the hem of the dress on the dummy. "We had to be very careful what we put on Rena."

"Is that why the photograph session Sunday was canceled? Her clothes weren't ready?"

"Who said they weren't?" The question was asked without expression but her eyes were suddenly very cold.

"I . . . I must have read it. In the newspapers." Horace was glad he had never had Berta in a classroom, either as a teacher or a student.

"The papers print a lot of garbage." Berta was picking her words carefully now. "Rena was new . . . for us. New to our style. Not as experienced as we are used to."

"But you chose her over another model? June, did you say?"

"I don't always make the decisions. Regrettably." She started to move around Horace.

"You sound as if you didn't like Rena."

"How could I?" With definite finality she went over to Franchard. Whatever she said to him made him look up at Horace. The look was one of barely concealed anger.

An hour later Horace was back in his apartment. He hadn't actually minded seeing Zoe back uptown, not to her hotel, of course. There was a cluster of expensive shops on Madison Avenue and Horace suspected Zoe, dress box firmly in her hand, was out to buy all the appropriate accessories she would need. He had hoped their conversation on the way would fill him in with some of the answers to the questions that buzzed through his head. He should have remembered Zoe in the rush she got from buying clothes was not going to be much help with facts.

"Well, of course the design business is profitable, surely you know that, Horace. Once someone has established their name, there's practically no limit to what they can pull in." She mentioned several designers that even Horace had heard of. "First the sensational designs. Then the ready-to-wear . . . that is if they can find a backer with deep pockets. After that they can go in almost any direction. A men's line. Designer sheets. Luggage. Perfume—you name it, somebody has to design it."

"Where do they find the time? Don't they usually do a couple of collections a year?"

"Horace, you are naive. They license their name out to companies that specialize. Technically they are supposed to supervise the designs, to give each item with their name on it, or initials, a stamp of approval." She sighed lightly. "Of course, I don't suppose half of them see what's being put out. But it can bring in millions. Sometimes more . . . as long as they're the current rage."

"Franchard is in that league?"

"Of course not, silly. You saw his space. He isn't a Dior or Calvin Klein. He was starting to get there a couple of years ago. But then, well, there were all sorts of rumors. Drugs, they said. Mismanagement. It could be a dozen things. But at his level, one bad step and you're off the ladder."

"Only now he's starting up again?"

"With a big help from dear Celeste. Frankly, I would have thought with her important promotion she would have gone for somebody brand new. A personal discovery, that would help her career. She's always had a kind heart. But after seeing Franchard's designs, I think she's made a good choice. He's definitely going to be a success." She gave him her smile that deepened her dimples. No surgery, if she'd had any, had destroyed those. "The look on your face when you saw me! Every woman in the world wants to see that look on the face of the man she cares about."

This was getting into tricky territory even for Zoe, for she leaned forward to the driver. "You can let me out here, driver." She turned back to Horace. "You *do* have money for the cab fare, don't you, darling?"

"Yes, of course." Must remember to get to the bank tomorrow, Horace thought. Even with Zoe picking up major expenses, escorting her was not cheap.

"I'll have the limo pick you up at seven Thursday. So don't forget. It's black tie." She half opened the door, clutching her large box carefully. "And you might try getting a haircut before then. There's no point in overdoing the shaggy-professor look."

And she was out of the car. As always after one of their meetings, Horace felt exhausted. He gave the driver his address and leaned back. Luckily there were cigarette butts in the ashtray in the door, a pleasant change from the wads of damp Kleenex people were leaving there more and more often. The driver, he noticed, had already lit his cigarette.

Damn it, Horace thought as he started to relax, there was something more he had wanted to find out. Not necessarily from Zoe, he thought. With her mind on a grand dinner party she was like a child looking forward to her birthday. But something at the studio. What *was* it? Something he'd seen? Or not seen? Something the woman called Berta had said? All right, so she didn't like Rena, models weren't always popular, at least not with the staff of a designer.

He thought of the sketches in Franchard's hands. Maybe that was it? In his brief time in the designer's office there had been no sign of an easel set up with a sketch board. No sketch board at all. Then he remembered reading or hearing about some designer who did all his work in bed.

Horace, he thought to himself, understanding Disraeli is a lot easier.

If he had hoped for a quiet respite when he got home, he was to be disappointed. Ginny was seated at the kitchen table, an empty glass and a bottle of what looked like vodka beside her. Good God, don't tell me she's a secret drinker, Horace thought. Ginny looked at him as if he were a stranger, then a small frown crossed her face.

"You're home early," she said, speaking in a perfectly normal voice.

"Are you drinking vodka at this hour? It's not even five."

"You caught that?" Suddenly the frown was gone and she was beaming with smiles. "And I wasn't saying anything! I hope Natasha Kinn thinks the same thing."

"You're playing Viola as a drunk tomorrow? When I left here you were deep in Shakespeare."

"That's my comedy-classic scene. This is my modern one. You have to do two. It's from an original play we did a reading of in college. I figured an original play, she'd have no one to compare me with. I'm supposed to be this alcoholic pregnant ex-prostitute who's contemplating becoming a lesbian."

"Just as I've always pictured you," Horace said dryly.

"An actress has to stretch. Now, why don't you go away . . . there's a pile of phone messages for you."

So much for her interest in Rena. And Zoe. "Aren't you curious about Franchard's?"

"Not now, Horsey! I've got to work on making this seem like real vodka." She studied the half-full bottle carefully. "Just how drunk would Donna-Jo be by this time?" She was clearly talking to herself. Then she looked up at Horace as if surprised to find him still in the room. "I won't be able to fix dinner tonight, you'll have to eat out. I've another hour's work at least on motivation, then I'll have some vegetables or something before I meditate. And to bed early." She turned back to the bottle and started pouring more water into her glass.

Horace made his way into his study.

Ginny had scrawled down several phone calls, several of which were from Axel Gruen, which Horace had no intention of returning. Newspapers or television must have told the photographer of Horace's connection, vague as it was with Rena's death. And with his portfolio. The last message was from Mark. Odd Ginny hadn't mentioned that he'd called again.

He stood there by his desk before picking up the phone. What was it that he needed to remember seeing at Franchard's studio? He had a feeling it was important. Or if not that, at least something that bothered him, sort of the way your tongue feels around your mouth to see if a filling had fallen out.

He picked up the phone.

"Professor? Glad you called. How was your trip to Franchard's?"

"Nonproductive, if you're referring to the murder, which I presume you are. Not that I expected it to be."

"I tried calling earlier but Ginny seemed distracted. I thought she might like to know . . . that both of you would like to know . . . that Paco has been released on bail."

"How did that happen?"

"A lot of pressure. A certain amount of pull." Horace could hear the weariness in the younger man's voice. "Hell, Professor, you know how things work in this city."

"The law firm that Franchard hired?" Something flickered across Horace's mind but disappeared. "I didn't know they had that much influence. Not in a murder case."

"The case against Navarez was pretty weak to begin with. Anyway, I thought Ginny would like to know, but I don't think she even heard me."

"She was getting drunk on a bottle of water."

"What?"

"Actresses, Mark. She has an audition tomorrow."

"Yeah." Mark remembered Cheryl rehearsing her songs. No room for anything or anyone else. All right, Ginny was attractive, but no point in going overboard with an actress.

A thought crossed Horace's mind, one that he had been chasing since he had left Franchard's. "Tell me, Mark . . . you said Paco is released on bail. How much would that be?"

"A hundred thousand. Pretty steep for a delivery guy, huh? Or whatever he is."

"If I remember correctly, that means somebody has to put up ten percent in cash? To make the bail?"

"That's right. Why do you ask?"

"Who could that have been?"

"Franchard. At least that's what Margolus told me when I finally caught up with him. Boy, he's been ticked off all day! Apparently the higher ranks in Homicide are getting involved with the case. And he's no guy to take that lightly.''

"This law firm you mentioned, that's working for Franchard?'' Horace looked down at his desk. It was messy as usual, but there was one thing that was not on it, something that had been clearly on the designer's desk. "What would they charge for doing this sort of . . . what do I call it? Favor? For the designer?''

"Their rates could go as high as five hundred an hour to a thousand. What are you after, Professor?''

"I'm not exactly sure. They'd bill for what? Three, four hours?''

"Probably a whole day. They must have been phoning everybody up to the governor.''

"That represents quite a bit of money.''

"Can you hold for a second, Professor? I've got a call on my other line.''

Mark must have been surprised when Horace agreed with unusual mildness. In the silence Horace was adding up the sum of money in his head. Franchard had probably spent nearly twenty thousand dollars today, just to free Paco. And the designer had not struck Horace as the generous type. Mark came back on the phone.

"Sorry, Professor. It was Axel Gruen again. He's been after me all day to get his damn portfolio back.''

"Yes, I even have a few messages from him. Have you got it?''

"That's something else that's weird. Margolus turned it over to me about four o'clock. I don't know whether it's because he doesn't consider it important, which would be pretty dumb of him because technically it's evidence, or because he's not about to hand over anything to help the guys above him. Anyway, I don't know how I'm going to get it to him. I'm supposedly on paperwork all tomorrow. And I'm not about to spring for a message service.''

"Perhaps I could be of help, Mark?'' Horace made a conscious effort not to sound too smooth. "I live not far from Gruen and I *did* know him years ago. It wouldn't be any problem for me.''

"Great. Tomorrow lunchtime?'' What he said next made Horace have the feeling that Mark was grinning slightly. "Your lunchtime, I mean. Not mine. Say, about one-thirty?''

Did everybody in the whole city know that Horace liked to sleep late? A clear invasion of privacy! Still, it gave Horace a wedge to get what he wanted.

"One-thirty would be fine, Mark. And could we meet at the dead girl's apartment?''

"What?"

Before he could get a chance to say no, Horace went on with what he hoped was an innocent-sounding request. "You know my niece is looking for an apartment. And with her having an audition tomorrow, she won't have time. I thought I might just check it out for her. Would that be possible?"

Mark hesitated for a moment. "I suppose so. I think the police stickers are still up although they've finished all their tests." He took another moment before agreeing. "Okay. I guess I can get the keys from Margolus or the Sixth Precinct."

"Good. I'll see you at one-thirty, then."

"You have the address?"

"It's been in the papers, Mark," Horace said gently but with just the slightest hint of sarcasm. Why did everybody think he was an old idiot? But he put the phone down quickly, before Mark could change his mind.

Before he called Axel to tell him his precious portfolio would be returned to him tomorrow, he took a moment to sit and look at his desk. Twenty thousand dollars at least Franchard had spent to get the release of a young man. All that with a thick pile of unpaid bills on his desk. Even before his retirement Horace had always been prompt in paying his bills, always with a shadow of a childish fear that banks could crash overnight and there'd be no money left.

Of course, not everyone was as punctilious as he was, he reasoned. Still, it couldn't help but raise questions about the two men. What exactly was their connection? Sexual? Somehow Horace doubted that, the young man who had delivered Rena's pictures had not seemed the type, not that Horace was sure there was a type anymore. Drugs? All the mentions of Paco had brought up his place of birth was Colombia. And there had been talk, as Zoe said, that the designer had had drug problems. Was that why the shoot had been canceled Sunday night?

He shoved aside the notes on Victorian parliamentary law and reached for the page Ginny had left with Axel's phone number. A lot of questions, and no answers. Taking one more day off his book wouldn't hurt that much.

He punched the numbers of the photographer.

WEDNESDAY

CHAPTER SEVEN

To Horace's surprise, he slept well that night after a comfortable dinner by himself next door at Le Mirabeau. Getting up for once was no problem. The apartment was pleasantly quiet. The table in the dining room was neatly set for breakfast, with a note from Ginny that she would be out for most of the day. However, there was fresh coffee waiting to be heated, yogurt in a dish in the refrigerator (Horace had trained himself not to call it an icebox anymore, although it had taken time), fresh squeezed orange juice, and waiting for him as he sat down, the morning papers.

Oddly, or so Horace thought, Rena's murder was barely reported, and then on the inside pages. Of course there had been another earthquake in California and the Mideast was erupting again but he was still a little puzzled. In the past as far as he could recall, when a beautiful woman in a glamorous industry had been found dead, it had made the front pages for several days. Still, this could mean that the police were keeping what they had found to themselves and not necessarily that the story was no longer news. There was also no mention that Paco had been released on bail.

By one o'clock, hair cut and a visit made to his bank, Horace took a cab downtown. It was another warm but comfortable September day although the papers predicted rain later on. No sign of clouds yet, Horace noticed as he turned into Bank Street. He liked this section of the West Village although it always made him feel too big, as if he leaned against a wall, the whole block of buildings would collapse like a row of dominoes. He was glad to see Mark was waiting outside the building, portfolio in hand.

"You just missed the landlord, Professor" was Mark's greeting.

"Landlord?"

"You did say you wanted to see the apartment for Ginny, didn't you?"

"Yes, of course." This is what you get for sticking your nose into something that's none of your business, he thought. You tell one lie and then another and before you know it you're stuck with a series of made-up stories you have to remember. "Has he been in the apartment?"

"With a crew. Cleaning up."

That answered a question Horace had often wondered about. Who did clean up after a messy murder? Somehow he couldn't see Margolus or anybody else on the police force doing it. Not at the cost of overtime with the city's budget problems.

"And from what he said," Mark went on, "I don't think Ginny's going to be able to afford this place. He plans to raise the rent almost a thousand dollars a month."

"Can he do that? Isn't it rent controlled? Or stabilized or something?"

"He makes a few improvements, rents it furnished, he can go as high as he wants. Still want to go in?"

"As long as we're here."

Horace followed Mark down the three steps to the door below the main stairs at the front of the house. Rena's apartment was clearly what was euphemistically called a "garden apartment," when actually it was the basement of the brownstone, although Horace supposed there must be another basement under this that held boilers and pipes and fuse boxes. Mark opened the front grilled-iron door. A new lock, Horace noticed as he bent his head. With another key Mark started to fumble with the lock to the apartment. There was still bits of yellow tape around the edges of the door, signs the police put up to denote a crime scene. Someone, either the landlord or the police, had broken through them.

"Actually this door should be sealed," Mark said almost to himself. "But that landlord looked like a pretty tough customer. A few strips of tape weren't going to bother him. Not with the first of the month coming up. He'll probably have an ad for the place in this Sunday's *Times*." With a little effort he unlocked the door and held it open for Horace to enter.

Whatever Horace may have expected, Rena's apartment was not what he had imagined. No sordid rooms like other recent murders. No blood-stained floor. Not even a wall solely devoted to pictures of the dead model. Of course, not all models were narcissists, but still . . .

Instead, what faced him was one long room, stretching from the front of the house to the back. From where he stood he could see through windows to bits of a garden. There was no particular style about the room, nothing that could be neatly labeled "American antique" or "French provincial." It had a quiet, empty look (although there was plenty of furniture) that said it had been furnished economically, efficiently, and with no particular quality that would have made it inviting to a guest. There was a Victorian sofa (fake) and behind it a long table that could have seated four for dinner if Rena had been so inclined. Instead, it was piled neatly with a few fashion magazines. Beyond that, against one wall, was a king-size bed. No footboard, Horace noticed, always important when you're tall, as Rena had been. The bed had been stripped, probably by the police, the sheets, pillows, and a neutral-colored quilt neatly folded. At the end of the room was a desk and chair.

As he walked toward the desk he saw without really noticing there was a large armoire, bedside tables, an archway to the kitchenette and a closed door. He opened the door. A long array of various colored clothes hung precisely on the iron rod. There was a second door opposite the bed, near the archway into the small kitchen. A minuscule bathroom was behind it.

Mark hadn't moved beyond the sofa. "Is it what you expected, Professor?"

"I don't know what I expected," Horace said thoughtfully. "Is this it? I mean, the whole of the place?"

"Garden out back. Do you want to look at it?"

"Not yet." He stood at the desk and turned around carefully, taking in the whole long room. Back when the house had been built, probably in the middle of the last century, this space must have been divided into a kitchen, a pantry. Maybe a storeroom. Possibly even the dining room. Looking up, he could see faint marks on the ceiling where the partitions would have been before this had been converted into what he could only call a studio.

"Mark, Rena was lying to Ginny." What was interesting, Horace realized, was he didn't find the conclusion surprising. "There's no spare bedroom, small or otherwise. Unless she planned on Ginny sleeping on the kitchen floor."

"You're sure she said she had a spare room?"

"That's what Ginny said. She wouldn't have been mistaken about that. It was to be a hundred and fifty a month." He heard Mark's faint whistle. "Yes. I know. Unbelievably cheap for New York. Only there's no room here." He walked through the thin archway into what was designed to be the kitchen and probably had been a closet of some kind at one time. The tiny area, like the rest of the apartment, was what real estate ads called "broom clean." The landlord's workers had done an efficient job.

On the one narrow counter, lined up like soldiers, were a series of boxes that had contained the essentials for eating. Horace picked up one or two. They were empty. If there had been anything hidden in them, either the killer or the police or whoever had cleaned up the place would have found it. Even the garbage can was empty.

"Why would Rena have lied about something like that? She must have known Ginny would have found out on Monday. Hell, even this sofa wouldn't fold out."

Both men turned to look at the Victorian sofa. Only a child of six could have slept on that.

"Because she never expected to have Ginny as a roommate," Horace said slowly. "I think it's fairly obvious why she called Ginny last weekend and made the offer. Made it at the very last minute. It gave her an excuse to send her portfolio to Ginny, care of me. She wanted it out of this apartment, and she wanted it out Sunday night. The night she was killed."

"Yeah, but she could have ..." Mark's voice trailed off as he thought of any other possible explanation.

"Could have what? Look at the size of that thing."

Mark looked down at the portfolio he was still holding.

"You couldn't mail that. It wouldn't fit into a locker at a bus station or Grand Central. Even Federal Express might balk at it. Not to mention she seems not to have had anyone she trusted to send it to."

"Except Ginny." Mark frowned and put the folio down on the sofa. "Only what was so important about the folio? You went through it. Ginny. Me. The police. It's just pictures."

"Which reminds me." Horace started moving through the long room thoroughly. The armoire contained the clothes a young woman wouldn't put on hangers: lingerie, panty hose, folded slips. "What did this room look like when you and Margolus got here?"

"A mess." Mark frowned, trying to remember what he had seen. "She was on the bed, facedown on one of the pillows. The armoire doors were open, everything shoved on the floor. Chairs overturned and the sofa ... Wearing pajamas and a robe. No sexual attack."

"A struggle?"

"I'd say a search."

"For what? Something small." Horace was almost thinking aloud, obviously not expecting an answer. He moved to the desk. "Was this disturbed?"

"Drawers pulled out and emptied on the floor."

Horace started opening the desk drawers. Whoever had cleaned up had not been as careful as they had been about Rena's clothes. He opened a second drawer. Nothing that wouldn't have been found in any young woman's desk.

"If you're looking for an address book, the police took it. I imagine they're checking out any names that might be in it." Mark moved closer to the desk. "You expecting to find anything?"

"I'm not trying to outguess the police, if that's what you're thinking," Horace said quietly. "I'm sure they've been very thorough."

"Then what are you looking for?"

"Things I would expect to find."

"You mean personal letters? A diary? They also took her appointment book, in case you're wondering."

"Mark, a professional model . . . she wouldn't just have one portfolio of her pictures, would she? Shouldn't there be a scrapbook, a collection, copies of her résumé that she could show to other possible employers?"

"Maybe she kept all that at her agency? It's the Classic Agency. She signed with them just days ago. I got that out of Margolus."

"I suppose somebody's already checked with them?" But Horace didn't really expect an answer. He began to go through the contents of the desk again. No stack of unpaid bills, that was the first thing he noticed. He picked up the dead girl's checkbook. The next thing he saw as he flipped through it was the late model had done what he did, stapled the canceled checks back to their original stubs. There were her rent checks (already far too high for this space, Horace thought), health club dues, places with unlikely names that Horace presumed were beauty salons, checks to expensive department stores, drugstores, weekly checks to cash, always at the same amount. "Walking-around money," Horace had always considered it, but with a busy model probably taxi money.

"What about her purse? Did she have credit cards? Snapshots of friends, personal items?"

"You mean like . . . condoms or something?"

"No." Horace wasn't after that, although it raised another point. "Who had been in the girl's personal life? She must have had one. Even Ginny had originally thought she was asked to be a roommate to protect Rena from some rejected lover."

"Nothing we could find. Although she had birth control pills in the bathroom and a diaphragm in one of the bedside tables. Want me to look and see if it's still there?"

"No, thank you." That closed off the one other possibility that Horace had unwillingly considered, that perhaps the dead girl's interests in sex concerned someone of her own gender, which would have been a bad mistake if she expected Ginny to share her interests. This wasn't something he intended to discuss with Mark, feeling a reluctance to go into what he was sure the younger man would consider a prurient interest.

"She wasn't a virgin, if that's what you're wondering." It was as if Mark had read his mind.

"But no photographs of boyfriends. No photographs of herself." Horace reached next for a folder containing bank statements. The deposits listed were good, but nothing that would have allowed Rena mink coats or diamonds if she had desired them. Underneath the bank folder was one containing records of stock dealings. Here the sums were higher. Whatever Rena had been, she had invested wisely, but, again, not extravagantly.

"Damn it, Mark, this isn't the apartment of a model!" Horace knew he was letting his frustration get the better of him. At least when he had gone to Franchard's there had been things that puzzled him. Here there was nothing. "I mean, considering her looks were her living . . . what is here? Jars of cosmetics? Mirrors with lights around them? Angled mirrors so she could check her appearance from all sides? Pictures of herself in various poses? Taken by different photographers? There isn't even a bulletin board with the ads she posed for. This apartment could have belonged to anyone, a rising woman executive, a banker, a lawyer."

"You should see my apartment." Mark couldn't resist a grin.

"You know what I mean," Horace answered crisply. "This apartment's a complete void. No matter how thoroughly the landlord cleaned up, no matter what the police took, there should be some sign that *somebody* lived here. And there isn't. Nobody leads that sterile a life."

"You think whoever killed her took everything that was personal?" Mark sneaked a look at his watch. He was going to have to get back to his office fairly soon.

Horace began to move around the room again. "They couldn't have. Not if it had to fit under a cape, as everybody seems to think they did. Whether it was Paco or not. There's no fireplace where the murderer or even Rena could have burned anything." He swiveled around to look at Mark directly. "What about garbage? Did the police check that?"

"Nothing. The usual stuff. Empty cartons of takeout food, newspapers, designer water bottles. She obviously didn't believe in recycling."

"Vacuum cleaner bag?"

"Empty. Dumped out on the kitchen floor." Mark couldn't help finding it somewhat enjoyable to see his former professor stumped. They had become like two kids trying to play detective, and not doing a very good job of it.

"Nothing in the refrigerator?" Horace took a step toward the kitchenette. "In the ice trays?" He was trying to think of all the places people had used in the past to hide things from burglars.

"Everything dumped. Ice included."

"Linen closet?"

"Sheets and towels all over the place. Whoever the killer was, he was thorough."

Horace snorted and began pacing the long room again. What wasn't in this apartment that should be here? No books, except for a pile of paperbacks on the far bedside table, now neatly stacked. Two mysteries, three books on financial planning. No romances, he noticed. No signs of liquor bottles either. Not unusual, he supposed. A model had to stay healthy to keep her looks. He reached for the fashion magazines. They dated back over a year. Flipping through them, he found certain pages carefully turned down. These were the pages where Rena Varmont was in one of the ads. So she did keep some record of her career! It was the first sign of humanity that Horace had been able to find since he came into the apartment. But the ads were small.

Mark was peering over his shoulder. "Interesting face. Beautiful, I guess."

"Not your type?"

"I suspect she'd scare the hell out of me if I'd met her." He glanced at his watch again. "Look, Professor, I really think I should be getting back to the office. I don't want to rush you, but I don't think there's anything more we're going to find here."

"You've been very patient. Put it down to an old man's curiosity."

"You're not old . . ." But Horace had walked back to the desk and was looking out at the garden, ignoring the compliment. The garden in the September sun looked neglected. Whatever Rena had been, she certainly hadn't been interested in using the small outdoor space. "I suppose the back door was locked," he said. There were three locks and a chain on the door to the outside. All shiny. All new, he suspected.

"And the windows. Whoever got in, she obviously knew them."

There was a bench and a chair near the kitchen windows. A soggy section of the Sunday papers was on one of them. Obviously the landlord's clean-up crew had ignored the garden. However, they had done a complete job in the apartment. It made Horace wonder if he could hire them now that he was without a cleaning woman. Probably way beyond his price range.

"All right, Mark," Horace said at last. "I'd better call Axel and tell him I'm on my way with the portfolio." He picked up the phone but there was no dial tone. "It's not working."

"Probably turned off by the company. The landlord or the police must have notified them. My guess would be the police. They even took the tape from her answering machine." He walked over to stand beside Horace. "I do have to get back, Professor." Mark couldn't help repeating what he knew Horace would not want to hear. "Don't mean to rush you."

"I'm just curious. It's supposed to be a sign of intelligence," Horace responded amiably. He picked up Rena's checkbook. He passed the canceled checks to the stubs of checks that had not been returned yet from the bank. They'd be with next month's statement, he presumed. The last entry was for a sizable check to Always Available Locksmiths. It was for well over three hundred dollars and dated the Friday before Rena had been killed.

"When did you say Rena signed her contract with the Classic Agency?"

"About a week ago."

"And before that?"

Mark felt as if he had been asked a question he should have studied beforehand. Livsey was still his professor, he thought miserably. "I don't know. I think she was free-lance."

Horace smiled amiably. "I'm sure the police have checked that out, Mark. It isn't really your job, is it?"

Mark felt suddenly relieved. What was it about a former teacher that still awed you?

"I guess we'd better be going. Shall I take the portfolio?"

Mark realized he wasn't quite off the hook. He felt his face beginning to turn pink. "There is something about that portfolio. I . . . I guess I should have mentioned it earlier."

Horace continued to stare at him, an enigmatic look that suggested everything from that he was failing the course to that he had raised a question that Livsey hadn't expected.

"The police found something in the portfolio. They didn't think it was very important, but they photocopied it, just in case." He pushed the large fake-leather envelope onto the desk and unzipped it. "It was behind one of the pictures." He took out the copy of the page. It was a newspaper clipping, clearer than the original probably had been.

Horace studied it carefully. It was a news story from one of the tabloids, the date five years ago. It told of a car accident involving a model named Diane Chaumet, age twenty-seven, who had apparently skidded her car into an embankment on one of the roads leading to her Connecticut home on a rainy night. There was a blurred picture of the car against a concrete embankment and a large shot of the model in a very striking pose. The only personal thing about the clipping was that the name of the agency she had worked for was the Classic Agency. Those two words were clearly underlined.

"Why didn't we spot this?" Horace asked. He looked around the room. Not anything that resembled an ashtray. He supposed he could hold off a little longer.

"It was behind one of her pictures. I guess we didn't think to look. Anyway, it's five years old." He handed the copy of the clipping to Horace. "The important thing is that she was listed as a successful model. I suppose Rena must have put it there as the sort of agency she should be under contract to." He couldn't tell whether Horace was accepting this. "Maybe we should have looked further?"

"We didn't have all that much time," Horace said in a tone that was as forgiving as he could get. "Still, it's interesting Rena kept this."

"You know how people tuck things in the back of things, meaning to reread them someday?" Mark's answer seemed weak even to himself. "I mean, this woman died before Rena got to New York. They weren't related, Margolus told me they checked on that. The fact that the name of the agency was underlined seems to be the important thing."

"I suppose so." Horace's smile was what he hoped was pleasant. "I really mustn't hold you up any further, Mark. I appreciate your catering to me." He folded the copy of the newspaper clipping and put it into his jacket pocket. He didn't for one moment think the clipping was something Rena had hidden casually in her portfolio. "You don't mind if I keep this, do you?" As if to hide his interest, he added, "Ginny will be curious about it, I'm sure."

"No. I guess it's all right." Mark watched Livsey zip up the plastic portfolio of the dead model's pictures. "You're going up to Gruen now?"

"That is what was planned, wasn't it? Give my respects to Detective Margolus."

Mark followed the professor out of the apartment, carefully locking the two doors behind them. Both new locks, Horace noticed again. Always Available Locksmiths. He cursed silently to himself for not having gone through every page of the phone books on Rena's desk. All right, not as good as an address book or an appointment book, but with the tiny print of the phone book pages these days, people had a tendency to mark the numbers they called for easier viewing. However, it was too late to go back into the apartment again.

Mark shook Horace's hand and headed to the right. Toward the subway, Horace thought, and moved left, toward Hudson and hopefully a cab that would take him uptown.

An idiot, that's what he'd been not to have checked behind the photographs of the album. People tucked things in there that were ... or could be important sometime in the future. Oddly, his legs weren't hurting. While it was only two blocks, still, looking back, he was glad he didn't have to keep up with Mark's brisk pace.

Take all the time you need, Horace, he told himself, and felt for the folded paper in his jacket pocket. Probably it was unimportant. At least the police, or at least Mark's report of them, had suggested they thought it was unimportant. But in all of his examining the dead girl's apartment, it was the one thing that had some indication of the aspiring model's life.

No, he thought as he crossed Bleecker Street. The second thing. New locks on every door, two days before she was killed.

One week after signing with the Classic Agency.

Horace now knew one more thing about the late Rena Varmont. A difficult, ambitious liar, yes. Not a girl involved with anyone; that would have come out by now.

But most important: a girl who was scared.

I am not scared, Ginny told herself that Wednesday morning. I am not going to be scared. She kept repeating this to herself as she made her own breakfast and Horace's. However, it stayed in the back of her mind as she prepared for the audition. Black tights, dark brown turtleneck sweater, and over it a loose neutral-colored sweater too large and long really to be called a sweater but something in which she could pass for a Renaissance page for Viola's speech and loose enough at the neck to slide down to one shoulder for the drunk speech.

To her embarrassment, she had slept soundly the night before. I should have been too nervous to sleep, she thought, tying her hair back with a dark ribbon (she could pull that off for the drunk scene). A real artist should be a mass of nerves, facing a great actress and hoping for a scholarship. I'm making up for it now, she thought as she slung her big carry-all bag over her shoulder and started for the subway.

Fortunately she had remembered from June the routes to take and found herself in the Murray Hill section of Manhattan well before her appointment at eleven. It was a clear day after all the rain, and she hesitated before entering the building in the East Thirties. It was, as she remembered it, two attractive town houses that had been remodeled into one to house the Natasha Kinn school and to provide rehearsal space as well as an apartment for the former actress on the top floor. I wonder what that's like, Ginny thought, realizing she'd probably never see it. She looked around the block before going up the front steps of the left building. This was where she had auditioned in the spring in one of the practice rooms before a group of three, two women and a cadaverous-looking man that she recognized as a constantly working character actor. Today would be the first time to see Ms. Kinn.

God, what do I call her? Ginny thought. Maybe it won't come up. Maybe I'll just sink through the sidewalk right now and won't have to meet her. She took one last look at the sun-splattered street, the small but still-green trees along the block, and hurried up the stairs.

Inside, it was as she remembered it: a modest space with a window separating the area from the receptionist. Ginny remembered the girl from her first audition. She can't be much older than me, she thought. She was greeted with a cheerful smile.

"Scholarship audition?" the girl asked after she slid back the glass partition.

"Yes. I'm Ginny . . . Virginia Karr."

"N.K. isn't down yet." The girl indicated the grille of a small elevator beyond the partition. "Do you want to wait in the little theater? That's where she'll be holding the auditions."

"Auditions?" More than one? Abruptly, Ginny felt her confidence coming back. Competition, eh? She could handle that.

Something of what she was feeling must have shown on her face, for the receptionist smiled reassuringly. "There's a ladies' room right down the hall, if you want it."

Did she look sick? That wasn't what Ginny was feeling at all! "I'm fine. I think." She tried to smile back at the friendly girl.

"Don't worry. N.K. doesn't bite," said the receptionist. Then she added with another smile, "At least, not very often."

Ginny followed her directions and went through the narrow double doors to what was the "little theater." N.K., huh? That solved the name problem. The auditorium itself was small, barely three rows, and the stage wasn't much larger than Uncle Horace's living room. It reminded Ginny of off-off-Broadway theaters. Better get used to it, she thought to herself, that's probably all you'll get a chance at for years and years.

The stage was lit, which made it possible to see that she was not alone in the dark of the theater. A young man was slouched down on the far side. He didn't raise his head as Ginny came in, which she thought was just as well. She didn't feel like conversation. Still, it was good to see it was a man, obviously also here to audition from the way he was mumbling over a crumpled script. Maybe they had one scholar-

ship for men and one for women? Ginny dumped her bag on a seat
and moved toward the stage. Ever since she had been a child, taken to
the theater for the first time by her parents, a theater, any theater, had
drawn her. A lighted stage, even one as empty and bare as this one,
never failed to make her feel as if she were finally home. Her real
home. There were a couple of folding chairs on the stage, she noted as
she moved closer. And a bench. What would a stage be without some
kind of a bench, she thought. To be used as a love seat, or a table or
a platform for some noble speech.

The doors at the back of the small theater opened with a bang and
Natasha Kinn strode down the aisle toward Ginny. She was not a tall
woman, although slightly taller than Ginny and as she came closer
Ginny could see the fine lines that creased her face. Her hair was the
same shoulder-length cut she had worn throughout her career, only now
the stagelights picked out the mixture of gray that had worked its way
through the thick gold that had made her almost a beauty. What was
it Uncle Horace had said? "No great actress is a conventional beauty,
too limiting." And there was no doubt Natasha Kinn had been great.
There was still that aura of success and authority about her even now,
when she must be close to or maybe over sixty. Ginny also noticed
that despite the cape that hung from her shoulders and a series of bright
scarves tied loosely around her neck, the actress's figure, never her best
feature, was now at the point of being almost beyond stocky. Perhaps
it was that and not the lessening of important scripts that had led to
her retirement.

"Good. You're on time. It's Virginia Karr, right?"

Time had not changed that voice; it was still rich and thick, what
one critic had called "honey over fire." Ginny could only nod. Natasha
held out her hand. "Glad to see you. Shall we get down to business?"

The next half hour passed so swiftly, Ginny couldn't believe it when
she came down from the stage and looked at the watch in her bag.
(Neither Viola nor the prostitute would have a wristwatch, she figured.)
She felt the audition had gone well, she'd even heard N.K., as she was
beginning to think of her, chuckle a couple of times. The actress came
up to her where she fumbled with her satchel. "I think you're going
to be part of our group," she said with a solid thump on Ginny's
shoulders. "I'd like to talk to you after the next audition," she said.
"Do you mind waiting?" It was a question, not a demand, as if the
two women were equals.

Ginny resisted the temptation to answer, "Years and years, if necessary," and merely said, "Of course not."

Natasha turned from her and called over to the young man still slumped in his seat. He hadn't laughed, Ginny thought sourly. Tough for him. I'll wait outside. But she looked back as she reached the doors at the rear of the little theater. He looked familiar somehow. Tall and lean and good-looking, she guessed, although there was no expression on his sulky face. Trying to be the romance-novel hero, she thought. Not easy to pull off with longish blond-brown hair and the standard jeans every actor seemed to wear on- or offstage these days. As she went out the door she heard him start into one of Stanley Kowalski's most famous speeches from *A Streetcar Named Desire*. Thin voice, she thought, and either he was trying a new approach or he hadn't really memorized his text. Let him be my only competition, she thought as she quietly closed the doors behind her.

Only what was there about him that seemed familiar?

It was barely five minutes before the young man came out of the theater, angry now instead of sulky. Behind him, Ginny could hear Natasha's voice, not loud but clearly one that would have carried right out to the street. "A major part of an actor's preparation is learning the lines, Mr. Bowers. Not to mention working on a voice that can be heard and a modicum of talent. Tell Miss Karr I'll be with her in a few minutes."

This last was almost lost as the young man, his lips thin with rage, tried to slam the swinging doors shut behind him.

"Damn bitch!" he muttered under his breath. He glanced at where Ginny was sitting. "You're supposed to wait."

Standing there in the sunlight that was coming in from the long windows that faced the street, Ginny finally remembered where she had seen him. She'd been so dazed before the audition, she hadn't really thought about him other than as another actor.

"You're a model, aren't you?" Now she knew why she hadn't recognized him at first. In Rena's pictures he had always been in elegant dinner clothes, the long hair smoothly brushed back, his eyes glowing as he placed a fur coat around her shoulders or fastened the catch of her bracelet. Axel Gruen's pictures in the portfolio!

"And a damn good one! I don't know why I have to bother with all this acting crap. But Katya thought . . . aw, the hell with it." He had an expensive attaché case with him, Ginny noticed for the first time. He clicked it open and tossed the script into it contemptuously. The case was full of pictures of Bowers, photographs, enlargements of ads he had appeared in, not to mention a hairbrush, a couple of bottles of hair gel, and some other bottles that she might have expected to find in a wealthy lady's boudoir.

"It's Mr. Bowers, isn't it?" It seemed silly to Ginny to call somebody "Mister" when he was probably only a few years older than she was. "Can you talk for a minute?"

"The name's Jon. And I already have a steady lady."

Whatever his problems, modesty wasn't going to be one of them, Ginny thought. "I think you've got the wrong idea. This isn't an approach." Ginny had met too many young men with high opinions of themselves to take his remark as an insult. "It's just that I saw you in photographs. With Rena Varmont."

"What photographs? Oh . . . that old jerk, Axel Gruen, I'll bet. They didn't even make good glossies."

"I was going to be her roommate," Ginny went on with the smile of a forgiving nun. "Of course, after her murder . . ." She felt a sudden rush. Maybe it was coming down from the audition, but she suddenly felt curious about Rena again. "I mean, you must have known her, didn't you?"

Jon muttered something under his breath while he pretended to be fastening the snaps on his case which were already closed.

"Didn't you?" Ginny repeated.

He looked up at her now, his dark eyes blazing, "What you want me to say? Too bad about her death? Nice girl? Great future? She was a total bitch."

One of his favorite words, Ginny decided. Or maybe he just didn't like women very much. That can happen with male models. "I just thought you might tell me something about her." Ginny smiled as mildly as she could, wondering if Mark had talked to the young man. "I didn't really know her very well."

"She was a total pain in the butt. Only one week at Classic and she was like . . . I don't know . . . some big movie star. Had to be shot from the left. Overhead lights. Pinspot on her eyes." The memory of Rena seemed to make him even angrier.

"The shoot on Sunday . . . were you going to be in that too?" Ginny did what she considered the unforgivable thing for a woman of this age; she looked up at him through batted eyelids as innocent as if she were playing a twelve-year-old. "It must have been such a big step forward for poor Rena. I mean, *Elegant* magazine, a new designer . . ."

"I've been in *Elegant* lots of times." Talk about Jon's career seemed to calm him down. "Not to mention there's a strong possibility of a big deal. I mean a real big deal. Symbol for a whole new men's collection. Hotshot name." He looked at her slyly now. "Can't talk about it, bad luck. But luck's going my way these days."

Not if you're going to be a spokesman, Ginny thought. Your voice is too thin. "That sounds wonderful," she said, trying to keep her attitude virginal and adoring without gushing. "But tell me about Sunday. It's such a shame Rena couldn't make it."

"Hell, it wasn't her fault. Somebody ripped the dresses. Like ... deliberate sabotage." The sulky look came back on his face. "Not that I cared. I was only going to be in one shot. Lot of good that would do me."

"Sabotage, you said?"

But Bowers was not about to be dissuaded from his irritation. "That old creep Gruen comes up with the idea of following the *Elegant* woman through the day ... you know, business suit, cocktail dress, evening gown ... that's the one I was to be in, with my back to the camera, of course. All Gruen could think about was Rena. And one in a lacy robe in bed. I wasn't even in that one, for God's sake." He stared at Ginny but she felt he wasn't really seeing her. "I mean, how elegant are these women supposed to be if there isn't a man around at lights-out?"

"You have a point there," Ginny added lamely.

"But if Katya pulls this deal off ... the big one ... screw 'em all. They'll shoot me from the left side." He swiveled to show Ginny his left profile. It didn't look any different from the other side, Ginny thought. "See the difference? I won't need to act or any of this other crap. Just rake in the money." He took a long look at Ginny, covering her from shoes to hair. To her surprise, Ginny felt herself blushing. Silent pictures, she thought as he smirked at her reaction and headed out the door. That's what he should be doing. But that's what being a model is, isn't it?

From behind her she heard the deep, throaty voice of Natasha Kinn, this time tinged with amusement.

"Never get mixed up with a bad actor, dear. It's always a disaster. Believe me, I've married two of them."

CHAPTER EIGHT

It was a fairly long ride from the West Village up to Axel Gruen's apartment, giving Horace plenty of time to think. Outside the taxi the few trees they passed had that dusty, dead look that meant autumn was rapidly approaching, although the afternoon stayed warm. Horace was happy that the driver was the silent type, a dying breed Horace found before turning his attention back to his thoughts.

Face it, he told himself, the trip to Rena's apartment had been a total waste. Well, not total. It perhaps told more about the dead model than if it had been full of personal items, pictures, love letters, brands of cosmetics. The very emptiness should be telling him something. He pushed aside the portfolio for the moment and took out the copy of the newspaper clipping the police had found tucked behind her pictures. He tried to read the newspaper clipping again with more care.

Diane Chaumet. Where did she fit into this . . . or, rather, into Rena's life? Horace hadn't thought for a moment that the clipping was unimportant, not after Mark had showed it to him. It's the details, he told himself. That's what any crime . . . and all history is about. Details missed, details arranged. Coincidences that weren't really accidental. The article wasn't very long, most of the page was filled with the two pictures, one of the smashed car. A convertible with the top down. That meant . . . what? A dry evening, obviously. He studied the article again. No, it had not been a dry evening. Earlier it had rained and the roads were still slick enough that if the model had been speeding, she might easily have skidded. Diane had been wearing no seat belt, but of course that wasn't a legal requirement then. But a model? Hair getting soaked with rain? That didn't sound logical. Of course the rain might have ended and she might have stopped to put the top down. But that didn't fit with the image that she was hurrying to get to her country house for the weekend. Connecticut. Where Rena had come from.

But the police had told Mark there had been no connection they could find between the two dead models. And Horace had enough respect for the police to believe they would have checked thoroughly. Might even have gone to the house itself, although by now it was undoubtedly owned by someone else, all traces of Ms. Chaumet removed forever. The article ended with a brief mention that Diane had just been released from Manhattan General Hospital earlier that day. No mention of why she had been in the hospital.

He studied the accident picture once more. Damn. He needed his reading glasses. He pulled them out, unfolding them from their tiny case. When he had started needing them the year before, a step he had delayed as long as possible, knowing it was out of vanity, which he tried to persuade himself he had only a minimal amount. He had picked these as something that looked casual, not really necessary. Although his optometrist had said with that unfailing mournfulness that always grated on Horace's nerves that once he started with reading glasses he would need them for the rest of his life. A thought Horace hoped to delay by picking the smallest ones he could find.

Glasses on, Horace studied the two pictures again. Not much could be seen in the accident photo, it had been shot from the back of the car in what was definitely nighttime conditions. All he could see of the model was the back of her head, slumped over the steering wheel, and beyond that the cracked glass of the windshield and part of the crumpled front of the car. A blur beyond that of a stone embankment. A short sentence saying the accident had occurred once she was out of the city, on a country road near her home. Surely that would be a road she knew fairly well?

He turned his attention to the other picture. This was a standard professional shot, one that Axel Gruen might have taken or some other expensive photographer. Must ask Axel about that, Horace thought as the cab moved into Central Park West.

The picture was different from the ones of Rena in the portfolio, just as the model was different. For one thing, the girl was blond, with a radiant smile. She had been posed looking backward over one semi-bare shoulder, making the most of her long eyelashes and high cheekbones. When did high cheekbones become the necessity for beauty, Horace wondered. Probably in the thirties with Garbo and Dietrich and Crawford. It was not only a lovely face, but there was something more to the late Diane Chaumet, not the girl next door, unless you had lived next door to Grace Kelly. Also deceased, Horace reminded himself.

Also in a car accident. But with Diane there was a hint of fun as well as sexual appeal. A girl who would enjoy watching a football game or even playing in one as well as the perfect lady to escort to the opening of the opera.

Twenty-seven. Horace knew age was becoming an obsession with him. Was twenty-seven old for a model? Not this one, surely. She could have gone on for quite a few years, even considering a youth-oriented culture. Her apartment, her house, wouldn't have been empty of personal belongings. Her date book would have been filled. Beautiful, she certainly was, but men, even cautious men like Mark, would have found her approachable. Horace found himself smiling a little. If she had been in one of his classes, he probably would have upped her grade, even if she had the brains of a pack of gum. But he suspected, as he studied the photograph, that she would have been much brighter than that. The type that would have always had the quick, correct answers.

The taxi turned into Eighty-ninth Street. Axel's apartment was an odd number, which meant it was on the north side of the street.

"Stop here, driver," Horace said. He got out of the cab slowly, lugging the large portfolio behind him, the newspaper copy stuffed hastily in his pocket. God, he missed Checker cabs, with room for the passenger. After he paid the silent driver, he stopped to look at the building in front of him. Built in the early years of this century, he suspected, when the West Side was just becoming fashionable. The buildings on the block were all different designs, some with the gabled roofs that had been stolen from Dutch architects, some Art Nouveau with tiny balconies, some renovated to look like the Federal period. New York's first real break from the block after block of identical brownstones.

At least five stories, Horace realized. Dear God, I hope Axel has an elevator. Stairs hit Horace's calves and thighs like strings that had been pulled too tight. Axel's buzzer listed number six. I'm not going to like this, Horace thought. Why am I not home writing about Gladstone and his work with the London prostitutes?

"Yes?" It had been several years but Horace recognized Axel's voice at once.

"Axel? It's Horace Livsey. I've brought you your portfolio."

There was no answer, just a firm, persistent buzz that released the outer door. There, at the end of the narrow hall was a small door wedging itself in apologetically next to a slightly sagging staircase. An elevator! Horace approached it carefully. The building didn't look as if much care had been taken on its maintenance. Damn thing probably won't work, he thought glumly. But the door opened easily, and the grate, and soon he was being moved slowly, although with noisy creaks, up to the top floor. I must lead a good life, Horace thought, hoping this wasn't tempting fate.

The elevator opened opposite Axel's apartment. The small man stood there holding open a large metal door that might have been more appropriate to a bank vault. For a brief moment the two men stared at each other.

"Horace Livsey." Axel said it carefully. Not exactly a welcome greeting, Horace thought. But not unfriendly. Noncommittal was perhaps more accurate. Then a small smile appeared, enough to show Axel's slightly yellow teeth. "Come in, old friend." He stepped aside, allowing Horace to pass him.

As always, Horace was startled to see how deep some of these buildings were. Unlike Rena's apartment, this one still had its odd partitions, dividing it into different rooms, each opening onto the next. Where Horace stood, there was still a trace of what might be called a front parlor. Hardly a living room. Except for an old television set pushed uncomfortably in a corner, the furnishings could have been something from the previous century. A tufted sofa and an ottoman, Oriental rugs on top of Oriental rugs. A massive chandelier (its prisms gray with dirt and much too large for this room) hung from the ceiling which needed painting worse than Horace's apartment. There were plants in jardinieres struggling to stay alive. And I think I need a cleaning woman was Horace's first impression.

But the walls were what really struck him. Whatever they had been painted originally (and that could have been decades ago, Horace realized) they were almost invisible now. It seemed at first glance as if every inch of space was covered with expensively framed photographs. Models in high-fashion clothes from high-fashion designers. Celebrities swathed in furs, all of them looking younger than they could have been when Axel had photographed them.

One whole wall was covered with what Horace recalled from Paris days: mood shots of the Seine with fog rising, an empty Place de la Concorde. A street alley. A kiosk in the rain, with tattered posters of revues long closed and forgotten. The opposite wall was like another shrine.

Here Axel had framed and hung what Horace remembered as one of Gruen's most successful series. It was ladies' stockings, and it seemed to Horace they were still stockings then, not pantyhose or tights or whatever they were called now. It had been for a firm called Regal and had featured famous women from all over the world. A two-page spread, Horace remembered. With a slogan that had been as imitated and kidded

as much as the ones for the Maidenform bra and What Becomes a
Legend Most furs. For Regal it was "The Most Famous Legs in the
World Wear Regal": one page showing the legs (skirts still near the
knees in those days) and the other page a closeup of the lady owner
of the legs, carefully airbrushed to total glamour. Dietrich was one, and
Betty Grable and Josephine Baker. As well as one former First Lady
and a famous novelist. Several European princesses obviously happy to
be paid for showing what they walked on and in.

"A sensational campaign, that Regal." Axel had apparently noticed
Horace's eyes moving around the room. Gruen sighed heavily. "My
most famous success. Money rolled in in those days, dear Horace.
Everyone wanted me. *Vogue. Bazaar.* Europe. Even when they had
other photographers under exclusive contract. It was Gruen they needed.
Gruen they wanted. I could command any price."

His accent had grown heavier. Horace found himself searching his
memory. "Wasn't there something . . . ?" he started to ask.

Axel's face turned red with anger, from the top of his open shirt all
across his bald head. "You mean . . . *la scandale*?" He turned his back
on the Regal wall. "One foolish mistake! The lady was starring on
Broadway. Period clothes, of course. Only when I photographed her,
the legs . . . they were impossible. Suitable for a piano, you would say.
Nothing would help. Not shading with makeup. Not darker colors. Not
even putting her in boots, and they were revolutionary at that time.
Regal screamed. I screamed. But she had a contract. So I slipped in
another model . . . just for the legs. But one of those dreadful gossip
people. Somehow they found out. Was the actress blamed? Was Regal?
No! Just me. As if I had done something criminal, like murdering her."
He started toward the next room of the apartment, gesturing Horace to
follow him. "Not that I wouldn't have been justified in doing it." He
stopped in the hallway to look back at Horace.

"After that . . . poof!" He flicked his hand in the air as a magician
might. "From there on it was downhill. Suddenly I'm old-fashioned,
suddenly I'm not 'with it' as they said. Suddenly I am too difficult. As
if I hadn't always been difficult." He was passionate about it now.
"An artist has a right to be difficult! He wants to do his best. I am not
a subway machine where you take a strip of pictures for a quarter. I
create beauty!"

Horace noticed in the late afternoon sunlight that the bristles of
Axel's bald head were now silver, as was his chin. We grow older, he
thought. And in the world of fashion, that can be even more fatal than
to be a professor in a world that wanted only computer experts.

"But you've kept on working," Horace said tactfully.

"Bah!" It was a snort of disgust from the photographer. "Bits and pieces. No exclusive contracts. No big travel allowance. Thank God, dear Diana Vreeland is no longer with us, she would be shocked at what has happened to me."

Diana ... that reminded Horace he was not there just to talk about old times. Diane Chaumet, that was what he wanted to hear about. And Rena.

Axel straightened a little, his head up, clearly, suddenly, more cheerful. "But now, Horace, things are going to be different. You will see. So will the fashion world. Big things will be happening. Come back to the studio."

Horace followed him into the next room, still carrying Rena's portfolio. Why hadn't Gruen asked about that?

The next room was a bedroom, or at least it had been made into one. Small, it barely contained the large double bed. Three walls were completely covered with still more Oriental rugs, hung from the ceiling. The other wall had peeling paint and one small window that let in very little light. In contrast to the front room, this enclosed space seemed almost neat, the bed made with bright designer sheets, the floor covered with still more eccentrically designed rugs. Could be suitable for a harem, Horace thought. Axel had gone on ahead. A single spot on the bed held some light from the window. A hairpin glistened. Horace picked it up unobtrusively. So there was a lady in Axel's life. He wondered who. Certainly Axel was no more attractive than he had been all those years ago in Paris. He had given up wearing black, he was in tired jeans and a soiled work shirt. Not the right clothes for a man Horace knew had to be seven or eight years older than he was. Denim, if it had to be worn, should be the cloth of young people: not with gray hair showing through at the neck, or pants that only the truly thin could carry off. Axel was hardly fat, but time had given him a small pot belly. Not attractive, Horace thought.

He dropped the hairpin back on the bed. Did women still use hairpins, he wondered. Of course, the bedroom might have been the dressing room for whatever models Axel still used.

"Aren't you coming?"

"Yes, of course, Axel." As Horace passed through the next doorway, he noticed a stereo speaker over the door and, glancing back, one more over the door to the living room. Was Axel trying to stay young with the blasts of modern music? Or did the models require it?

But by now he was in the room beyond. Axel's studio. He had obviously knocked down walls (probably without the landlord's permission, knowing Gruen) and made the rest of the long apartment into a large work area. Beyond were two small rooms with their doors open, obviously meant to be a kitchen and a bathroom but from what Horace could see, their main purpose must have been to be a darkroom for Axel to develop his pictures and a storage space for his supplies. A small table separated the rooms. It held a china bowl full of odds and ends of what Horace supposed were camera parts.

The room he stood in now was probably the most bizarre Horace had ever encountered. The wall to his right was covered with an enormous stark white sheet of paper flowing down from a thick roll of the same paper attached to the ceiling. Background, Horace thought, moving carefully past the tripods of lights and silver umbrellas that he knew were part of the shading a photographer needed.

The floor was bare linoleum, battleship gray. And the rest of the room . . . Horace could only stand stock-still and stare. If the first room had cluttered walls of pictures, this large room was as close to what Horace could imagine a second-hand camera shop might look like. Every inch of space, all the way up to the ceiling (which was mostly skylight), had been hung with cameras—small ones, large ones, one that looked like it dated back to the days of daguerreotypes.

"Not Luis Daguerre," Axel said as if he had read Horace's thought. "Fox-Talbot, a contemporary and, in my opinion, a much superior artist." He touched the large black box, mounted on its own tripod, with an almost loving gesture. Horace noticed that the early camera was bolted to the tripod which in turn was securely screwed into the floor. "It is huge and awkward, but it produced the first beginnings of successful art." He smiled as he turned slowly around, standing carefully in the same space. "And very valuable.

"Look carefully, my friend. Here there is an entire history of photography. The old Brownie cameras. The first Kodaks." He pointed to another large black box hung on one wall: "A ten-by-eight view camera fitted with a twelve-inch f/6.3 with a Commercial Ekbar. Cecil Beaton used one like this for years. Big and difficult, but the negatives . . . so easy to work with." He moved along the walls, not having to watch where his small feet were taking him, touching the objects fastened to the wall: some hanging from their straps on nails, some on little shelves he had obviously built himself. "And here the Hasselblads, of course. Then the Rolexes." He looked back at Horace. "I hated them at first, but now . . ." He touched another row of cameras. "And the Mamiya, the best of the Japanese in my opinion."

There must be over a hundred cameras in this studio, Horace thought. "It's . . . like a museum, Axel," he said tactfully, although he felt those dozens of empty lenses staring down at him had a spooky effect. Not a place he'd like to be in for long. That, rather than the Regal scandal, might have frightened people away.

"A museum? Ah, my friend, that is where they are going. I have put it into my will. But whoever gets it, they must be all in one room. The Axel Gruen room. So the world can see there were more and better photographers than Avedon or Bresson. And there will be more, now that I am starting the new phase of my career." He caught the questioning look on Horace's face. "Oh, yes, Horace. Soon there are to be contracts again. The Classic Agency, Katya and Philip admire my work."

Katya and Philip. The Classic Agency. Horace was remembering the newspaper reports of Rena's murder. She had been found by the owner of her new agency, Philip McKay. He shifted the portfolio that was still in his hand to his other hand.

"That's ... wonderful, Axel." Why hadn't he taken the portfolio? He must have seen Horace holding it.

"They will see. All of them. Age has nothing to do with a real artist. Out of date! They dare to call me that? Was Karsh out of date? Steichen? Well into their eighties and still they photographed! Skill and talent, they do not age."

"But models do." Horace held up the portfolio like a tray, presenting it to Gruen. "I brought the portfolio. You said you wanted it?"

"Oh, yes." Axel stood there, silent for a moment. Then he took the portfolio and placed it almost casually on the floor in the corner.

"Hadn't you better check it? To see that everything is there?"

"Hardly necessary, now that the girl is dead."

What is this? Horace asked himself. The guy has been driving everybody nuts to get this back and now he treats it like junk mail? "I thought you wanted it. You know it was delivered to me. Well, care of me. For my niece."

"Yes, I read that." Axel could not have seemed less interested. "Rena was to be in the *Elegant* shoot. Celeste will pick someone else for me to photograph. Some modern clothes-hanger. But I will make her beautiful. And I have the right to veto her decisions, of course."

"You have that good a contract with *Elegant*?"

"Celeste? Oh, yes. All the way from when she began at the magazine we have been friends. And now that she is at the top ... ah, it will be like old times again. She gives a small dinner party tomorrow night; naturally I will have to be there." He dismissed it with a shrug as if chic dinner parties were one of the more annoying duties that success forces on one.

"I'll be there too," Horace said mildly.

"You?" This clearly surprised the photographer. "I do not think of you as the social type." The implication was clear that in a gathering of the famous and wealthy, Livsey would be a total oddity.

"Courtesy of my ex-wife." Horace smiled amiably. "You remember Zoe? She's now the Countess Sirelli. The count is dead, but she retained the title."

That seemed a simple explanation to Gruen, for he nodded. "Ah, yes, the beautiful Zoe." He studied Horace. "But wasn't there a banker after you and before this count?"

"It's a long story." Whatever tactful approaches Horace had planned to make, he decided the smug photographer could do with a bit of a jolt. "Tell me, Axel ... did you ever photograph a model named Diana Chaumet?"

Horace might have expected any reaction rather than the one he got. Shock, anger at Livsey's prying, curiosity—anything but the carefully blank expression on Gruen's face. "Chaumet? No. I can't recall anybody with that name. But these models, they come, they go."

"She 'left' about five years ago. A car accident." Axel still showed no signs of emotion. Horace might have been talking about the weather. "She also was with the Classic Agency."

"I think they meet the buses." Axel smiled at his own humor. "Or at least Katya would. Attractive girls come in from out of town, all young, all ambitious." He sighed. "So few of them have what it takes to make it."

"Then you wouldn't know anything about this newspaper story of her accident?" Horace pulled out the crumpled page in his pocket and handed it to Axel. "It was in Rena's portfolio."

"The Classic Agency," he muttered as he skimmed the article. You're not really reading this, are you, Axel, Horace thought to himself. Is it because you really have no interest in it or you know it very well already? Or are you hiding something?

"I suppose somebody must have sent poor Rena this clipping when they knew she wanted to be a model. Not unusual."

He seemed about to crumple it and throw it away but Horace held out his hand. "If you don't want it, I'd like to show this to my niece. She was going to be Rena's roommate." No reason to mention there had been no spare bedroom in the dead model's apartment.

Axel handed over the paper without protest.

"What did you think of Rena?" Horace asked. Axel's face remained expressionless.

"She was ... I thought at first ... interesting. Like all models, cheap. She wanted her pictures for free. Someone, I forget who, had recommended me." Axel shrugged. "But the more I worked on her, the less I thought her chances were."

"The Classic Agency didn't think that. They signed her to an exclusive contract just last week."

For the first time, Axel showed a little wariness. Horace suspected he was wondering how he knew that. "I didn't say she was without possibilities. She was young, though models get younger and younger each year. And she had determination, that is always good."

A phone rang somewhere, probably in what had been built as the kitchen.

"Excuse me. I must take that." He moved quickly to the end of the long room.

Horace heard his voice on the phone. "Yes? Yes, Katya. . . . No. Not today. I can't." There was a short moment of silence, then: "We will discuss it privately. Tomorrow morning at the meeting. You know what I am demanding." Axel's voice was harsher now.

Horace considered it time to leave. He walked back through the small bedroom, losing the sound of Axel's voice, although what was being said was clearly not what the photographer wanted to hear. In the front room he stopped. The steel door had too many locks on it for him to slip out quietly. He looked around the room once more. He was missing something, he felt. Only what?

Details, he told himself, and looked around again. Not the wall of Paris pictures, he knew them only too well, and with too much nostalgia. Not the shrine to the Regal campaign. Not the furniture—he suspected it had all been moved from the various European apartments Axel had inhabited in his lifetime.

He turned to face the other wall, the glamour shots, he supposed he would have described them. What was it that bothered him? He scanned the wall quickly. Axel might be in any moment to let him out. Finally, on the next to bottom row, he saw it.

A photograph of Diane Chaumet. The same one reproduced in the newspaper clipping now safely back in his pocket. Horace leaned over. Was that an inscription on the photograph? He squinted, there was no time for reading glasses. The writing was for once not a celebrity scrawl, but neat and flowing. "Love and much thanks, dearest Axel." And it was signed "Diane."

Horace could hear movement from the far room. He straightened and quickly went over to the wall of Paris pictures, and was studying them as Axel came into the room.

"I really must be going," he said politely.

"We see each other tomorrow night," Axel said. He did not sound overjoyed about the prospect as he unbolted the heavy door and pressed for the ancient elevator.

"I'll look forward to it," replied Horace affably. "And I'm sure Zoe will too."

He was safely going down in the elevator, when he realized Axel had not thanked him for bringing the portfolio.

And why had he lied about knowing Diane Chaumet?

I can't lie to Uncle Horsey, Ginny thought as she sat at the kitchen table. Not only because I don't want to, but because he wouldn't believe me anyway. Darn it, this should be the happiest day of my life! A full scholarship to the Natasha Kinn School! And the strong possibility that N.K., as Ginny was learning to call her, would be able to arrange housing.

But, and that was the problem. Not until January. Four months, or almost. Horsey would never let her stay that long. Not if she made three meals a day of all his favorites, not that he had that many. But N.K. was insistent she start with the fresh semester, casually dismissing Ginny's hesitantly mentioned current housing problems with an airy "Perhaps you could commute from your parents' home in Connecticut."

An hour and a half by train each way! And N.K. wanted her to audit classes until January. Plus working on monologues, already assigning her the letter scene from *The Country Wife*. N.K. had said, "You have a real gift for comedy. Anybody with a voice can make people cry. To make them laugh, that is hard. I was never very good at it."

She had been generous with her time, giving Ginny at least half an hour before disappearing. Ginny was lucky, she knew it. Natasha had already assigned her certain tasks, scripts to buy or borrow from the library to study. Informing her that with the scholarship she would be expected to spend a certain number of hours a week helping out at the school, answering phones, opening mail, arranging class hours for the members who were already working actors, cataloguing the wardrobe room.

"And pictures. You must have those as soon as possible," the actress had said, swinging back her gray-gold hair imperiously. "I want you to go to auditions, lots of them, before January. You won't get cast, of course, nobody ever does at first, but it will test your determination and harden you to rejection." She smiled cheerfully.

"You are not to mention me or the school, naturally, not until you have been with us at least half a year."

"No, of course not." The mention of pictures suddenly cleared Ginny's mind of the daze she had been in. "I've heard of a photographer," she began tentatively. "Axel Gruen. Is he good?"

"Axel Gruen?" The older woman's eyes widened. "Good Lord, he must be a hundred and two!" She seemed oblivious of the fact that Gruen was probably her age or maybe even younger. "I thought he died years ago. He wanted me to do some kind of ad for stockings. But I was being very, very serious in those days. A Tennessee Williams play that season, and, of course, *The Three Sisters* the next year. I turned him down." She stood and stretched, almost as a dancer might. Her figure may have thickened, Ginny thought as she watched her, but her carriage and grace were still there.

"No, my dear, what you need, I think, is somebody more modern. Some of the students have gone to a new young man, Oliver Tomorrow I think he calls himself. Not personally interested in women, they tell me, but he can capture them on camera. Ask around."

She then went on to describe the kind of regime she expected Ginny to start: dance and movement classes at the school, auditing the scene classes, an hour a week with one of the teachers as they went through the monologues she was to have prepared.

All that and she wants me to spend three hours a day commuting, Ginny said to herself glumly as she left the school.

So now she was back on West End, wondering how on earth to approach Uncle Horace. Not that he was an ogre or anything, but four months was asking a lot of him. The phone rang and she got up in panic. Oh, God, don't let Natasha have changed her mind.

But it was Mark on the phone.

"How'd it go?" he said.

"What? Oh, the audition. You remembered." Points for you, Mark, she thought. "I got the scholarship. But it doesn't start until after the first of the year and I haven't figured out a way to get Horsey to let me stay here."

"You will." His voice changed, Ginny could sense he was struggling with awkwardness. "Listen, I called to ask you to do me a favor. I didn't want to bother you before, with the audition and everything. And by the way, congratulations. And it's about Rena ..."

Rena! Ginny hadn't really thought about her since she left the school. I'm shallow, she thought. And self-centered. And, pride sneaking past her self-flagellation, a damn good actress!

"Yes, Mark? About Rena?"

"You have a little free time now, don't you?"

"Until January, it seems. Why? What do you want me to do?"

"The Classic Agency has been on the phone, they want somebody to clear out Rena's stuff, I guess they have some sort of locker there for their models. And the landlord has been pestering the D.A.'s office. He wants Rena's clothes and stuff out of there before Sunday."

"But I thought maybe . . ."

"You haven't seen the professor today, I guess." Mark described his meeting and the price the landlord was going to ask for any new tenant. Ginny whistled softly. There went that hope of a place to stay. But Mark was continuing. "And there wasn't any spare room either. Your uncle thinks she must have been lying to you."

"Oh, damn it!" She should have known all along it was too good to be true. "Then why should I do any favors for her?"

"Because there doesn't seem to be anybody else. No family. No *close* friends or anything. The agency is going to take care of the funeral—cremation, I think. But the personal stuff . . . anyway, it wouldn't exactly be for Rena. It would kind of be for me. I'm up to my ears in paperwork down here. But I could meet you at Rena's apartment after you'd been to the agency. We could figure out if there was anything you wanted, and where to send the other stuff, Goodwill maybe, or the Salvation Army."

He could practically hear Ginny's mind working in the silence. "I'll take you out for dinner afterward. A good dinner. I promise."

New as she was as an actress, Ginny was not inexperienced when it came to young men who were attracted to her. "It had better be a very good dinner," she said, softening it with what she hoped was an engaging chuckle. Anyway, wasn't tomorrow night the night Horsey and Zoe were going to some fancy party? "As for the clothes, I think we can send them to Natasha Kinn. She was saying the school had a wardrobe department." All right, Rena was taller than average, but things can be shortened and struggling actresses never had the money for good clothes.

"I'll meet you at Rena's at what? Six? Seven?"

They settled on six-thirty, mainly, Ginny thought with a small smile of amusement, so that he could go home and shower and change first. Maybe she could use that as an argument with Uncle Horace that she needed a chaperone to live with in this wicked city.

But Mark seemed to have his mind on other things again. "Incidentally, you might like to know your original hunch was right. The autopsy reports are in and Paco seems to be in the clear. He was definitely identified as leaving the apartment before midnight. And Rena was killed sometime between four and seven the following morning.''

And he hung up.

Maybe he wasn't as charmed by her as she thought, drumming her fingers on the bare table.

And then she heard Horace's key at the front door.

THURSDAY

CHAPTER NINE

It was well past noon the next day before Ginny started for the Classic Agency. She'd spent the morning thoroughly cleaning the apartment, trying not to disturb Horace while he slept, and leaving him strictly alone while he had his breakfast: yogurt and coffee cake, at his request. When he disappeared into his office, she had started from the back of the apartment and worked her way forward as quietly as possible, although there wasn't much she could do about the vacuum cleaner noise.

She knew it was the least she could do after last night. She'd blurted out her news and the need of a place to stay at least until January the minute he had walked into the kitchen. He seemed oddly preoccupied as he got himself a glass of water and opened his long array of vitamin bottles on the top of the refrigerator, popping them into his mouth like salted peanuts. She was afraid at first he hadn't heard her.

Instead, he looked at her, still as if he weren't really seeing her. Ginny suspected this was probably one of his traits that had led Zoe to divorce him, that absent look, as if whoever was in the room wasn't really there. But he *had* heard her after all.

"I suppose it won't be too bad," he said absently as he put the tops back on the bottles. "You're bound to go home for Thanksgiving and Christmas and probably New Year's. And with all of these things that Ms. Kinn wants you to do before January, it's not as if you're going to be here that much."

He was clearly startled when Ginny jumped up and hugged him enthusiastically. The fog seemed to clear from his face and he looked at her with some amazement. "This isn't charity, Ginny. There are my books to be dusted. And shopping. And an occasional dinner, as long as you stay away from the witches' recipe in *Macbeth*."

"I'll be a mouse," she had said. "And as for food, Julia Child will be so impressed, she'll take up pottery."

"I'll be sure and tell her the next time I see her."

But that abstract look was on his face again. Ginny took no chances; she called her mother the next minute and had Horsey repeat the offer, which shook him out of his preoccupation for a moment or two. She realized her mother could not have been happier, but there was a certain amusement in her voice when she talked to Ginny again as if she had expected this all the time.

It was only when they were having dinner together at the restaurant next door that Ginny began to think that it had not been kindness, love, or the desire for a clean apartment that had led Uncle Horace to change his mind.

He told her about his day: Rena's apartment, visiting Axel, the lie about the dead model Diane, and showed her the newspaper clipping. He even asked about hairpins.

"Do women still wear hairpins?" he asked, relaxing over his martini. Ginny had tactfully decided to stay with plain tonic-and-lime, she didn't want him to think her acting scene had been based on experience.

"Not usually. Maybe with very long hair. But then I'd think it would be bobby pins." She thought of the girls she knew, clips and hot rollers, but hairpins, no. "Maybe an older woman?" she ventured.

"I can't see anybody in Axel's studio being over thirty," he said, taking a long sip of his drink. "And he certainly doesn't have a cleaning woman."

She'd already told him about Mark's phone call and suddenly the pieces were beginning to fit together. He was offering her a roof over her head because he was really intrigued with Rena's murder. And without her and Mark he might just be excluded from the investigation. Ah, my stuck-in-the-mud old Horsey! Ginny smiled to herself, careful not to show what she'd figured out. Uncle Horace had always been a demon for facts; that was what made him a good historian and kept two of his textbooks still in print. Now with a murder almost literally on his doorstep, he wasn't going to just settle back into his grumpy, academic-retirement rut. So at least Rena's murder had been good for something.

But Ginny knew she was going to have to move tactfully. Any hint that Horace was actually curious would bring his defenses up and send him scuttling back to the privacy of his study. So throughout the meal she kept the conversation on what each of them knew. Her meeting with Jon Bowers at the school clearly interested him.

" 'Better things to do than acting,' " he repeated. "And Katya recommended him. That would have to be Mrs. McKay, wouldn't you think? Co-owner of the Classic Agency.'' His eyebrows came together as he chewed over this and the chicken in front of him. ''I mean, he *did* say Katya, didn't he? There can't be too many women with that name.'' He looked at her across the table as if he were really seeing her. ''Do models usually go to acting classes?''

''Some commercials have dialogue,'' she replied. ''And most models want to move on to bigger things: a movie career, going on the road to sell whatever product they've been seen in the ads, big bucks in that.''

''I should have been born beautiful,'' he said reflectively. ''See what you can find out at the agency tomorrow. About anything.''

''I'll do my best,'' she said obligingly, hoping he wouldn't catch the smile tugging at her lips.

So now she was on her way to the Classic Agency. To her surprise, the building in the East Fifties was not an office building, sleek and modern, as she expected. She should have known the address was too far east for that. It was a very stylish town house, something one of the smaller countries with large resources might have chosen for their U.N. embassy. The outside seemed to have been freshly painted in cream, the stone cornices above each window sandblasted back to their original tan. The front door on street level was a glistening, gleaming black, the brass plate beside it quietly announced here was ''Classic, Inc.'' This is over three million bucks in real estate, Ginny thought as she opened the door.

Inside was a wide open space with a graceful staircase sweeping up to the floors above, the floor itself a checkerboard of wide black-and-white marble squares. Directly in the center was a delicate desk (Louis Something, Ginny thought as she approached it, and probably genuine). On the desk were two phones as pink as the one single rose in a tall glass vase. And behind the desk was a delicate-faced young man in an impeccably tailored suit. He glanced up and down her figure quickly and seemed to come instantly to the conclusion she couldn't possibly be there for a modeling job.

You needn't have been so fast about that, Ginny thought. I *do* have good bones.

''May I help you?'' He clearly implied there was nothing about her he could have any connection with except possibly to direct her to whatever real address she was looking for, and then only if she groveled a bit.

''I'm Virginia Karr,'' said Ginny in a cool, level voice. Hell, she'd faced Natasha Kinn, this twerp wasn't going to get to her. ''I was a friend of Rena Varmont's. The district attorney's office asked me to come here and collect her things.''

"I didn't know she had any friends." This was almost inaudible, but the mention of the district attorney's office seemed to impress him, for he stood up, carefully smoothing his jacket. "Her locker's in the back." He was obviously weighing whether Ginny was important enough actually to show her, or if a simple wave of his manicured hand was sufficient.

Before he could make up his mind, they both looked up at the sound of angry voices above them, cut off in the next moment as if someone had come out of a room and shut the door firmly.

A trim, handsome man in his forties came down the staircase quickly. You're out of place here, was Ginny's first thought. Not that he wasn't as well dressed as the receptionist, but he wore his clothes easily, as if he hadn't thought about them since he got dressed that morning and probably had just grabbed the first suit and tie in his closet. But he wore them with the casual grace of a man who didn't have to worry about weight problems or his height (well over six feet, Ginny felt) or his looks. This is what a male model should look like, Ginny thought. Handsome, of course, but not aware of it or the impression he made. Deep blue eyes with faint crinkles around them and strong hands and wrists.

"Julian, Mr. Gruen would like some tea. India, not China. Would you ask Matilda?" The young man instantly snapped to attention, pressing a button on the left phone and talking into it quietly. His eyes never left the man as he finished coming down the stairs. Oho, thought Ginny. I'm not the only one who finds this guy attractive.

The tall man appeared to notice Ginny for the first time. He came toward her, holding out his hand. "Sorry, I didn't mean to be rude. Can I help you? I'm Philip McKay."

Good grip, Ginny thought as she shook his hand. Not one of those bone-crushers some men use to show their macho side, but nothing soft or limp either.

"I'm Ginny Karr," she answered. "I was going to be Rena's roommate. The district attorney's office sent me over to pick up her things."

"Not a very pleasant job, is it?" His face was serious now. "She never said anything about planning to have a roommate."

I'll bet she didn't, Ginny thought. Since she hadn't really planned on it anyway.

"You're the girl who was in the newspapers, aren't you? The one she sent her portfolio to?"

"Yes." Should she mention that the portfolio had been brought back to Axel? If he was upstairs, she decided it was up to him to mention it. Before she could think of anything more to add, there was a sharp voice from someone on the balcony above them.

"Philip, would you also tell Matilda I want some more coffee? Hot, this time. And I imagine Celeste will want some too, since Axel is determined to be difficult for the rest of the day. And a diet something for Franchard."

"Yes, Katya," Philip McKay said with a touch of weariness, and took the receiver from the willowy receptionist as Ginny looked up at the balcony.

So this is Katya McKay, Ginny realized. Tall, elegantly thin, dressed in a beautifully tailored blouse and skirt. She found Katya staring down at her. It was an uncomfortable feeling, the same look the receptionist had first given her, as if she had been summed up and found wanting. Ginny held her gaze, not about to give Katya the pleasure of looking away first. You're a handsome woman, she thought. A strange word to use, but the first to come to her mind. Chiseled features, slanting eyes, mahogany hair pulled straight back into a tight chignon covered in black velvet net.

Ginny found herself wanting to shiver, which was silly on a warm September afternoon. But Katya McKay had the same sort of glittering fascination of an exotic and deadly snake, something you might shrink from in a jungle.

"You're Horace Livsey's niece, here for Rena's things. Good. The sooner they're out of here, the better." With that she turned aside as if she had no further use for Ginny.

"You might say thank you, Katya." Philip McKay had put down the phone by now. "After all, she's saving us a certain amount of trouble." His tone was polite, but there was no doubt he spoke with authority. Whatever had attracted him to her in the first place, he was clearly not awed by her authority any longer.

"We're taking care of the bitch's funeral, isn't that enough?" Katya's eyes were fixed on her husband's face, almost as if it were a battle they had been through before and one that she had not always won. So you're another one who didn't like Rena, thought Ginny.

"She has enough fees coming in to cover the expenses," he said quietly but firmly. "It is the least we can do."

"But we've all done much more than the least, haven't we, my dear?" This direct challenge from his wife caused Philip to look away. Ginny could see a small vein in his temple throbbing. Boy, something's going on here, she thought, and decided she'd better keep her mouth shut. Katya's thin red lips had twisted into a sardonic smile. "Checking up on her so early in the morning. So thoughtful."

"I'll be up in a minute, Katya." The weariness in Philip's voice was now clear to everyone.

"And try, just for once, to get Matilda to hurry." With that Katya turned and disappeared down the hallway above them.

There was an uncomfortable moment of silence broken only by Julian subtly clearing his throat.

"I'm afraid you find us all under a strain, Miss Karr." The smile and the genuine warmth of McKay were back as he looked at Ginny. "Of course, none of this is particularly helped by the fact that they called us about the autopsy. Now that Paco's been cleared and we know that Rena died between four and seven-thirty Monday morning, I seem to be back as the principal suspect."

"Somehow I don't believe that." Ginny was as surprised as Philip by what she had said. It wasn't as if she had any reason to come to his defense other than she liked him. And certainly there was enough tension between him and his wife to suspect that there might have been more than business between McKay and Rena.

He smiled again, warmly. "Nice to know I have somebody on my my side." He turned to the receptionist. "Julian, could you show Miss Karr where the lockers are? And we'd better start seeing the ladies now. Are they all here?"

Julian snapped into efficiency, picking an elaborate folder out one of the drawers of the desk. "Elaine's still doing the cosmetic spread, but she swears she'll be here in half an hour. And Suzanne has a callback in an hour for that runway show next week. She has to leave in twenty minutes."

"Better send her up first, then." He turned away and started for a small door under the stairs, probably to charm the absent Matilda into speed. As he reached the door he turned back to Ginny. "Sorry to be rude, Miss Karr. If you'd like some coffee, I'm sure Julian could get you some. It's just that Celeste has scheduled the *Elegant* spread to be reshot this Sunday. Everything's always a deadline." He smiled slightly and went through the door.

Manners, Ginny thought to herself. Not much of that left. She didn't even mind that he had called her "Miss" instead of the ubiquitous "Ms." It made her feel young and rather delicate.

"It's through here." Ginny caught the impatience in Julian's voice. Without McKay around, he was back to his arrogant self. He walked over to the double doors that must have originally opened onto a front parlor when the house was first built. He didn't look back to see if she was following him.

As soon as he opened the doors, Ginny could hear a babble of female voices. "... One look at her wedding gown and I knew that marriage was never going to last." The woman speaking put down the tabloid she had been reading aloud to the other women in the room.

No, not women, Ginny thought as she followed Julian in. They all seemed incredibly young to her eyes, even though their makeup was complete and perfect, enough that to a man it would look natural. Ginny knew better. There were at least ten models in the room, all in different hairstyles (and hair colors), all dressed with the same casual richness Rena had worn since she came to New York.

In person they were not beautiful, not to Ginny's eyes. The tall ones had increased their height with high heels. The younger ones, still aiming for the never-out-of-date gamine look, were in ballet slippers, their hair cut to wisps around their faces, emphasizing their wide, heavily made-up eyes.

"Suzanne, will you go upstairs, please?" Julian issued it like an order as he consulted his appointment book. There was an instant moan from the others. "Sorry, girls, but her highness wants to start the parade now."

"Listen, Julie, I've got to leave by two. The dentist is replacing my front caps." This from one of the giantesses who clearly stood in no awe of the young man.

"You'll be next, June. Meanwhile you might show this young woman Rena's locker." Obviously, remembering Ginny's name was more than could be expected of him.

June moved with practiced grace toward the end of the large room. She was stunning, with skin the color of the dark tan people with a two month vacation hoped to acquire. Her long hair was dyed silver, laced into jangling cornrows with silver beads. The other models with moans and sighs and much looking at wristwatches settled back on the large, comfortable divans that filled most of the sunny room. Ginny felt like a pygmy following the tall model ahead of her.

June led her through another room, smaller and efficiently neat and officelike, into a corridor that was half in darkness. Flicking on a light switch, June marched through the wide hallway toward the end of a line of lockers, painted as the corridor in soft pastels.

"Rena's the one at the end. That's what you get when you're the new girl." June moved as if to go back to the waiting area. Ginny, being behind her, came around to plant herself in front of her. The girl might be tall and striking, the kind that would photograph well, but Ginny suspected she was younger than she was.

"Did you know Rena?" She was prepared for evasions or more dislike, and it stopped the model more effectively than her position.

"Rena? No. Not really. She only signed here last week." She tugged down her turquoise sweater as if to make the most of her small breasts. "I'd seen her at calls sometimes, when she was sent by other agencies. Small-time ones." She sniffed slightly, as if to imply being signed by the Classic Agency placed one in another, more rarified category. "Kind of a loner."

"Did you like her?"

"What's to like? Look, we were all up for the same jobs. That doesn't make you bosom buddies. She kept her mouth shut. Showed up on time. Must have had something I didn't see, if she got the *Elegant* shoot. Even if it was with that old poop Gruen."

"The *Elegant* shoot is important, I guess." Ginny moved away from the model toward the last locker. Funny, it didn't have a padlock on it, the way the others did. She tried the door; it wasn't even locked. To her surprise, she found June right behind her.

"You get a four- or five-page spread in *Elegant,* you're tops. Your price per hour can go up a couple of thousand. I'm not kidding. I had just one page about six months ago, suddenly they're calling from all over. Two trips to Paris. One to Italy, although I can't say I'm crazy about Italian photographers, they get a little too personal when they arrange the gowns, if you know what I mean." She smoothed back her rows of silver hair. "But when you're hot, you're hot and you got to rake it in while you can."

Ginny was only half listening as she gazed at the contents of the locker. Hair rollers and cosmetics were shoved onto the top shelf. Below there was a stack of photo albums, not as large as Rena's Axel Gruen portfolio but thick and heavy. Nothing much was hanging from the rod that held clothes. Lord, she thought, how am I going to get all of this out of here?

"Look, you want me to ask Matilda for some trash bags? You're never going to be able to carry all that junk otherwise."

"That would be a help." I'll have to take a taxi, Ginny thought. Damn! Another expense. She decided to put that off for a moment. After all. Horace had asked her to find out anything she could. "Tell me about this *Elegant* shoot." She got down on her knees and started piling the albums of pictures on the pale-carpeted floor. "I can't help wondering why Rena didn't make it. Or at least call in."

"She must have called." June allowed herself a small frown, rather as if it were a wicked indulgence such as going off her diet. "Or the agency called her. See, the dresses weren't ready. Or they were ripped or something. It was a Sunday, so I wasn't here. But there's no way she would have missed it. Not with the rest of us circling like sharks to get it. And her just being signed when none of us thought she was that terrific." June shrugged. "Of course, that could be jealousy. We're all lousy with it in this business. Only I never really saw her as a runway type. Didn't have the flair. Still, maybe in pictures . . ."

Ginny had finished emptying the bottom of the locker, putting a pair of expensive leather boots on top of the albums. She stood up and started going through the clothes on the rack. June was already fussing with the contents of the shelf.

"You're not going to want any of this stuff, are you?" she asked. "Nobody likes using other people's makeup. But Matilda has two nieces, ten and twelve, I'll bet they'd love it."

"Terrific." One less load of stuff to carry. She flicked through the clothes on the rack. A couple of sweaters. Two raincoats, one serviceable, one expensive. "You want any of this?"

"Wouldn't fit." June was shoveling out the contents of the shelf into her long arms. "I'll go back to the kitchen and see if Matilda's got bags for this stuff."

Still with her arms full, she hesitated. "Funny about there being no padlock on Rena's locker. She was always very careful about that."

"Maybe the police broke it off?"

"Could be. They were all over the place Monday. Not that they'd have to cut it off or anything. Mr. McKay keeps a list of the combinations in his desk." She shrugged. "Some of the girls would forget their own names if they didn't have an assignment sheet."

"Mr. McKay's office?"

"The room we went through. Most of the business is done upstairs, where Madam's office is. I think he uses it only to sleep in when he can't stand the sight of her anymore."

"Not a happy marriage?"

June sighed theatrically. "Honey, the stories I could tell you!" She was about to move, when Ginny pulled out the last item on the rack.

It was a black cape, full and long. The kind Paco had worn when he came to Horsey's apartment. And behind it was shoved a wide-brimmed black fedora. The costume the murderer was supposed to have worn, Ginny thought. "June, is this Rena's?"

The model looked at the cape and hat carefully. "I never saw it," she said, the frown reappearing. With one long finger she touched the material. "Kind of heavy for September." She shifted the bottles and jars in her arms. "I'd better get those bags. With my luck, Julie-Baby will pass right over me if I'm not back in the arena when Suzanne is through."

The trash bags weren't exactly glamorous, but Ginny managed to get a cab almost as soon as she stepped out of the front door of the Classic Agency. Horace would want to see the photo albums, she was sure. Not that she didn't as well. And Mark would want to see the cape and the black hat. Why were they in Rena's locker? There could be at least a hundred reasons, Ginny thought. Well, maybe one or two. The murderer might have seen Rena wearing the cape and hat and figured it was a good disguise to leave her building. Or the murderer might have stuffed them there sometime after Monday morning, which made whoever had killed Rena very familiar with the Classic Agency. Not Philip McKay, Ginny decided loyally, knowing she probably would not have felt the same if he hadn't been so nice. Now, if he had murdered his wife, that she could understand. . . .

It was simpler to go back to Horace's apartment and unload what she had collected. Also, she wanted to call the Kinn school and see if they wanted Rena's clothes for their wardrobe department. That would solve one problem. And she probably should get at least slightly cleaned up if Mark was taking her to dinner.

To her surprise, Horace wasn't in the apartment when she got there. The door to his office was open and from the clutter of papers on his desk Ginny had the feeling he had probably not been able to concentrate on his work. That is, if her theory about his curiosity concerning the murder was correct.

She dumped the albums in the spare room, taking a minute or two to flip through them. Yes, they were all by different photographers, unlike the Gruen portfolio. She could see now why the portfolio might have had a special importance to Rena. Somehow the other photographers had not been as successful as Gruen had been. She was still beautiful, of course, or, rather, attractive. But somehow she belonged in the more stylized photos Axel had taken. The modern lighthearted but sexy look obviously was not comfortable for her. In some pictures she looked almost plain. Only Axel had managed to blunt the almost hostile defiance in her eyes and turn it into something smoldering and elegant.

The thought of that sent Ginny scurrying to her own back room and tiny closet. She wasn't going to push her luck by asking for the spare room. Anyway, the maid's room, while small, had light, and no matter what she might have to rehearse, Horace would hardly be able to hear her from his part of the apartment. Only what to wear? She had a fairly complete wardrobe, but what went with cleaning out a probably dusty apartment and then a dinner with an intelligent young man? Men were lucky, she thought not for the first time. With a blue blazer and gray slacks they could go anywhere.

It was six-twenty-five when Ginny arrived at Rena's apartment. This time she carried trash bags and walked with the supreme confidence that she knew what to do with whatever they were going to clear out. That nice receptionist had practically swooned over the idea of Rena's expensive clothes. Ginny decided to scrap her first idea of black slacks and a turtleneck and wear a proper dress. It was fresh out of the cleaners and with the end of September approaching this might be her last chance to wear it.

Mark, she noticed, had spruced up himself too. Not bad-looking, she thought as she approached him. Not in the Philip McKay category, of course, but not repulsive either.

"You're on time," he said cheerfully.

"No, I'm early," she replied serenely. "And so are you."

This brought an easy grin to his face, and they went down the two steps to the iron gate that led to the entrance of Rena's apartment.

Their first disagreement, minor as it was, concerned Ginny's plans for disposing of Rena's clothes. Mark seemed hesitant about the dispersal of her things to private people rather than, as he suggested, a police warehouse which is what Margolus had told him was the usual procedure, at least until the murderer had been caught and tried.

"It's just that lawyers sometimes want jurors to look at the actual objects of a crime scene," he protested.

"You're going to lug a bare bed into a courtroom?" Ginny asked, using what she thought was a reasonable tone of voice. "And what about her clothes? Is there any reason they can't be given away? I mean, you still have what she was wearing when she was killed, haven't you?"

"The police have them. Pajamas and robe." Mark was beginning to feel not quite so happy about all of this. What Ginny was saying was reasonable enough, but he knew how weak it would sound when he reported it to Margolus. "And the landlord is keeping the furniture."

Ginny was moving restlessly around the long room that was Rena's apartment. She wasn't looking at it calmly and quietly as Horace had. Women, Mark thought. You couldn't be rational with them.

"You could take the checkbooks and the contents of her desk, that

ought to satisfy any attorney. Or the police. Grab a trash bag.'' She
pulled one out of the box and handed it to him before wandering around
again. ''I don't think the police are going to have any interest in her
underwear or pantyhose. And if they have, they should be ashamed of
themselves.'' She started dumping the contents of the drawers under
the armoire into another bag. ''I vote we just leave them outside with
the garbage.''

''Don't you think that sounds a little . . . well, callous?''

''Listen, this is a girl who lied to me about letting me be her roommate. A girl I've seen maybe three times in the last two years. If you
think I'm going to get all mushy about her, you're wrong.''

Women are definitely the stronger sex, Mark thought as he went on
emptying the desk drawers.

''That's funny.'' Ginny was behind him, but there was something in
her voice that made him look up. She was standing just inside the
small bathroom.

''What?'' It couldn't be anything important, the police had been all
over the place probably half a dozen times.

''There's no hair drier.''

''So? Maybe she didn't believe in them.''

''Mark, you must know enough about women to realize practically
every single woman in America has at least one, sometimes a second,
for traveling. And Rena had shoulder-length hair, at least shoulder-
length. There wasn't one at the agency either.''

''Maybe the police took it.'' He was trying to remember the list of
objects they had removed. The list was on his desk downtown. He
should have brought it. Mentally he ran through the pages he had been
given. No, he couldn't remember a hair drier.

Ginny moved toward the bed where she had spread out the black
cape and hat. ''And what about these?''

''I know enough about women to know that hats and capes like
that are fairly common.'' No point in letting Ginny think he was a
complete virgin.

''No labels,'' Ginny said thoughtfully, looking at the cape and hat
carefully. ''Or if there were any, they've been cut out.'' She reached
into her trash bag and pulled out the tall boots that had also been in
Rena's locker. ''No labels on these either, although I think they're
Ferragamo.'' She turned the boots over in her hands. ''Nearly new too.''

''I guess I'd better take those,'' Mark said, and began to shove them
into the bag that already held the dead model's records. This is going
to screw up my plans for a grand dinner, he thought. You don't wander

into a terrific restaurant carrying full garbage bags. What place do I know in the Village that she might like?

But Ginny was talking again. "Doesn't all this seem a little . . . well, *strange* to you, Mark? I mean, here's a girl, almost plain when I knew her in college. Last week she signs with a top agency as a model. But no one seems to like her."

"Not even you."

"I was counting on a place to stay," she answered crisply. "But that wouldn't be a reason to kill her. And somehow her portfolio is important and yet Uncle Horace said Gruen didn't even look at it. And the clipping about another dead model. An apartment as sterile as a hotel room. And now the clothes Paco or whoever the murderer was was wearing are in her locker at the agency."

"We don't know that they were the clothes the killer wore. Not now that Paco has been cleared." Why couldn't his week with Homicide have been a simple case of mugging or a gang murder? "Especially since McKay was here at the time of her death."

"Near the time of her death," Ginny corrected him. "Come on, I'm getting hungry. And I don't think there's anything more to do here."

Almost the same words Horace had used, Mark thought as he glumly started packing up Rena's belongings. Why the hell did I suggest dinner anyway?

CHAPTER TEN

Why the hell did I agree to dinner anyway, Horace thought angrily that same afternoon. I could have got out of it, I've gotten out of other invitations of Zoe's. He shuffled the papers around on his desk. Nothing was making sense today. He would have liked to blame it on the noise Ginny had made with the vacuum cleaner, but he knew that wasn't it. He'd always been able to work through it, days the cleaning women had been here. Here and gone, he thought mournfully.

When he heard Ginny leave for the Classic Agency, and he had to strain hard to hear her, she was being so quiet, something he knew wouldn't last, he got up from his desk and wandered aimlessly through the apartment. Damn it, Ginny had already laid out his tuxedo, the studs in the shirt, the one job he always managed to mess up.

No point in thinking about Zoe and the coming dinner party. No point in fiddling around with English law either. And yet it wasn't even two o'clock. Research, he decided, that's what I need, relying on the age-old strategy of a writer who doesn't feel like writing. A trip to the public library, that would get him back to Victorian England. Only when he finally got there, by the circuitous route of the New York bus companies, he headed for the periodical section. There were four papers five years ago, he recalled. All right, so he was curious about Diane Chaumet. No crime in that, was there? At least it would give him something to talk about at dinner.

You're lying to yourself, Horace Livsey, he told himself as he settled in front of one of the microfilm machines, the rolls of film in their neat boxes at his side. You don't want to talk about the late Ms. Chaumet tonight. You want to ask questions. He settled in and started twisting the dials of the machine to the date of her accident.

Two hours later he rewound the last film and leaned back. My eyes hurt, my legs hurt, my back hurts; I'm going to be a great dinner guest tonight.

And he'd learned nothing.

There had been more details about the young woman's death. Nothing was wrong with her car or her brakes. True, she had been released from Manhattan General Hospital earlier that day, but the hospital sources reported she was in a perfectly healthy condition, certainly able to drive a car. There had been no signs of alcohol or drugs in her system. She did have a slight bandage over one eye that he noticed in one of the photographs in one of the tabloids, but surely not enough to obstruct her vision, not driving familiar roads. Apparently she had been well liked; the head of her agency, Philip McKay, had been quoted as saying "It was a tragic loss." There were pictures of her service at the Frank Campbell Funeral Home. McKay was there, and a sharp-featured woman in a dress that looked dark enough for mourning but too chic to denote sadness. McKay's wife and co-owner of the agency, the lines under the picture said. The place apparently was full of friends. He even noticed a blurred picture of Jean-Claude Franchard.

One picture he studied for a long time. It was of Celeste Lanier, his hostess for the dinner this evening. She was identified as one of the editors at *Elegant* magazine. She seemed genuinely distressed, even in the murkiness of the reproduced photo, leaning heavily on the arm of a man busily shooing away inquiring photographers. No mention of who he was.

Horace had read through several more days of the newspapers, straining a little as the story drew less and less space. The death was ruled accidental. Only in one of the gossip columns was there an item that held anything Horace hadn't already known.

The column was by one of the more sharp-tongued ladies and, while phrased carefully to avoid the possibility of a lawsuit, she implied that Diane had been in the hospital for cosmetic surgery. What she also, with clearer phrasing, hinted was that the operation might have been botched, ending Diane's career as a model and raising the possibility that her death had not been an accident but could perhaps have been suicide.

Horace read the item several times, finally copying it down, word for word, in the notebook he always carried. But the lady was notorious for putting out false information to stir up interest in her column, and Horace felt it was the kind of item that might have appeared after the death of any relatively famous person. Presidents, millionaires, politicians, and, of course, movie stars—after any of their deaths, somebody was bound to suggest the demise was self-induced.

A dirty world we live in, Horace thought as he got up painfully and stretched.

Still . . .

Promptly at seven he was at the doors of the Stanforth Hotel. Since they had already met at Franchard's, Zoe had decided they didn't need a half hour of conversation to "catch up," as she had put it. The limousine driver had announced their arrival to the doorman and in less than five minutes (unusual for the always-late Zoe) she came through the revolving doors of the hotel. She was wrapped in a large lace shawl in vaguely Spanish style but Horace could see she was wearing the dress she had picked out at Franchard's. She smiled brightly at Horace as she got into the car and smoothed her skirts; parties for Zoe were what a glass of champagne might be to anybody else. Horace had learned years before that a simple kiss around the region of her hair was all that was allowed before a party. Not that he minded, it was sufficient to look at her. Effort had clearly been made. She barely looked forty and a very attractive forty at that.

"Now, you are going to talk tonight, aren't you, Horace? Not just stand against the wall looking like an aged Heathcliff." These were the first words out of her mouth as a greeting.

"I'll talk, Zoe, my dear," he responded placidly. In fact, there were so many questions floating around in his head, he suspected he might easily monopolize the entire evening. Careful, he told himself. He wasn't a policeman, he wasn't a detective, he was an innocent by-stander, and the less people thought he was interested in Rena or Diane Chaumet, the more he was likely to learn.

Celeste's apartment was in one of the large gray buildings that lined Park Avenue. Horace could never understand why this was such a desirable address. All the occupants could do was look out at each other through the slightly parted lush drapes that seemed to be obligatory in these buildings. The apartments facing the East River he could under-stand, although most faced the barren, deserted island that had once held hospitals and the flat, colorless land beyond. Now, Riverside Drive, that at least had space and views. Even West End had a variety of architecture and a lively family feeling. But New Yorkers considered Park Avenue or Fifth to be the ultimate diploma announcing their success.

Still, in the case of Celeste Lanier, it must be the start of success, for her apartment was only on the third floor, "treetop level" as the real estate ads tactfully put it, although the only trees to view were stunted and tired. But there was a white-gloved doorman and expensive-looking wood paneling in the lobby. No elevator man. But on Celeste's floor Horace noticed that there was only one other front door. Low floor or not, Celeste had definitely arrived.

Before Horace could push the buzzer, the door was flung open wide with a grand flourish. The man standing there made Horace feel instantly as if he had come to the wrong place. The man was round and pudgy, had clearly avoided exercise as much as Horace but had not stayed away from fattening foods. He was somewhere in his late twenties or possibly early thirties, but definitely of another generation from Horace or Zoe and very possibly of another world. He was wearing an orange velvet coat with black satin lapels (his one concession to formal attire), purple crushed-velvet trousers, Moroccan slippers, and in place of a starched shirt and tie a white turtleneck and a wide batik scarf, knotted intricately and held in place with a large turquoise pin.

"Hello, you beautiful people. I'm Oliver Tomorrow and I've had an absolutely rotten day." He stepped aside to let Horace and Zoe come in.

Oliver Tomorrow, where had Horace heard that name before? As if the question had been written on his forehead, the man instantly went on.

"Yes, of course you've heard of me. Artist, photographer, today's genius, and that's a beautiful dress," he added as he helped Zoe untangle herself from her lace shawl.

"Thank you," replied Zoe, completely unruffled by the flamboyant young man. "It's a Jean-Claude Franchard, from his newest collection."

"Filthy scum that one, but he's obviously got his talent back. But scum he still is, after stabbing me in the back. *I* was supposed to do the *Elegant* shoot and he knows it. Instead of that boring old creep Gruen." His eyebrows went up to nearly the edge of his sparse, ginger-colored bangs. "Celeste has put me on guard duty at the door until everybody arrives. She knows I can hear an elevator open four blocks away." He waved vaguely toward the large living room behind him. "Hordes of Celeste's nearest and dearest are in there or due any minute."

"Isn't the choice of a photographer usually up to the magazine's editors?" Horace asked mildly. Luckily Zoe was still occupied with untangling some of the lace of her shawl with Oliver's help.

"Celeste and her helping hand!" Oliver continued. "Loyal, of course, the darling girl has always been that. But to be saddled with someone as outré as Gruen!" The eyebrows went up again. "I mean, loyalty can go just so far, she has her own career to think of. But she has promised me the next issue.'' He sniffed slightly. "That is, if I'm not in Milan. I'm booked so far ahead.'' He freed Zoe from the last of her entanglements. "There, dearie, all clear and no harm done.''

The elevator door behind them opened and Oliver stepped forward to welcome the next guests.

"Celeste's gentleman friend?'' Horace whispered as they moved toward the living room.

"Hardly.'' Zoe still had on her party smile but the sarcasm she put into that word would have withered flowers.

The room they entered was large and carefully decorated. Red material had been tightly stretched across the walls, raw silk or something like it, and the furnishings were handsome, a mixture of modern and comfortable (large chairs and sofas) and French antiques: chests, picture frames, odd little stools clearly never meant to be sat on. The room held about ten people as they entered but could easily have handled close to forty; obviously being the managing editor of a top fashion magazine required space for large parties. Beyond the main room Horace could see what probably was generally an extension of the living room but was now filled with several tables draped in beautiful linen and gleaming with silver, expensive china, and tall candlesticks, the candles not yet lit. Unlike many of the top social parties Zoe had dragged him to, this was obviously going to be a sit-down dinner, not an annoying buffet where you had to juggle plates, knives, forks, napkins, and wineglasses on your lap. Zoe *had* promised an excellent meal.

"Your usual, Countess Sirelli?'' A young man in a white linen jacket had quietly appeared at their side. "A kir royal?''

"Yes. How kind of you to remember.'' Zoe looked at the young man, clearly recognizing him but at a loss for his name. "I'm sorry. It's Joseph?''

"John.'' The young man smiled slightly. "I served you at the Buchmans' last spring.''

"Of course! You're with Bountiful Banquets, aren't you? Now I'm sure I'm going to have a perfect evening. How's the career going?'' Whatever Zoe's faults, she never forgot a face or the person wearing it.

"Two weeks summer stock and I think I'm up for a commercial.'' Then, remembering his job tonight, he turned to Horace. "What can I get you, sir?''

"Just a plain ginger ale,'' Horace replied. He would dearly have loved a vodka martini but he'd learned long ago that cocktail hours in New York tend to stretch out indefinitely. And if he was going to make a fool of himself asking questions, it was better he did it sober. Besides, he could see an array of wineglasses at each setting on the tables in the far room.

"Nonsense, Horace, you'll be bored in no time with that." Zoe looked at the pleasant young man. "A vodka martini on the rocks, John, if you would, with a twist."

The young man bowed and disappeared. Before Horace could say anything more to his ex-wife (and what could he say except it was rather pleasant that she still remembered his tastes?) a young woman came up to them, holding out both hands in greeting.

"Zoe, you are absolutely gorgeous! This summer obviously agreed with you and nobody wears a Franchard dress better."

The ladies exchanged polite air-kisses, giving Horace a moment to regard the woman. Celeste Lanier. He recognized her from the blurred picture of Diane Chaumet's funeral. She had to be in her late thirties, he supposed, but the cheerful smile on her face made her look ten years younger. Not tall but with a quality about her that any princess might have envied. Her silver-blonde hair was cut fairly short and Horace suspected the silver was not part of some careful streaking in a beauty parlor but the beginning of gray. Only gray was too drab a word for her. Zoe moved to one side to introduce Horace.

"Celeste, you've met my ex? Professor Horace Livsey."

"I—I don't think so. I think I would have remembered." This was not said in the artificial way of social flattery but as if she really meant it. Horace looked down at her and took the hand she offered. There was something fragile about her, as if she might break if you held her too tight. Victorian, he thought as he looked into her large blue eyes, a lady to protect and cherish, although there was nothing of the past in her long gauze tunic and wide trousers, sprinkled with sequins.

"It's a pleasure to meet you," he said, resisting the impulse to bow and kiss the hand he still held.

"And if Horace says that, he means it," said Zoe, watching them with some amusement. She knew the signs when Horace was attracted to a woman but she also knew that practically no one could resist Celeste's charm. The silver in her hair didn't matter any more than the tiny lines at her eyes; men would always find Celeste Lanier attractive, if she lived to be ninety. It was something that happened when you were a genuinely nice lady; a quality Zoe could turn on occasionally but seldom had the patience to keep up for very long.

"Are you getting a drink?" Celeste asked as she stepped back after Horace had released her hand. "Is there anyone you want to meet? Or don't know?"

"Darling, go be a hostess, we'll mingle." There was no point in letting Horace get too charmed.

Celeste had given a quick glance at the front door, where Oliver was holding forth with a newly arrived couple. The McKays, Horace realized, recognizing them from the newspaper photographs. The afternoon at the library had not been wasted, nor, he admitted to himself, his daily reading of the newspapers.

"I'm afraid it's mostly the fashion crowd tonight, Professor Livsey." Celeste was looking at him again. Another attractive quality about Celeste was that she seemed to give her whole attention to whomever she was talking to. "I hope you won't be bored."

"I'm sure I won't be." She left them then just as the young man arrived with the drinks on a tray. Zoe handed Horace his glass and drifted casually over to one of the tall windows. It was swagged with what Horace guessed was a sort of gold brocade, opulent and yet somehow not garish. The lady has taste, he thought. The silk curtains beneath the drapes were billowing softly and Zoe edged them closer to the window.

"Since I've never known you to have a martini without smoking, I guess you can do it here." Her eyes flickered about and she picked up a delicate china dish with a matchbook on it. "Celeste has even thought of ashtrays." She took Horace's glass and placed it on the dish deftly as he reached for his holder. "And yes, she's a remarkable woman, and yes, I adore her but don't get any romantic ideas."

Cigarette lit, Horace retrieved his glass. "Don't be absurd, Zoe. She's probably young enough to be my daughter."

"Just possibly, if you started early. Anyway, she always has a string of beaus." Zoe glanced around with an air of casual indifference. "I wonder who the current one is?"

"She seems rather gentle to be an editor in chief, especially in this fashion business. It seems rather cutthroat, the little I've learned about it."

"I suspect Celeste can cut throats with the best of them. You don't get to be the editor of a premiere fashion magazine by being Little Nell." Zoe took a small sip of her kir. "Although somehow nobody ever gets angry with her. Or at least they don't stay that way." Zoe nodded and smiled at several people around the room, which was beginning to fill up. "See those ladies? All of them must have been hoping to get the *Elegant* job and probably would have sacrificed several pedicured toes, their own or others, to have it. And yet here they are ready to break the very excellent bread Bountiful Banquets will provide."

"She's really that successful?"

"Nobody above her but the publisher." She mentioned a name even Horace had heard of, the owner of several major magazines as well as television stations, cable networks, and one of the finest private art collections in the country.

"Will he be here tonight?"

"Unlikely. And it's 'they.' His wife very wisely never leaves his side." She smiled up at Horace. "No, darling, he's not her beau. And the last I heard, they were in South America. He believes in putting people in charge and letting them make their own decisions."

Zoe was still glancing around the room but she managed to whisper to Horace, "Don't make a point of it, but I think the number-one man in Celeste's life is over there talking to old Mrs. Phelps."

Horace had enough social skills to be able to flick an ash in the china dish and yet still glance indirectly across the room. A handsome-looking man in his late forties was talking politely to an imposing woman considerably older. He was probably better-looking in a tuxedo than wearing anything else, Horace decided before realizing he had seen the man before. Wasn't he the one Celeste had been leaning on as she came out of Frank Campbell's after Diane Chaumet's funeral service? "Do you know who he is, Zoe?"

"A Dr. Bosley. He just happens to be one of the best plastic surgeons in the city, which makes him right up there with the really rich. He probably knows half the faces in this room, both before and after." She glanced back at Horace, aware he hadn't taken his eyes off the man in the far corner. "And no, darling, he didn't do me. Not, of course, that I've ever had anything done," she added quickly.

"But models might have had something done, wouldn't they?"

Zoe was used to Horace wandering off to what seemed like different subjects but this was beyond her. Before she could think of an answer, Celeste had reappeared at their side.

"Zoe, love, could you do me a favor?" Important editor or not, she looked like a small girl asking to go to the circus. "The McKays are here and they're apparently not speaking to each other. Again. Could you sort of go over to them and act as a buffer while I rescue Malcolm? He can't want to be stuck with Mrs. Phelps all evening."

"Malcolm?" asked Horace.

"Dr. Bosley. Haven't you met?"

"Dr. Bosley ..." Horace pretended to frown. "Isn't he attached to Manhattan General Hospital?"

"Why, yes, you know him?"

Suddenly he was aware Zoe had moved through the crowd, and he and Celeste were for a moment alone. If ever he was going to get a chance to talk to Celeste about Rena and Diane, this might be it. "I was just asking Zoe about your new job," he began tactfully. Most successful people like to talk about their work, even when hosting a party. "It must be a major crisis, a model dying just when you're planning on her pictures for your magazine."

"Rena, you mean?" Suddenly she shook her head in embarrassment. "Of course! She sent her portfolio to you. Or was it your niece? I read about that in the papers. Good Lord, the police must have been buzzing around you since Monday!" There was genuine sympathy in her voice. "They certainly spent enough time with us at the magazine. Half of my writers are working tonight to make up for the hours they lost in the questioning." She allowed herself a glance in the direction of Dr. Bosley, but there were now enough people in the room that he was no longer visible from where they stood by the open window.

"Such a strange thing to do," Horace said quickly, hoping to keep her attention. Another man in a white jacket was passing around canapes, which seemed to keep most of the crowd occupied. "Sending the portfolio to me . . . all of them pictures by Axel Gruen."

"He had a real talent in photographing her. And models are all a little strange anyway. I could tell you stories about some of them that bring a new meaning to the word *bizarre*."

"But you had picked her for this—what do you call it?—photographic spread?"

"She's signed with the Classic Agency, that means something about her was special." She made a small grimace. "I didn't quite see it, I have to admit. That's one of the problems in fashion. There's always a whole new trend coming up that you're supposed to stay ahead of. Axel thought she had the possibilities to be one of the best. The new wave." She smiled up at Horace. " 'New waves' come in about as often as they do at the Hamptons."

"Could she have become that successful?" That was fairly direct, Horace realized, so he amended it with the sort of dazed look that he knew he didn't do very well. Apparently Celeste didn't catch it.

"Truthfully—" She paused for a second, looking out at the billowing curtains of the open window. "In my opinion, I don't think so. She was beautiful, at least when Axel photographed her. Tall. Slim. The figure to wear clothes. Striking."

"But not the superstar type?" He was pressing a little hard and he knew it, but Celeste didn't seem to notice. "I mean, what does that take?" He was adding this lamely but at least it seemed the innocent remark of an outsider.

Celeste paused for a moment and what she said next surprised Horace. "Professor?" It was almost a whisper. "Could I steal a cigarette from you?" Horace fumbled for his pack. For the first time he was aware he should have carried the solid gold case Zoe had given him years ago when it was accepted that people smoked. As he lit Celeste's cigarette, he had a fleeting thought she might have been evading his innocent question.

"Malcolm hates me to smoke," she said in a gentle voice. "But when you start having big parties." She grinned self-consciously as she pulled in her first puff. "I get nervous, don't tell anybody. Even with the best caterers in New York." She looked at him then, and for the first time her face was serious, the little-girl look gone. "You've asked an interesting question. What makes a successful model?" Now she smiled, as if she had solved a difficult question. "Strange, but I think it's a sense of humor."

Obviously, he was looking at her with some puzzlement. "I'm serious. All the great ones, past and present, have it. Suzy Parker, Jean Shrimpton, Lauren Hutton ... it's like the ability to play charades. Without humor you can't really throw yourself into the weird attitudes the photographers or advertisers want. It doesn't mean you don't take the job seriously ... all the best do, but there's also laughter behind it." She smiled almost apologetically to Horace. "I must be boring you."

"Not in the least." He'd had only half of his martini but he knew he was going to have to move carefully. "And did Rena Varmont have that?"

"Rena?" It was almost as if she had forgotten the dead model. "No. I don't think so. I could have been wrong. I have been before." She was gazing around the crowded room now, ready to move back to being the hostess of the sort of party that would make the society or gossip columns the next day.

Now or never, Horace thought. "And Diane Chaumet? Did she have that special quality?"

This had caught Celeste's attention. For a moment her face seemed saddened—to the point where Horace wished he had kept his mouth shut.

"Diane? She was a darling." But Celeste looked at him sharply, the kind of look Horace suspected anybody on her staff who was late with a deadline might get. What had Zoe said? *She could cut throats with the best of them?* "Did you know Diane?"

"I think I met her once or twice." Horace hoped he was learning to lie better. "Zoe and her parties ... I think I was introduced." Back it up with something, he thought. But not too much. Lying was becoming easier, he realized. "A beautiful blonde, as I recall."

"And a charmer to everyone. I was just starting to move up at *Elegant* then, but she always had time to stop in and chat." Celeste looked up at Horace again, adding quickly, "Not because I was important or could get her jobs, just to be friendly." Her eyes moved around the room again.

Horace knew he had only a few seconds left. "Tragic, her death. Did I hear something about it being suicide?"

This snapped Celeste's attention back to him. "That's impossible!" She was almost indignant. "I saw her that last afternoon at the hospital, we were discussing new assignments, when she could take time off to get a vacation, boyfriends. She was in great spirits."

"I don't think Zoe told me what she was in the hospital for." Horace made a fast note to himself that he had better fill his ex-wife in on what she was supposed to have told him.

"Some female thing, I think." Celeste was back to waving at new arrivals.

Horace never claimed to be totally knowledgeable about female anatomy, not, at least, below the surface, but he doubted seriously if any female condition would result in a bandage around the eyes. Before he could mention that in some kind of offhand way, he heard a man behind him.

"Celeste? I thought we agreed, you had given up smoking." The man was the doctor Celeste had pointed out across the room. Somehow he had managed to extract himself from the elderly woman he had been talking to. His tone was lightly humorous but there was no doubt he felt he had the right to reprove his hostess.

"Darn it. You caught me." Celeste hastily put out her cigarette. "Malcolm, you know Professor Livsey?" Before either of the men could answer, she had floated away toward the door where Axel Gruen had just entered. "There's Axel. I'd better keep him away from Oliver or there'll be pistols at dawn. Or maybe Rolexes. What do photographers fight with?"

Dr. Bosley looked after Celeste with an amused smile on his face. "There goes one tactful lady," he said. "They could use her in the State Department." He looked at Horace, the smile still on his face. "No, I don't think we have met, Professor. But of course I know who you are. The newspapers were full of the dead model sending her portfolio to you."

Horace could see he was curious enough to want to know whether there had been some romantic link between Horace and the late Rena Varmont but had obviously decided after one look at Horace's gray hair that was not likely. Age, damn it, Horace thought, wondering if he would be dismissed so casually if he were a multimillionaire.

"You're a plastic surgeon, Doctor?" Time for attack.

"I suppose that's what you would call it." The doctor was clearly braced for the questions that must devil him at every party: Whom have you done? And is it true about so-and-so? Or painful or expensive?

Horace decided to get to the point. He had a feeling dinner was going to be announced soon. If he wasn't at Dr. Bosley's table, conversation would be over for the evening. "Celeste and I were just talking about the late Diane Chaumet . . . my ex-wife and I had met her years ago. Did you know her?" That was a bit blunt but the doctor was already looking around the room for better company.

"Chaumet? No, I don't think so." He frowned a little, as if someone had questioned his bill. "A model, wasn't she?"

Do you forget funeral services that quickly? Horace wondered. It was only five years ago. "Died in a car accident," Horace added.

"Never met her. Nor did I know Rena Varmont," the doctor added, obviously clearing the decks preparing to move away. "Which is going to leave me out of most of the conversation tonight. Old Mrs. Phelps could talk about nothing else. Apparently she was able to get the messenger boy who brought you the portfolio out on bail. This between her work saving the whales and sitting on most of the museum boards in the city." He grinned and looked suddenly a lot younger. "Hope you're not stuck with her at dinner."

"Stuck with whom?" Axel Gruen had joined them, arriving quietly without their noticing. Tonight he was carefully dressed for the occasion in a beautifully tailored black velvet jacket and the requisite tuxedo trousers. Horace suspected that not only were they brand new, a sign of his future prosperity, but had never been worn before.

"Mrs. Phelps, Axel." Dr. Bosley's smile was gone. He was polite, of course. Horace suspected he'd be polite in a vice raid, but nothing more.

"Ah, yes, a daunting lady. I thought you'd be talking about poor dead Rena. Everybody else is."

"We didn't know her," said Bosley calmly.

"Really? Such a delightful girl." Was there more than a little skepticism in Axel's voice? It was hard for Horace to tell. He'd been standing for almost half an hour and his legs, always his weak point, were beginning to ache. Unfortunately, the one chair nearby looked as if it could have held only a very thin and quiet three-year-old.

"You were one of the last to see her, weren't you, Axel?" It seemed a simple enough remark but apparently it was the exact thing Gruen wanted to hear from Horace.

"Oh, yes. That last Sunday afternoon. Everyone has been asking me about that."

Or have you been volunteering the information? Horace thought.

"Tell me, Livsey, have they made any progress on the murder?" Gruen's smile was sardonic rather than pleasant.

"I'm sure I wouldn't know."

"And I thought you were in the middle of the investigation."

"I'm not under suspicion, if that's what you mean." Before he had to add to that, the young man who had given him his first drink arrived holding a silver tray and a full glass.

"May I offer you the other half of your drink, sir?" It was the tactful question the best caterers and their staff used when giving a guest a refill, obviously invented to ease men whose wives or lady friends were keeping a sharp eye on their alcoholic intake. Horace had heard it before at the parties he had escorted Zoe to, much more diplomatic than what went on at academic cocktail parties, when the host usually said, "Ready for another?" He put down his empty glass and picked up the full one gratefully. Zoe was seated on one of the comfortable sofas and he made a move toward her. "Thank you ... John." At least he'd gotten that name right. He smiled at Gruen and Bosley. "I think it's time I rejoined my ex-wife. At least socially." He moved away, not expecting an answer, and there was none.

The next half hour the party flowed smoothly; the conversation, at least around Horace and Zoe, had moved on to more general matters than the murder of a model. It was time to put the investigation to rest, Horace realized. Still, he noticed Gruen making a point of speaking to the McKays. Whatever he said, and Horace had his suspicions, they did not take it happily. Katya, slim and as immobile as if she were modeling her crimson evening gown instead of wearing it, flushed and her eyes glittered angrily. McKay, for the first time at the party that Horace had noticed, reached out and touched her arm, almost as if he were cautioning her. And Katya, to Horace's surprise, took a submissive step back, moving away from his hand, her composure back. Axel turned away from them, a triumphant grin on his face.

"What was that all about?" Zoe asked, noticing that Horace had been clearly staring at the three.

"I think our old friend has just cemented a business deal. One the McKays are not happy about."

"Horsey, have you been snooping again?"

Before Horace could come up with a plausible story, a group of ladies had surrounded Axel and his voice was clear enough for nearly all the room to hear.

"Yes, dear Celeste is signing me to a long contract. I won't be working exclusively for *Elegant,* of course. One has only so many hours in the day, you know. But I'll be doing all of Jean-Claude Franchard's shows, naturally." There were exclamations of praise sufficient to turn Axel's bald head pink.

Which, looking back at it later, Horace thought was one of the worst examples of bad timing he'd ever seen in a social gathering.

For Franchard had just come in the door, his tall frame looming over the pudgy Oliver Tomorrow, still on duty welcoming guests.

Franchard's face was livid with anger, his eyes full of rage as he stared at Gruen's back. If looks could kill, Horace thought.

He took a swallow of his glass. It was going to be an interesting evening after all.

CHAPTER ELEVEN

It was not going to be an interesting evening at all, Ginny decided before they had ordered. Mark had taken her to a little restaurant around the corner from Rena's apartment, tucked into the tiny basement of a building on West Fourth Street. It was obviously not his first choice and he was being cranky about it, insisting on changing the table they had been first given (which was perfectly fine, Ginny thought) for one in the back room.

She would have expected his mood to have improved when she had transferred all the things he felt he should turn over to the police into a large tote bag they had found just before leaving Rena's apartment. The other clothes were still in the trash bag that he had helped carry to the restaurant. Now that they were settled, he still seemed on edge, pushing silverware around the table and not even glancing at the menu.

"I could do with a glass of wine," she said since he hadn't bothered to offer and the young waiter was hovering around them anxiously. Luckily, at this hour the place was practically deserted.

"Sure. Sorry." He ordered two glasses. But when they arrived he was still frowning. Maybe he was more concerned about Margolus and what the police would think of their removing things than he let on.

"Have the police discovered anything new? About Rena, I mean?"

"No." His tone was definitely surly. "I wish you could tell me more about her. You're the only link we seem to have."

"We've been all through that." This must be what he'd be like questioning a hostile witness, and she wasn't liking it one bit.

"The college you met her at . . . that was expensive, wasn't it?"

"Fifteen thousand a year. About." She thought of her father sighing

136

as he made out the tuition checks. Not that Daddy was poor or close to it, but it *was* an awful lot of money.

"Where did she get it?" He was aware the question had come out more brusquely than he intended. "I mean, you said she only had this aunt she lived with, a nurse or something?"

"A retired nurse." Ginny shifted a bread stick on her plate. This was definitely not going to be a pleasant social date between two young people.

"Retired? That would make the aunt how old?"

"I don't know. I just met her once or twice. In her fifties, maybe."

"Young to retire."

"Maybe she inherited some money or something."

"Possible." He glanced at the menu as if nothing on it looked appealing. "Still, wouldn't Rena have mentioned that? If the aunt was planning on putting her through all four years of college?"

"Rena wasn't exactly the chatty type. I've told you that." Ginny was getting a little cross, part of it being that she was hungry. "Let's order." Might as well get this meal over as soon as possible.

But still, after their first course arrived Mark kept going back to Rena and her aunt. Not that Ginny wasn't intrigued by the death of someone she knew, although she didn't know her well, but there were other things going on in the world to talk about.

"What hospital did the aunt work at?"

"For heaven's sake, Mark, how would I know?"

"I was just wondering." He realized he was being rude, and took a deep breath. No point in getting Ginny angry at him. "One of the weird things about this damn murder is that clipping in the portfolio. About Diane Chaumet. It said she was released the day of her accident from Manhattan General. It just hit me that maybe Rena's aunt was somehow connected with Diane. Worked at that hospital, maybe."

"And if she did, so what? Rena's aunt died, what? Three years ago?" And before he could interrupt, she added, "From perfectly natural causes. Heart attack, I went to the funeral."

"A lot of money spent on the funeral?"

"I don't know what funerals cost!" He was being a real pain.

"There must have been some money. If Rena could just pull up stakes and move to New York. Doesn't it take time to get started on a modeling career? Was there a house to sell? Something like that?"

"No, they shared an apartment. Nothing grand."

"Did the aunt do any work after she retired? You know, private nursing, somebody's companion, something like that?"

"How would I know?" A little more of this and she was going to make a fast exit and settle for a sandwich at home. And to think she had taken her best summer dress out of the cleaner's bag for this!

"Look, I'm not trying to be difficult, but nobody seems to know anything about Rena. Complete blank. You saw the apartment. Margolus says everybody they've questioned acts like Rena was a total stranger. All the police have is that damn portfolio, the clipping slid behind one of the pictures, and you."

Ginny sighed. "I didn't kill her, if that's what you're working toward."

"I know that. Only, I remember the people I went to college with, the things they said, pieces of information that, if they got murdered, might be helpful."

"I'll just bet you do!" Ginny knew both her voice and her temper were rising. "Do you go around taking notes on everybody you meet? Just on the off chance somebody might kill them?"

"Of course not! But lots of times people remember more than they think they do. That's all I'm asking." He tried to smile, it was not as ingratiating as he hoped it would be, he could see Ginny was pressing her lips tightly together as if she were preparing to give him a sharp piece of her mind. "Try to understand that if I can help the police on this, it could mean a nice boost to my career."

"Is that why I'm being treated to dinner, somewhat reluctantly? To help your career?"

"I didn't mean it like that. You're a very pretty girl. I like you."

"Is that all you'd remember if I got murdered?"

"No. I'd remember you have a blazing temper and a very stubborn streak." Two could get angry, he thought, only he wasn't prepared for what happened next.

Ginny stood up, pushing her chair back violently. "You are a total pain in the ass, Mark Franklin! I've been helpful and cooperative and every other damn thing a concerned citizen could be. Now you're treating me like I was on the witness stand, and I don't like it one bit!"

He stood up too, knowing he had lost whatever advantages he may have had with her. "You're probably going to be on a witness stand and facing a lawyer tougher than me."

"Good." Her voice was clear ice now. "But it'll be a courtroom, where I'm sure the judge will see he at least has good manners." She took a swift couple of steps away from the table, pausing only to throw over her shoulder, "And you can take all the stuff we took from Rena's apartment to your precious Margolus. I wouldn't want him to give you a bad mark or anything."

In movies, Mark thought glumly as he watched her go, the hero would dash after an indignant young lady. Only in life it didn't work that way. There was the wine to pay for and the half-eaten first course. He slumped back down in his chair again. Might as well finish his meal here. There'd be plenty of time to take all this junk down to Homicide afterward.

It was barely midnight when Horace left Zoe's suite at the Stanforth. He had been surprised that the party had ended early, but he reminded himself in the busy world of working New Yorkers, Thursday was still a "school night" and people had to be at their jobs early and clear-headed. Cocktail hours might stretch on, but dinners (especially by the best caterers) flowed swiftly and smoothly and only the unemployed like himself lingered for an after-dinner drink. Finally Zoe had raised a finger and beckoned him, and they were out the door shortly after ten. At that they were among the last to leave.

Of course, Zoe had made up for it. In more ways than one, Horace thought, grinning to himself as he rode down in the hotel elevator. First had come a very good brandy while Zoe questioned him about the people he had talked to and why. Fortunately she was as interested as he was in the death of Rena Varmont as well as Diane Chaumet, whom it turned out she *had* met once and while Horace had been escorting her. Odd, he had no recollection of the late Ms. Chaumet.

Then, to both of their surprise, one thing led to another. First, the Franchard dress was tricky to unfasten and with no hesitation, Zoe had turned her back to Horace for help with the hooks and zippers. She was wearing black lace underclothes beneath the dress, the promise of the gown had obviously struck a chord with her. And then his hands were around her, enjoying the feeling of her delicately scented skin. . . .

And somehow they were in the large bed in the next room. Their lovemaking had the excitement of something new, but also the wonderful comfort of each of them knowing what pleased and aroused the other. The damn thing still works, Horace thought as he leaned back afterward, his arm around Zoe's bare shoulders. If it were not for the inevitable questions Ginny was bound to ask the next day, he could cheerfully have stayed there all night.

Zoe, however, had never been one to let anyone but servants see her in the morning, and with an ungracious shove had pushed him out of bed. "We can have lunch together Saturday," she said, mentioning a favorite and very expensive restaurant she adored. "And discuss the murder then." She watched him struggling into his clothes. "And we're going to have to do something about your legs."

"Nothing wrong with them. They reach the ground." His voice was muffled as he pulled his dress shirt on over his head. He was not up to replacing studs at this hour.

"You didn't fool me, coming to sit on the couch next to me. You were practically limping. It's those cigarettes." She ignored the fact that they had shared one in comfort just a few moments before. "You're never going to be able to go to dances this winter if you can't stand for half an hour."

"You always said I was a terrible dancer anyway." It was getting to be like the old days of their marriage.

"You were all right. No, you were rather good. Although you never did manage to learn how to signal when you wanted me to reverse"

Oddly, it was not an acrimonious discussion. Horace felt it was the special kind of intimacy that had happened in recent years when Zoe and he had occasionally gone to bed together, when both were uninvolved. He looked at her lying in bed, the sheets demurely tucked around her.

"I love you too," he said with a smile. "Just not every day."

"One o'clock. And don't be late." She turned off the bedside light and snuggled down in the covers contentedly. It was obviously up to him to let himself out.

Only, outside the hotel, the weather had changed again and there was a fine mist that promised to turn the night into still one more of the rainstorms that had plagued the city recently. The doorman was inside talking to the desk clerk, and rather than attract attention, Horace felt it better to hunt for a taxi himself. Walking toward Madison Avenue a little slower than he had in the past, the rain really began to come down. This means I'll have to get these pants pressed again before Zoe's next social gathering.

He ducked under the awning of the bar on the corner and surveyed the avenue for an empty taxi. Plenty of occupied ones, he noticed. But a rainy night in New York . . .

He edged farther back under the awning. Would it be better if he went inside for a drink and let the traffic clear? Probably not, plus he had already swallowed more alcohol that evening than usual. That meant indigestion through the night and less than the usual amount of sleep. It had been enjoyable with Zoe, but at a certain age a good night's sleep was often almost as desirable.

He glanced casually into the bar. It was nearly empty, which considering it wasn't that late surprised Horace. Still, his nights of stopping in for a nightcap after a pleasurable session with a lady were well past him. But in the far corner he could see one couple, deeply engaged in conversation, the man holding the woman's outstretched hand in a gesture that only people sexually involved would be using. The young man was facing the street, and Horace realized with a shock that he recognized him. Jon Bowers, the model Gruen had photographed with the late Rena Varmont.

Horace couldn't see the lady's face, her back was to him. But he recognized her from the evening. Not only had she been at Celeste's party, she had been at Horace's table at dinner, an amusing if slightly catty conversationalist. Only what was Katya McKay doing holding hands with one of her male models at this hour, and he was fairly sure it *was* Katya. There couldn't be that many dresses of that color and design out tonight in New York.

But before he could look again to be sure, an empty cab moved slowly up the street. Horace flagged it. His curiosity wasn't sufficient to allow him to get soaked any further.

Mark had finally tracked down Margolus in his office, still lugging the tote and trash bags Ginny had left him with. He hated feeling he had made a damn fool of himself with her. She was absolutely right, of course, which only made him feel worse. Monday he would have finished his week with Homicide and he'd probably never see her again. And a good thing too.

He hadn't expected to find Margolus in his office at this hour, and one look at the detective's face told him the rest of the night was not going to be any better.

"Where the hell have you been?" The burly detective snarled as he walked in, feeling something like a garbage man with what he was carrying. "I've been calling all over for you."

If this was any sign that Mark was welcome, it didn't come out that way. "I was helping the professor's niece clear out Rena's apartment." He put down the bags. "Here's all we've removed. I thought it better to bring it down here."

"You thought right." Margolus shoved aside the paper plate that contained the last crusts of a sandwich and a paper container of dead coffee. "Our brilliant district attorney has changed his mind again. Pressure or no pressure from real estate guys, that apartment is getting sealed back up." He scowled at the telephone as if he expected somebody to call and contradict him. "Whoever heard of emptying a crime scene just three days after a murder?"

It was not a question Mark was prepared to answer. "Has something happened?"

"A lot. You find out anything from the girl?"

"Not much. I tried asking her about Rena but there wasn't anything

new." Mark sat down, uninvited. "You know, I've been curious about
that clipping we found. I'm just wondering if there could be some
connection between this Diane Chaumet and Rena. Something we
haven't thought about."

Margolus snorted. Why must amateurs keep fouling up a perfectly
clean-cut murder? They were always thinking dumb things that just
complicated an investigation. Photographers and clippings and portfolios
when Margolus knew the answer was perfectly simple. The messenger
boy had done it. Probably had the hots for the model, shoved her down
even if she was taller than he was, and then muffled her yells with the
pillow. Open and shut. Only there had been all this hanky-panky about
some society woman getting fancy lawyers to give him bail, the autopsy
saying it happened around dawn . . . so what? The guy could have come
back, if actually he had ever left.

And now this wet-behind-the-ears lawyer was going off about somebody's accidental death five years before. God, was this day ever going
to end?

"What are we not supposed to have thought of?" he said, not sparing
the sarcasm. "The two models were aliens from outer space?" For
once he didn't enjoy his own humor.

"Is there any way we could find out how much money this dead
aunt of Rena's had?" He could tell Margolus was not going to be
receptive to the idea. "Her will would have been filed for probate, there
would have to be bank records somewhere." He added in what he
hoped was a positive manner, "This woman had planned to send her
niece to a college for four years, with a heavy tuition. And the statements we found in Rena's apartment showed she had a fairly decent
stock portfolio." Margolus was still staring at him with total disdain
on his broad face. "Isn't that a little strange?" Mark added lamely. "I
mean for a nurse who retired early?"

"Let's get one thing straight. We don't have the time or the muscle
to go checking into bank accounts of dead women who lived in Connecticut. Personally, I couldn't care less if the aunt was smuggling guns
or running a bordello or bagging food at the A&P. She is not our
problem." He leaned forward, his scowl deepening, a thing Mark didn't
think could happen. "We got one dead body. We got a whole crazy
fashion business that barely seems to know her. And we've got one
guy who was heard having a fight with her the night she was killed."

"Back to Paco again." Mark might have known this would be the
approach Margolus would take.

"That's right, Sonny. Back to Paco again. And just in case you think
I'm some kind of bigoted racist or got a one-track mind, there's a

couple of things that have cropped up today that, since you're supposed to be learning from me, you ought to know."

The detective was not above playing his own game of suspense. He stood up and stretched, never taking his eyes off Mark. "Navarez was supposed to show up in court this afternoon to answer a few questions—"

Mark broke in. "I thought he was out on bail?"

"That doesn't make him a free citizen." He snorted in disgust. "Don't they teach you anything in Criminal Law? Bail just means he can get out of jail. It does not mean he can leave the county, the city, the country. It also means if there are further questions to be asked, and believe me, there were . . ."

Mark suspected the further questions were ones Margolus had come up with and nobody else, but he decided this was the time to keep his mouth shut.

". . . Only your poor, picked-on messenger never showed up. And his boss, who sprang for ten thousand dollars cash, swears he doesn't know where he is. And that means our major prime suspect is hiding out or on the run."

"Didn't he have to turn in his passport? Isn't that a requirement for bail in a murder case?"

Margolus was smiling now, smug and superior. It was in a way more menacing than his scowl. "He didn't have a passport. He had a green card. And guess what? His green card is fake."

Mark could only stare at him.

"That's right. Forged. He's an illegal immigrant. This Franchard guy swears he didn't know it." Margolus rubbed his stomach gently. The sandwich obviously wasn't sitting very well. "Only I don't believe that phony designer for one minute. If I had my way, he'd be behind bars too, only I'm told he's clear. And got money.

"In any case, Mr. Franklin, our sole job now is to track down one Paco Navarez and rearrest him as the principal suspect of the murder of one Rena Varmont. That's presuming we can find him." The sarcasm was back in his voice. "And since one of your fancy lawyers got him sprung in the first place, maybe that should be your job tomorrow." He sat back down in his chair, pushing the bags Mark had brought in aside. "You find him."

Mark didn't even bother to say good night.

All around the city that night, people were sighing with the relief that Thursday was finally over, and tried to settle down to sleep.

One of them was the murderer of Rena Varmont.

FRIDAY

CHAPTER TWELVE

I'm actually up at nine-thirty, Horace realized with some surprise the next morning. I'm not only up, I'm awake, alert, and feel great! Of course, a complete night's sleep had certainly helped, and he knew perfectly well that his time at the end of the evening with Zoe had been responsible for that. He didn't even have a hangover. Improper as the thought was for a man of his age, he couldn't help thinking there was a great deal of therapeutic value to sex.

You're a dirty old man, he thought, but he couldn't stop smiling. Why, he might even make breakfast for Ginny for a change. Only she was already up and sitting morosely at the kitchen table with a cup of coffee in front of her. She looked up, startled, when he came through the swinging door.

"Sorry, Uncle Horace. I haven't set the dining room table or started on your breakfast yet."

Bleak and flustered, Horace realized. Wasn't she supposed to have dinner with young Franklin last night? "Don't worry about breakfast or the dining room table," he said cheerfully. "I can eat here and I can get what I need myself." As he opened the refrigerator door he glanced at her. "Have you had anything besides coffee?"

"Peanut butter and jelly sandwich last night." Her mood was not lightening.

Not the time to ask about Mark, Horace thought. "How about some yogurt? Apple sauce? Coffee cake? Thanks to my wonderful niece, I have a well-stocked refrigerator. I could probably even manage to boil some eggs."

"I'm not hungry."

This from Ginny? Horace took out what he needed and sat down at

147

the table opposite her. "Would this have anything to do with our Mr. Franklin?" he said tentatively.

"He may be yours, he's certainly not mine." She took another swallow of her coffee and made a face. "What grade did you give him?"

"In my course? B plus."

"Should have flunked him." She got up to pour them both coffee. "Only then you'd have to see him all over again."

"I gather last night did not go well?"

"All he wanted to talk about was Rena's aunt. I walked out on him. And to be honest, I hope I never see or talk to him again."   .

"I thought he was quite taken with you?" The course of true love was not running smooth. Still, Ginny and Mark had met only a few days ago. There would probably be hordes of young men before true love came along.

As he tried to think of a tactful question, the phone rang. Ginny picked it up with the speed of a girl expecting to be called.

"Hello?" She set her mouth suddenly in a grim line, reminding Horace of how her mother looked when she was genuinely angry. "Look, Mr. Franklin, I've told you everything I know and I really don't want to get involved any—" She was abruptly silent, and it was obvious to Horace that what she was hearing was not what she expected. "I'll see if he wants to talk to you." You could freeze ice cubes with that voice, Horace thought. "It's Mr. Franklin. It seems he wants you. Personally, I would recommend you get your own lawyer first."

This was clearly announced and definitely meant for Mark to hear. Horace repressed a smile and took the phone.

"Good morning, Mark. And how are you today?"

"Lousy, Professor. I'm sorry to disturb you, but something's happened." He hesitated for a moment. "I'm glad you're up. Ordinarily I wouldn't call at this hour."

"I've had my share of teaching morning classes, Mark," Horace replied breezily. Time to stop this myth that he was a total drone. "I'm quite capable of intelligent discussions before noon." He heard Ginny sniff indignantly. "What has happened that's so important?"

"Axel Gruen's dead. Murdered."

That's blunt enough, Horace thought. Thank heaven he'd slept and had the start of breakfast. "When?" he asked. "And how? And where?"

"Apparently it was last night, Professor. Or very early today. A downstairs neighbor went to walk her dog around seven. The elevator seemed stuck on Axel's floor, so she called the super."

Horace remembered the apartment: The elevator door opened on a tiny hall opposite Axel's steel door. But Mark was still talking: "They found Axel in his studio. The local precinct notified Margolus, he got me, and we're here."

He hesitated again. Clearly he was unsure of his standing in Livsey's household. "The thing is ... well, Professor ... the place is a mess. I mean, a real mess. Like at Rena's apartment. As if someone *was* searching for something. And I thought ... well, Margolus thought ... since you had come here to deliver the portfolio, you might know if something is missing. Since we hadn't been here before." He added lamely.

There goes my morning with Queen Victoria, Horace thought, and was surprised to find he didn't mind a bit. "Of course, Mark. I'll be glad to come over." He added with a slight edge of formality: "Just as soon as I finish breakfast." No point in letting them think he was at their service whenever they wanted him. Anyway, he suspected getting up at nine-thirty was not going to become a steady habit. There was a snort from Ginny, which Horace felt might be some kind of signal. "Would you like to talk to Ginny again?"

"What I like and what Ginny likes seem to be two different things." Mark didn't sound happy about that either.

"I'll tell her," Horace replied amiably. "Give me half an hour." He hung up the phone and went back to his breakfast, wondering how long it would be before Ginny started asking questions. He didn't have his watch on, but he estimated it was no more than three seconds.

"What was that all about?"

"Axel Gruen's been murdered." Years of being a teacher had taught him to underplay an important fact as well as any actor.

"You're kidding? How?" Suddenly her eyes were wide open.

"Mark didn't say. But apparently the studio is ripped apart, the same as at Rena's. As if somebody had been searching for something. Since I seem to have been the only one to have visited the studio when it was intact, Mark and Margolus want me over there to see if I can find anything that's missing." He thought of the dozens of cameras hanging on the walls of the studio. They had seemed menacing then, but he suspected he was going to like them a lot less now. "Oh, he sent his regards to you."

"No, he didn't." Ginny's face was grim.

"Well, something like that." Horace reached for another slice of coffee cake and the butter. "Would you care to accompany me?"

"Absolutely not!" But he could see she had briefly considered it. Nothing like curiosity to get you over a bad mood. She leaned forward, her face serious. "Wasn't Axel at that party last night?"

"Yes. And having the time of his life." The fact of the photogra-

pher's death began to hit Horace now. After all, at one time he and
Axel had been friends, or at least acquaintances. Now all Gruen's grand
plans to revive his career were over. But he had one triumphant evening,
Horace thought, for the first time feeling a twinge of sadness. Not the
worst way to go . . .

"Horace? Why would somebody kill Axel?"

"I thought you weren't interested in murder anymore?" That was
unkind, he realized as he said it. No point in teasing her.

"Natural curiosity. Anyway, why would anybody kill him?"

"That, my dear, is going to be something the police will have to
figure out." No point in encouraging Ginny or himself that it had
anything to do with either of them. But as he finished breakfast, he
noticed the sour look on Ginny's face was gone, to be replaced by what
he could only describe as a thoughtful expression.

It was closer to forty-five minutes before Horace arrived at Axel's
building. Fortunately the elevator was working again, and as he threaded
his way through the police cars, news cameramen and women, uniformed cops and sightseers, somebody gave him a badge that admitted
him past the yellow ribbons that marked the whole building as a
crime scene.

The steel door to Axel's apartment was open when he reached the
top floor. Here the front room seemed as crowded as a party, Margolus
in the middle of plainclothes and uniformed men (and two women
officers, Horace noticed). The look on Margolus's face was no more
pleasant than it had ever been. He spotted Horace as he got out of the
elevator and pushed his way through the crowd.

"Finally got here, uh?" It wasn't much of a greeting.

"I have a life, Mr. Margolus. And it includes breakfast." Horace
wasn't going to be rude, but a few ground rules were going to have to
be established if he was to be pulled back into murder.

"This isn't my idea to have you here." Margolus glanced around
impatiently. "This wouldn't be happening if I had my regular partner.
But Sanders is having his appendix out so I'm stuck with the kid
lawyer."

"Where is he?"

"In the studio." He shoved through the crowd, allowing Horace to
move into the front room. Impossible with all these people to discover
if anything was missing here. Horace noticed all the pictures were off
the walls.

"Margolus, is the body . . . ?"

"We just took it out in the body bag. Autopsy, of course. Although it was pretty obvious what caused his death. Whole back of his head was bashed in.''

''What was he wearing?''

This stopped Margolus, who looked back at Horace with some curiosity. ''Tuxedo pants, starched shirt, no tie, black velvet jacket on the bed,'' he answered automatically. Horace had the feeling he had been asked and repeated that information several times already this morning. ''Why?''

''Because I saw him last night at a dinner party. He was wearing that then. Which I think means he hadn't gone to bed at the time he was killed.''

''I'm going to want you for questioning.'' Margolus moved back to the people around him, leaving Horace free to go through the bedroom (bed still made, he noticed) into the studio. In contrast to the front of the apartment, nobody was in the big studio except Mark. He didn't look as if he had spent a good night.

''Morning, Professor. I'm sorry about all this.'' He continued to stare down where masking tape had marked off a section of the floor. Where they must have found Axel's body, Horace realized. I thought they used chalk.

The next hour made Horace feel he was on a completely purposeless visit. Gradually the apartment had emptied, leaving only Mark and Margolus to wander around, in Horace's case somewhat aimlessly. As far as he could see, none of the cameras had been touched, they still lined the walls, staring down at the three men with the wide, unblinking eye of their glass lenses. The rain had started again, making the studio darker than Horace remembered from his first visit, splashing the skylight above them with a steady beat. He had spotted that there seemed to be only two tripods facing the long sheet of white paper; he was fairly sure he had seen three. When he mentioned it, Margolus nodded grimly.

''The murder weapon.'' He touched one of the two remaining tripods, dusty still from having been inspected for fingerprints. In fact, there seemed to be a layer of the same dust all over the apartment. Nobody could say the New York police weren't thorough. ''Light,'' Margolus went on, lifting the tripod. ''Aluminum. Photographers need that to carry it on location shots.'' He set the tripod back down on the floor with a thump. ''But lethal. You get banged over the head with one of these, you might just get stunned the first time. But multiple blows ...''

''There was more than one blow?''

''Looked that way.''

Mark picked up the tripod. "It was the same type as this, Professor. The murder weapon, I mean. Which makes it sort of a unisex weapon."

"What are you talking about?" Margolus obviously considered the word *unisex* to border on the obscene.

"Just that a woman could lift it. Swing it. Do as much damage as a man."

"It was a man, Franklin." Margolus's natural belligerence had returned. "It's our old buddy Paco. Same M.O. as with Rena."

"Paco?" It was Horace's turn to look confused.

"He's apparently jumped bail, Professor. He was supposed to show up in court yesterday for further questioning, but he didn't. He's not at his boardinghouse. Franchard swears he hasn't seen him. Margolus thinks he killed Gruen as well as Rena."

"Illegal immigrant. You didn't know that, did you, Livsey? Phony papers."

"And why would he kill Rena? And Gruen?"

"Say they found out about it. Threatened to turn him in. Kid doesn't want to go back to Colombia, decides to get rid of them."

"Why would they want to turn him in? I don't know about Rena, but Axel certainly had enough experience moving rapidly from one country to another that he would have, if anything, sympathy for an immigrant, legal or not."

"I still think there's drugs involved in this. Maybe he was their pusher. They didn't pay up, so he slammed them."

"There were no traces of drugs in Rena's body. I read the autopsy report." Mark said it boldly, standing directly in front of the detective. "And I'm willing to bet five bucks you won't find any in Gruen's body either."

"Then they were threatening him for some other reason." Margolus was not about to be dissuaded from a favorite theory. He looked around the studio, almost ignoring Mark and Livsey. "Jeez! A pile of cameras here. Like a museum."

"He planned on giving them to a museum. His own room, he mentioned that to me." It wouldn't be a pleasant place to be in, Horace thought, but Margolus was clearly fascinated with the cameras hung on the wall, touching them reverently.

"That's where they belong, all right. Practically the whole history of photography here."

"You know about cameras, Detective?"

"One of my first assignments. Developing crime shots. Enlarging. Copying. Learning how to develop lousy film so nothing gets lost." There was almost a pleasant expression on his face, as if he were remembering earlier, happier days. "You learn a lot of things on this job, Professor. Some of them very . . ." He hesitated, clearly wanting to choose the right word for this intellectual old guy who seemed to crop up every time he turned around. "Some of them are very . . . significant." He pulled himself back to the present with a little effort. "Okay, suppose you start looking through this place and see if you spot something missing."

But an hour later it was Margolus who found something.

Meanwhile Mark and Horace had gone through the bathroom/developing room and the crowded kitchen, opening and emptying boxes of supplies. As far as either of them could tell, there was nothing strange or missing, although as they opened the last carton Horace suspected they wouldn't know if something was suspicious or not. It hadn't been work Horace enjoyed doing. I might as well have been cleaning my bookshelves, he thought. That, at least, would have been productive.

Margolus was in the bedroom, prowling around, ripping off sheets and pummeling pillows to see if anything had been hidden inside. Mark had gone over to the table between the kitchen and the bathroom, and was rummaging through the drawer. This must have been where Axel kept his papers, as Mark handed him a checkbook and a stack of bills. Unpaid, of course, and dating back several months. Horace thought about the bills on Franchard's desk as he fished for his cigarettes and holder. Damn it, his lighter was out of fluid! And of course he had no matches with him. He glanced through the bills silently. For a supposedly luxurious business like fashion, nobody seemed to have any money. Maybe there were matches in the kitchen.

But in the clutter of the china bowl on top of the table, he spotted what looked like a lighter. Deliberately staying oblivious of Mark's look of concern, he reached for it. But Mark handed him Gruen's checkbook instead.

"Take a look at this, Professor. A balance of maybe five hundred dollars. Hard to tell with Gruen's bookkeeping. But he sure wasn't rich."

Horace remembered his conversation with the dead man, the exuberance he had displayed the previous night. "He thought he was going to be." Horace also remembered only too clearly the look on Franchard's face when he heard Axel brag about doing all of the designers' photographs. He fitted his cigarette into his holder and picked up the custom-made lighter from the bowl after he had handed the checkbook back to Mark. Just as he was starting to light it, he heard Margolus bellow from the door to the bedroom.

"Hey, put that out! You may be able to smoke in your own apartment, but you can't here. Not with all this photography stuff around. This is a crime scene, I'm not having it go up in blazes because you got some kind of addiction."

Horace sighed. Life was not easy these days, he thought as he shoved everything back in his jacket pocket.

Margolus was not through yet. "Hey! Where's the stereo?"

Mark and Horace turned to look at him. Margolus was up on a metal chair looking at the speaker over the door to the studio.

"What stereo?" It was Horace's turn to feel like the slowest student in class.

"The one that goes with these speakers, Professor." There was more than a slight edge of sarcasm in Margolus's voice. God, I must have sounded like that in classrooms a thousand times, Horace thought as he and Mark moved toward the doorway.

"The guy has two speakers in his bedroom." Margolus was spelling it out with exaggerated patience. "So what comes through them? You want music, you got to have a stereo. Or something." He climbed down from the chair but continued to look up at the doorway above him. Then he swiveled around and stared at the speaker over the archway to the living room.

"You remember seeing a stereo here?"

Horace was going through the images of his meeting with Axel. There had been so much to see: the pictures displayed in the front room, the distinctive Oriental rugs hung on the bedroom walls, which he had presumed were either an attempt at European luxury or to muffle sounds, the long room with the one-eyed cameras staring down at him.

"I . . . I don't remember seeing a stereo." He felt like a complete idiot. This was what he got for trying to be a detective. Why wasn't he back in his office, safe in the middle of the last century?

Mark was roaming around restlessly. "No signs of records, Detective Margolus. Or discs or anything." He looked at the detective, feeling foolish, not wanting to see the expression on Horace's face. If the professor was embarrassed, that was only natural, he didn't belong to the generation that felt music playing in the background was as important to functioning as air to breathe.

"But there could have been a stereo, right, Professor?" Margolus wasn't letting Horace off the hook.

"I suppose so." Horace was fumbling for words. "I just didn't seem to notice it."

"Just the kind of thing someone like Paco would steal. I'll have to send out an alert to hock shops, not that that does much good. But if

Paco's on the run and needs money, that would be a fast way of getting it. On any street corner, especially around this neighborhood.''

Ignore the obvious ethnic slur. Ignore the fact that this was a perfectly good neighborhood. Ignore the fact that your temper is rising. Horace told himself all these things as he slid past Margolus into the small bedroom. ''Perhaps they're not really speakers at all,'' he said almost absently. He was in big danger of making more of a fool of himself, but all he could see in his memory was that tired television set in the front room. All right, so he didn't play music very often in his own apartment, but he did have a stereo and occasionally used it.

''No sign of a pawn ticket in Gruen's papers,'' said Mark. ''If for some reason he had pawned it.'' He wasn't going to leave the professor out on a limb if he could help it.

''So. No stereo.'' Margolus moved the folding chair back into position. ''Mark? See if you can find a screwdriver.''

Franklin and Livsey realized at the same time that this was new. Margolus had actually called Mark by his first name. Mark scurried for the crowded kitchenette. There had been standard screwdrivers there.

Margolus was efficient, Horace and Mark didn't have to look at each other to realize that. The first box came off with very little effort, as did the back.

''What do you know?'' It was the first time either of them had heard the detective express any surprise. For a change, it was a whisper, not a bellow. He held the large box in his hands, twisting it slightly. It hadn't come completely away from the wall, there were wires still attached that seemed to disappear into the wall behind where the speaker had been placed. There was a glint of gray-black metal, and Margolus turned it around to show the two men standing below him.

''That's a camcorder! Like they use in banks.'' Mark was clearly stunned.

''A version of it. Almost small enough to be a palmcorder.'' Margolus climbed down from the chair, leaving the box dangling from its wires. He moved the chair over to the other speaker and repeated the process. ''Another camera,'' he announced as he got the last screws out. He stepped down, this time bringing the speaker and the camera inside with him. He didn't look at Mark or Livsey as he fiddled with the back of it. ''No tape.'' He said it without any disappointment. He obviously hadn't expected any.

''I'd say Mr. Gruen was up to some very dirty tricks.'' He stretched up and placed the speaker close to where it had hung. ''Focused right on the bed.''

Mark had taken the chair and was checking the first camera. "No tape here either."

"Looks like the murderer got what he wanted." Margolus had a smug smile on his face.

"I doubt that." Horace was surprised at his own voice. "If he was after whatever pictures Axel took in this bedroom, he wouldn't have taken the trouble to screw the speakers back in place." He looked straight at Margolus, still holding the second camera and speaker. "I think you'll admit whoever would kill somebody, possibly two people, would hardly spend unnecessary time here." He went on as if explaining a difficult point to an obnoxious student. "Certainly not a frightened young man like Paco."

Mark had disappeared back into the studio, tracing the wires. "Come here," he called out. He had found a door tucked behind the array of cameras, a door with no handle. Somehow he had managed to get it open. The three men stared at the inside of what was clearly a closet. Of course, thought Horace. A closet. Axel would have to have had one, why didn't I pick up on that when I was here? You're getting feeble-minded, he told himself, although to be honest he really hadn't been here that long. And even the police in their search had missed it.

Like every other part of the apartment, this cubicle served two purposes: clothes were hung carelessly from a rod and beneath them was a shelf with what looked like some sort of taping machine as well as a monitor to replay tape. For once silent, Margolus fished around with the equipment. "No tape here either." He glanced back at Horace. "So there goes your idea that the killer didn't take it."

"You think all this has something to do with his murder?"

"What else? Maybe he was blackmailing somebody."

Horace remembered the stack of bills and the nearly empty check-book. "Surely blackmail would have brought him a certain sum of money." He stepped back to look at the bedroom. The heavy rugs, the brilliantly colored sheets, what could Axel have photographed so discreetly? He flipped the light switch by his hand. Suddenly the room was carefully but completely lit. Not too bright though. He turned to Margolus. "Those cameras, they can take pictures in this light, couldn't they?"

Margolus looked at the camera in the speaker he still held. "Sure. They use them around banks and security guards so as not to alert anybody suspicious."

"What do you think Axel was photographing, Professor?"

Horace hated the suspicions that had formed in his mind. "Gruen was at the bottom of his career, or at least he had been until he got these promises of employment from Celeste at *Elegant* and from Franchard.'' He debated telling Margolus about the look on the designer's face that he had seen the previous night, and decided against it. Looks were not evidence and he had no desire to get someone else into trouble. ''Perhaps Axel was augmenting his income by shooting pornographic movies?''

''You some kind of expert on pornography, Professor?'' This was Margolus at his worst.

''No.'' Horace decided a heated defense of his virtue or honor or whatever was being called into question was foolish. ''But I believe a great deal of these films are distributed by organized crime. They would pay in cash. Which,'' he added to Mark, ''is why Axel's checkbook balance was so low.''

''You think people making dirty pictures would be so shy he'd have to take the movies secretly?''

''I wouldn't be surprised. Male anatomy doesn't always work when it knows it's under inspection. He could let whatever twosome or group or combination go about their business without their feeling he was part of it.''

''You know, for a college professor, you gotta dirty mind.''

''You should read some of my history books,'' Horace said equably. But Margolus was already heading for the phone. Nobody apparently had turned that off yet. Mark and Horace could hear him bellowing to somebody to send experts over.

''Shall I take a look at the front room, Mark?'' Horace moved out of the bedroom. The room was still cluttered from the police investigation, and again there seemed to be dust from fingerprinting all over the room. Each of Axel's pictures had the same thin layer, but now they were all piled in a heap on the floor. Horace bent slightly.

''What are you looking for, Professor?''

''A picture of Diane Chaumet. It's gone.'' He straightened and looked around the room carefully. ''Of course, several other pictures seem to be missing too. I can't be sure.''

''Diane Chaumet.'' Mark's face was as grim as Margolus's. ''I knew she had something to do with all this.'' His eyes narrowed. ''Maybe the other pictures were taken to throw us off?''

''If there were other pictures taken. I can't be sure.''

''Okay. You guys can go. I'm going to wait for the camera experts to get up here.'' Margolus stood in the bedroom doorway. He seemed about to add something. . . .

''I know,'' said Horace. ''We're not to leave town.''

Once out on the wet street, now nearly back to normal, Horace stopped to fish for his cigarettes. Damn! His lighter was still dry and he had forgotten to hunt for matches. Not that he could have lit anything in this rain. He felt something else in his pocket and pulled out the lighter he had picked up in Axel's apartment. It was long and elegant, obviously expensive, a special design.

"Removing evidence." He looked at Mark. "Margolus will probably have me in Rikers Island for this." He turned the lighter over in his hand. It was beautifully monogrammed with two initials.

D.C. Diane Chaumet, he thought. He shoved it back in his pocket. "Mark, there's a cab, grab it." He was getting soaked.

"Something wrong, Professor?"

"I think it's time we had a seminar, you, me, and Ginny if she's home. We'll get lunch, if I have to make it myself."

"A seminar? On what?"

"What the three of us know."

He grabbed the handle of the taxi door.

CHAPTER THIRTEEN

Ginny was home, and while her greeting of Mark wasn't exactly cordial, she was clearly more interested in what had happened than in being angry. Mark walked around her warily as if expecting any moment she might spring at him. Lunch was simple.

"Zoe called," Ginny said as they were starting their sandwiches. "She'd heard about Axel's death and had tried to contact you and Celeste. Apparently she couldn't get through to her at the *Elegant* office and Celeste's home phone had so many outgoing messages on it she couldn't even leave her name." She picked at a piece of lettuce, not looking at either of them. "From what she heard, Celeste is still going on with the shoot this Sunday and she is leaving messages for Franchard and Oliver Tomorrow and half a dozen other people to reach her as soon as possible."

"Maybe we should have had her here for the seminar."

"What seminar?"

I didn't know you could leave that many messages outgoing, Horace thought briefly. He really should have read beyond page three of his instruction book about the answering machine.

"Your uncle feels we should pool our knowledge."

"I just meant that all of us seem to be going off in different directions. Margolus is obviously convinced the killer is Paco."

"He isn't. I know he isn't." Ginny was being indignant citizen again.

"I don't really think so either." But Mark said it in a hesitant way, as if he weren't totally convinced. Still, there was no point in having Ginny angry again.

"Unless there's a serial killer loose, which I very much doubt, or two separate killers are in this, which I also doubt, I think we should

159

start by trying to find out what links there are between the two killings.''
Horace had no intention of letting his "seminar" be taken over by
anybody else. "What have we? An unknown model who just, unlikely
as it seems to many of her peers''—he nodded at Ginny for her contri-
bution—"had signed with a major agency and been given a very lavish
photographic spread for an important magazine. We have a photographer who apparently insisted on her.''

"A photographer you think has been making dirty pictures for a
living.''

"You don't have to be crude about it, Ginny. It's only a theory.''

"But he was considered washed up. You told me that, Professor.''

"Talent doesn't die, Mark. Those photographs of Rena were stunning.
And considering how beautiful Franchard's clothes are . . .'' Horace had
a brief flash of Zoe in her blue gown. "I'd say it was an advantageous
combination all the way around.''

"Only why did she send her album to you? Or to me?'' This was
Ginny at her most practical.

"With the clipping about Diane Chaumet tucked in it?'' Mark wasn't
about to let go of the one fact he seemed to be the only person to
find curious.

"A dead model. Five years ago. Possibly a suicide.'' Horace told
them about the item about Diane's death he had found in the gossip
column.

"But you said Celeste told you last night that she had seen her that
afternoon and she was in great spirits. That doesn't sound like somebody
about to kill herself.''

"Unless somebody saw her after she saw Celeste.'' Horace chewed
on the last bite of his sandwich, obviously unaware of what he was
eating. "She left the hospital later that night.'' He got up and stretched.
"And what connection does all this have to Rena? Or Axel?''

"You said he lied about knowing her.'' Mark was making notes,
Horace noticed with approval.

"Was it a lie? Or had he actually forgotten?'' Axel was older than
Horace and yet he hadn't remembered meeting Diane Chaumet until
Zoe had told him. A beautiful girl like that, he should have remembered.

"And there's Jon Bowers saying he didn't need a career as an actor,
he was going to make a fortune as a model. Then you spot him playing
footsie with Katya McKay.''

"I didn't say I was positive it was Katya, Ginny.''

"A Franchard dress? She'd be wearing one to a party for him. There
can't be that many around town. He hasn't designed in a couple of
years. Zoe told you that.''

"My ex-wife has not always been known to be an accurate reporter."

"About clothes she would be."

"And with a pile of unpaid bills on his desk," Mark chipped in. "Plus according to the lawyer who sprang Paco, he had to put up a percentage in cash to get Navarez out on bail."

"Who has now very inconveniently disappeared." Horace took his dishes over to the sink. "Who also was illegally in this country."

"Margolus thinks somebody was threatening Paco." Mark knew it was not a popular opinion, at least not at this table, but if it was a seminar, as the professor called it, better to get the opposition's point of view in here too.

"How could they threaten him? He didn't have any money. He didn't have any important contacts." Ginny could see the young man as he had stood in the door on Monday morning. Was there a scared look on his face? She didn't think so. But she'd hate to have to testify there wasn't.

"There's another thing that bothers me." Horace still seemed to be chewing, although there was nothing in his mouth, it was a habit Ginny had seen before when he was puzzled. "Both Axel and Rena were hit from behind. Now, that suggests to me that whoever killed them—if it was the same person—was someone they knew well enough to turn their backs on. Not to mention letting them in their front door."

He studied Mark carefully. "No sign of illegal entry at Axel's apartment, Mark?"

"No, sir."

"And yet he had a series of locks on that door. It was steel too, he obviously considered his cameras valuable. And new locks on Rena's doors." Horace sat down again. "No, I think we can be reasonably sure the killer was somebody both Rena and Axel knew. At least well enough to let them in at night."

"That seems to narrow it down to most of New York City." Mark sighed.

"New York City's fashion industry." It was Horace's turn to sigh. "Which doesn't narrow it down very far."

"There's the thing about no padlock on Rena's locker. And June, the model who showed me the locker, was sure it was there Monday."

"Not on any police list the police have," said Mark. "I checked over all of the stuff they have this morning." He was still smarting from Ginny's questions of the night before. "No hair drier either."

"When was the shoot last Sunday night canceled? Does anybody know?'' Lunch and an abject Mark had definitely cleared away the last of Ginny's bad mood.

"Axel said that nobody bothered to tell him. And Rena saw him in the late afternoon. So it wasn't canceled then, or she certainly would have mentioned it."

"Could she have been sick or something? Suddenly?'' Mark still felt the clipping of Diane Chaumet was getting lost in this discussion.

"No. From what that model told me, you'd have to be dead to miss this chance.'' Ginny felt a little tremble up her back. After all, Rena *was* dead.

As if he knew what she was thinking, Horace broke in. "But she didn't die until sometime near seven on Monday morning.'' Where had he put his cigarettes? In his jacket on the back of his chair. But as he reached for it, Ginny turned to Mark and gave him what Horace could only describe as an embarrassed smile.

"Mark, I think I owe you an apology."

This was Ginny at her best, open and honest, and the young lawyer couldn't have reacted with more astonishment if he had been kicked by a horse.

"Last night,'' Ginny went on. "You asked me about Rena. If I remembered anything about her from college. That one year. I didn't then, maybe because I was mad or hungry or both.'' She could see Mark was about to interrupt but she went on quickly. "No, I behaved very badly. And I'm sorry. But I got to thinking when I came home. There was only one remark that Rena made that I remembered ... and believe me, I've tried to think of others. But it was during a biology lab experiment. The teacher held up a dead frog that we were all supposed to dissect."

She gave a little shudder. That had been the least favorite part of one of her least favorite classes. "Anyway, the teacher said, 'We have here an ordinary frog ...' and Rena whispered, 'Imagine being dead and having somebody dismiss you as "ordinary." ' '' Ginny looked at the two men who were watching her. "I know it doesn't sound like much. But doesn't it kind of prove ...'' She went on hurriedly. "Rena never would have missed that shoot? Never! Someone must have called it off and told her."

"Couldn't have been Axel. Even if he was lying, he wouldn't have the power to cancel something like that. And he wanted it as much as Rena.'' Damn! His lighter still didn't work. Horace fished around in his jacket, what was that bulky thing doing there? He pulled out the lighter he had picked up at the dead photographer's. He looked at it carefully now.

"D.C.," said Mark, watching him. Diane Chaumet, he'd bet a month's salary on that. "And you got it at Axel's?"

"It was in a bowl with a pile of odds and ends, camera lenses, empty boxes of film, screws and nuts and bolts, probably for the tripods." He started to open it but it seemed stuck on something.

"Axel didn't smoke, did he?"

"I never saw him smoke." Horace let his mind go back before dinner, back to the days in Paris. "No, I guess being around highly flammable material like photographic supplies, he never started." He tugged at the top of the lighter without success.

"Anyway, that wouldn't be there from five years ago." They had finally got around to Diane. Aware they were staring at him, Mark took the lighter from Horace. "I mean, if it was a sentimental gift he treasured, he wouldn't just leave it lying around. Not with people, models or whatever, in and out of the place." He managed to get the top back.

"I'll be ..." He handed the lighter back to Horace. "That's no cigarette lighter. Or it isn't now." He pointed to the flat white unit tucked into the silver case.

"What is it?" asked Horace, putting the lighter case and its contents down on the kitchen table carefully, as if it might explode.

"I'm not going to play with it," Mark said, also careful not to touch it. "But it looks to me like a tape from an answering machine."

'Rena's!" Ginny was practically bouncing in her chair with excitement. "I'll bet you anything it's Rena's!" She grabbed Mark's arm. "On your list, was there anything about the tape from her answering machine?"

"No." Mark was frowning, not looking at her. "And there should have been if the police had it."

"Wouldn't they have noticed if it was missing? If they checked everything out?"

"I've only been involved with Homicide this week," Mark answered carefully, not taking his eyes off the silver object on the table. "But they could have overlooked it. Or Homicide might have thought the precinct took it and vice versa."

"Let's play it!" Ginny was standing, her cheeks bright with excitement. "Horsey, you've got a machine on your office phone." She was already to start for the hall.

"No," said Horace firmly.

Both Mark and Ginny stared at him. He had put enough emphasis on one word to stop a firing squad. "This goes directly to the police. Untouched by any of us. If it is what we think it is, we're not going to take a chance on tampering with it and destroying possibly important evidence." He was aware he was sounding like an old movie about Scotland Yard. "Mark, I want you to take this to Margolus right away. Tell him how we ... I ... found it. If he wants me to go to jail, tell him I'll be in all afternoon."

He fixed them both with a stern stare. "And no playing games. Either one of you."

——— CHAPTER FOURTEEN

Only as it turned out, Horace wasn't in the apartment all afternoon.

Mark left almost immediately, the lighter carefully wrapped in a clean handkerchief, not that there was much possibility of finding fresh fingerprints now. He stoutly resisted Ginny's pleas to accompany him, and was happy that Horace agreed. Mark wasn't too sure how much longer he could have held Ginny off, especially since she had actually apologized and was regarding him as a human being again.

After he left, promising to call if he had any information, Ginny, totally subdued for once, started piling their dishes into the dishwater. Horace went down the hall to his office, filled his lighter, and settled in for an uninterrupted cigarette. But he found himself unable to think about anything except the two murders.

Suppose the tape hidden in Diane's lighter was Rena's? That meant that Rena or her dead aunt, the retired nurse, must have known the model who had died in an accident—or was it suicide?—five years ago. Couldn't have been Rena, the girl would have been only seventeen then. The nurse? Had she heard or seen something, that Diane had given her such an expensive gift? Or maybe it hadn't been a gift. Maybe the nurse had found it left behind and with the lovely Chaumet woman dead that evening there had been nobody to return it to? That seemed more logical ... but only if Rena's aunt had worked at Manhattan General Hospital. And there was every probability she hadn't. Nobody except Mark seemed to be interested in following that up. Certainly Horace had no way of finding out about it. And Rena didn't smoke. Ginny had been clear about that.

Ginny stuck her head in about half an hour later to say she was off to the Lincoln Center Library to see if she could get copies of some of the scripts Natasha Kinn had assigned her to study. Horace only grunted in reply. Axel was still on his mind, and now that he was alone in the apartment he found for the first time that total silence wasn't helping his thoughts one bit.

If what was in the lighter was a tape from an answering machine, either Rena's or possibly someone else's, she could have shoved it into the clutter in the china bowl on the theory Axel wouldn't notice it. That would make her sending the portfolio of her pictures taken by Axel to Ginny, via Horace, a further precaution. If anything happened to her, and something brutal had, she might have reasoned the pictures would lead Ginny or Horace (or the police if it came to that) to Gruen. And it had.

That destroyed one half-thought Horace had been forming, that somehow Axel and Rena were involved in something together. If they were, Rena certainly hadn't trusted Axel very much. Surely if she had told him about the tape, he would have said something. Or would he? He ended up dead as well.

No, it seemed to Horace, Rena hadn't trusted Axel. And she couldn't very well have sent just the tape to Ginny, little as she had known his niece, Rena would have guessed, correctly as it turned out, that Ginny's first thought would be to play the tape.

The phone shocked him. Could Mark be calling with information already? He grabbed it fast before his tape kicked in, relieved that Ginny was out and there was nobody to pick up the extensions.

Only it wasn't Mark.

The girl's voice, and it was barely louder than a whisper, sounded both very young and very frightened.

"Is this Professor Livsey?"

"Yes. Who is this?" Was there a slight accent? He couldn't be sure.

"My name, it is not important. But I must see you. Please. You can help someone who is in serious trouble."

English was not her first language. Spanish, Horace thought. The woman at the dry cleaner's spoke like that, only not so scared. Could this be something to do with Paco?

"Is this something to do with Mr. Navarez?" He knew he was taking a chance of frightening her into hanging up, but if she was brave enough to call him, maybe she would trust him.

"Please! Don't say his name! But I must talk to you. Today. *Please.*" There was such a desperate urgency in her voice now that Horace had the feeling she was already regretting calling him.

"All right. Tell me where and when." He was almost as surprised as the girl on the other end that he had made such a fast decision.

"Five this afternoon? There is a restaurant called the Peking Moon."
She mentioned the name of a street that Horace knew was somewhere
in Chinatown.

"How will I know you?"

"I'll know you." She was calmer now, a little confidence in her
voice. "We saw your picture in the papers."

And she hung up.

Ginny hadn't come back by the time Horace left the apartment. He
wasn't sure he could have kept from telling her where he was going
and he wasn't absolutely positive he wanted to. Still, he did write
"Peking Moon, five pm" in his appointment book, closed it firmly,
and placed it under some papers. It was silly, he thought, the girl had
sounded as if she couldn't swat a fly but still there was somebody loose
in the city who had killed two people and maybe it was time Horace
started acting like a sensible adult.

He was fortunate in getting a cab driver who was not only silent but
also knew how to get to the Peking Moon without instructions, which
Horace couldn't have given. Chinatown, as well as the appeal of Chinese food, had always been a mystery to him. Partly that was because
it was difficult to eat in an Oriental restaurant by yourself, he admitted.

The Peking Moon was crammed into a narrow street filled with stores
selling strange foods, souvenir shops with bright-colored banners outside, and the odd shops to be found in underdeveloped and overcrowded
sections of the city: shoe repair stores and cut-rate outlets selling everything from tiny cameras to used television sets.

The Moon was clean and small, halfway between a restaurant and a
diner. A row of booths and, on the opposite side, a lunch counter.
Horace needn't have worried about finding the girl, there was only one
person in the place, facing the door, with a menu held up to half cover
her face. As he came nearer, the girl, for she seemed hardly more than
a child, lowered the menu. Her eyes were big and dark, her hair neatly
combed, a loose sweater (with holes at the elbows, Horace noticed) and
blue jeans below it. She tried a tentative smile. It wasn't successful.

"You called me?" It seemed the only greeting he could make since
he didn't know her name.

"Yes, Professor. Please sit down."

As he slid into the booth opposite her a man peeked out from the
swinging door at the back of the café. The girl waved him away
impersonally.

"I didn't order anything for you, I haven't much time," she said apologetically.

"Suppose we start with your telling me who you are." Horace tried to put it gently—the girl opposite looked ready to run at any sudden movement on his part.

"My name is Inez." She hesitated. "I won't give you my last name." She leaned forward. "Did you tell anybody you were coming here? About me calling?"

Strictly speaking, Horace hadn't. A note in his appointment book wasn't exactly telling. He shook his head. "Is this about Paco?"

"The police are all over the city looking for him. Just because he's illegal." She added that with a thin edge of bitterness. It just made her look younger. You should be doing high school homework, Horace thought, not mixed up with murder.

"They searched his room. Did you know that?"

"I imagine that's standard procedure. I'm sure they had a search warrant."

"And that makes it right? Paco didn't do anything!"

"He jumped bail. And he lied about his papers."

"He couldn't go to court! He knew they'd find out about the papers, they'd never let him out again."

"You know where he is?"

She was silent for a moment, biting her lower lip. "He's staying with me. That's why I can't tell you my last name." She stared at him defiantly. "I don't trust you. But Paco . . . he said you seemed intelligent. A professor. We have great respect for professors in our country."

"You're Colombian too?"

Suddenly she seemed close to tears. This was clearly all too much for her. "Yes." She said it softly so that he had to bend forward to hear her. "And my papers, they aren't legal either. Not yet." She added that hastily looking around as if she expected a policeman to walk in any moment.

"That's all right, Inez." Horace tried to make his voice comforting. "Tell me about Paco."

"He is a wonderful boy." She twisted a paper napkin in her fingers. Her hands were much older than the rest of her, callused, hard from work. "Yes, he gets angry sometimes. He hates the way they exploit him."

" 'They'?"

"Franchard. The factory. Everybody. You are illegal, they can make you do anything they want, pay you anything they want. You can't complain!'' She put down the shredded napkin. ''Because they don't hire you if you are a legal. They know you can protest then.''

''Paco is with you, you said?'' Horace knew she wasn't going to give him any more information than absolutely necessary. ''Where is that?''

She closed her lips firmly.

''Please, Inez. I'd like to help you both if I can.'' A foolish statement, Horace realized; still, Franchard had put up bail money and Mark was with the district attorney's office. Maybe he could do something after all.

''Paco had nothing to do with murder. He would never do that.'' She may have been frightened, but she was prepared to fight for him. ''I can prove that, but I . . . I just wish there was some other way. . . .'' She stared at him, her eyes wide again. ''Do you think if two people are in love but can't get married, God will forgive them for sleeping together?''

Horace fumbled for a reassuring answer. ''I think God is a lot more tolerant than human beings, Inez.''

She relaxed a little. ''Paco said that too. Not that it matters. I love him so much.'' She leaned back, as relaxed as Horace had seen her since he came into the Peking Moon. ''It's not that he doesn't want to marry me. He does. Only my family, they look down on him. 'What is he?' they say. An errand boy for a man who makes women's clothes. That is not the husband they want for me. A store owner. Or somebody with clean fingernails. Somebody who is a citizen who can make me a citizen. That's what they want. So they say no. Paco talks to them and talks. He will not always be like what he is now. Everybody shouts and gets angry.'' She stared at Horace as if defying him to contradict her. ''If he didn't kill then, he would never kill.''

Not necessarily true, Horace thought, but this was not the time to interrupt with practicality.

She controlled herself, but she couldn't look at him. ''Paco slept with me last Sunday night. He's been in my room since he was freed. He was with me all Sunday night. All last night.'' She raised her eyes to look directly at Horace. There was no doubt she was telling the truth. ''He could not have murdered that nasty model. He could not have murdered that arrogant photographer.'' She allowed herself a small smile. ''Oh, yes, Paco tells me about these people. But he could not have killed them. He was with me. Both nights. We don't sleep. Last night we couldn't even make love. We only talk, talk, talk about the trouble he's in. This morning he makes me promise to call you.''

She looked exhausted, as if this confession had taken more out of her than she expected.

"How could he have spent both nights with you if your parents did not approve?" Horace broached it cautiously. This is the kind of question Margolus and Mark would ask.

"My parents, they were sent back to Colombia. They tried to organize all of us who work at the factory. All we wanted was twenty-five cents more an hour. Is that so much?"

Horace had no idea what a quarter would mean to their wages, but he was getting the idea it was the difference between total misery and the edge of poverty. He shook his head.

"They don't want me here in New York, my parents. But I cannot leave Paco. I keep my mouth shut. We all have different names at the factory for safety. So the owner turns in only my parents. They put me with my godmother, very strict. Only last week she has to go to the clinic. Something bad with her lungs. All the loose threads in the factory. The windows don't open. Cold in winter, it makes us work hard. The summer, hotter than Colombia!" She seemed to retreat into her head, remembering. "But no streams, no mountains, no cool air like at home . . ."

"So you have a room, and Paco is there?"

"Pictures of him all over. Television. Newspapers. He does not dare go out." Courage was coming back. "But he didn't kill those people! He was with me! I *swear* that. Monday my godmother comes back. Where can he go then?"

Horace had tried to think of a list of questions on his way down, but they all seemed jumbled in his mind now that he had met the girl. Girl? Child was more like it. Dickens's London, he thought. We haven't progressed very far in a century after all.

"Tell me about Sunday. When did Paco come to your room?"

"It was after eleven. He didn't want to stay. He had this big flat package that she wanted him to take to you. But . . . I . . . I persuaded him. It was starting to rain. He had only that wet cape. I told him the next morning would be soon enough to deliver it. She had not even given him subway fare." She broke into a string of angry Spanish words that Horace suspected her family had never heard her say.

"So the portfolio . . . and Paco were with you all night long?"

"Yes. Only . . . do I have to say that all out loud to people? My parents, the shame, they would never speak to me again." She set her face grimly. "But if that is what is necessary to save Paco, I will do it."

"There may be another way. If the police find the real killer first."

"They won't. Paco is so easy to blame it on." She made a move as if to leave.

"Please, Inez. A few minutes more? There's so much I don't know, that nobody seems to know." She moved back into the booth again, her eyes wary.

"I know ... and so do the police ... that Paco picked up sketches and samples sometime Sunday afternoon to take to the photographer Axel Gruen. But when did he pick up the portfolio from Rena Varmont?"

"Around ten."

"Why was the shoot canceled? Do you know?"

"Somebody did not want it to be done." She started to say something more, then changed her mind. "We make all Franchard's clothes, that's how I first met Paco. He wasn't like other boys. My parents are wrong, he is going to be somebody."

"Your factory makes Franchard's clothes?"

"Not for a while. The owner, he was angry. 'No more credit,' he says." Inez was clearly more at ease talking about this than about Paco. "Then one month, two months ago, there is money. A lot of money. We start working again. Old orders are put to one side. That never happened before. Franchard himself comes down there, not just Paco. Big nuisance, but it was work and we get paid on time."

"Did you make the clothes that were to be photographed Sunday?"

"Of course. I am very good with the delicate stitches. The beads, the embroidery." She glanced up at the clock on the wall, her face that of a frightened child again. "I have to go now. I'll be late for the night work."

"You work both days and nights?"

She was smiling bitterly at him as she stood. "You think there should be laws against that? Maybe with twenty-five cents more an hour I could work only one shift." She shrugged. There was no self-pity on her face. "Life is not always easy, Professor."

"The clothes for Sunday? They were finished? They were not ripped or ...." He struggled to find another word. "They were ready to be worn?"

"They were perfect. Mr. Ohalow, he would not let anything leave the building that was not perfect. Now I must go." She picked up the small purse that had been on the bench beside her. "I can't tell you anything more. Only Paco didn't do these terrible things. Make the police understand."

She moved quickly toward the door. Barely five feet, Horace realized. And no food on the table that had been between them. Would she go hungry, or did she maybe have something hidden at the factory? He got up slowly. His legs were aching again. As he started toward the door, he left a tip on the counter for the time they had spent.

The streets were oddly empty when he got outside. Too early for the dinner crowds, he realized. He could see Inez farther down the block. Luckily she did not look back.

She was heading toward a large brick building on the other side of the narrow street, a building Horace suspected had not been cleaned since it had been built decades earlier. Fire escapes zagged down the walls. Grimy windows closed, he noticed.

Inez was about to cross the street, when a long, expensive-looking car pulled out from where it had been parked in front of the building. The driver apparently was in a hurry or careless, for as he swerved out, he almost seemed to be aiming the car at the young girl.

"No!" Inez screamed, loud enough for Horace to hear. She squeezed back between two parked cars, covering her face quickly. The driver hesitated and then, looking back in Horace's direction, shifted gears and roared off down the street.

Was it deliberate? Inez scurried quickly across the street and into the dark entrance of the factory, not looking back.

But the driver had and Horace had recognized him.

What was Dr. Bosley doing in Chinatown?

CHAPTER FIFTEEN

On his way home Horace debated with himself about what the girl had said. Actually, it wasn't much of a debate; he had already made up his mind not to mention the meeting to anybody. Not now, at least. Careful as the girl had been, it would be easy for the police to find her at the factory and either follow her to where she lived and capture Paco or simply get her address from her work records. That is, if they kept records, which Horace was beginning to doubt.

No, this information he could keep to himself. He didn't believe Paco had committed either of the murders and he did believe Inez. Which makes me some kind of an accomplice, he realized. To think a week ago he had his own quiet life, no Ginny, no Zoe, and definitely no murders, unless he wanted to touch on Jack the Ripper over a century ago.

As he went into the elevator of his building he could only hope Ginny was still out. Peace and quiet was what he needed. Only when he opened his front door, there were three people in the living room, who all turned to face him: Ginny, Mark, and Margolus. All right, Horace, he thought. Come up with a good lie about where you've been; they obviously expected him to say something.

"What was on the tape?" he said immediately. A good attack usually works best.

"Quite a bit." This from Margolus. He looked at the coffee table, where there was a portable tape machine.

Not mine, thought Horace, wondering for a second just where his was.

"It was recorded from Rena's tape. It was her machine."

Horace had never seen Mark look so serious. Ginny looked sober too.

"And? What is on it?" He moved into the living room. "I should apologize, Detective Margolus, for taking the lighter, it was a pure accident." Somehow Horace had a feeling they weren't all there to arrest him.

"I guess you did us a favor." The words came out reluctantly from under Margolus's thick mustache. "Not that we wouldn't have found it eventually. Monday we're planning a thorough search; it's a crime scene until then."

"Not tomorrow?" Ginny faced him surprised.

"On a weekend? You know what the city thinks about overtime for police? Not to mention all the so-called experts?"

"Homicide made a copy of the tape," Mark interjected tactfully. "I thought ... well, we all did, you might like to hear it."

"It's a real lulu." Margolus sat down on the couch. "It's Rena's all right. Your niece identified her voice."

"It starts out strange, Horsey." Ginny sat down beside the detective, clearly eager to hear it again. "You know, most people just have 'leave a message after the beep' and that sort of stuff."

Gratefully Horace moved to his favorite chair. Obviously they were not interested in where he had been. Which saved him having to think up a plausible lie. "Suppose you play it for me?"

Mark leaned over and pushed one of the tabs on the recorder. The volume had been turned up, for the voice Horace heard almost boomed through the room.

"This is Rena. It's Sunday afternoon. You know who you are. Just remember I'll be expecting you tonight after the shoot. Because there is going to be one, don't kid yourself."

Mark pressed the stop tab. "Pretty threatening, wouldn't you say, Professor?"

Horace leaned back in his chair. The voice was not what he expected. This was no shy, inexperienced young model. This was the voice of a very determined young woman who knew exactly what she wanted and had every intention of getting it. Rather like the picture he had been shown by Mark and Margolus last Monday morning. Unbelievable it was only four days ago.

"Sounds to me as if there was some question about her being photographed."

"Sounds that way to me too. And the rest of Homicide." Margolus reached over to start the tape again. "Wait till you hear who called her."

"Do it one at a time, Mr. Margolus." Ginny had put her hand on his arm. "It's so confusing with all the voices."

Margolus grunted and pushed the button.

The first voice Horace heard startled him, because he had been think-ing about the man ever since he had left Chinatown.

"Rena, this is *Doctor* Bosley. I don't know what this is all about or what you think I can do about it, but I assure you, I have absolutely no reason to see you. Whatever you know or think you know, this is totally absurd. Call me back when you get this and give me one good reason why I should meet you tonight."

There was a click as the message ended and the heavyset detective turned the machine off again.

"Dr. Bosley. Anybody know him?"

"Plastic surgeon. I told you that, Margolus." Mark was being very careful in the way he spoke to the detective.

"You, Professor Livsey? You know him?"

Careful, Horace told himself. If he got into what he saw or thought he saw in Chinatown, it would lead the police straight to Inez and Paco. "I met him the other night," he said carefully. "At a dinner party. I didn't even know he knew Rena."

"Would he have known Diane Chaumet?"

Margolus turned on Mark, all of his frustrations erupting in anger. "Will you forget that damn woman, Franklin? That case was closed five years ago. It's the two bodies we got this week that we have to worry about."

"Why was Bosley at the dinner party, Uncle Horace?" Ginny was clearly more in control than the other two.

"I think . . . or at least Zoe hinted that he was a beau of Celeste's." He looked at Margolus, wondering just what the detective might ask next. "That would be Celeste Lanier. The head of *Elegant* magazine that was doing the shoot."

"What's a beau? You mean they were sleeping together?"

"I couldn't possibly know that." Horace shifted uneasily in his chair. "I believe they have been friends for a long time."

"The professor says he was with her at the funeral of Diane Chaumet." Mark was like a dog who wouldn't give up on a bone, Horace thought. So did Margolus. With a grunt he turned to Ginny.

"You know anything about this Bosley?" She shook her head. "Okay, let's go on to the next one." He pressed the tab down again.

"Rena, are you mad? Are you absolutely crazy mad?" Horace recog-nized the voice instantly. He whispered the word *Franchard* to the others as the tape continued. "I have done everything I possibly can for you, and you know it! Whatever little tricks you think you have up your sleeve, you cannot destroy me. You cannot hurt me!" The voice became more controlled. "But I can hurt you. Oh, yes, don't think you have me in your claws."

There was a bang on the tape as the designer slammed down the phone. Ginny pushed the button to stop the machine.

"You said 'Franchard,' Professor?" Margolus stared at Horace, but his voice was if not deferential at least curious.

"I happened to visit his . . . establishment." Horace was also remembering the furious look on the designer's face when he had heard Axel bragging about being his special photographer for the future. Should he mention it? "He was also at the dinner party the other night. It was, I believe, being given in honor of him."

"He say anything about this Rena Varmont at the time?"

"No, Detective. But I didn't have much chance to talk to him; we were seated at different tables."

"Sounds like a big party."

"Why would Rena want to see him? Especially after the shoot, he would have been there, wouldn't he?" Mark scratched his chin thoughtfully.

"He's also the guy that got Paco Navarez out on bail . . . was he using him to do his dirty work? You know, bump off some model that was causing trouble, then got scared Paco would talk and got him out? Probably got him all the way back to Colombia by now." Margolus was clearly not about to give up his favorite suspect.

"Bail he couldn't afford." Horace cleared his throat, slightly embarrassed. After picking up the lighter that morning, he wasn't too happy about mentioning he had snooped around the designer's office. "At least, I believe he had some financial problems." Horace thought of what Inez had told him. "Or at least had had them in the recent past."

"What did he mean by 'tricks'?" Thank heaven Ginny was getting the discussion back on the track, thought Horace. "I can understand the part about he had done everything possible, I mean, all the dresses were fitted for her."

"Until they were ripped," added Horace. When had that happened? And who had done it? Nobody seemed to know.

"Exactly. Or was he just being excitable?" Ginny turned to Margolus. "Models can get so fussy about how they look, Detective."

"Could she have been holding him up for more money?"

Ginny considered what June had told her at the agency. "I doubt that, Detective. She stood to make a great deal from this spread. One of the models at the agency told me that," she added carefully. "I don't think it was money she was talking about."

"Although Franchard was going to need a good chunk to pay the lawyers who got Paco out." Mark thought of Phelpsie and his father's lavish offices. "That firm doesn't come cheap, and they don't wait to be paid."

"Okay. So maybe she knew something about money. Maybe she knew something about the doctor. That means blackmail, right? Only over what?"

"Figure that out, Detective, and you might have the murderer." Only Horace couldn't understand how Rena could be blackmailing anyone.

"The next voice, I think it's Mr. Gruen's," Mark said tactfully. He pressed down the tab. Instantly the room was filled with the slightly guttural voice of the dead photographer.

"Rena, my child, you sound very harsh on your machine. You catch more flies with honey than vinegar, if you remember that saying. Now, I shall be expecting you as arranged this afternoon. Don't worry about the shoot, they wouldn't dare cancel it, not this late. Everything will go well. Only don't forget to bring my things back to me. Remember, they *are* mine."

Mark stopped the tape. "Those last words. They sounded kind of threatening as well." He looked at Margolus, prepared to let him make the judgment.

"Yeah. Maybe not enough to kill her if she forgot, but I'd say your buddy Gruen is capable of treating anybody who crossed him with more than sharp words."

This was addressed to Horace, who realized he was somehow right in the middle of all this. He'd seen Paco, he knew all the others, even to their voices, which neither Margolus nor Mark did, nor Ginny. They weren't just being kind or considerate in bringing a copy of the tape up to him.

They weren't thinking of him as a suspect. That was something. Hopefully from what he had seen and heard poking around that the murderer didn't think so either, although the car incident in Chinatown had not been reassuring. Only why would Bosley want to hurt Inez? Because she knew something that might cause him trouble?

"Are there more messages, Mr. Margolus?" Keep it polite, Horace told himself.

"Yeah. Paco. Listen to his voice." He reached over and started the tape again.

"Listen, Miss Varmont, I am busy today. You know that. I have to go to the factory for the clothes, I have to take samples to Gruen. I must be back for the shoot at the agency. You must understand. I cannot take your orders. I have work to do, important work. And nobody, and I mean you, is going to stop me!"

There was a click as the machine went quiet. For a moment everyone in the room was silent.

"Not exactly the mild little victim you described, eh, Professor?" But Margolus didn't seem as definite about his feelings concerning Navarez as he had been before.

"Perhaps Rena's message was not for him? After all, he did pick up her portfolio for her."

"Later." Mark stood up and started moving around the room restlessly. "Paco seems to have been a busy guy that Sunday."

Busier than you think, Horace thought to himself. Now was definitely not the time to mention Inez. "Is that the last message?"

"One more," said Ginny. She pressed the button again.

Another voice I recognize, thought Horace as he heard the tape. He had sat next to Katya McKay for the whole dinner, not that there was any question of her identity, she announced that herself.

"Rena, my dear child, it's Katya. I can't possibly think that nasty little message on your machine was meant for me. You know I want to help you any way I can, as I am sure you want to help me. So there couldn't be any possible reason for us to have a late-night meeting, now, could there? With everything going so well? Or possibly could this message be for Philip? Or Celeste? You have a lot of people to worry about, dearest, but surely I'm not one of them. Remember what we talked about. Ciao till later, Rena."

Mark stopped the tape and pressed the button for rewind. "That's it, Professor. Five rather strange phone calls. All implying something. Only I can't figure out what." He slumped down on the sofa beside Ginny.

"Or perhaps implying five different things." Horace leaned back in his chair, trying to remember each of the conversations. "Have you questioned the five again, Detective?"

"Not yet, Professor. But we will. We tried to set up something this afternoon while you were out. . . ." Horace took a deep breath, waiting for the inevitable question as to where he had been, but Margolus wasn't looking at him. "They're coming in tomorrow. All but Paco. No trace of him yet. Seems there's some kind of panic with all of these people, getting a new photographer, new models, all for some magazine deadline."

"There's a lot riding on that magazine deadline, Mr. Margolus." Ginny smoothed her skirt and proceeded as tactfully as she knew how. "It's the first issue under Celeste's management, it's a big comeback for Franchard, they're using the Classic Agency town house as the setting. . . . It's not as if anybody is avoiding being questioned."

"Somebody is. And I'm willing to bet that somebody is the killer."
Margolus started for the door, waving Franklin to stay where he was.

So much for working together, Mark thought as the front door
slammed.

After Margolus was gone, the three of them remained seated in silence for a moment. When Horace heard the elevator arrive at his floor
and go down again, he began to relax. Somebody had better know what
he learned, he had come to realize. This business of carrying around
suspicions, opinions, and observations that might or might not be important was not a very prudent thing to do.

"Mark, if I tell you some thoughts of mine, can I expect you to keep
them to yourself?" It was tentative, and Horace felt he was opening
doors that he probably should keep closed. "At least until Monday?"
Paco would have no place to hide then.

For once Mark was not the subservient ex-student he had been since
meeting Horace on Monday. "That depends. As an assistant district
attorney—"

"Would-be assistant," Ginny broke in.

"All right, 'would-be,' I'm supposed to be an officer of the court.
Or at least an advocate of the law. That means revealing to the police
all information that might be pertinent to the two murders."

"Don't be so pompous, Mark." Ginny wasn't angry; oddly, her voice
was more that of someone who was aware of his faults but still liked
him anyway. "Horsey isn't withholding evidence or trying to shield a
killer, he's as interested in solving this as we are." Shouldn't have said
that, she thought. It was just the sort of remark to make her uncle
retreat back into his shell. Only Horace was making no move to get
out of his chair. "And it's only till Monday," she added.

"I don't know if what I have is relevant to the murders," Horace
began slowly. "It's just odds and ends of things. Only I don't want
anyone innocent getting into trouble." He proceeded to tell them a
(slightly) laundered version of his meeting with Inez, leaving out only
that he had seen the factory building she had entered, but mentioning
Bosley's presence. He also told them of the look on Franchard's face
when Axel had announced at the dinner party his future connections
with the designer's work.

Mark and Ginny listened in silence. That was something Horace had
not expected, the reversal of roles between teacher and student that had
made Mark so easy to talk to had become that of lawyer and possible
client. Horace didn't like being in that situation at all.

Finally, Mark spoke. "You really believe this girl Inez was telling the truth?"

"Yes."

"And Dr. Bosley? You make it sound as if he were trying to kill her."

"That's conjecture. And I'm probably wrong. I can't see any reason why he would do that, any more than I can see any motive for him to kill Rena or Axel."

"Plastic surgeons involved in the fashion business?" Ginny frowned. "That's weird."

"Unless he was involved in some way with the late Diane Chaumet." Mark, Horace realized, was no more about to give up his favorite motive than Margolus was to give up pinning the murders on Paco.

"That doesn't make sense either, Mark." Ginny was clearly more puzzled than angry. "Anyway, we don't know he knew her. Or Rena's aunt, for that matter. If you're trying to connect the two of them, which seems to be your major suspicion."

"Okay, so I seem hooked on this. Only what was that damn shell of a lighter, holding Rena's tape, doing at Axel's? It must mean something, and it had to come from Rena." He looked over at Horace. "And you said Diane's picture was taken from Gruen's walls. After he had denied knowing her."

"I said I thought it was missing. I couldn't be sure."

"We'll find out Monday. If the police are really going to do a thorough search." He grabbed the tape machine in front of him as if he'd like to shake the answers out of it. "I just wish we had the authority to ask questions of somebody at that hospital. If there was a connection between Chaumet and Rena, somebody there might know."

"Proving your theory?"

"Ginny, I don't have any theories!" It came out of him more explosively than he had expected. "Anyway, Professor, I suppose I can keep my mouth shut about Inez and Paco and all the other stuff until Monday. I probably won't see Margolus until then anyway." By which date, Mark realized, his week with Homicide would be over. He could leave all of this until the case came to trial. Oddly, it didn't give him the serene feeling he was hoping for.

The telephone rang. Horace got up reluctantly. There hadn't been a phone call this week that had been pleasant as far as he could remember. He went into his office. It was, as a fitting end of a rotten day, Zoe on the other end.

"Horsey? I've been trying to reach you all afternoon."

Not a good beginning, Horace felt, noticing for the first time the light on his machine was blinking. And she knew he hated being called "Horsey."

"Zoe, you've got me now. What is it you want?"

"Testy, testy! I thought with retirement you might mellow."

Some retirement, Horace thought. And there was an edge to Zoe's voice. Surely their encounter after Celeste's dinner party had shown he had no need to mellow?

"Zoe, I'm rather busy at the moment. What is on what I occasionally call your mind?"

"There's no need to be nasty, Horace." She was shifting into her beguiling voice; that meant she wanted him to do something he had no intention of doing. "First, I just called to remind you we're on for lunch tomorrow at La Côte Normande. One o'clock, dear Horace, and don't be late."

Damn! He'd forgotten that. He tried to think of a fast excuse but nothing was coming.

"I can tell by that sigh," Zoe went on without waiting for a reply, "that you are thinking of an excuse. Don't even try." Beguiling was moving swiftly into her martyred tone. "After all, I do certain favors for you. . . ."

They had known each other long enough that Horace had no doubt she was referring to their very pleasant sexual encounter of the previous night. "I rather thought the favors were mutual," he added dryly.

"Don't be coarse. And I want you to keep the afternoon free."

"I am not going to another dress salon!"

"I wouldn't dream of taking you. But I've got you an appointment with the famous Dr. Sleeper. I was at his table at Celeste's dinner party last night. A charming man who has made an exception to see you on a Saturday afternoon."

"I don't need a doctor!" Zoe couldn't be suggesting plastic surgery, could she? But he realized he was still fussing over the sight of Dr. Bosley.

"You most certainly do! You told me yourself you can barely walk three blocks."

"My back operation . . ."

"You can't blame everything on that! Anyway, it was two years ago. It's high time you did something about all those aches and pains you keep complaining about. Dr. Sleeper happens to be an expert on cardio . . ." She hesitated a second. "Well, whatever it is that means not enough blood is getting into your arteries. With your long legs and your age, it's time you saw someone about getting your circulation going properly."

"My circulation was perfect last night."

Zoe was not about to play the modest maiden with her ex-husband. "Lying down maybe. But I want you standing up and able to dance. You're seeing Dr. Sleeper tomorrow if I have to chloroform you and drag you there myself." After an announcement like that, it would be unlike Zoe not to finish off with one final zinger. "You might be interested to know that Dr. Sleeper is eighty-two and walks four miles a day."

"Probably running from pushy ladies. Now, Zoe, I will not have you interfering with my life. Many years ago a very nice judge took that privilege away from you!"

"Horace, darling, I'm only thinking of you." Beguiling, Horace noticed, had suddenly come back. "Anyway, it's no distance from the restaurant and it'll make me feel so much better."

"Where is this elderly quack holding forth?" Whatever the fee, it would add toward deductions and who knows, this specialist might have something effective, a pill, or something easy to manage.

"He's at Manhattan General Hospital. The annex to it."

It looked like Mark was going to get his wish. Somebody with a good reason to wander about chatting with anybody old enough to remember Diane Chaumet.

And the murdered model's aunt.

SATURDAY

CHAPTER SIXTEEN

La Côte Normande did not necessarily serve the best food in New York, although that opinion changed with the tastes of the various food critics and the rare shift in chefs. It was also not the most expensive restaurant in the city, although it was securely lodged in that range. But for several decades, despite stiff competition, it had remained the choice luncheon spot for the East Side social set whether they were American or European. And after all, what did food matter if all you were going to have was consomme, a glass of white wine, and perhaps a few leaves of lettuce? Which seemed to Horace the favored lunch. One came to La Côte Normande to see, to be seen, and to exchange the latest gossip concerning love affairs, business deals, and unprintable scandals.

Horace arrived promptly at one, to find Zoe already waiting in her favorite booth, just inside the entrance where she could see everybody and everybody could see her. She looked, Horace thought as he came in, not only incredibly young and attractive but meticulously made-up and beautifully dressed. It was clear this was her opening public announcement to social New York that she was back in town and expected to be invited everywhere.

He brushed a kiss on her cheek and slid carefully into the booth beside her.

Her first words as he fumbled in the pocket of his jacket were, ''This is a no-smoking section, Horace, and you're just going to have to live with it.''

He glanced around at the rest of the room, hoping to see a vacant table, but for a Saturday the place was crowded. ''Why aren't all these people out closing their summer homes?'' he grouched.

''That's what servants are for. Anyway, they were predicting rain.''

She leaned forward. "I must say I'm a little surprised. Since I'm away so much, I thought Saturday would be a good day to establish myself with Mario again."

Horace had known for years that Mario the maître d' had an imperious way with certain customers and had been known to turn away Texas millionaires when the restaurant was almost empty. One with social ambitions did not offend him. The good side was that he did not accept personal tips.

"Then let's get this thing over with." He opened the enormous menu. He might as well make this the main meal of the day, as he suspected from the previous night's conversation that Mark was intending to ask Ginny out tonight for a proper date. That meant Le Mirabeau or a sandwich for Horace.

"Don't be difficult, Horace. You know you can be charming when you want to be."

Horace wondered if that was a somewhat late compliment for their involvement Thursday night, but before he could suggest it, not preparing to be tactful in the least, Zoe let out a little sound of surprise.

"Now, there's an interesting combination!" As always, Horace was amazed that Zoe could address him, read the menu, and still be able to see everybody in the room. He started to twist in his seat to see what she meant. "Don't look now!" Zoe whispered. "Philip McKay just finishing lunch with Celeste Lanier."

"Probably business. Isn't that fashion spread supposed to be photographed tomorrow?" And weren't they both supposed to be questioned by Margolus today?

They were approaching their table now, and for a second Horace thought he saw a faint flicker of surprise in Celeste's eyes. But it was gone before he could be sure, to be replaced by a wide smile, Philip hovering behind her.

"That's what I like to see," Celeste said cheerfully. "Divorced couples being civilized together."

The usual greetings were exchanged, and before Zoe could offer, Celeste said politely, "Could Philip and I join you for a minute?"

Horace noticed this also came as a surprise to Philip but not necessarily an unpleasant one. When they were seated and the proper drinks had been ordered and delivered, Celeste was clearly in the best of moods.

"You'll never guess where Philip and I spent the morning," she announced with a wide smile. Horace could guess but he wasn't about to interrupt. The less people knew about his involvement with the police and the two murders, the better. "The Homicide Department!" She said it with the air of someone who had just climbed the Himalayas. "Fingerprinted and everything."

"Which I still can't seem to get off my hands," added McKay.

Zoe obligingly moved Celeste's story onward. "What on earth for?"

"It seems they're questioning everybody they can find who was involved with both Rena and poor Axel. And that's us. They even had Dr. Bosley down there, and Katya. . . ."

Horace wasn't happy about this. He was counting on Bosley being far away during his visit that afternoon to Manhattan General.

"But, Celeste, haven't they already questioned you?" Zoe smiled at Philip. "Both of you?"

"A lot," said Philip, fiddling with his glass. "Now they wanted to know specifically where we were last Sunday afternoon."

"And why and when the shoot was canceled," added Celeste.

"Where were you?" That came out blunter than Horace could have wished, but it seemed to have no startling effect on either McKay or the lovely editor.

"We were at my office, going over the dummy for the next issue of *Elegant*. Trying to find the right spot for Axel's four-page spread. Then we went down to the agency. Axel was going to shoot the *Elegant* woman there that evening."

"Only he didn't." Apparently neither one of the couple was surprised by Horace's direct remarks.

"Only he couldn't." Philip took a good swallow of his drink. "Katya was busy getting the agency to look like a private house again. You know, flowers, candles, all that stuff. Then the messenger arrived with the clothes, all carefully wrapped in plastic. . . ."

"We didn't even pay attention to them until about seven. The makeup people had to have their space, the hairdressers were going crazy trying to find outlets." She turned to Zoe. "You'd think it was an opening night on Broadway. So there the dresses were hanging, all perfect, we thought, until Jean-Claude arrived and unwrapped them."

"He went ballistic," said Philip, shaking his head as if he still wasn't used to the passions of temperamental designers.

"What had happened?" Zoe wasn't being a hostess anymore. She leaned forward as eagerly as a child reaching for candy.

"They were ripped, darling." Celeste sighed heavily. "I don't mean hems hadn't been finished, or seams not sewn, I mean practically destroyed."

"Franchard swears they were perfect when he sent Paco the messenger with them. I thought he was going to have a heart attack, and then he went paranoid and claimed everybody, including us, was out to get him.''

"Remember, Philip, he also included seven French designers, and three Americans, and no, Zoe, I won't mention their names, that could get into slander.''

"Some of whom probably don't even remember who he is.'' Philip was clearly not in sympathy with the designer.

"So you had to cancel the shoot?'' Horace had finished his plain tomato juice, all he allowed himself in the middle of the day, and placed his hands in his lap. What a time not to be able to smoke! "That would be after seven?''

"And, of course, everybody was either on their way or not home.'' Celeste drummed her fingers on the tablecloth. "Which meant we had to pay all of the makeup and hair people anyway, and left me with four empty pages for a magazine that goes to press next Tuesday.''

"But you're redoing the shoot tomorrow, aren't you?'' Zoe might have the attention span of a hummingbird, but certain details stayed firmly in her mind.

"Yes, and that's really why we're crowding in on you and Horace. I want you to come. It's going to be a fabulous thing, completely the opposite of Axel's idea, poor darling. I've managed to get Oliver Tomorrow''—she turned graciously toward Horace—"you met him at my dinner party, didn't you, Horace?''

Horace had an image of the flamboyantly dressed young man who had greeted him. "Yes,'' he said, making it as dry as possible. "I met him.''

McKay grinned. "My feelings exactly. Only he's the hottest guy in town at the moment, which may not please Franchard, because he's likely to get more publicity than Jean-Claude. Still, publicity will help *Elegant*'s sales.''

"And I do want the first issue to be a success.'' Celeste was almost wistful as she said it. "Oliver has some strange ideas, but he is good. He's taken over La Picassa for the evening.''

Zoe and Horace looked at each other in total bewilderment.

Celeste laughed. "I know. I'd never heard of it either. But it's supposed to be the hottest new disco in town.'' She turned to Philip. "Or is it an after-hours spot?''

"Both, I think. God knows I've never been there. I don't think they let anyone in over 26. But Oliver thinks it might make startling pictures to photograph Franchard's high fashion in a down-and-dirty West Village bar. Or whatever they call it.'' Raising his eyebrows, he added,

"I suspect he knows the place thoroughly. And I won't go into the reasons."

"We're getting a very clear picture just the same, Philip," said Zoe soothingly. "Only why would you want us?"

"Background, ducks. Can you bear that? Chic New York society in Franchard dresses . . . you've got to wear your blue . . . against black leather, heavy metal, and whips."

"A far cry from the day in the life of the *Elegant* woman," Horace couldn't resist adding.

"Poor Axel." For a moment Celeste's lovely face was serious. "He was so counting on this. And I *am* going to do a nostalgia piece in a couple of more issues, once I feel I've really got the job nailed down. But for now . . ."

"I might not be able to make it," Horace said, carefully moving his legs to an area where Zoe couldn't (he hoped) kick him. "But I know somebody who could." It might be a good idea to have Ginny on the scene. A plan was half forming in his mind. "My niece. She's young and attractive and surely there should be someone to be a contrast to the hairy apes."

"I'm not going to take that as a crack at me," Zoe said with some asperity.

"It's a terrific idea, Horace. Tell her a black turtleneck and black tights, and don't worry, if she's under forty, she'll have them. No colors though, I don't want Franchard throwing another fit."

After setting time and location, Celeste and Philip left. Horace noticed he took her arm as they left the restaurant.

"That was curious." Zoe hadn't missed it either. "No mention of Katya. I mean, why isn't she with them for lunch?" A small bowl of clear soup had been placed in front of her, but it could have been water for all the attention she paid it. "Too bad Philip McKay isn't free. He's the kind of man Celeste should marry."

"People who should marry and people who do aren't always the same."

Zoe was quick enough to realize he was referring to her desertion of him many years before, although he did understand Avery Banning had always been the one true love of her life. Subdued, she applied herself to her soup.

Like a mother taking a reluctant child to school, Zoe accompanied Horace to the door of Manhattan General. In a way, Horace was almost glad, as the hospital had several entrances, a result of additions and annexes built around the original building, and he knew he had a tendency to get lost.

Dr. Sleeper's office was on the third floor of what seemed to be the most modern of the annexes. Here Zoe left him. She was not in a terribly good mood even though at least twelve people had stopped by their table during lunch to welcome her back to the city, offering a variety of invitations that should have made her blossom at her popularity. But it still rankled that Horace would not accompany her Sunday to La Picassa. At the door of the doctor's office she kissed Horace briefly on the cheek. He almost thought she was about to say ''Now be a good boy'' before she marched off to the elevator.

The nurse was older than the others they had seen in the hospital and showed Horace in to the doctor with a cheerful smile. Dr. Sleeper, as Horace had suspected, was a lean, trim man who looked several decades younger than his age. The appointment was brief; obviously whatever charm Zoe had exerted on the doctor Thursday night had faded, and with a desk piled with paperwork Dr. Sleeper was no more eager to see Horace than Horace was to see him.

He checked pulse points in Horace's ankles, said there were no pills for his circulation (a disappointment) and that he needed to give up smoking and walk every day, gradually increasing the distance. And no, angioplasty wouldn't help the arteries, not if Horace continued smoking, the pain and blockage would probably return in a couple of months. Horace was out of the office in fifteen minutes and damn irritated.

As he headed for the elevator, he saw a familiar figure standing waiting for the doors to open. Dr. Bosley. So he had his offices here? Horace spotted the door to a men's room and ducked inside. He contemplated a fast cigarette while he waited for the doctor to disappear but realized he would probably set off every alarm in the building. Five minutes later he looked out. The corridor was empty.

After the police had interrogated him he must have come back to his office to clear up paperwork the way Dr. Sleeper was doing. Horace couldn't think of any other reason why a plastic surgeon would have office hours on Saturday. The annex, of course, was also convenient for any patient who wanted to keep cosmetic attention private and confidential.

At the elevator there was a board listing offices. Bosley was farther down the hall. Why not try it, Horace thought. After all, if Diane Chaumet was a part of these murders, although dead for five years, perhaps Bosley had been her surgeon. And if the gossip column had been correct about the botched job . . .

He put on what he hoped was an ingratiating smile and opened the door of the doctor's office. Inside, a pretty girl of about Ginny's age was staring at a desktop full of letters, manila folders, and what might be X rays. The look on her face was one of total dismay.

"I'm sorry, the doctor has left for the day," she said without looking up.

"That's all right. I didn't really need to see him. I just thought I'd say hello." She looked up at him then, as if surprised to hear a male voice. "We're . . . friends," Horace added somewhat lamely.

"You just missed him. And now I've got to do all these files and bills." She clearly wished she were anywhere else.

"There must be a lot of files," Horace said sympathetically. "I mean, hasn't the doctor been here, oh, at least five years?"

"I guess so. Anyhow, I just started last month. And the old files are someplace else. I don't know where he took them. I guess when you have as successful a practice as he has, they just took up too much room here."

Or maybe there was something in one of the old files Bosley didn't want anybody to see, Horace thought. He made his apologies and went back into the corridor.

It was quiet now and empty, no doctors or nurses or possible patients in sight. Sorry, Mark, Horace thought. Dead end. And he winced a little at the expression.

Perhaps not.

Making up his mind, he walked back to Dr. Sleeper's office, not feeling any particular pain in his legs. The cheerful nurse was still at her desk.

"Professor Livsey? Did you forget something?"

The perfect opening remark, Horace thought. "I can't seem to find my eyeglass case," he said. "I just wondered if I dropped it in the doctor's office."

"I'm always doing that." She stood up. She had a pleasantly ample figure and pink cheeks that owed nothing to makeup. "The doctor's left, I was just about to leave myself, but if you want me to help you look . . . ?"

No wedding ring on her left hand, Horace noticed as he did with all women over thirty-five. He made an effort to smile charmingly. Apparently it worked, as she ushered him into the room Horace had left less than ten minutes before.

As they searched around the desk and examining table for the case that was safely in Horace's pocket, the nurse continued talking, apparently glad to have company. Sleeper hadn't looked like a man who enjoyed social conversation. So much for being lean and trim, Horace thought.

He managed to work the nurse's talk toward Bosley, mentioning he'd just missed him in the hall.

"There's a busy man!" The nurse, who by now had insisted Horace call her Nancy, stopped and looked at Horace. "You wouldn't believe how his practice has grown! Everybody seems to want to be younger and more beautiful these days." She sighed slightly, as if facing the fact no surgery could possibly make her twenty again and a size eight.

"I suppose a lot of celebrities need it. For professional reasons. And models." He hoped it seemed just a tactful remark.

"He gets them all. The names I could tell you I've seen going into his office!" She smiled coquettishly. "But I won't. Professional ethics, you know."

"Of course." Keep your voice low and soothing, Horace. "I think a friend of a friend of mine was one of his patients . . . say, about five years ago? A model named Diane Chaumet?" A bit too direct, he thought, but the nurse, eager to continue talking, snapped at the bait.

"She was a darling! Irene Varmont and I thought she was just about the nicest patient we'd ever had."

"Varmont?" Please, keep on talking, Horace thought.

"Yes. Same name as that girl that was murdered last Monday. I wonder if they were related?" She had settled into the doctor's chair now, the search for the eyeglass case clearly forgotten.

"You two were . . . in the operating room? You and Ms. Varmont?"

"No." She stared at him, her eyes narrowing. This question had been a bit too close to interrogation, Horace realized. "Of course not. That's for specialists."

"I just thought . . . since you said my friend's friend was such a good patient."

"In the operating room they're out of it. It's later, that's when you find out if people are nice or just plain ornery." She leaned back, her mouth twisting a little as she looked back on the past years. "Believe you me, when this opening came to work directly for Dr. Sleeper, I jumped at it. Handling the private patients, especially the ones who want to get cut up just so they can look better, they can be a bunch of spoiled brats. Like you'd nothing else to do but hold their hand and tell them everything came off beautifully, whether it did or not. Wanting attention every five minutes like they were the only people in the whole world in pain. Pain they asked for," she added.

"I suppose cosmetic surgery is painful?" Horace felt his charm slipping, and the nurse was studying him carefully.

"It's the waiting they can't stand," she said after a moment. "They expect to come out of surgery and look twenty years younger instantly."

"I guess they don't realize it takes time for swelling and bruises and ... things to go down." What a perfectly idiotic remark to make, Horace thought. Fortunately the nurse didn't think so.

"You got that right." Nancy smiled benignly. "Of course, they're all terrified that something went wrong with the operation and they'll come out of it deformed or weird or something."

"Surely not with someone as skillful as Dr. Bosley?"

"All of them. Talk about fragile egos! Even Diane Chaumet." Her attitude softened a little. "Of course her looks were her profession. But still, why she would want surgery, I'll never understand. But somehow she'd convinced herself that one eyelid was a little lower than the other. You know these models. They're already beautiful, but they all worry about looking better. As if they weren't perfect already."

Horace realized she was reaching the end of her desire to talk when she glanced at her wristwatch. Surreptitiously, he slipped his glasses out of their soft case and prepared to drop the case on the floor. "Does it take long to recover? From the surgery, I mean?"

"They leave practically at once if they have someplace to go and recover. Where they won't be seen by their dearest friends. I remember Irene, that's the other nurse that was taking care of this Chaumet girl, she was concerned that she might not have anyone to look after her. But Diane was determined to hide out in the country. Not that she didn't have friends. Lord, the flowers that arrived every day! As much as some of the movie stars. We had to take loads of them to the other rooms."

"So she hadn't kept her trip here a secret?"

The nurse gave him a long, appraising look. She's on guard now, Horace thought. Damn it!

"You really are interested in Diane Chaumet, aren't you?" The smile had disappeared and Horace felt it wasn't going to come back.

"Not exactly." Pick the right words. "Actually, it's Irene Varmont. My niece knew her briefly when she was a child. Then she lost track of her, but I remembered she'd known this Miss Chaumet."

"Irene retired early." The nurse got out of the chair and started for the door. "I don't think you left your eyeglass case here, Professor." She obviously expected Horace to follow her out, but with her back turned it gave him the chance to drop the case on the floor by the desk.

"Here it is!" He held it up triumphantly. He moved toward the doorway in what he hoped was a nonchalant manner. "Ah, well, I suppose at her age Miss Varmont had earned her retirement."

"She was younger than I am!" The nurse was almost indignant, as if she had been personally attacked for being too old to be competent. Age, Horace thought. Bothers us all. "No, she just told me she'd come into some money. Some investments that paid off in monthly dividends, she was always very closemouthed about that. It certainly wasn't her age that made her leave."

"Of course not." Nothing like striking a nerve to get the truth, Horace thought. Must remember that for the future. "I mean, look at you ... the very prime of life." He was rewarded with a flirtatious smile. "Now I really must thank you for being so helpful about my glasses case. I'm sure you have a pile of work to do."

"Nothing that can't wait until Monday."

It was an innocuous statement, but Horace had the feeling she would be available for coffee, drinks, or maybe dinner if he suggested it. Only he had the idea there was going to be nothing more she could tell him about Diane or Rena's aunt. "I really should stop in and see Dr. Bosley, just to say hello, Nancy."

"He won't be able to tell you anything more about Diane Chaumet. Or Irene. I don't think he had anything to do with that operation." She held the door to the hall open and the smile was gone from her face.

He suspected he hadn't fooled her for a second.

Saturday night was the longest night Horace felt he had spent in years. Ginny had been home when he came back from Manhattan General, hair in curlers and rushing around in a bathrobe, clearly preparing for a date with Mark. She claimed it was "totally unimportant" but Horace had never seen her make such elaborate preparations before. And no, Mark wasn't going to pick her up, they were meeting at the restaurant.

Which meant Horace had no sounding board for the ideas that were wandering around in his head. Since Mark had been so determined that Diane Chaumet was somehow linked to the deaths of both Rena and Axel, Horace considered Mark's nonappearance at the apartment a sign of plain laxness. I should have given him a C, he thought as he slumped into his office. Before she left, Horace said quite definitely he wanted to see the young lawyer Sunday at noon.

"I may not want to see him then," Ginny replied airily, waves of a light perfume surrounding her.

"*You* may not be necessary. Just tell him" had been Horace's parting remark.

From there on the evening went downhill. He made a sloppy sandwich and a drink and tried to interest himself in television that consisted mostly of reruns of shows Horace had never watched in the first place and firmly decided never to watch again. He tried to concentrate on his book, but after a couple of fruitless hours in which he wrote three sentences and promptly tore them up, he gave up pretending he could concentrate on anything except the murders.

I should never have gotten myself mixed up in this, he found himself saying through the course of the evening. The fact that he hadn't done it completely of his own free will, or curiosity, didn't help. Yes, he had been shoved into the middle of it, but he could have stopped there.

The problem, of course, was that he had about a hundred questions and no answers at all.

"Look at it logically," he found himself saying out loud. For no good reason he found himself remembering a line supposedly said by Jane Austen (although he had never been able to track down the quote): "I write about love and money," she was reported to have said. "What else is there?"

What else indeed? Apply the same theory to murder, Horace, he told himself. Money. That was the easier of the two. Nobody, except possibly Rena's dead aunt, had any, or any that seemed suspicious or questionable. Dr. Bosley, of course, but he was in a lucrative profession. Axel didn't. The quick look at Rena's accounts showed she didn't have anything that seemed excessive. The McKays? A profitable business Horace was sure, but nothing they hadn't built up together over the years. Nothing that could have led to the sudden unexpected murders of two people in one week. Celeste? A salary, undoubtedly good but also nothing she hadn't earned herself. Paco? Not a penny clearly. Franchard? Deep in debt, but still able to summon up enough resources to get the messenger or whatever he was out of prison. But he had wealthy patrons for that.

Oliver Tomorrow?

Horace frowned at the thought of the flamboyant photographer. Sure, getting the *Elegant* shoot away from Axel might be a sufficient reason for murder, but then, why Rena? Besides, he was apparently very much in demand, with correspondingly high fees. No, that didn't seem to work.

And love didn't work out any better. Granted that Philip McKay had lunch without his wife and with Celeste, but that didn't indicate a sizzling romance, not when the lunch took place in one of the most socially popular restaurants in New York, where people were bound to see them together. Besides, supposedly Malcolm Bosley was the man in her life and had been at least since the death of Diane Chaumet five years before. Katya McKay (if it had been her that he had seen in the bar late Thursday night) and the young model who was boasting of a "great new career" according to Ginny? That was a possibility. But the young man—what was his name?—oh, yes, Jon Bowers, would have nothing to gain from either of the deaths. Rena was no competition and Axel had already photographed him and well.

Paco and Inez. Horace didn't want to think about them, at least not as liars and killers. Besides, what reason would the young man have to kill a model and a photographer? Admittedly, Rena's voice on the tape showed a harsh and cruel side of her personality, and if one wanted to believe myths of hot-blooded Latin temperament, Paco might have been driven to fight back.

And fatally.

Only why would he want to kill Axel? Not to mention that for both nights of the murders, Inez was prepared to give him an alibi. Of course, she could be lying.

And it could be the killer was a complete outsider. Or that there were two killers.

Damn! Horace got out of his chair and looked at the overflowing ashtray on his desk. He really should cut back. His legs ached and so did his back. He stretched and looked at the clock. Not eleven o'clock yet. He suspected it would be several hours before Ginny returned to the apartment, with or without Mark Franklin. Why had he ordered him to be here Sunday noon? All he had were vague ideas and not many of those.

But he knew the answer. Monday Franklin's connection with Margolus and Homicide would be over and Horace and Ginny and the young lawyer would be on the outside looking in. Eventually the police would track down Paco, especially if he had no place to hide Monday, when Inez's godmother came out of the hospital. Paco would be tried for murder—somebody always came forward to say they had been suspicious of his behavior for months—Inez's alibi as an illegal alien, unmarried to the boy, would be discredited. She'd be deported. He'd be in prison. And in a month or two the whole thing would be forgotten.

Except that Horace knew he wasn't going to forget.

SUNDAY

—— CHAPTER SEVENTEEN

Around eight on Sunday morning, Horace gave up trying to sleep and got out of bed. Washing and shaving didn't improve his mood, only he wasn't exactly sure what his mood was. Puzzled, of course. And confused, which he didn't like at all. But unlike most of his thoughts of the night before, what he was considering seemed the logical next step, even if highly dubious.

Ginny appeared at ten, surprised that her uncle had fixed his own breakfast and had left coffee warming for her. Horace was pleased that Mark had agreed to come to the apartment and that apparently their evening together had gone well. By noon, both of them were prepared for the young lawyer's arrival, Ginny having already made a fresh and better pot of coffee. . . .

"You want me to call Margolus? At his home?"

"You have the number, don't you?"

"I . . . I can get it."

Ginny watched the two men with quiet amusement. It wasn't that Mark was afraid, exactly. It was just that it was fascinating to watch him weigh the specific request of his ex-professor versus the definite anger the homicide detective would display over Horsey's idea.

"You do see that it might bring the killer out in the open, don't you, Mark?"

"Possibly." Mark was clearly torn by the decision. "Not necessarily. And you know Margolus. He likes everything done by the book. And this isn't in any book, I can tell you."

"I'll be happy to talk to him." Horace said it calmly. He had a backup idea if the detective turned them down.

Ginny watched Mark as he went to the phone. Last night had been a pleasant evening, the restaurant charming, and the food excellent. It had not been a romantic evening, something she felt Mark was as reluctant as she to start. Instead, they had talked about all sorts of things, not the murders but their future plans, schools they had gone to, friends they might have in common (they had several, it turned out). It was the way friendships begin, much better than moving into hot-and-heavy romantic overtures, or hints of overtures. Afterward, he had seen her politely to the door of Horsey's apartment building, kissed her on the forehead, and told her how much he had enjoyed the evening. She had enjoyed it too, and found to her surprise she didn't miss the awkward fumblings in the taxi and heavy breathing that ended most dates these days. No, not romantic, but both of them had known this was not the last evening they would spend together.

Now he was at the telephone, writing down a number. He hung up and looked back at the two of them in the living room. "He lives in Queens," he said. Before they could make any comment, he was punching in the number.

"Mr. Margolus, please," he said into the phone. Good Lord, he'd forgotten the man's rank. Was he a sergeant? A lieutenant? They had been calling each other by their last names all week. While he waited, he looked again at the professor and Ginny. She looked particularly pretty this morning. "She's gone to get him, Professor. He's putting up storm windows."

"In September?" Ginny was totally unprepared for this. Even her mother didn't start reminding her father of that particular household chore until the middle of October.

"Margolus? It's Mark Franklin." Mark was back talking on the phone. "Have you a minute?" Apparently the detective was happy to take a break from what he had been doing. "Thank you. I'm at the professor's . . ."

The two in the living room could hear the loud tone of Margolus's voice, if not the words. Horace walked over and took the phone out of Mark's hand.

"Mr. Margolus, I have an idea that might be of some help to you and the police. Yes, about the murders. I was wondering if it would be possible for you to come to my apartment about six tonight?" Almost as an afterthought he added quietly, "And could you bring the keys to Axel Gruen's apartment?"

Mark looked at Ginny, who merely shrugged.

"Yes, I understand that," Horace went on after patiently listening to what were clearly objections on the detective's part. "But could you at least bring them? If you don't approve of what I have in mind, you can make your decision then. I just feel there is something we need to discuss, and with the police going in tomorrow—'' Margolus had definitely interrupted again, but now the tone was low enough that Ginny and Mark couldn't hear his voice from where they were sitting.

"Thank you, Inspector. I'll expect you around six. Don't rush, if there are other things you have to do this afternoon, I'll understand. And with our still having Daylight Savings Time, what I'm thinking about should probably happen only after dark." The professor seemed about to end the conversation when he added: "By the way, there is still a policeman guarding the building, isn't there?" The answer seemed to please Horace. "Good. Make sure he stays there."

He hung up the phone and walked back to the living room. "He doesn't like it, but I think he's curious. My estimation of his intelligence has gone up."

"You want to get into that apartment again. But why?"

"Mark, you heard him say the police are going to go over the place thoroughly tomorrow. If there's something there that the killer hasn't found, it might be a good idea if we found it first."

"But we know what the killer was looking for. Rena's tape." Ginny turned from Horace to Mark. "Isn't that it?"

"Perhaps." He looked at his niece, smiling happily. "Only this is where you come in, Ginny. The killer may not know that the police are going to search the place again tomorrow. If there's something more than the tape that the killer wants, if we can get word to the people we consider the major suspects tonight at the *Elegant* photographic session at La Picassa, it might just bring him—or her—out to do a little searching tonight."

"A trap? With a cop at the door?" It was her practical voice, Horace noted, another echo of her mother.

"Perhaps Margolus can persuade the policeman to make himself scarce . . . or at least not openly visible."

"And how are we going to tell everybody we've been talking to about the search tomorrow?"

"That, Mark, is going to be Ginny's job. You've been invited to the shoot, my dear. By Celeste herself. For background."

"A dress extra," Ginny remarked, thinking it frustrating and totally normal that her first job was going to be way off-Broadway and for no pay.

"Background but talkative. And hopefully observant. If anyone is missing after you have spread the word, try to note who it is." He hesitated for a moment, then started for his office. "I'll look up the phone number of Axel's apartment, you can call us if you see anything strange—''

"I have the number, Uncle Horace," Ginny said serenely. "Remember? I gave it to you that morning when you were being so stubborn."

"I am never stubborn," Horace replied. "And you are to be careful. Stick close to Zoe. The people you can't talk to, she can."

"The countess is going to be there?" Mark couldn't keep the surprise out of his voice.

"I have a feeling a great many people are going to be there." He pinched his upper lip thoughtfully; somewhere he had read that was supposed to relieve cramps in the legs. "And I wonder what they're all thinking about this afternoon?"

Zoe, the Countess Sirelli, wasn't thinking at all, she was fuming. It was just like Horace to fob off going with her with no excuse whatsoever. And while Ginny would be compensation, Zoe belonged to an era where a lady was not seen outside her home after dark without a male escort. Especially wearing an elaborate evening gown. She thought of various men she might call but discarded the names as quickly as she thought of them. Everybody has a job, she thought, unless they were too decrepit to get up and down stairs, which wouldn't work tonight. Sunday evening was a night the others wanted nothing more than a quiet dinner and early to bed, to face the pressures of their business week ahead.

She'd already phoned Celeste petulantly, and she promised to find a suitable escort, but the editor was handling a thousand last-minute details and she was far from sure she had even heard her.

Damn Horace! He could perfectly easily have accompanied her!

"Sure, I suppose I could accompany the countess," said Jon Bowers when Celeste called him. Well, well, well, he thought. Chief Boss Editor at an important magazine. She was going to owe him big after this one. "Although I should be a little angry that I wasn't considered for this shoot." That was a lie, he was good and angry.

"Jon, darling . . ." Celeste's voice was smooth as silk. "It's women's clothes and men's whips. Not really how I see you. It'll be just background if that," she added hurriedly. "And of course I'll pay the Classic Agency your usual fee, just don't tell the countess."

"Of course not. And you can skip the fee." He thought he heard her sigh with relief, these shoots could go on for hours. "I'm sure you'll find other uses for me. And not in the background. In the future,

I mean." He knew Celeste had gotten the idea, there was no point in pressing it.

As he hung up, he wondered if he had a clean dress shirt. Good idea to be there tonight. Show Katya he wasn't tied to her. Especially when they both knew what had happened. She had more to lose than he, so it would be good to have other options open. Not to mention a good chance to be seen by Oliver Tomorrow. A little light suggestiveness when they were introduced, and Jon would make sure they were, wouldn't hurt, although Jon had no intention of following through with the photographer.

Still, if that's what it took to get ahead . . .

"How am I supposed to plan setups when I don't even know what that silly twit Franchard is sending? And Celeste's on the phone all the time. I can't get through to her!" Oliver Tomorrow was close to a screaming rage that he knew was only nerves, but if he really let go, it might dispel the headache he got if he didn't let his creative side out. And the slim young man in front of him didn't help his mood. God, how he hated the East Side types who thought because they were thin and still in their twenties just the sight of them was enough to turn him on. Or, actually turn off his anger.

"Mr. and Mrs. McKay will be there early," said Julian patiently. "They've checked the availability of all your favorite models, some that aren't even part of their agency." God, how he hated these "artistic" types who lived in lofts and wore weird clothes! He was definitely getting out of here before the photographer asked him to help lug his equipment to La Picassa. Not with him wearing his new Paul Stuart suit.

Oliver was looking through the pictures, discarding them on the floor as he flipped through the pile. "Oh, God! Can't Celeste do anything right? These were my last month's favorite models. And the clothes? What am I supposed to do about the clothes? It could destroy my whole mise en scène."

"I suppose you could call Franchard. He'd know what he's sending," said Julian, unable to resist a small, slightly superior smile.

"That nervous Nellie? Why, oh, why am I stuck with comebacks?" But as he was yelling, he remembered the red dress on that bitch McKay at the dinner party, and the blue job the countess wore. Could be interesting. And a wealthy countess is always a good connection to have. He'd call Franchard. After all, there were certain dangerous things they had in common. . . .

"It'll be all right, Johnny. You'll see."

"Don't call me 'Johnny,' Berta! Jean-Claude! How often do I have to tell you."

"I'm your sister, you don't need to put on the front with me." She held him cradled in her arms as she had so many times before, from his childhood on.

"But suppose they find out?"

"No one's going to find out anything. We've covered all that. All we have to do is destroy what they mustn't find. You'd better think about how to do that."

"And if I can't? I'm not ready for this! I'm not!"

He was close to tears but he knew she would hold him until he calmed down. He leaned against her bosom, feeling the warmth of her body soothing him, her hands patting him gently on his back. As always, she had taken care of everything. At least twenty outfits were carefully wrapped in plastic and hung on the rack. Beautiful clothes, they both knew it. And tonight there would be no damage. Berta would take them down in the van herself and no one would be able to ruin them. Or him.

"Johnny, Johnny, relax! We've been through so much together. And nobody knows anything yet. . . ."

"They're talking! I know they are!"

"But they don't *know* anything. We stopped the rumors before. To-night we'll stop them again. For good. The worst is over."

"But Paco . . ."

"Paco is . . . dispensable. He's done all we needed him to do." The phone was ringing. She detached herself from her brother and reached for it. "Just do as I tell you and everything will turn out all right. It always has before, hasn't it?"

She could tell he was beginning to relax. Please, she thought to herself, no more bad things. Just let us get through tonight. No more bad things.

Dr. Malcolm Bosley was moving back and forth before the picture window of his elegant co-op apartment. For once the sight of the placid East River brought him no pleasure. Damn it, why didn't Franchard pick up the phone? He heard Berta's voice.

"It's Malcolm, Berta. How's Jean-Claude?"

"Frightened and shaky. I was about to call you but the photographer was calling."

"You didn't mention my name?"

"Of course not."

"I just wanted to warn you. I'm going to be there tonight. Celeste's escort supposedly. Not that she'll have any time for me. But this has got to work out, there's too much at stake.''

"You don't have to remind me. I don't know you, you don't know me. Jean-Claude you can just nod to. After all, you did meet him at that dinner party.''

"He hasn't said anything to anybody? Jean-Claude, I mean?''

"He knows what you've done for him, he'll be quiet. But if you could bring something . . .''

"Not again! You both promised never to ask again!'' He could feel his anger rising. He didn't have anything like that in the apartment, and to get to the hospital . . . "How can I do that? I have to pick up Celeste!''

"Just a sedative. A mild one. Please?'' It was so unexpected to hear her plead, it shook him for a moment.

"I'll try. Just tell him to keep his damn mouth shut!'' He banged down the receiver.

"Quiet, Paco. Quiet.'' She whispered it softly in English, less chance of anyone understanding in the other rooms of the hall. "You know it's impossible.''

"After all that has happened? All I've done? I can't stay away!''

"Maybe the police will be there? They're clever. I don't know how much that professor believed, or who he may have talked to. . . .''

He turned away from her in the bed, but she knew without seeing that his face was set, his mouth determined. "They won't recognize me.'' He rubbed his unshaven chin. A week now. It was almost a beard. With a cap and dark glasses, he could get by, he knew he could. If only Inez would help. "You must get me in there! Just let me have one more chance! Just one more.''

"You said that the last time.'' She said it wearily, not bothering to whisper. He'd win her over as he had before, no matter the consequences to both of them. "Two people dead, Paco. How do we explain that to God when we see Him?''

"God is for the next world. Here we have to do what we must ourselves.'' But he turned to hold her close to his body. She'd agree, they both knew that.

"Come on, Katya, we both know you weren't home that night!''

She continued to brush her long hair, not bothering to look in the mirror at her husband standing behind her. "We both know that, do we? And how would 'we' know that?'' It had been years since Philip could anger her or make her afraid.

"I checked your bedroom after the party."

"My, so athletic! You actually climbed the stairs after all these years? Not for a romantic reason, I'm sure." Take that dart, she thought to herself, fishing around for a hairpin. "Snooping around again?"

"Hardly. But after Sunday . . . or, rather, Monday morning, when I couldn't find you . . ."

"You didn't look very hard. It was in my appointment book. Hairdressers."

"At seven in the morning?"

"Does it matter?" She put down her pins and swiveled on the stool to face him. "After all, there's only your word you checked on me Thursday night. But several people—Julian and Mattie for example— know you didn't come home at all last Sunday night."

"I was here. It was . . . simpler to sleep in my office."

"With the door conveniently locked. Not a very good alibi."

"And yours?"

"You think I'm capable of murder?"

"I think we both know what we're capable of." There was a coldness in his voice she hadn't heard for a long time. She found herself shivering in her thin robe.

"Especially when we don't get what we want." He started for the bedroom door.

"I always get what I want, Philip." She flung it at him before he could leave. "Haven't you learned that by now?"

But he had left the room

Almost six o'clock, the killer of Rena Varmont and Axel Gruen thought. What had the police reluctantly admitted in the past? After twenty-four hours, if they didn't have a suspect or an informer, the trail grew progressively colder. It was almost a week since Rena had died. Thursday evening for Axel. And nothing to worry about so far. Nothing to worry about once this evening was over.

And there'd never be a reason to kill again. That was a promise. If only nothing else was discovered . . . but that was impossible. The killer had searched both apartments so thoroughly. Nothing existed to lead the police any closer.

Only nothing more must be found. Ever.

CHAPTER EIGHTEEN

Harold Margolus sat on the couch in Professor Livsey's living room and listened in silence. He was surprised at himself, considering what he thought of the professor, considering also he was giving up a Sunday evening. At least he didn't have to put on a suit or tie for what was technically his day off. And there was a certain logic in what the older man was suggesting.

"And who is going to spread the word tonight that the police are going into Gruen's apartment tomorrow?" Margolus looked around at the others.

"I am." Ginny had changed into the ordered black tights and turtleneck. She had scooped her hair back and crammed it under a black leather cap. Something about the gesture reminded Horace of something he had meant to think about, but it was gone before he could capture it. "After all, I'm an actress."

"And my ex-wife will be there, ready to spread the gossip." Horace leaned back in his chair, resisting the urge to light a cigarette. This was no time to get on the detective's nerves, not when he was being surprisingly cooperative. "Now, Mr. Margolus, I don't guarantee that anything will happen . . ."

"You just want you, me, and Franklin to wait in Gruen's apartment and see if anybody shows up?" Ordinarily this would have come out as a sneering assessment of amateurs playing at detection. Oddly, it was strangely flat to Horace's ears, more of a statement than anything else.

"It just seems to me that Rena's answering machine tape might not be the only thing the killer is looking for. I mean, the lighter shell with the tape and the initials D.C. was right out there in the open."

"Could be like Poe's 'Purloined Letter.'"

207

It was Horace's turn to be surprised. Somehow he had not expected
the policeman sitting opposite him to be knowledgeable about one of
the classics of criminal fiction. And to know the best place to hide
something was in clear view.

"What's the matter? You think none of us read?" This was clearly
a challenge from Margolus.

"If I did, you've taught me a lesson in humility," answered Horace mildly.

"Margolus . . ." Mark began hesitatingly. Damn it, why couldn't he
think of the man's rank? "Is this likely to get you into trouble?" Mark
realized he sounded like a wimp, but somebody had to consider the
law in this room. "Going into a crime scene without permission?"

"I have automatic permission as long as I'm on the case." Margolus
was still unusually calm. He felt like smiling but held it back. He could
see he had shaken up all three of them by his attitude. Good! Let them
know he wasn't some immovable dumb jerk they could impress with
their education and degrees. "I've already checked with the precinct.
When we get to Gruen's place, the policeman will walk away, checking
his watch as if he were due for a break. At that time two plain-
clothesmen will take their places, one in an unmarked car down the
street with a full view of the front door. The other, apparently a drunk,
will lie by a disposal in the back. They both have walkie-talkies. They'll
notice anybody coming in or going out."

"Including us?"

"Definitely including us, Professor." He shifted in his seat. "These
guys were part of the first investigation. They know the names and faces
of all the tenants in the building. Anybody else they can notify us."

"You think this might really work?" It was a question Ginny didn't
want to ask, but things were going so smoothly, it worried her.

"No. I think it's dumb." This was more like the old Margolus. "You
think every possible suspect in the two murders is going to be at this
disco tonight and be so scared of a police search tomorrow that they're
going to try and break in before then? When everybody will notice
their absence? And presuming they have some way of getting past
Gruen's steel door, the grilles on the windows? If they were that anxious
to break in, they would have done it before now . . . and noticed a
policeman at the door.

"Just how dumb do you think this killer is? He's going to arrive
tonight and find nobody at the door after hearing from some gossip
there might be a thorough search tomorrow?" He shifted his bulky
body to get more comfortable. It was his turn now. "Maybe some street
punk. But not all these high-class suspects you've figured are all tied

together." He turned to Mark. "And all involved in Diane Chaumet's death too."

"Then why are you going along with the professor's plan?" Mark looked genuinely puzzled.

"Because maybe *I* want to look at the place again before a band of experts start falling all over each other. There are a couple of things that bother me about that apartment." It gave him some amusement to see the blank looks on their faces. "Also, Autopsy is now wobbling on the time of Rena's death. It may have been earlier, closer to three or possibly two Monday morning. Seems she was hit first, then smothered later."

There was a moment of awkward silence in the living room. Ginny broke it as tactfully as she knew how. "It's . . . considerate of you to let us help, Mr. Margolus."

"Detective. Second grade. Only lieutenants use titles."

Mark exhaled. Must remember that. But Ginny was going on.

"You're sure you're not inconveniencing yourself? I mean, your family . . ."

"It's my mother and dad. I've got my own apartment in their house, they're getting older, they're safer with me downstairs. They'll be all right tonight. They're used to my weird hours." He glared at them defiantly with a look that said plainly, You want to make something out of my still living with my parents?

Nobody wanted to make anything of it at all.

It was getting darker as Ginny made her way to La Picassa. Zoe had called to inform Horace somewhat loftily that she had an escort for the evening, so Ginny had made her way alone to La Picassa by subway and foot. The darkness was less because the days were getting shorter than as if more of the rain that had swept the city for most of the week was making a return appearance. Or was about to. She was glad she had grabbed a raincoat before she left the apartment, though more for respectability than protection from the weather.

Fortunately there was already a crowd gathering in front of the club, otherwise she might never have found it. New, it might be, and "hot," but it sure was obscure, she thought. No street address, of course, but no sign either. She'd expected something in neon or maybe spray-painted on the wall of what was clearly an old and long-abandoned warehouse. Instead, there was a small plaque fastened insecurely to a wide door. From his blue period she thought, then realized this was the feminized version of the painter's name. Why, she wondered, making her way through cables and wires that were being unloaded from a large truck in front of the building. Nobody seemed to be at the entrance, so she walked in boldly.

Once inside, a harried young man hurried up the steps to her. He had long hair, half orange, while the other half hung in limp purple strands. "I'm sorry. Private party tonight." He was clearly wavering between the excitement of the event and fear that something was going to go wrong. A spread in *Elegant* could move the whole place for at least fifteen minutes into the center of public attention. Ginny could see he was already dreaming of it being a new hot night spot, and from there? Who knew?

"It's all right," Ginny said soothingly. "I'm here at Celeste's invitation." The man in front of her blinked unknowingly. "Celeste Lanier. *Elegant* magazine," Ginny explained patiently. "I'm part of the shoot."

"Oh, sure. Oh, yes!" The young man burbled on happily, clearly relieved not to have to eject her. "It's just that I wasn't informed who was supposed to be admitted and who wasn't. Hank promised to be here early with a list, but he hasn't shown up yet and there are all these people asking about voltage and watts and backup generators." He mopped his brow and in the darkness Ginny could see he was totally confused. "All *I* know about electricity is you flip a switch and light is supposed to come on."

"Me too." Ginny tried to make it sound reassuring. Then switching to what she thought was a professional attitude, she asked, "Anybody else for the shoot here yet?"

"No. And I thought it was supposed to be about seven." He ran his fingers through the orange side of his hair. "Isn't it about that now?"

"A little later, I think." No way could she read her wristwatch in this light. "Suppose you show me where the models are going to dress? Maybe I can help get that organized."

"Oh, sure! Oh, yes!" Ginny got the feeling that in his eagerness to please and get ahead in New York, he would answer every request that way. "I guess it'll have to be the ladies' room and the storage area in the back. I tried to clean it up, but we didn't close until after seven this morning and there's just been a zillion things to do." He paused at the bottom of the steep staircase to look back at Ginny, who was edging her way down carefully. "Would you believe I haven't been to bed at all today?"

"They really overwork you, don't they?" She reached the bottom of the stairs. Her eyes were adjusting to the darkness. In front of her there was a big room, concrete-floored, a long bar along one side, tables crowded into the space remaining, allowing for a large dance area. Opposite the bar was a semi-enclosed booth for the disc jockey. She suspected there were more amplifiers than she had ever seen in her life attached to the walls around the room. "Are there any lights here?"

"Not many." The young man seemed to take it as a personal failing on his part. "There never are many, but with the new electric equipment coming in, I don't think I'd better turn what we have on." He smiled a little apologetically. "I could light a few candles?"

"I think the models are going to need more than candles. And the hairdressers. And I know the makeup people will. Let's see the space you've got for them."

"Oh, sure. Oh, yes. It's to the back." He moved carefully through the tables to the back of the huge room. "I wish Hank would get here."

So do I, buddy, Ginny thought as she made her way after him. The place was a long way from anything her aunt Zoe had ever seen, and the thought of the models and their Franchard clothes in this cellar made her wish she had settled for just sneaking into a dead man's apartment.

They started out shortly before eight, each of the men having consumed several large sandwiches first. Not a night for martinis, Horace decided, settling as did Mark and Margolus for a beer. Mark had made a trip out and returned with several flashlights (Margolus had his own, large and lethal-looking). Tactfully, he had also brought an assortment of gum and hard candy balls for Horace. My God, does it take two murders for me to cut back on smoking, Horace thought as he stuffed them gratefully into the pockets of his oldest corduroy jacket.

When they arrived at Eighty-ninth Street, Margolus parked his car carefully and, motioning the others to wait, went up to the policeman on duty. Their conversation was brief and the detective signaled Mark and Horace to get out and follow him. Horace noticed the crime tape had been removed. The policeman would stay at his post another half hour, Margolus informed them as they squeezed into the small elevator. After it had creaked to a stop, he pushed back the grille and fished for the keys to the apartment. Once inside, he looked back at Mark and Livsey.

"No lights, got it? If there's any chance your little idea is going to work, we'd better not have anybody outside seeing lights on." Mark and Horace nodded. "I'm going to check on the studio first. You two check this room and the bedroom." He didn't wait for a reply.

"I'll take the bedroom," Mark said. Why am I lowering my voice, he wondered. It's not like anybody could hear us. "At least that way I can see what Margolus is up to."

So Mark was as mystified as Horace over the detective's whole approach to this evening. Horace fished in his pocket for his flashlight.

There was still enough daylight coming in from the windows that he could see almost everything in the living room. It was in the same disorder it had been when he had come with Mark the morning after Axel's murder. Pictures taken from the wall and thrown anywhere on the floor, the sofa cushions ripped (He presumed by police—unless the killer had been here already? But that wasn't possible, not with a guard at the door).

"I'll see if I can find Diane's picture," he said to Mark before the young lawyer moved into the next room.

There was still a thin layer of the dusting for fingerprints floating around everything he touched. Might as well get at it, he thought as he crouched down on the floor and started going through the framed mementoes of the dead photographer.

An hour after Ginny had arrived at La Picassa, the place was crowded with people. About fifteen hairy, black-leathered men had roared up with their motorbikes and were settled somewhat restlessly against the wall near the disc jockey's booth. Aside from occasional shouts for music, they had remained quiet, drinking one beer after another from the six-packs they had brought with them. For whatever reason, and Ginny suspected it was rather because the place didn't want to go up before the State Liquor Board to apply for a license than because the owners disapproved of drinking, no liquor was served. However, caterers had arrived (supplied by *Elegant,* they briskly informed the nervous young man) and set up on three of the tables supplies for sandwiches, soft drinks, ice, and plastic glasses. The beer drinkers moved in a swarm toward them.

Next came the makeup and hair people, about twenty of them, Ginny guessed, trying to take in everyone who entered. Almost instantly they began squabbling about lights, fixtures for the hairdressers, lighted mirrors for the makeup people. Next, looking drab as unpainted walls, the models arrived. June, the friendly girl who had helped Ginny at the agency, was among them, but she seemed barely to recognize her. Next came Franchard and Oliver Tomorrow. Now the wrangling began. Oliver wanted the models in extreme hairstyles, the designer held out for smooth, straight-back hair not to distract from the dresses. These were being carefully brought down from the street by a large woman and her assistant, a small Latino-looking girl. Horsey's Inez, Ginny thought, trying to stay out of the way.

Only Celeste's arrival quieted the noise. With swift efficiency she moved among the warring parties, settling the models on chairs in the storeroom, arranging with a large, burly man with a clipboard (the missing Hank, Ginny suspected) about where lights were to be plugged in. Mirrors appeared miraculously and racks for the clothes.

An amiable-looking man had accompanied Celeste. Unlike the *Elegant* editor who was in a sweater and blue jeans, he was faultlessly dressed in evening clothes. He looked around La Picassa with what Ginny decided was a permanently raised eyebrow. She suspected before he sat down on any surface, he would wipe it clean with several paper napkins.

The McKays arrived next. Whatever their personal feelings might be, they had obviously been through an expensive fashion shoot in a difficult location many times before. Katya moved directly to the models' area, followed by Jean-Claude and Celeste. Mr. McKay, clearly not planning to be photographed, huddled with the lighting experts that had been hired for the evening. Almost at once a new noise was added to the area as a relief generator started up. Soon the photographer's assistants—and he seemed to have one for every finger of his hands—were moving about, hoisting lights on tripods, filling small cameras, adjusting silver umbrellas.

It's like a movie, Ginny thought. And how was she going to drop the news of the police search in the middle of all these people, each intent on getting his own way with their equipment? Fortunately at this moment Zoe descended the stairs cautiously, holding up the skirt of her blue evening gown. Behind her, carrying a hamper, came the one person Ginny had not expected to see, the sulky, terrible actor she had auditioned with at the Natasha Kinn school. That's a strange couple, Ginny thought, but remembered Celeste had promised to find an escort for her aunt. Zoe, safely on ground floor, beamed a radiant smile around the room, clearly prepared to make an adventure out of the evening. Unfortunately nobody was paying any attention, which caused the smile to wilt a little.

The crowd was now so dense that Ginny knew Horsey's former wife couldn't possibly recognize her. She started through the crowd, only to be accosted by the photographer.

"No, no, no! Too normal! Much too plain-American-girl for this. Who sent you?" Oliver Tomorrow glanced around, an assistant rushed to his side immediately. "Omar," he directed to the eager young man, "make her distinctive. The sort of 'pet' of the club. Like 'Nobody' in *West Side Story*. And don't whine that was before your time." Tomorrow turned away, and before Ginny could protest, Omar had grabbed her face.

"Cap's all right," he said appraisingly. "All black's good." He took out a grease pencil. "I think cat's whiskers, that could be interesting." Before she knew, Ginny could feel him designing her cheeks. She tried to resist, but he was stronger than he looked. "And just a teeny-tiny death's head on your forehead." He whipped out a red pencil and finished his work. "Yes," he said approvingly. "Gives you an air of decadence. Not that it'll show up in the pictures, most likely, but it adds ambiance." With that he moved swiftly after the photographer.

Thank God I didn't bring a purse and a mirror, I hate to think what I look like, Ginny thought. She eased her way through the crowd—was it getting bigger?—toward Zoe. Obviously what had been done to her face was a complete disguise, Zoe barely noticed her. She and the model had spread a cloth from the hamper over a small table and opened a bottle of champagne. She had also brought tall glass flutes, a small bowl of roses, and, waiting for the appropriate moment, an unlit candle in a silver holder. What were Celeste and Oliver Tomorrow going to make of this? Ginny shuddered. But that wasn't her problem.

"Zoe, could I speak to you for a minute?"

The light was fading fast in Gruen's studio. Horace had searched through the pictures on the floor. Not a sign of the one he had seen of Diane Chaumet. He got up carefully, to find Mark standing in the doorway to the bedroom.

"Do you know what Margolus is doing?" Mark was still speaking in almost a whisper but Horace couldn't blame him. If anything was going to happen, it was going to be from now on. "He's opening every camera in the studio. I mean, every one!"

"He's a photography expert," Horace said patiently, keeping his voice low. "I'm sure we can trust him not to injure anything."

"But what's he hoping to find?"

"Film. Remember the cameras we discovered focused on the bed? We didn't find anything, tape or film, did we?"

"Somebody could come here for that," Mark admitted grudgingly. "How are you coming?"

"No Diane Chaumet. But just to be sure, let's try to put these pictures back on the walls in their original places. At least then we can see if anything else was taken." He had divided the pictures on the floor into three piles for each of the walls. "You take the Regal ads, I'll do Paris. Whatever is missing, I suspect should be in the last pile. At least that's where I saw her picture."

"We'd better get moving, it's almost pitch-dark in here," said Mark as he reached for the framed photographs.

Ginny had whispered her message to Zoe, who, obviously bored with Jon Bowers, immediately rose, champagne glass in one hand and bottle in the other, and began to move through the room to the people Ginny had specified. Years of drifting through cocktail parties, receptions, and state functions had trained her to be able to approach anybody and start a conversation. Talk about working a room, Ginny thought enviously. Never in her life would she have that much confidence.

However, she tried to keep close to Zoe just to catch the reactions as Zoe gossiped. That's what she was here for, not to be made up for Halloween. But she could never get close enough to hear the actual conversations. Technicians, men in leather, lighting people, and makeup personnel swarmed around her. Only by stretching could she get the slightest glimpse of the people Zoe was tracking down.

The reactions she saw surprised her. Good heavens, she thought, Horsey was right. Nobody is taking this news well. The McKays, for example. He had listened to Zoe patiently, but almost at once his face was suddenly grave. Katya, Zoe had caught on the run. Mrs. McKay's reaction at first was annoyance at the interruption, but she forced a polite smile on her face. Only when Zoe had moved on did the smile fade. Katya McKay glanced swiftly at her husband, who was watching her. There was a dangerous glint in her eye, and her mouth, never voluptuous, had thinned to a dark red line. There was a sardonic smile on Philip McKay's face now. He's not as handsome as I thought, Ginny decided.

Oliver Tomorrow barely listened to Zoe, moving her carefully through the crowd to fasten her next to three hairy men clad entirely in black leather. But the assistant hurrying behind him had heard Zoe and the look on his face was one of panic.

Zoe next swerved to the models' area, forcing Jean-Claude and his bulky female assistant to halt in the doorway. This was the strongest reaction. Franchard looked quickly at the woman at his side, but her face remained implacable. He swayed a little but the woman put her arm around him, forcing him to remain standing. Behind them, huddling close enough to hear, was the girl Ginny called "Horsey's Inez." Clearly she had heard Zoe gossip and her small face was pale with fear.

They cleared the doorway, Franchard and the woman following Zoe as she attempted to move away. Obviously the designer was anxious to ask Zoe more questions, the woman with him keeping her face expressionless. Only Ginny could see she had tightened her grip on the designer's arm.

Now Ginny could see into the dressing area. She edged closer. The models were in the in-between stage of being prepared: base makeup had been applied, hot rollers were on the four heads, except for June, who was being swathed in a sort of silk turban. This was the stage when the false eyelashes were being added with exact and demanding care. But behind them, near the rack of dresses, was a small male figure. He had a black cap and turtleneck, dark trousers and sneakers. There was a beginning of a beard on his sallow face. But what caught Ginny's attention was with all the shadows and patches of darkness in the ill-lit space; the lights being concentrated on the models and the photographic setups, he was wearing dark glasses.

It's Paco, Ginny thought. But she couldn't be sure, he had ducked behind the rack of clothes as if he had sensed someone was staring at him. And it was now too crowded to get into the models' area.

Why would Paco be here? Then she remembered her instructions. Damn! Zoe had just moved away from Celeste, no chance now to catch her reaction. Ginny scanned the editor's face, but it seemed no more worried than any professional determined to get the assignment finished as quickly and efficiently as possible.

She had better luck with the man who had accompanied Celeste into La Picassa. Like birds of a feather, both of them being the only men in tuxedos, he had joined Jon Bowers at the table Zoe had set up. The look on Bowers's face was not a happy one, and when Zoe smoothly took her place at the table greeting the man Ginny couldn't identify, she continued her conversation as if she had never left her escort. That must be Dr. Bosley, Ginny decided. When Zoe leaned forward to whisper her news, his face turned red. Or at least it seemed red, for the lights were being turned on, colored gels were being slid into their brackets, furniture was rearranged at the far wall.

At that moment the disc jockey who seemed to have appeared from nowhere turned on the music and the volume. The blast of sudden sound was as violent as an earthquake, even for someone Ginny's age who was used to loud music. Ginny could see Zoe was squealing as she fished in her hamper for cotton balls to push into her ears.

It's all right, Zoe, Ginny thought. You've done what you were supposed to do, and before the evening really starts.

Music. Then lights. Then a surge of movement as the models came out of their area.

Showtime, Ginny realized.

"That's the last of them." Horace looked around the room carefully. It was time for a flashlight but by now his eyes were getting accustomed to the gloom. All of the pictures that had been scattered on the floor were back on the walls, if not in their original places, at least as close as Horace could remember.

And there was only one empty spot, the row near the floor that

Horace had to bend over to see when he had come to Axel's the first time.

"Diane Chaumet?" Mark wasn't whispering anymore.

"The only one missing. Not very clever of the murderer." So Mark had been right, Horace realized. Was that what the killer had been after? If so, their evening here was a waste of time and energy.

It was then they heard Margolus. It was too dark to see him but he must have been filling the doorway to the rest of the apartment.

"You guys want to come here? I think I've found something."

—— CHAPTER NINETEEN

The clothes were stunning. Since Oliver Tomorrow had come onto the scene late, he demanded to see all of the dresses and, after each model pirouetted in front of him, she was hurried back into the dressing area to change into another outfit. Ginny tried to decide what made the clothes so distinctive. Bright colors, of course, and interesting use of fabrics (who would have thought denim could come in a vibrant shade of pink and still make an attractive and yet efficient-looking daytime suit?). But there was more than that to Franchard's clothes. They seemed to have no category to them, they were not just for wealthy women of a certain age who need to camouflage tired areas of their bodies, but they were not so freakishly young that only emaciated waifs could wear them. Hemlines varied but the tailoring was superb; each design seemed to flow gently around the models' figures. At least three of the outfits Ginny would have bought in a minute, not that she could have afforded the prices. But with a shrewd eye, she realized that by the following spring, less expensive copies would be available in a store in her price range.

Celeste seemed to be everywhere at once. The idea of poor dead Axel doing a day in the life of the *Elegant* woman had clearly been discarded. Now it was Oliver Tomorrow's idea to shock the eye not just with the clothes but with the grimy background and brutal-looking men in leather. Each time he arranged a pose, the model would seem amused or faintly superior, as if she knew that wherever she went, a cave like La Picassa or dinner at the White House, she could stand out as being best-dressed.

And beautiful.

That was it, Ginny decided. These clothes would make every woman feel gorgeous. The models were definitely rising to the occasion, and Ginny could feel that maybe for the first time in a long while they were wearing clothes that showed them at their loveliest. Clothes that already they were talking to Franchard (Ginny suspected) about buying for their own personal use. Celeste, wisely, was playing no favorites. Apparently she had decided that all of the twenty designs should be photographed, choices for the magazine spread to be made later. Oliver Tomorrow (for once) made no complaint, he seemed ecstatic at the idea of capturing the women in this setting whether they were wearing a design meant for daytime wear or a full evening gown. (June looked particularly spectacular in that.) Ginny noticed that Zoe, having borrowed a pen and paper from someone, was busy jotting down outfits she had every intention of purchasing at once.

If Franchard has been out of favor these last few years, Ginny thought, he sure is back now!

The first serious shot was ready: two huge, leather-clad men were facing each other with fierce expressions on their faces, ready, obviously, to fight over the model in a green-beaded outfit who stood between them, an amused smile on her enigmatic face. The background was a wall of whips and chains, carefully arranged by one of the assistants.

At last everybody seemed to be ready. Even the disc jockey had turned the music down, whether because of interest or orders, Ginny couldn't guess. Two assistants hovered behind the photographer, each holding a loaded camera. Like a surgeon, he reached behind him without looking, the camera placed swiftly in his hands. "More lights," he called out. There was a sudden blaze on the group as the lamps revved up to top level.

At that moment, every light in the room went out.

Mark and Horace stumbled carefully through the dark bedroom after Margolus. There was a brief flash of light, allowing them to see their way into the studio part of the apartment. Margolus had hung a blanket from the bed over the doorway to close off the few lights that he had turned on in the studio. Through the skylight above, Horace could see a full moon. Nothing would be seen from the street, the few lamps were draped with material Margolus had found in the apartment, dish towels, and pillowcases. It made for a soft but steady illumination. Better than total darkness, Horace thought. Or flashlights.

Margolus was facing them, a flat square object in his hands. "Is this what you were looking for, Professor?" He handed it over to Horace.

It was the photograph of Diane Chaumet.

"Where did you find it?" asked Livsey.

"It was behind that roll of white paper he'd got hanging from the ceiling. And not just behind it. Hung on a nail in the wall."

"If the killer was after that picture, why would he do that?" Mark was frowning.

"Because the killer didn't do it." Horace was trying to sound as if he had expected this all along, but he knew he hadn't. But it was becoming obvious to him now. "Axel didn't want anyone to know that he had known Diane. He concealed it."

"That doesn't make sense. This was his apartment."

"With a lot of visitors, Mark." Horace studied the photograph again. What was her connection with the photographer? With Rena Varmont? Five years after her death, Axel had been so afraid someone might realize he had cared for the dead model that he had hidden the photograph after he suspected Horace had seen it. But he didn't have to worry about Horace. It was the killer of Rena that had frightened him into concealing the picture. Only he had felt so strongly about Diane, he couldn't bear to destroy the photograph.

"You mean someone like Rena?" Mark had taken the picture of Diane from Horace.

"Hardly. We know she was here last Sunday afternoon. And the picture was in its proper place when I saw it Tuesday." Horace was surprised that Margolus hadn't wrapped the picture carefully before touching it, but then he realized the only fingerprints on it would have been Axel's, dead since Thursday. The killer wouldn't have touched it. "No, Axel was being careful. Whatever he was up to, he didn't want anyone to know how close he had been to Diane Chaumet." He handed the picture back to Margolus. "You'll notice that's a very affectionate inscription she's written on it." For a second the image of the dead photographer came into his mind—bald, gnomelike, perpetually middle-aged until these last years. "Not that it's a romantic inscription, although he may have desired her. Practically any man would. But from what I've heard of her, she was a kind creature, she wouldn't have hurt his feelings by rejecting him, but she wouldn't have encouraged him to think they could have a love affair."

"So he could have loved her and maybe she never knew it?" Mark was clearly impressed. You're a romantic after all, Horace thought, knowing the young attorney was considering various other unconsummated affairs from Cyrano on.

"She would know it, Mark," Horace said quietly. "Women always know. But the best ones arrange it so no one gets hurt."

"Only someone did. Diane. In an accident."

"Boy, you just can't leave that woman alone, can you?" Margolus was definitely not a romantic, Horace realized.

"If it was an accident." Horace let that one sink in for a moment. "There were rumors of suicide. And after this week, how can we be sure there wasn't a murder? Things can happen to cars."

"You want the police to go back five years to see if anything was wrong with this woman's car? You crazy, Professor?"

"No. I'm trying to think like Axel." Horace moved around restlessly. "I suspect Diane was a very important person in his life. I'm sure he mourned her sensibly. And I don't think he ever forgot her." He smiled at Margolus. "You don't forget people who are . . . were . . . important to you, as you get older. As a matter of fact, sometimes they become more valuable than the people you see every day."

"Could we possibly get back to the two dead bodies we have this week?" It was clear Margolus was getting impatient.

"Except we *are* back to them." There was new confidence in Mark's voice. His theory about Diane being important was beginning to pay off. "Axel photographed Chaumet, probably loved her. Without result. And Rena's aunt was one of Chaumet's nurses in the hospital." He looked at the detective straight in the eye. "I'd say there has to be some kind of connection. I don't think anyone would believe that many coincidences."

"You know, between the two of you, I could start beginning to believe in the tooth fairy," Margolus grumbled.

"Did you open all the cameras, Sergeant?" Horace was on the other side of the studio, looking around at the walls.

"Yeah. Why? There was nothing in them, if that's what you're after. Of course for some of them nobody's made film of that type for years, some of them decades."

"And this?" Horace was standing by the large boxy camera on the tripod that was by far the most prominent piece of equipment in the room.

"That's an antique."

"I know. Axel told me it was one of a photographer named Fox-Talbot. A contemporary of Daguerre, he said."

Margolus moved over to where Horace was standing. "That's no Fox-Talbot." He ran his fingers over the black box. "The lens might be, but the casing, no way. It would have been bound in leather at that time." He moved his fingers around the large camera. "The screws holding the swivel, they're modern."

"As are the screws holding it to the tripod. And the floor. Holding it very firmly." Horace felt around the front and the back of the ancient camera. There might be certain modern additions to the trophy Axel had treated so carefully, but there was enough vintage materials attached to what was basically a large black box that only an expert could have detected that it had been pieced together.

"What would be inside a camera of this age?"

"Space mostly." Margolus was getting curious himself now. "Ridges for the glass plates they used before film was invented. Fixtures for light. A timer of some kind, it could take an hour to get a print in those days, at least an hour. Of course, the timer might not be attached. That length of time a clock would do."

"How would you get the plates in?"

"You'd slide them in at the top, I think." Margolus was almost apologetic. "I'm more up on modern cameras." He ran his fingers over the top of the case again. "I guess I must be wrong. No openings here."

"No openings." Horace had already examined all the sides of the camera, bending over with his flashlight to see the underside of the case. "But I suspect it's been opened. And not back in the last century."

Margolus started tapping the sides and the top of the box. "Sounds hollow."

"It would be, wouldn't it? After all this time?" Now Mark was touching the camera.

"Maybe." Horace straightened up. "Margolus, could you get the lenses off this? Without damage?"

"I can try." He started swiveling the large dim glass circles in the front of the camera. One of them began to move slightly. "I feel like I'm cracking a safe," he joked.

"It's very possible," said Horace, watching as the lens moved slowly to the left.

——— CHAPTER TWENTY

Dark.

Pitch-black dark. Ginny didn't try to move; with this many people surrounding her, she couldn't have gone anyplace anyway. After the first second the noises started, human voices, some cursing, some moaning, and above them all she could hear Zoe screaming loudly.

Almost at once she started to smell the smoke. Great, she thought. No lights and now a fire! She had images of a front page of a tabloid: DOZENS DIE IN DISCO FIRE. Slowly she started to edge herself toward where she figured the stairs to the street were. Franchard, practically in tears, was yelling, "Save the clothes!" over and over again. Oliver Tomorrow (Ginny was sure it was his voice although it had lost its esthetic edge) was bellowing curse words Ginny had never heard and hoped never to hear again.

Above all this, some man yelled that the stairs to the street were where he was standing. Another man (Philip McKay? Ginny wasn't sure) was shouting, "No need to panic, it's not a fire, just blown fuses. Move calmly toward my light." A flashlight broke the darkness. The leather-clad men were carefully assisting women toward the light, starting with the models and then moving on to the female assistants. Women and children first, thought Ginny, like the *Titanic,* wondering if she would pass as a woman in her outfit and makeup.

Slowly the panic began to subside, although the pace of the people hurrying up the narrow stairs increased when a flash of flame spurted out on the far brick wall. One of Celeste's staff seized a fire extinguisher and splashed the area at once. The flame went out but the smoke increased, as did the smell of the flames.

Up the stairs, Ginny told herself. Where is my raincoat? No time to worry about that now. One of the burly motorcyclists practically lifted her over an overturned bench and set her feet on the staircase. She was helped up to the street by the young man with the multicolored hair. He kept repeating over and over again like a mantra, "Oh, hell, Hank will kill me." To Ginny that would seem to be the least of anyone's worries.

Outside, she found herself gasping for air, although it probably had been no more than a few minutes since the lights had gone out and the small fire started. The street was crammed with trucks and rescued equipment, and over and around all of it a fog seemed to be descending on the area. The Hudson River, Ginny thought. Right across the street.

She tried to find the people she had been told to watch, but with so much movement going on, it was impossible. Especially now that night had closed in along with the fog. Somewhere, from not far away, she heard the sound of a fire engine or maybe two. People were either moving in furious activity to protect the equipment being brought up from the cellar disco or were standing numb with the fear they had repressed while down in the darkness.

From the corner of her eye Ginny saw a wisp of Zoe's blue dress as she disappeared into a waiting limousine. Adventure or no, Zoe had clearly had enough of the evening and was heading uptown. As her long car disappeared, Ginny was unable to see if anyone was with her.

Damn! She checked the area. Where were the two men in tuxedos? If they were still here, she couldn't spot them. A thin young man ran swiftly past her, thrusting himself into the crowd around the entrance of the disco. It's Paco, all right, Ginny realized. She tried to fight her way through the crowd which had grown larger from curious passersby, but it was impossible. Great! More people, just what I didn't need. Some of them seemed overage housewives (where around here could they live? Ginny wondered) in tired robes and slippers. Some more men in black leather also had appeared and were starting up conversations with the men who had been in La Picassa. It's not a cocktail party, Ginny thought angrily, but it was becoming one now that everybody seemed to have come out of the building safely.

The fire trucks appeared, sirens blaring. Three huge trucks, and a couple of cars with the fire department logo painted on them. Hoses were whipped out and the men disappeared down the stairs. Ginny could hear moans of anguish from one or two men. Not pain. The sound suggested they owned the club. You wanted it "hot," Ginny thought to herself. Well, now it's going to be very wet and very hacked up. Then, with a cynicism that surprised her, she realized the place would probably reopen in a matter of weeks with a new name, like "The Wreck" or "Damaged Goods."

She pushed her way forward. The crowd was getting thicker. She thought she saw Celeste calming one of the models. Franchard was with the stolid woman examining his clothes on a rack. How did they get that out here? Ginny wondered, but the efficient-looking woman at the designer's side looked capable of lifting the whole building to get what she wanted.

The sound of the generator starting up broke through the crowd noise. Lights started coming on again, this time focused on the bare walls of the building and including the fire trucks. Gradually firemen were emerging from the building, eyeing the four models huddled together with obvious interest. The models, still in their Franchard designs, were looking back at the firemen, clearly intrigued.

"That's it, guys! We skip the interior!" Oliver Tomorrow was back in command. "Sex, that's what I want! Sexy looks from the firemen, provocative looks from the models!" He whispered something to the man who seemed to be in charge of the fire team. He wasn't wearing a helmet, like the others, but the blue uniform of a man of authority. Ginny pressed closer. All she could hear was something about a donation to widows and orphans and the man replying if they got a call they would all have to leave.

"Ten minutes! Just give me ten minutes!" Oliver was shouting. Not waiting for an answer, he grabbed June, bright as a flame in a multicolored orange-red chiffon dress and centered her among the firemen, ordering them to point their hoses on her. "No water! No water!" he kept shouting. The firemen grinned. From where she was standing, Ginny knew it would make a startling photograph. For all his affectations, Tomorrow was clearly able to improvise, and do it quickly and well, in a way that would make an unforgettable picture.

"More lights!" the photographer yelled. This is where I came in, Ginny decided. Time to circulate among the crowd and see who was left of her list of possible murderers.

Only before she could move, the man Tomorrow called Omar shoved up beside her, holding a lamp with a long cord to the generator. "You! Hold this!" he commanded, pushing the light into her hands and simultaneously moving her through the crowd watching until she was right beside Oliver. "And don't twitch!"

The photographer edged her two feet closer to one of the trucks. More firemen had gathered there and were looking up admiringly at a model in a long gown of cream jersey that hugged every part of her body. Someone had gotten them into their black-and-yellow raincoats.

Tomorrow kept snapping pictures, stopping only to hand his camera behind him to an assistant who snapped a freshly filled one into his hands.

Horsey is going to kill me, Ginny thought, struggling to keep her arms from wavering as they held the special spotlight. What with all the noise, confusion, and lights blazing down on the scene, there was no way she could tell who was still in the crowd.

And this could go on for hours!

Margolus had taken off the first lens and was working on the smaller glass disc behind it. This took a little more effort. Mark and Horace watched him. I hope I'm right, thought Horace. But whatever the murderer was after had to be there! Axel had no safety deposit box, no safe, no false-bottomed carton of equipment. If he was concealing something so dangerous someone would kill to find it, it had to be in the large camera.

Unless, of course, I'm just a stupid old fool.

There was a faint click, hardly loud enough for anyone in the room to hear it. And the whole front of the camera, strangely looking like a large birdhouse now without the glass lenses holding it in place, slipped down off the camera. It would have fallen to the floor except for the two faded silk cords that kept it attached to the box.

Mark and Horace crowded closer as Margolus, flipping on his large flashlight, focused the beam on the interior of the box so carefully and tightly screwed to the floor. All three of them could see the inside was filled with papers and files and odd objects. Margolus stepped back and glanced at Horace.

"Well, Professor, it looks like you were right."

— CHAPTER TWENTY-ONE

A minute later, as Margolus began to remove the contents of the camera, he began to regret his concession to Horace. He took out the top file and flipped it open.

"What the hell's this?" he demanded, handing the open file to Livsey. "Nothing but a bunch of watercolors."

"Not exactly." Horace looked at the pages in his hands. Very familiar, he had seen the same or at least ones that were similar in Franchard's showroom, tacked to the walls. Only these were different. He realized the difference at once. There was no edge clipped off on the bottom left-hand side of each page. Instead, there was a large, clear scrawl of a name.

Paco.

Of course, thought Horace. There was no "Franchard" scrawled on the opposite edge of the paper as there had been on the designs he had seen. Nor were these the simple fashion sketches suggesting a mood that Horace had seen in newspapers when he hurried past the fashion pages. These were meticulous drawings showing seams and colors and how each outfit would move on the body.

"What are they, Professor?" Mark had edged closer, to stand by Horace's shoulder.

"For one thing, the reason Franchard had to have Axel photograph his new line. Only it isn't his new line. These designs were drawn by Paco."

"The messenger boy?" Margolus took one of the sheets. "How do you know he did these? Maybe he was just copying Franchard's work?"

"These are originals, Margolus. They all were. Only the ones in his showroom had Paco's signature carefully clipped off."

227

"You mean Franchard was taking credit for Paco's work?" Mark frowned. "I don't know much about fashion, but don't all top designers have assistants? There's nothing wrong in that, is there?"

"Not if you're established. But Franchard was making a comeback, after all sorts of rumors that he'd had personal problems. Drugs possibly. A nervous breakdown." Horace tried to remember the things Zoe had told him about the industry. "If word got out that he wasn't able to design this collection, that would have been the end of him. Backers would disappear, or, worse, go after his talented new assistant, which they will now."

"An illegal immigrant." Margolus was obviously not aware of the big money involved in launching, or, rather, relaunching a name designer.

"Which gave Franchard a very strong hold over him." No wonder Inez was so afraid. Between Paco's illegal status and her own, Franchard had the young Colombian designer in his grip.

"Which explains why Franchard was willing to spring for cash and an expensive law firm to get Paco out of jail on bail fast." Mark thought of his old classmate's determination to free the young man. "Some messenger boy!"

"While the designer could continue to bully him into doing odd jobs as well as designing his whole collection." Horace looked through the rest of the designs. One of them was of the beautiful dress Zoe had worn in the showroom and to Celeste's party. The boy had enormous talent, it was right there in front of him.

"Okay, Franchard was cheating the kid. Exploiting him. Only why would Paco kill Rena and Axel? Franchard's the guy I would have thought he'd want to bump off." Margolus was still confused by all the apparent importance of a few dress designs.

"Paco wouldn't have wanted to kill Rena. Or Axel. Not if he suspected they knew what Franchard was doing. I told you at the time, Detective, that Axel wasn't the type to turn in anyone who was an illegal immigrant." Horace closed the file carefully, making sure the edges of the pages were squared neatly inside. This would be evidence someday in some courtroom, he realized. "And I don't think Paco's ambition would have led him to murder the designer. Not at this point, at least. He was getting a first-class chance to display his talent, plus training in the very big business of the fashion world. No. He didn't need credit now. He's young, ambitious. He could afford to wait for a bit."

"Only how did Franchard find him?" Mark knew he was sounding like a pedantic lawyer again, but he hated unsolved questions.

"Margolus may have the answer," Horace went on a little more tactfully as he looked at the detective. "We do tend to associate Colombia with drugs. Possibly Franchard went down there for a personal supply, discovered the boy, and arranged to bring him back. Illegally, of course."

"Only what the hell are the sketches doing here?" Margolus was getting impatient. There was still other stuff hidden in the camera.

"I suspect Rena had a hand in that. She may have seen Paco at work. Obviously she managed to get her hands on these original sketches."

"And brought them to Axel?"

"Yes, Mark. You've been concerned about a connection between Diane Chaumet and the murders of this week. Rena comes to New York three years ago. She does what any ambitious young woman would do . . ." Horace thought of what Ginny had said the first morning she had come to his apartment. "She would have looked up any contact, no matter how remote, that might help her in the career she had chosen. Possibly her aunt had mentioned Axel Gruen to her. Possibly Diane had mentioned Axel to the aunt."

"A lot of 'possibles.' " Margolus was not about to be convinced.

"Not that strange," Horace went on. "Diane was in a hospital. Axel, no matter how broke he might have been, would undoubtedly have sent flowers. With a card." Horace put the file down carefully on the top of the narrow cupboard. "What must have shocked Rena was to discover how far Axel had fallen out of favor. Still, he made a portfolio of pictures of her. That started her career. She may not have trusted him much, which is why she sent the portfolio to me and left the tape of her machine here, where sooner or later somebody would discover it and trace the phone calls made to her the day she died."

"Phone calls by her murderer?"

"Perhaps. At least enough to frighten her."

"And the sketches?"

"Models go up for all kinds of calls, just like actresses. She could have gotten her hands on them then."

"And brought them here? That sounds like blackmail." Margolus moved restlessly. "Only it can't be blackmail. We didn't find any money." He moved back to thrust his large hand into the opening of the camera. "Unless it's in here."

"I don't think you'll find money there, Margolus." Horace was beginning to realize how narrow his thinking had been all week. Would he have wanted money more than the chance to continue teaching? "Blackmail needn't always be about money. Axel could have used these sketches to blackmail Franchard into demanding Celeste use him

as the photographer for the spread in *Elegant* magazine. He would have been back on top, or at least his ego would have convinced him that he would be. Money was secondary. With the magazine exposure, he would have convinced himself he wasn't too old to be a success again."
Horace smiled a little dryly. "Believe me, I know the feeling."

"There's other stuff in the camera." Mark was also getting impatient. "If Axel and Rena could have blackmailed one person, there could be others."

Margolus moved first, pulling out a manila envelope. Opening it, he pulled out several rolls of film and several photographs. One glance at the top photograph and Mark noticed a blush rising in the burly detective's face.

"Good God, take a look at these!" The detective handed a couple of the pictures to Horace and Mark.

These were not artistic shots. And they certainly weren't fashion, since neither of the two people photographed on the bed in Axel's middle room were wearing any clothes. Katya McKay and the male model Jon Bowers.

"Athletic, isn't he?" Horace remarked after a moment. Their positions indicated that they had been involved in a variety of sexual activities, some of which looked more painful than pleasurable to Horace, but, he admitted wryly, people knew more about how to achieve sexual satisfaction these days than he had when he was young.

"Blow-ups." Margolus seemed embarrassed by the word, although technically that was what the photographs were. "From the film." He stretched out a length of film and held it close to the nearest lamp. "Yeah. Talk about pornography!"

"So again you were right, Detective," Horace said smoothly. It was time they made peace with each other. "And if you can move away from the couple's . . . activities, you might notice that the very colorful sheets and pillowcases are different in each picture."

It was something Margolus had not noticed, and he tried to concentrate on the edges of the photographs rather than the entwined bodies. "And what's that supposed to mean?" he asked gruffly.

"That the affair had been going on for some time. Or had happened at least five separate times." He pointed to the different photographs. "Nobody gets up in the middle of a romantic encounter to change the sheets." He put the photographs back in the manila envelope. "I wondered, the first time I came to see Axel, why his bed was made with such new expensive linen. Colorful linen. And I noticed a hairpin on the bed. Of all of the ladies we've seen in this murder investigation, only Katya McKay had hair long enough to need pins." He cleared his throat, reluctant to go on, but it was time to be completely honest with the policeman. "I also am fairly sure I saw Mrs. McKay and the young man having a quiet drink in an out-of-the-way bar after the dinner party Thursday night."

"You could have told me!"

"I wasn't positive, Margolus. And I didn't think it was my business to go around spreading gossip."

Margolus snorted. Clearly he felt Horace had done worse things than telling the police what he had seen, false lead or not. "If they were having such a wingding affair, why would they come here? Didn't they know this guy Gruen was slime?

"That one I bet I can answer." Mark was surprised at the way the other two men looked at him. "She's a married lady, not on good terms with her husband. He's an ambitious young model . . ."

"Okay, we get why they were doing it. But why here?"

"Because, Sergeant, where else could they go? Some hotel? Somebody could spot them. The bill would have to be paid with a credit card, that's another record they wouldn't want to come out. They couldn't go out of town, New Jersey or someplace, she wouldn't be able to explain why she was out of the office for so long. Which was also her home. Same thing for Bowers's place . . . could be in the wilds of Brooklyn.

"But she knew Axel, must have from years before. Knew he could probably use some extra money. Anybody spots her—or Bowers—coming into a photographer's building, they both have a perfectly airtight reason."

"Until he showed them the pictures?" Horace was smiling, both at Mark's conclusions and his specific knowledge of how quiet affairs can be conducted. Better not mention that to Ginny, he reminded himself. Horace was in enough trouble with two murders.

"Axel might have shown them. Or Rena. That's probably how she managed to get Katya McKay to sign her for the McKays' agency. Ginny told me the other girls didn't consider Rena in their class. I figured that might be jealousy, but now I'm beginning to think it might be—"

"Blackmail," Margolus broke in. "I didn't know you could blackmail so many people with no money being exchanged."

"Careers." Horace had reached into the camera for the next file. It was larger than the rest and felt as if it contained thick documents. "And we have another little target that Rena and Axel must have set their efforts on." He handed the file to Mark. "You're the lawyer, Mark. What do you make of this?"

The file was marked "Bosley." Axel had been surprisingly efficient in what he had collected. Mark flipped through the pages. "Looks like copies. One of the deed of ownership of a building on Chavel Street . . ."

"Chinatown. I was there Friday." Horace remembered the diner and the frightened girl who was sure Paco was innocent.

"Somehow I don't see you in Chinatown."

"It was an . . . impulse, Detective." Horace wasn't going to reveal everything to Margolus. Not yet, at least. "It's a section of factories mostly. I seem to remember that someone told me Franchard's clothes were made there."

"Boscard Corporation." Mark looked up at the two men. "Combination of Bosley and Franchard?"

"So?" Margolus was not impressed. "Nothing illegal about the doctor forming a corporation. You told me he was a plastic surgeon? They must be hip deep in money. Got to invest it somewhere."

Mark had gone on to other papers in the file. "Boscard also owns the building."

"Still no reason for him to be blackmailed. If he was."

"Oh, he was being blackmailed, Margolus. A sweatshop factory with perhaps illegal workers—" Horace hesitated, it wasn't the time or place to discuss Inez. "He must have been breaking several laws. And if not, not a very good reputation for a society doctor to have."

"Sorry, Professor, I don't buy it."

Horace reached for the rest of the file. There was a thick envelope that also showed signs of age. It wasn't sealed. As he lifted the flap, photocopied sheets slipped out and onto the floor. Picking them up, he found they were copies of personal checks. One a month. Made out to the same person, signed by the same person. All covering a period of three years. He handed some of the copies of the checks to Margolus and some to Mark. "A steady two thousand a month made out to Irene Varmont and signed by Malcolm Bosley. Not Boscard. Bosley himself." He smiled as he watched Margolus. "Again you're right, Detective. There *was* money involved."

"Which stopped when Rena's aunt died." Margolus wasn't to be pacified. "Now I suppose you're going to want me to look into her death!"

"I understand from my niece it was a perfectly natural death. But it left the girl with a certain sum of money and investments. It also explains how the aunt could have retired and still had enough to send the girl to an expensive college. Not that she stayed there," he added.

"Rena might have found this." Mark was chewing the thought over. "But the money seemed to have stopped then. So she couldn't have been able to do anything to Bosley.'' He put the copies of the canceled checks back in the envelope. ''Anyway, why would she want to? What could a plastic surgeon do for Rena? Ginny never said anything about her having surgery. And what good would it do Axel?''

''Bosley could introduce them to his lady friend, Celeste Lanier. A rising editor at a chic fashion magazine. Or, in Axel's case, push for the photographer to have another chance.''

''Still not good enough, Professor. Not good enough for steady money every month. There has to be something more.''

''What else is in that file, Margolus?''

The detective pulled out a rather tattered manila envelope. What he pulled out looked like copies of medical reports. ''Either of you two ever heard of a place called Golden Shores?'' he asked.

''Very expensive rehab. For very rich drug addicts,'' Mark answered promptly. ''I had a girlfriend in college whose father was in and out of there a couple of times.''

''Let me see that.'' Horace took the pages from Mark. These two had the faintly sepia tone of copies that went back a few years. He put on his reading glasses. ''Jean-Claude Franchard,'' he read aloud. ''Legal name John Felt. Admitted by his sister, Alberta. Admitted and released several times. Released each time to his personal physician, Dr. Malcolm Bosley.''

''A plastic surgeon? Why would Bosley be his personal physician?''

''Because he was a doctor. And could obtain the drugs Franchard wanted legally. Franchard's sister must have loved that, Mark.''

''Why would the doctor want him on drugs?''

''I don't think he did. But I could imagine our designer friend claiming he needed the stimuli to design. Bosley had a lot of money sunk into Franchard's reputation. Not to mention the factory. He might not have liked doing it, but he did it.'' Horace handed over the papers to Mark. ''Take a look at the bottom of the pages. On every one there's a list of attending nurses. Irene Varmont appears on practically every page.''

''So she knew about Bosley giving him drugs.''

''And if she knew, Rena knew. Or found out after her death. Which meant Axel knew. That's probably how Rena's aunt was able to make copies of the Boscard Corporation papers. Bosley must have had to have Jean-Claude's signature during his spells in Golden Shores, not hard for a clever woman to make copies that were in the hands of a sick patient.''

''That aunt was some piece of work!'' Margolus thought he was

beyond shock after all his years with the police, but the pictures and
then this clearly shook him.

"So supposing Rena tried the blackmail again . . . that would give
Bosley a good reason to kill her and Axel." Mark realized it made
sense at the same time as Margolus.

"You want me to pick up this guy Bosley, Professor? I can send out
a bulletin through the walkie-talkie?"

"He's not going anywhere, Margolus. Not tonight. Unless it's here."
Horace felt his feet were back on solid ground again. It had not been
his original theory, if theory wasn't too strong a word for an idea that
had been picking at his brain all week: that Diane Chaumet's operation
had been botched by Bosley, that Rena's aunt knew it and had been
blackmailing the doctor. Life is sometimes more complicated than something as obvious as a doctor, a patient, and a nurse.

"Rena and Axel . . ." said Mark thoughtfully. "Boy, they sure were
networking their careers every way they could."

There was a small buzz that froze all three men. Margolus moved
first, reaching into his raincoat pocket for his walkie-talkie. "Yeah?"
The others could only hear a faint mutter. "Got you. We're ready."
He clicked off the machine and replaced it in his coat. He shoved the
papers in his other hand into the camera and pulled out a gun. To
Horace, it looked larger than a cannon.

"Looks like company's coming."

"Man or woman?"

"Cop in the car couldn't tell. Pants, raincoat, hat, hunched under an
umbrella." Margolus was moving toward the front of the apartment,
not caring if the others followed or not. "But not a tenant, or anybody
who's visited a tenant this week."

Mark was right behind him. Horace lingered for a moment. There was
still one scrap of paper at the bottom of the improvised safe. He pulled it
out. Naturally I'm curious, he tried to tell himself, not wanting to admit
that if there was going to be gunfire, he wanted to be as far away from
it as possible. Alone, he could hear the rain on the skylight above him.

It was a slip of pink paper, torn off a pad. The lettering on the top
of the sheet was embossed: "From the Desk of Celeste Lanier," it said.
Written on it, under some doodles, in what was clearly a feminine hand,
was a series of names:

Celeste Lanier
Celeste Lanier McKay
Celeste L. McKay
Mrs. Philip McKay

The small page had been crumpled as if it had been discarded in an office wastebasket. Only somebody had carefully picked it out, somebody curious and ambitious. My, you were a busy girl, Rena, Horace thought. He felt a sadness as he held the page. It was the sort of thing schoolgirls did when they were first in love, not efficient, successful lady executives. But human beings don't change that much, no matter how successful they become. Or even if they are nearing forty.

So Celeste was going to be Axel and Rena's next target. Whatever there was between the editor and the very married co-owner of the Classic Agency hadn't reached a point where Rena and Axel had gathered anything positive.

For the first time that week, Horace felt, if not glad that the aging photographer and the young model were dead, at least relief.

The blackmail was over.

But as he stood there he could hear the creak of the elderly elevator as it moved slowly up to the top floor. This was no visitor to some other tenant.

This was very probably the murderer.

Livsey moved toward the bedroom. Margolus was silhouetted in the dark living room as he stood against the windows. Enough street light came in to show he had the gun in both hands. Just as they do in television, Horace thought, as always surprised when life turned out to be as melodramatic as the media made it. Mark, he noticed, had stayed carefully in the bedroom, but somehow he had picked up one of the tripods as a weapon. After all, something like that had killed Axel.

There was a moment of silence, then the three heard the elevator door creak open. For another moment, it was as if all the men were holding their breath until they heard a key turn in the lock.

As the door opened on the dark living room, Mark reached out a hand on a swift signal from Margolus. As he switched on the living room lights, Horace heard the policeman yell, "Hold it right there, Doctor!"

But the man standing in the doorway was Philip McKay.

– CHAPTER TWENTY-TWO

"Dumb. Just plain dumb. I should have known it was a trap."
McKay sat hunched on the ripped sofa in Gruen's living room, his
head down.

"Philip McKay, I'm arresting you for the murder of Rena Varmont
and Axel Gruen. You have the right to remain silent . . ." This was a
new Margolus, direct and official.

"You can stop right there, Detective. I know the Miranda rights.
And I'm not saying anything until I have a lawyer."

"Not even that you didn't kill them?" Horace was calmer now that
the lights were on. He was surprised how sorry he felt for the man.

"Would it make any difference?" There was a tired despair in
McKay's eyes as he looked at Horace. "You wouldn't believe me
anyway. I'm not sure I blame you."

Margolus was busy on his walkie-talkie, Mark at his shoulder. Horace
sat down beside McKay. He had no handcuffs on him as yet, but Livsey
suspected that would be Margolus's next move.

"Suppose you tell me why you came here tonight?"

"I . . . I was looking for something." He ran his hand through his
graying hair impatiently. "I should have guessed when Zoe was chattering away that you'd have something to do with this. You've been in
it from the very beginning."

"What was the 'something' you were looking for?"

"I'm not saying another word without a lawyer!" It came out firmly,
McKay was getting his courage back. "This isn't going to be some
television movie where the killer confesses neatly in time for the closing
commercial." He was getting sullen, Horace knew. He picked up the
envelope with Katya McKay's pictures that he had gone back to the

studio for while Margolus and Mark were patting McKay down. No weapons.

"Would these be pictures?"

McKay took them wordlessly. "So she is involved with him." He looked at Horace, his gaze direct. "Where did you find them?"

"Does it matter? Or had you looked for them before? At Rena's apartment? After her death? Or Thursday night after the party, with Axel dead?"

"No comment." McKay had withdrawn into himself again.

"You'll have to talk sooner or later."

"Then it's going to be later." He shifted so that only Horace could see his face and hear his low voice. "Suppose I told you I didn't kill them? Suppose I told you I'd found these keys in my wife's dressing table, guessed that this was the place she had gone with her boyfriend. That I suspected Rena and Axel had some kind of hold on her. I could tell you where I had the keys copied, not that you'd believe me. Because if she could get in here, and I had copies, that just pushes me in deeper, doesn't it?"

"I'd say it doesn't look too good."

"Katya will be wonderful on the witness stand. A faint quiver in her voice. Dowdy clothes. The lonely wife who was seduced into an affair because her husband didn't love her anymore. That lady's quite an actress, Professor."

"Would she be right? That you didn't love her anymore?"

"Did I ever love her?" McKay wasn't sullen anymore. He seemed to have gone into some private place, some memory of the past. "I don't know if love ever came into it. Ten years ago I was just starting the agency. She was smart, clever. Not beautiful enough to be a model, although she had tried. Better business head than mine. Sexy, at least at first." He put his head down in his hands again. "Oh, hell, let's not go on with this."

"You never thought of a divorce?"

"Like seven times a day. You see, there was someone I cared about. I asked for a divorce then. Katya said yes. If I gave her the whole of the agency. Title to the town house. All our investments. I could be free. And dead broke." His face twisted in a bitter smile. "And Madam would have been damn sure my name would have been mud in the industry. I'd never get another job again." He sighed heavily. "I was a little old even then to go back to selling ties at Brooks Brothers."

"Could she have hurt you that badly?"

"Sure. A word or two that Philip McKay makes passes at models, lady editors, women designers. Who'd trust me after that? And now, of course, it would be worse.''

Margolus came over to them. Considering the smallness of Axel's living room, Horace wondered how much he had heard. "Okay, McKay, I'm going to have to put the handcuffs on you now. I'll take you downtown to be booked. The two guys on stakeout will accompany us.'' He turned to the young lawyer. "You and the professor stay here. Lights out. Just in case somebody else gets the bright idea to come in for a search.''

Mark nodded. McKay stood up obediently as Margolus snapped the metal cuffs on him, hands behind his back.

"When do I get a lawyer?"

"You'll get a phone call downtown.''

"Great! The only lawyers I know deal in contracts. And they're probably all on their way in from the country, a Sunday night.'' He turned to Mark and Livsey. "Not quite the way it works in movies, is it?'' He tried unsuccessfully to manage a small smile. "Anybody know a good criminal lawyer?''

Mark looked at him unhappily. "I'm sorry, Mr. McKay. I've been in real estate until I applied for the district attorney's office. Anybody I'd know would be less experienced than I am. And Detective Margolus will tell you I'm not very experienced.''

"You're all right, kid," Margolus said gruffly. "How about your wife, McKay? She'd be back from this shoot by now, wouldn't she?''

"Katya?'' His laugh had no humor in it. "She'd let me rot in jail for the rest of my life before she'd lift a finger.'' He let Margolus guide him toward the steel door. "I guess a night in jail won't kill me. Not after ten years with her. Maybe I can think better tomorrow.''

"The court will appoint someone. At least temporarily. Until you get your own representation.'' Mark realized it was feeble help to the man, but it was all he could think of at the moment.

"Sure.'' McKay stopped, almost colliding with Margolus, who was guiding him. He looked back at the two remaining men in the room. "Very clever, fellows. And very dumb of me.'' He turned to face the open door and then looked back once more. "Hang on to the pictures of Madam McKay, will you? I'm going to need them.''

And Margolus ushered him out the door. Mark moved to the light switch. The room was again in darkness. Horace went to the window. Through the rain he could see an unmarked car pull up in front of the building. A disheveled-looking man appeared from the back areaway of the building and climbed in. The backup.

Mark stood where he was. This hadn't ended the way he expected.

He waited an awkward moment for Horace to say something, and then when the professor made no move, he said, "If you want a cigarette, I promise not to tell Margolus."

Horace turned around. Mark couldn't see his face, but from the set of his shoulders, he knew Livsey hadn't heard him or at least wasn't paying him any attention.

"I think there's a telephone in the studio." He moved past Mark and headed to the rear of the apartment. He had written down the number to call his thanks after the Thursday dinner party. Now, if he could just remember it. "There's one person who might know of a good lawyer even on a Sunday evening," he said as he started to punch in the number. He still had the pink slip from Celeste Lanier's desk in his pocket. He supposed he was withholding evidence, but at least Celeste cared about McKay. Mark stood in the doorway behind him, watching quietly. Horace held the phone away from his ear so that the young lawyer could also hear. "Damn! It's busy!" He put the phone down abruptly. "I'm going to have to leave you here, Mark."

"Wait a minute, Professor . . ."

"I know what Margolus said. But lock the door behind me, and put the chain on. I don't think there are going to be any more visitors, but just in case, call information and get the number of the local precinct. Anybody tries to get in, call them at once. I'll try to get back as soon as I can." Horace looked up at the skylight. Rain was still splashing against the dusty glass. Not a night to have come out without a raincoat, but he wasn't going to leave McKay deserted.

And there were still a couple of questions in his mind. If he was correct, and by this time he wasn't too sure of anything, the real killer wouldn't be coming here.

Luck wasn't with Horace. It took over twenty minutes to get a taxi, by which time he was soaked through. Somehow, it didn't seem to matter, and the driver seemed happy to be heading for the East Side of the city. The question that had been picking at his brain ever since they had opened the camera-safe in Axel's studio suddenly was clear in his mind, clear and focused.

When the cab pulled up in front of Celeste's building, he realized for the first time what he would look like to an imperious doorman or the man inside at the reception desk: a shabby, disheveled bum probably. It was going to take all of his professional authority to get inside.

But there was no doorman out front tonight, and the man at the desk barely glanced at him when he asked for her apartment.

"Go right up," he said before returning to his newspaper. "She's expecting you."

Once in the elevator (no elevator man Horace remembered from Thursday evening), he tried to think about how to talk to Celeste. But there was no time for plans, the door to her apartment was half open. He walked into the entryway. Beyond was the scarlet living room. Celeste was seated on a sofa, her back to him.

"Put the film on the table by the door," she said, not moving. "How many rolls did Tomorrow shoot?" There was something strange about her speech, Horace thought. He moved closer. "I didn't bring the film."

She twisted to see him. Her hair was tousled and damp, as if she had just come in from the rain outside and had forgotten to dry it. But she was wearing a long, soft robe and in one of her hands she held a glass. No ice, and from the color she had made a strong drink.

"Professor Livsey. What are you doing here?" She was obviously making an effort to speak clearly but the hand holding the glass wavered. "I'm expecting the film from the shoot."

"So I gathered." Was she drunk? "Doesn't a photographer usually develop his own pictures?"

"Not an artist like Oliver Tomorrow." There was more than a little scorn in her voice. "And with a deadline Tuesday, we're not taking any chances. Hell, the man can't even load his own cameras." She made an attempt to rise but seemed to lose her balance for a moment, and sank back into the sofa. "The magazine will have professionals do it." She took another swallow from her glass.

Horace noticed that the coffee table in front of her was littered with sheets of pages, proofs he gathered for the new issue. There was also a bottle of scotch, nearly half empty. And a small bottle of pills.

"Why are you here?" Her voice was definitely slurred.

"I've got some bad news."

"God! This week! What else could I expect?" She took one more swallow from her drink, and tried to pull herself under control. "What's happened now?"

"The police have arrested Philip Mckay. For the murders of Rena Varmont and Axel Gruen." There was no point in trying to be diplomatic, Horace realized. However much she had been drinking, and he suspected it had been a great deal, only the truth would penetrate.

"Phil? You're crazy!" Now she did stand, bracing herself on the table in front of her. She swayed slightly, but not enough to fall. "Where? Why?"

"He came to Axel Gruen's apartment tonight. He . . . he claims he was looking for something to prove his wife had been unfaithful."

"Idiot! Didn't he know what Zoe said was a trap?" She moved away from the couch but her feet were unsteady and she reached out to support herself on the fireplace mantel. How much smaller this room looks than it had Thursday night filled with glittering successful people, Horace thought. "Hell!" She practically shouted the word. "I could have caught Katya sooner or later. We could have been together!"

"Maybe he was trying to protect somebody."

For a second she seemed almost sober, a small, catlike smile on her face that reminded him of how charming she had been the night of her party. "You mean . . . me?"

The smile slipped off her face. She forced herself to move back to the sofa, slumping into it as her hands reached for the bottle standing like a small tower among the papers. "Yes," she said ruefully. "That's Philip. Always the gallant gentleman." She repeated the word, making it into two: "Gentle. Man. Too nice for a bitchy world like ours."

"Too nice for murder, I think." He didn't like what he was going to have to do. And it probably wouldn't help anybody. Sober, she would deny anything he could get her to admit tonight. And with no other witnesses . . .

"If he was capable of murder, he would have done it to Katya. Years ago. Before you came into his life?"

"I was always in his life." Her face was grim now. Without her makeup her face was pale gray. "Maybe he didn't know it, not really. Not until lately. But I was there for him. In ways Katya could never be."

He had to take the risk now. It was a guess, but it was the only connection that made sense.

"More than Diane Chaumet?"

"He never loved her!" The color rushed back to her face, and her eyes were raw with anger. "She threw herself at him! All the men in New York after her, and she had to pick Philip." She faced Horace squarely. "Oh, yes. She went after him. She knew he was miserable with Katya. . . ."

"That's when he first asked his wife for a divorce?"

"First. And only time." She slumped back against the cushions of the sofa as if exhausted. "He wasn't about to try it again for me." She wiped one of her eyes, but there were no tears there. "An affair, yes. We could have that if we were very, very discreet. But marriage? No." Her thin shoulders hunched under her warm robe. "And I loved him. Really loved him."

"More than Diane did?"

"Who knows? She was twenty-seven. She knew her days as a model were almost over. She decided she wanted to settle down. Marriage. A family. All that suburban stuff. A couple of more years at big fees and she'd have enough that it wouldn't matter if Phil was broke from a divorce.''

''Only she didn't have those years, did she? You saw to that.''

Her eyes narrowed and she put her glass down on the table. For this moment, at least, she was cold sober. I hope she doesn't have a gun, Horace thought in the split second of silence between them. She was ready to kill him.

As he realized she had killed Rena and Axel.

''I don't know what you're talking about.'' Each word came out like a tiny sliver of ice.

''You went to see her in the hospital the day she left after the plastic surgery. The thoughtful gesture of a friend, I've been thinking all week. But tonight we found where Axel had been hiding things and something didn't quite make sense. Not until McKay came.'' He touched the pocket where he held the slip of pink paper at the bottom of the camera case. No need to bring it out now. Because that wasn't what was important.

''I think you'd better go now.'' It was almost a parody of a dignified dismissal, ruined by her reaching again for her glass.

''Not yet. You see, there were so many people involved. A plastic surgeon ...''

''Malcolm didn't operate on Diane....'' The words were almost inaudible.

''I know that now. But I was so busy trying to put two and two together that I didn't realize I should have started with one. And one.'' He took a step closer so that he could see her face. ''What did you tell Diane that afternoon? That the operation was a failure? That she'd never work again? That no man would ever be able to look at her without shuddering?''

''You can't prove any of that!''

''I think I can. One thing I've learned this week is how insecure everybody in your fashion world is. A frightened woman, knowing her career is almost over. In love with a married man. She hears this from an editor she trusts. She gets in her car and drives to the country. She knows exactly where she's going to do it.'' He stepped back. He felt no pity for Celeste now. ''Everybody would remember her just as she'd been. Young and beautiful.''

''It was an accident.'' But Celeste's voice was shaky. She reached for the bottle of pills and fumbled for a couple.

''I wouldn't take those if I were you.''

"You're not. And you can't prove I said anything to Diane to drive her to suicide."

"Not tonight perhaps. But I think a lawyer could make a pretty good case for it in time."

"Are you going to go now? Or do I have to call down and have somebody take you away?"

"It wouldn't do any good. The police have the evidence." His legs were suddenly very tired and he sat down opposite her. "Somebody heard you talking to Diane, didn't they? Her nurse, Irene Varmont."

"Irene's dead." It was a flat monotone.

Horace felt all the pieces fitting together. "Yes. After retiring from Manhattan General. A rather early retirement." He learned forward to shift the bottle of pills away from her reach.

"Leave them alone." But she didn't reach out to stop him.

"Tonight we found copies of checks. Checks from Dr. Bosley. Just from the time that Rena's aunt worked at Golden Shores part-time as a private nurse. That sent her niece to college. But—and I'll admit I've been a little slow about this—who had given Irene Varmont the money to feel she could retire and still support herself and her niece? At Golden Shores she could, and apparently did, blackmail Dr. Bosley and Franchard regarding Bosley providing drugs to the designer. But who had given her the financial support so that she could afford to quit Manhattan General and go into work as a private nurse? Was it her first attempt at blackmail? Was it what she had heard you say to Diane that afternoon, a lie she knew would destroy the model?"

"And I thought I was having an ex-professor of history for dinner Thursday night. It seems I was having Sherlock Holmes." Her hand was steady as she reached to fill her glass again. "Only not a very efficient Sherlock Holmes." She smiled, her face cold and set. "I think you're a little too old for that."

That stung. But the fact she was fighting back convinced Horace he was on the right track.

"Perhaps. But Rena Varmont had a tidy list of stocks when she died. A very comfortable sum for a model who wasn't supposed to be that good. Or that successful. Inherited from her aunt, I suspect."

"That has nothing to do with me."

"I think it does. Sooner or later we'll find her safety deposit box, see the certificates. And if we don't, the companies are all listed. Efficient, Rena. They'll have a listing of the transfer of the stocks from you to Irene Varmont. All of them. And the date they were transferred. Right after Diane's death."

"Go away." Her voice was still defiant but slurred. "It's no crime to give people money. If there is, I should sue Irene Varmont for blackmail. Only she's dead.''

''But her niece wasn't. How did she contact you? She didn't have much to go on, just what her aunt told her.'' He leaned forward. ''No. First she would have gone to Axel, knowing how he felt about Diane. She had enough evidence from her aunt's time at Golden Shores for the two of them to get their hooks into Bosley and Franchard. Axel may have been out of favor in the business, but he knew all the secrets. What did he do? Approach Katya? Jon? At any rate, sometime in the past couple of months he had proof of Mrs. McKay's infidelity. You'd give a lot for that, wouldn't you?''

''I didn't have a lot to give.'' She waved her free hand around at the luxurious room. ''Sure. I got the promotion I'd been working for for years. The grand apartment. Only no money yet. It might take a year to pay off all my bills.''

''But you had power. Katya was promoting Rena . . . the model must have shown her Axel's pictures. Franchard and Bosley were pushing the two of them. You started getting Rena jobs. You promised Gruen to revive his career.'' He leaned back in the chair. For a moment she made no move. Finally, she spoke.

''I couldn't do it. They weren't good enough. Not for this job. Not for my first issue. I could have been fired. Then I'd have nothing. Not Philip. Not my work.''

''You went to see Rena last Sunday afternoon. You weren't at your office.''

''You can't prove that.''

''I think I can. There'd be a sign-in book in the lobby of your office building, and a relief elevator man to take you up to the *Elegant* office. He won't remember you, because you weren't there. There'll be no signatures in the book, not yours or Mr. McKay's.'' He watched her as she poured herself one more drink. ''Makes it even more difficult for him, doesn't it?''

''So I saw Rena at her apartment Sunday afternoon. That doesn't prove anything. She wasn't killed until well after midnight.'' She was being defiant now, her face hard. It was a look Horace suspected her staff knew well if they made a mistake.

''No. But you sat in the garden with Rena. It was a warm, sunny day. The windows would have been opened. I suspect you were trying to persuade her to give up the *Elegant* assignment. Promising her future work. She wasn't having any of that. She'd begun to suspect about you and McKay. Maybe she showed you a memo slip you'd doodled on in your office.''

"That bitch!"

"And while you two talked, all the people who were trying to keep their little secrets from coming out were calling and leaving messages. You would have heard them, because Rena wasn't about to answer, not with you there. She'd have been fighting you all the way. You didn't kill her then. Maybe you hadn't even thought of it. But later, when you went to the agency, it began to cross your mind."

"She would have been on my back the rest of my career. Her and that tired has-been Gruen. I'd worked too hard and come too far to let that happen!" She didn't seem to be talking to Horace now, it was as if she were going back to the previous Sunday, remembering her feelings, her plans.

"You ripped the dresses so the shoot couldn't take place, didn't you? It would have been easy with all the commotion going around as the agency was being set up for the shoot. Ripped them and then rewrapped them. The shoot was canceled. Rena went to Axel. He lied to us about going to Franchards. He was at his apartment. Both of them must have been furious. And both of them must have been scared. They'd made a lot of enemies. So as protection Rena took the tape from her machine. If anything did happen to her, there were the people who had called her that afternoon, all of them frightened and angry. . . ."

"All except Philip." Her eyes were red now, but still no tears came.

"Rena put the tape in Diane's lighter case and hid it in the bowl in Axel's apartment. I doubt if she told him. She didn't trust him very far."

"A pair of snakes . . ."

"Not very nice, I'll grant you that. She'd also prepared to send her portfolio of pictures to my niece with a clipping about Diane. In case anything happened to her. Because several people must have called her that night. Only we'll never know, will we? Because there was no tape in her answering machine."

"So it wasn't me who killed her." She reached for the bottle of pills and swallowed a couple. "You'll have to go, I'm going to have to sleep soon. Monday's going to be a busy day."

"Yes. Somebody's going to have to get McKay out of jail. I was hoping you'd know the name of a criminal lawyer."

"They can't charge him! They can't, can they? Really?" She was like a frightened child now, begging for reassurance.

"I've told you. They've already charged him." Horace stood up. He didn't know what was in the bottle of pills, but if they were to help her sleep, they could be dangerous with what she had been drinking. If he could just get the bottle before she took any more . . .

"How did it happen?" he asked quietly. "Sunday night?"

"I . . . I called her. The line was busy, she'd taken the phone off the hook. I had to be sure the tape was intact. So I went to her apartment. She was sleeping but she let me in. She was still drowsy. She went back to bed. But she was sneering at me!" Celeste was shouting now. "I grabbed the first thing I saw, a damn hair drier. I only meant to shut her up."

She sank back in the sofa. "But then she started to struggle . . ." She looked up at Horace, eyes cold. "You can't prove any of this."

"Miss Lanier? I've got the film."

Ginny was standing in the doorway, holding a bulky package. Her face was smudged with dirt and what looked like bizarre makeup. She at least looked reasonably dry. If she was surprised to see her uncle, she gave no sign.

"How long have you been there?" Celeste forced herself to stand. It took more effort than it had before, but she managed it, swaying slightly.

"Long enough." She looked at Horace. "And you needn't worry about how Celeste got in and out of this building without being spotted Sunday night and Thursday. The man at the reception desk is asleep. Didn't even lock the front door." She faced Celeste. Horace could see no pity in her eyes. "But you'd have a key for that, wouldn't you? Not to mention there's a door to the service stairs down the hall. Three floors up, that would be no problem for you."

"You don't know anything." Celeste swayed again but grabbed the edge of the mantelpiece for support before she could fall.

"I think I do." Ginny put her package down on the marble-top table inside the doorway. "You didn't go to Rena's Sunday night to steal the tape from her machine. That's where we all got mixed up, or at least I did. You went there to make sure the tape was still there. You needed it for the police to find."

"Only it wasn't there." Horace realized this had been in the back of his mind ever since he had walked in here. "If anybody else had called that night, it wouldn't have made any difference. They would have thought the line was just busy. What they said that afternoon wouldn't have mattered. But it did to you.

"Then Monday you hid the hat and cloak and boots in her locker at the agency. All the models knew where McKay kept a list of the padlock numbers in his desk, in case they forgot."

"What did you do with the hair drier?" Horace moved closer to Celeste. She was standing straight now, not leaning on the mantel for support.

"The hair drier. Long hair. She was so damn proud of it." Celeste reached for her drink on the coffee table. The pill bottle was gone, Horace noticed, and Celeste had her other hand shoved deep into the pocket of her robe. She shook her soft, silvery-gold curls like an animal. "Like Diane. Like Katya. The long-hair girls. Not my style."

"Unlike murder?" Ginny was still watching her, not moving closer.

"You can't prove a thing. The hair drier is somewhere in the Hudson River. No fingerprints, even if you did find it."

"And Axel? He must have said something to you the night of your party, something that implied he knew what you had done. Now he did have a hold on you. Maybe you didn't think he was any good, but he hadn't survived all these years without being clever."

"I went to make him an offer Thursday night after the party. For the pictures he had of Katya and her stud. He laughed at me! Like Rena. That dirty old gnome laughed at me! Why should he sell me the pictures when he could have me and Katya both in his grip? Rena'd told him about the tape, only not where she'd hidden it. But he guessed what I'd done. No real proof. Just enough to make a very ugly mess." She pulled her hand out of the pocket of her robe and swiftly covered her mouth.

Ginny moved forward but Horace stopped her. "Whatever you've taken, Philip McKay will still go to jail for a very long time. Do you really want that?" he said.

"Whatever I want, it seems I'm never going to have it, doesn't it? No wonderful gentleman, no career. Not with two witnesses." She looked confused now. "Because I've said too much, haven't I?"

"It might not hold up in court." Horace reached out and put his arm around her shoulder. How thin she was, how fragile. Killer or not, for a moment he almost felt sorry for her.

"Even if I testify that Rena had told me what her aunt was up to?"

Ginny's voice was hard, flat. Horace knew she was lying but he could see Celeste didn't. His niece might turn out to be a successful actress after all.

"But the court might not believe me. You'd still be free."

"No. Dead." Celeste didn't look at Ginny. Her eyes were getting glazed.

"The easy way out? Just a nervous editor who unfortunately mixed sleeping pills with liquor to help her through a deadline!" Ginny's smile was cold. "And that would mean Philip McKay would still spend the rest of his life in jail."

"No!" It came out like a scream. Then, abruptly, Celeste cut it off. She stood straight. If Horace hadn't seen the liquor she'd consumed and the pills she had swallowed he would have sworn she was totally sober, totally in control of herself. She walked across the room to Ginny. She wasn't swaying now, it was the firm step of a woman who knows exactly what she's doing. "Get away from that phone!"

Ginny stepped back. Whatever she had managed to pretend before, she was a frightened girl again. She watched in silence as Celeste pressed some buttons on the side of her machine. While it was giving its warning beep that her standard message had been erased, she looked at Horace and Ginny. The smile on her face was almost sardonic. They made no move toward her.

"It started with a telephone tape last Sunday. Rather neat to finish it with one tonight, isn't it?" She brought the receiver up to her mouth. Bracing herself on the edge of the table, she began to speak slowly and distinctly into the phone.

"This is Celeste Lanier. It's Sunday night, September twenty-fifth. I hereby confess that I killed both Rena Varmont and Axel Gruen. Nobody knew about it. Nobody helped me. And I don't regret it one damn bit. They both deserved to die." Her voice rose a little, sour and harsh. "Have a nice day, world."

Now she swayed. Still she managed to put the phone down. "Is that clear enough for a courtroom," she asked as she faced Horace and Ginny.

She slipped to the floor before they could grab her. Horace knelt beside her, raising a hand as Ginny reached for the phone.

"Don't touch that!"

"I've got to call 911, Horsey. She could recover."

"She doesn't want to recover." He tried to ease Celeste's body on the thick carpet. She was still breathing. "There must be a phone in her bedroom, or the kitchen, use one of those. The police will need her fingerprints on this one."

Ginny stepped back cautiously, her eyes wide.

"And when you've done that, you might want to call Mark at Axel's apartment. He'll want to be here when the police come. And to see you home."

At that Ginny scurried out of the room. Horace bent over Celeste's body again. Her eyelids fluttered for a moment before they opened. "Diane's the only one I regret," she whispered. "You were right. She didn't deserve to die. That was the only real murder I committed."

Her head lolled back on the floor. Horace tried to find a pulse at her neck and her wrist. She wasn't breathing anymore.

She was dead.

Automatically, he looked at his wristwatch. Somebody would want to know the exact time. It was 12:05.

Not Sunday anymore. Another Monday.

He thought of the women. Diane, Rena, Celeste.

"Monday's child is fair of face . . ."